THE BLACK MANTLE

Books by

Andrew Watson

The Shadowbinders Trilogy

Harbinger of Justice

The Black Mantle

Storm of Shadows

Novellas

Silence is Silver

THE BLACK MANTLE

Book Two
of
The Shadowbinders Trilogy

Andrew Watson

The Black Mantle
Book Two of the Shadowbinders Trilogy
Copyright 2025 by Andrew Watson
First Edition: February 2025
ISBN: 978-1-7393400-4-9 (Hardback)
ISBN: 978-1-7393400-5-6 (Paperback)

Cover Design by Felix Ortiz
Map by Joshua Hoskins
Edited by Sarah Chorn

To my grandparents,

For reading to me my first stories and being the first to read mine

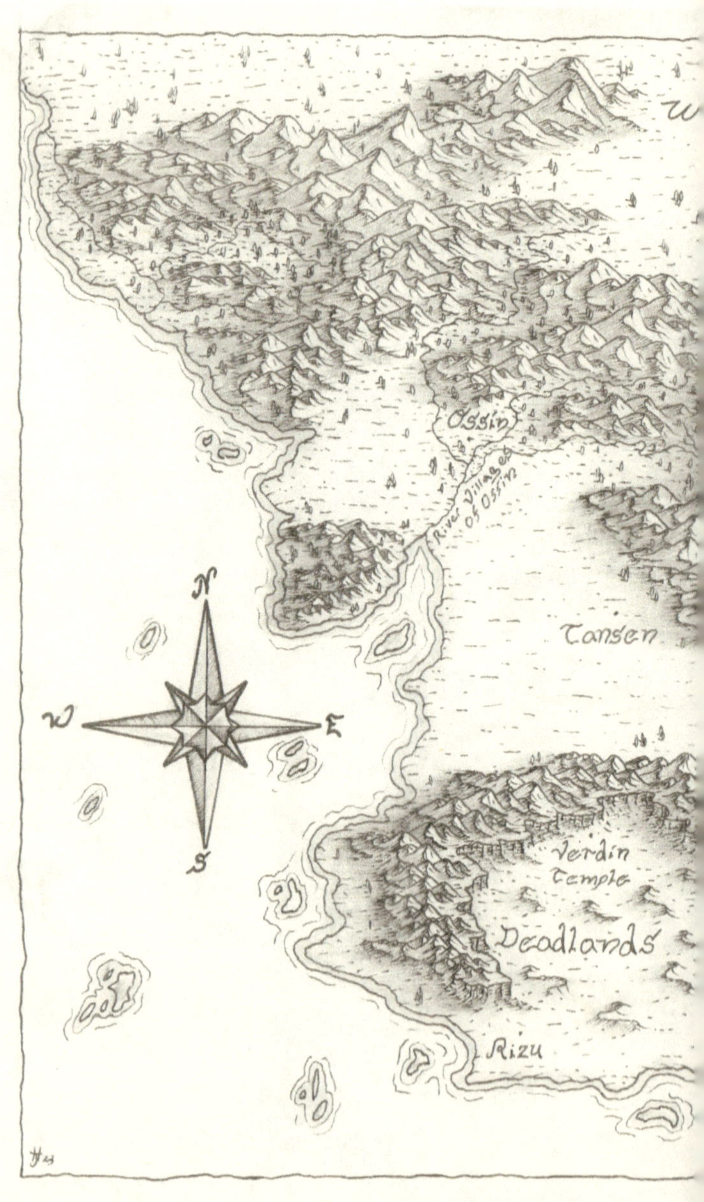

N
W
E
S
Ossin
River Village of Ossin
Tansen
Verdin Temple
Deadlands
Rizu

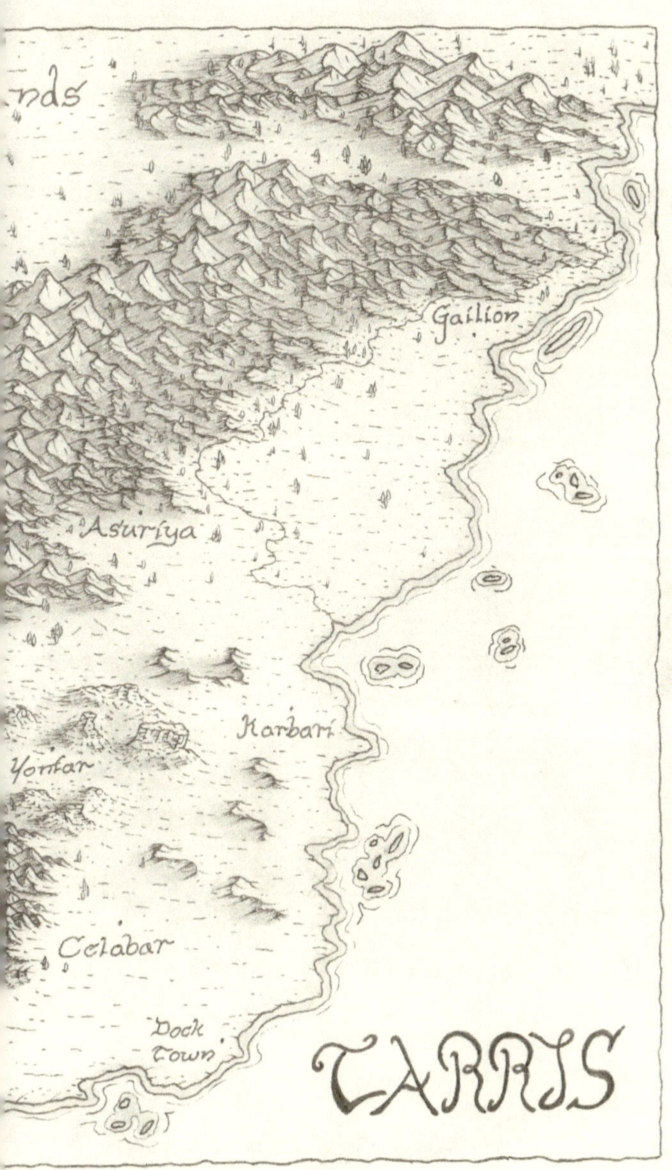

nds
Gailion
Asuriya
Karbari
Yonfar
Celabar
Dock
Town
TARRIS

The Story So Far

A recap of the events from book 1, *"Harbinger of Justice."*
Spoilers Ahead

Nya lives on the streets of the desert city, Yontar. She is forced to steal to survive. However after an unfortunate run in with a gang, Nya is caught and arrested. To shorten her sentence, Nya signs up for a secret project so that she can return to her sick mother who cannot care for herself. The project threw her, Kit, Styra, Drak and an Urdahl called Bas through a black rend and into a dark other world to be used as distractions for the dangerous creatures that live there. Bat-like creatures, known as husks, tear through the group killing most of the guards, scholars and Drak. After a perilous journey to reclaim the research notes, the others make it back to Yontar.

Upon returning, the guards wave a strange black dagger at those who survived. Nya felt a burning aversion to the blade, stemming from the creature that she picked up from the dark other world and that now lives in her shadow. Given the name Bom, Nya struggles to keep the shade under control.

Nya's mother beats her senseless in one of her tirades and in

Nya's defence Bom lashes out killing her mother. Horrified by what she has done, Nya sits in that attic, blood pooling at her feet, hugging the corpse of her mother until Kit finds her the next day. He cares for Nya as she comes to terms with what she has done.

After some time, they hear rumours of a man who has similar abilities to Nya and seek him out for guidance. There they find Kyan, a man bent on retribution and justice.

Meanwhile, Rai hunts for the truth about the shade that lives in his shadow. This leads him to a market square, where he is shocked to find his old friend that he thought long dead, Kyan. They were once part of an elite assassin group called the Seventh Sceptre that killed for the empress. But his old friend seems different.

As Rai approaches Kyan, he spots Nya in the crowd as her shadow bleeds around her. He steps in to offer help to the girl and strikes a deal with her: he will train Nya to control her shade if she enters Kyan's cult to learn his motives.

Nya and Kit join Kyan's Decreed cult and trek north into the desert. There they find the lost library of Nenelan, thought to be destroyed in the cataclysm that took the old capital of Tarris thousands of years ago. Within the ancient library, Kyan finds a tome that contains the location of the resting place for the deity Ma-atan, the Harbinger of Justice. Rai attempts to stop Kyan but Nya sides with the Decreed and betrays Rai, knocking him out.

While unconscious, Rai delves into his past at the Green Leaf Orphanage. There, he is an outcast until a new child, Kon, arrives and befriends Rai. Another child, Zin, known for being a bully, isn't pleased with the new kid siding with Rai, and the next day Kon is found bleeding out on the bathroom floor.

In his unconscious state, Rai continues to fall through a troubled past before finally starting awake. Then, along with Kit, he chases Kyan across the desert to Ma-atan's temple.

The Decreed arrive and wake the sleeping deity, but Kyan soon realises his mistake when Ma-atan starts slaughtering everyone in the temple. While trying to rectify his blunder, Kyan and many of his cult are killed. Together, Rai, Nya and Kit drag Ma-atan back into the pool of silverwater that it had been found in.

During the fight, Ma-atan rips Kit's heart out before inspecting it and plunging it back into the boy's chest. Nya screams as fury floods her and she opens up a connection to the dark other world that homed the shades. She pulls on the power there and forces Ma-atan back into the pool where its chains are reconnected, binding the deity once more.

A voice comes from the shadows and the connection to the dark place.

I see you.

Nya passes out severing the link and Rai rushes over to Kit to find him alive. But his heart no longer beats in his chest.

The remnants of the Decreed disperse and the company return to Yontar. Nya and Kit take up roles in the Patched Cloak inn and try to move past the horrific events at the temple. And Rai sets off to Tansen to inform the empress about all that has taken place.

For deities that were once thought to be myth, now roam Tarris, and a dark presence from another world has been awoken.

Prologue

6 years ago.

It had many names. The dead city. The cursed capital. But that's not how Wint saw it. Asuriya was a treasure trove for men like him. He stalked through the fringes of the outer city, his wide-brimmed hat keeping the burning Sun Eye's gaze off.

He stepped up to a derelict building. The door had caved in so Wint clambered over the rubble and into the living space. The top of a pan stuck out from beneath the rock. Bending down to inspect it, he noted that it was made of mud clay. *Not worth much*, he thought and stood. Many of the buildings had been picked clean by other crews. But most didn't dare go further into the city. All feared the blight that touched this dead place. Which is why only the most desperate were to be found here. Well, the most desperate, and Wint.

As Wint exited through a collapsed back wall, he saw movement. He reached for his sword but it was just one of his pickers. The kid stared at him like cornered prey. The boy couldn't have been older than ten years of age and dirt smothered his face. His brown hair was matted with sweat and dust.

"You aren't going to find anything out here, kid," Wint said. "Best to move further in."

The kid nodded and scampered off. There were fifteen of them out scavenging through the city for him. Poor lost souls drawn to picking for treasure hunters like Wint. It was dangerous work. The deeper one got into the city the more blight-touched creatures roamed. Kiren with six legs. Sand foxes with faces full of eyes.

Wint shuddered. He had done his time as a picker. Picked some fine pieces from the old capital in his day too. However, the treasure hunter always took a bigger portion of the prize. That was when Wint knew he had it all wrong. Taking all the risk and reaping so little of the reward.

"But look at me now," Wint whispered to himself.

He looked to the sky. It was soon time to saddle up. Even he wouldn't linger in Asuriya during dark hour. So Wint made his way back to the aya.

Gor, his mercenary, sat atop the beast's platform under the shelter of a tarp.

"Toss down the waterskin," Wint called as he leant against the aya. He caught it and took a swig as the first of the pickers started to trickle out from the city.

They lined up one by one and approached Wint with what they had found. Some cracked pots, warped pieces of metal, shredded books and one picker brought him a chair. It was the usual bits and pieces. He inspected each item and paid less than half of what it was worth before gesturing them onto the aya.

Wint sighed as he dropped a ladle at his feet and glanced over the meek haul. *Cowards can't have delved deep enough into the city.* He was going to need to find more desperate souls next time. Those willing to risk their lives to find the true treasure. Above, the Sun Eye began to dip. They needed to hurry if they wanted to set up camp at the usual cave. A couple of kids were missing but they often lost one or two. Wint cleared his throat and climbed up the ladder onto the platform.

"Gor, get us moving," he said. Wint cracked his back and was about to settle in for the long ride home when he noted the pickers huddling together and whispering. Wint searched their faces expecting to see his solemn street kids but instead they were lively, eyes wide and searching.

What is going on? Wint was about to ask when one of the pickers shouted a name and pointed back to the city. Wint followed the boy's gesture, staring back at Asuriya.

There, running between the buildings were two of his pickers. Their small forms weaving among the rubble of destroyed homes. One was clutching something tight to their chest. They broke out of the city limits and ran toward the aya, their faces wild.

They made it halfway to the aya when a kiren darted out from the debris. The wolf-like beast was warped by the blight of Asuriya. Its shoulders stuck out like blades and the tip of its tail had split in two. Its fur was patchy and wiry.

Wint looked between the kids and the kiren. They wouldn't make it. That much was clear. But what was the kid holding?

Wint knew the smart choice was to tell Gor to go. Smart choices were what kept one alive. Pickers were replaceable. Sunlight glinted off a metal sheen of whatever the kid held. Wint licked his lips.

Treasure, however, was not replaceable.

"Gor, ride for them!"

His mercenary looked at him like he was crazy. Maybe he was. But all it took was one piece. One single piece of treasure to set one up for life. He had seen treasure hunters retire on a single piece.

That was the magic of treasure hunting.

"Now!" Wint shouted.

Gor whipped the reins and the aya sped towards the kids. Wint spun and waved his arms. "Well, don't just sit there! Get ready to haul them up!"

It took another breath before the first picker moved to the side and leaned over the edge with their hand out. Soon a handful others followed suit. Wint stood at the platform's edge beckoning the boys on.

"Come on! That kiren won't leave much of you if you let it take a bite!"

That sped them up.

The kiren bounded over the sand. Its muscles bunched and pulsed with each impact. Their aya reared at the sight but Gor kept the dumb beast moving.

The kids threw themselves against the aya's fur, clutching with a frenzied expression. The other pickers called out and reached down to pull them up. One made it onto the ladder and threw himself up it and onto the platform but the second kid didn't have time.

The picker just climbed out of reach as the kiren snapped where he had been seconds before. The aya reared and whinnied. Wint held out a hand. The kid went to grab it but Wint pulled back.

"The treasure first, kid."

Worry creased the picker's brow but he threw him a black object. Wint caught it. A smile eased onto his face. A black dagger. Now that would fetch a pretty price. Pretty enough to retire? Perhaps. The boy called out. Wint ignored him and stepped back onto the platform inspecting his prize.

Other pickers leapt to try and pull the kid up but he slipped. The boy let out a feral scream as he dropped to the sand and the kiren descended upon him. The pickers cried out hanging over the edge of the platform. But all they could do was watch as one of them was ripped apart.

Wint glanced down at the dagger. The blade was completely black and not made of any material Wint had ever seen. He ran a finger over the edge and hissed pulling it back to find blood. "Still sharp after all these ages," he said in awe.

The picker's screams tore him back to the moment. He peered over to see the kid being ripped to shreds by the kiren. The other pickers glanced at Wint, faces pale, as if it was his fault the boy couldn't hold on for a couple more minutes. One picker threw up over the edge of the platform. Another took Wint's hand. He was one of the youngest boys and it took Wint a minute to realise he was the other kid that had arrived late with the blade.

"Sir, that's my brother! Please help him!" He was crying. This was the worst part about working with street kids. The Duat-damn tears.

Wint dropped down onto his haunches to match the boy's eyeline. "You know, your brother saved us. He is a hero. If I tried to help him he wouldn't be a hero anymore, now would he? Do you want to take that away from your brother? He'll hold the kiren off long enough for us to escape. Don't you worry." Wint ruffled the kid's hair and stood.

"Gor, ride for Yontar. We have our prize."

PART 1

1

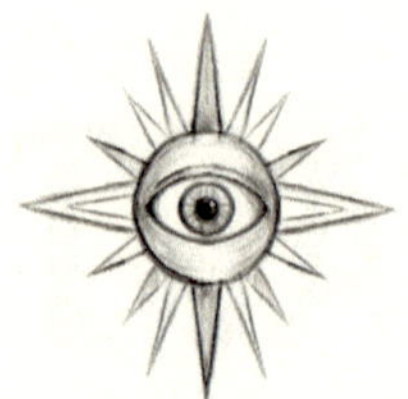

The Shattering of Bonds

22 years ago.

The Sun Eye sat on the horizon staining the Green Leaf Orphanage in red. Shadows danced across the courtyard, echoes of life blackened by the glare of a God. Rai watched the other children run around tossing a ball to one another. They squealed as the ball moved up the line. Whoever dropped it would be out for that round.

Lil, a scraggly haired girl with deep blue eyes met Rai's gaze before he turned back to his book. The other children didn't bother asking Rai to join them anymore. The answer was always no.

The light faltered as dark hour approached. All the children would be brought inside soon. Rai snapped his book shut, straightened from his perch under the great tree, and made his way indoors. It was best to beat the rush of other children flocking indoors for mealtime.

Rai's slapping footsteps rang up and down the empty corridors of the orphanage. Squeals from the children playing outside pierced the otherwise quiet interior. Rai spared no glances as he passed the darkened bedroom that he shared with nine others, but continued towards an open door aflame with candlelight.

The space had once been a reading room, the back wall still covered in books. But the tables and chairs had been removed to make space for the bed that now held Kon. Hovering by the door, Rai peered in and wondered, as he did every night, if Kon would want him there. It was his fault Kon was in this state after all.

Kon hadn't woken since the incident in the bathroom. The Mauts said he had slipped and hit his head but Rai knew better. It was Zin. He had done this. All because Kon befriended Rai rather than joining Zin and his crew. Rai could tell by the smirk Zin wore at breakfast that morning that something was wrong. When Rai had gone running to find his friend, Kon had been bleeding out on the bathroom floor.

But the Mauts wouldn't believe him, or didn't *want* to believe him. They didn't want to deal with the truth. Better to brush it off as a way of the world.

Kon's eyes were sunken, skin a sickly pale. Where once he was skinny, the boy was now frail. It had been a couple of months and Kon closer resembled a corpse than the lively boy Rai knew. Maut-Fer slid a spoon into the boy's mouth whispering something just out of Rai's hearing.

"How is he?" Rai asked.

"The same," Maut-Fer said. She sighed putting down the bowl. "It's possible he might never wake up, Rai."

"I know."

But I have to believe that he might. He didn't dare speak the thought aloud.

"You should go and play with the other children. I can take care of Kon," Maut-Fer said.

And pretend this never happened? Laugh with the others like my friend isn't asleep because of me?

And what if it happened again? What if he were to befriend another just to have them fall to the same fate?

Rai said nothing.

Maut-Fer gave Rai a sympathetic look, stood, and gestured to the chair by Kon's bed. Rai sat and picked up the bowl to feed his friend. His hand shook as he pressed the spoon into Kon's mouth.

"You need to join the other children, Rai," Maut-Fer said, placing a hand on Rai's shoulder. "You will try? For me?"

Rai didn't take his eyes from Kon when he lied, nodding.

Days were always moving but never changing. They became a stream blending into one another, forever pushing Rai forward to an indistinguishable tomorrow. The repetition allowed Rai not to think. If he just kept going through the motions perhaps Kon would wake up and shatter this nightmare.

Rai had never put much thought into the Gods but when Maut-Fer offered to bring him along to morning prayers, he accepted. If there was a sliver of a chance the Gods would hear him, Rai would take it. And there was a certain peace to praying that Rai hadn't anticipated. He had always thought praying was for those who wanted something, and although he did, Rai took respite in the process, and found himself looking forward to it each morning.

Keeping his head down, Rai shovelled in his breakfast. It was some sort of meaty stew but Rai didn't give it much thought. Early morning light poured in the windows as the rest of the children filtered into the feast hall. Raucous conversation clashed with the bubbling pots in the kitchens. But it was background noise, dull and far away. Rai could silence it if—

"Hey." A voice cut through the blur of sound.

Lil dropped into the seat beside Rai. He flinched as her tray crashed onto the table. She was new to the Green Leaf Orphanage, arriving after the incident with Kon and was one of the few who tried to interact with Rai.

Lil grinned at him. "Did you hear that the sky readers said it might rain today?"

Rain was rare in Tarris, only happening once or twice every couple years.

"Really?" Rai asked.

"No. It would be great if it did though, wouldn't it?" Lil said, between mouthfuls of stew. "You know, there are parts of the world where it never stops raining. They all wear big funny hats that have tracks in them to redirect the rain. I saw an illustration of them in a book."

Rai nodded and turned back to his breakfast.

"Not much of a talker, huh." Lil watched Rai eat, one eye brow arched, before leaning in. "I believe you."

Rai glanced up.

"About Zin. He's a bully and I wouldn't be surprised if he had hurt that boy. He might not have meant it to go that far but that doesn't make it any less his fault," Lil said.

She was the first one to mention Zin. No one else dared bring up his name when talking about Kon. Rai looked over to the rotund boy who sat at the far end of the feast hall as he jostled his friends and sprayed his food with his laughter. Carefree and unbothered by what he had done. Rai's fist clenched around his fork.

Lil went back to eating. Rai could tell that she didn't say it to quell him or get him to do something like the Mauts did. She meant it. She truly believed him.

"Thank you," Rai said.

Lil nodded. "A few of us are playing bevel ball after chores. You should play. Zin won't be there."

"I…"

"I'm sure your sleeping friend wouldn't mind if you took a night off. Maut-Fer will be there and he probably wants a break from you too," Lil said. She slurped the last of her stew and pushed away from the table. "We'll be by the tree." And with that she ran off, sliding her tray onto the counter and vanishing out into the corridor.

Rai stared at the door. He wouldn't go. He couldn't leave Kon. But he felt a surge of gratitude for the girl. She had asked.

With one final swish, the wiry brush scraped the last of the sand out into the courtyard. Rai wiped the sweat from his brow and leant on his brush. The unmistakable hiss of other brushes echoed around the orphanage. But some of the others were already playing in the courtyard having finished their afternoon chores. The sky was red, the Sun Eye coming to the end of its watch.

Lil stepped out from behind the great tree laughing as she tossed the ball to one of her friends. They seemed so relaxed. So at ease in a world that could take anything it wanted in the blink of an eye. How did they banish the terror that Rai felt climbing up the back of his throat even now?

But then, they were orphans. Loss was what tied them together. A bond forged after the snapping of another had to be stronger than the first. Strengthened by what was.

Lil caught his eye. She gestured for him to join them, then had to dive out the way as her friend threw the ball at her. Rai smiled when Lil hopped back to her feet, her hair sticking up on one side. Rai waved a placating gesture that could have meant anything and ducked back inside.

Rai passed down the corridor carrying the brush under his arm. He threw open the closet and tossed the brush inside. Taking a deep breath, Rai looked to his left which lead back to the courtyard and then right, which led to Kon's room.

Rai headed right. He couldn't leave Kon.

The light from Kon's room poured out into the corridor as a strip of orange. Maybe Lil was right. Every night he questioned if Kon would want him by his side. Wouldn't Kon be angry at him? Wouldn't he curse Rai's name and demand he stay away from him?

Rai wavered. The Mauts didn't know if Kon was aware of those around him or not. Would one night make a difference? Perhaps if he befriended Lil and her friends, they could come to morning prayers and petition the Gods to help.

Rai had avoided the others in fear of losing them like he had Kon. But cutting ties to those around him had the same result as them snapping. So why wouldn't he risk the possibility of creating bonds that could last forever?

Spinning on his heels, Rai headed for the courtyard.

That was the first night since the incident that Rai hadn't been plagued by nightmares. He had been wary joining Lil and her friends but they didn't look at him like a wounded sand fox, and they didn't mention Kon or Zin. They just played bevel ball until the lamps were lit for dark hour and Maut-Eln called them in. It was simple and easy, and Rai found himself present in the moment, not looking at what has been and what could be.

Rai woke before the Sun Eye had started its watch feeling refreshed. The other boys in his room slept soundly in the bunks around him, their steady breathing filling the dark. Birds chirped outside calling for Ova, the World Turner, to gaze upon them with its Sun Eye granting them light and warmth.

Creeping out of bed, Rai slid down the ladder and made his way out of the bedroom. The corridor was empty and silent save for the distant clatter of the kitchen making morning meal. Rai stretched. He started for the small shrine that he used for morning prayers and then stopped.

Maybe I should go check on Kon, Rai thought. Rai visited him after breakfast every morning but since he hadn't gone last night…

Travelling down the empty corridors, Rai made his way to Kon's room. He stepped in and froze.

Kon was gone.

His bed that had held him since the incident, gone. The chair and side table by his bed was gone too. The room was a reading room once more. A sinking feeling bloomed in Rai's stomach. Had Kon woken up?

Rai tore through the corridors, uncaring of the noise he made and who he disturbed. The morning glare added another worldly glow to sleeping orphanage. The dreamlike facade clashed with the nightmare panic clawing its way through Rai's mind. He skirted around a corner almost knocking over a tall vase sitting on the window ledge.

Shoving his way into the room with the small shrine, Rai panted, startling Maut-Fer. A row of painted clay statues were lined up in an ornate display. Each resembled the deities of different virtues. Rai opened his mouth to ask about Kon but he couldn't find the words. The look on Maut-Fer's face told Rai everything he needed to know.

Rai sank to his knees.

Maut-Fer bent down and wrapped an arm around him. "Hey, hey, it's okay. It's better for him to enjoy the Reed Fields of Aru than be stuck in a bed here, is it not? Dying is the way of the world."

The way of the world. The Mauts liked to use that phrase but Rai didn't know what it meant anymore. He felt sick. The pit in his stomach threatened to drag him to the floor. How could this be the way of the world? It was unfair and cruel. Kon hadn't deserved this.

And he had died alone.

Rai should have been there. He should have been by his side. Kon died alone while Rai was out playing *bevel ball*.

"I should have…"

"No, no, no. You can't blame yourself," Maut-Fer said, pulling him into a hug. "Perhaps Kon waited until he was alone. He wouldn't want to have upset you. This was easier."

But it wasn't. It was too sudden. He was just gone and Rai

couldn't do anything about it. He pressed his face into Maut-Fer's shoulder as the tears started to flow.

It shouldn't be this painful, Rai thought. The Mauts had given him the day off of doing his chores. Rai wished they hadn't. It left him alone with his thoughts as he wandered the orphanage.

He had barely known Kon. Rai had spent more time with him in his unwaking sleep than he did with Kon awake. But guilt was another bond. One that drained him and yet Rai clung to it like water in the desert. Guilt is addictive and insatiable and Rai had more than his fill.

Lil had come to him that morning. It was hazy but Rai remembered that she had said if he wanted someone to talk to he could come to her.

Rai hadn't responded.

The others were out in the courtyard playing, leaving the orphanage hollowed. This mindless walking was doing nothing to settle his thoughts. He didn't want to talk about it but Rai wanted to be near someone who understood. And Lil was the closest anyone had gotten to understanding.

As he made his way down a narrow hallway, whispers caught his attention as he passed Maut-Eln's door.

"Sad but necessary. There was no helping the boy." Maut-Eln's unmistakably stern voice was quieter than normal. Like she didn't want to be heard.

"I know but that doesn't change the pain it's caused Rai," Maut-Fer said.

Rai knew he should keep walking. This was a private conversation and he wasn't sure he wanted to hear what was being said.

"He'll get over it. At least he wasn't there when it happened."

"I wasn't sure he would leave Kon's side, but he went with Lil. Hopefully this'll be the start of him rejoining the others. No one will adopt an outcast," Maut-Fer said.

Rai started walking when Maut-Fer asked, "How did you do it?"

How did you do it?

Rai froze.

"The doctor gave me a bottle," Maut-Eln said. "Just a couple drops in his food. He promised me it would be painless."

An icy cold washed over Rai.

"It's a sad world we live in when it's easier to slip the boy poison instead of looking after him." Maut-Fer sighed.

"No one would have adopted him like that and we can't afford to keep him," Maut-Eln said. "It's a way of the world."

A way of the world. That phrase again.

Rai felt sick.

He understood now. It was a coward's phrase thrown out when they didn't want to face hardship.

Rai couldn't listen to anymore. He stumbled down the corridor and out into the courtyard, mind spinning. The Mauts had *murdered* Kon. The mothers of the orphanage killed one of their own.

Breathing hard, Rai pressed his hands against his knees. The world around him shifted in and out of focus. Rai was going to be sick or pass out.

A hand gripped his shoulder. Looking up, Lil was saying something, concern pressing lines into her face.

I wasn't sure he would leave the boy's side, but he went with Lil.

What were the odds that Lil had come to him on the day they murdered Kon? *He went with Lil.* Had they asked her to get him out of the way? Rai would have noticed a change in Kon if they poisoned his food.

Rai pushed her away. Then he saw it. It was just a flicker but he knew the feeling well. Guilt. A bond forged between them by the act of betrayal. She *had* known. She hadn't wanted to be his friend. She hadn't wanted to support him after Kon died.

"Rai…"

He turned from her and marched back into the orphanage. Rai had gotten it wrong. It was better to cut ties with those who got too close.

The shattering of bonds was pain unlike any other.

2

Home

Rai sipped on his ale peering out the window at the place he thought he'd never return to. The city that had born, rose, and broke him. Tansen, the capital of Tarris, clung to the horizon as little more than a blotch in the pulsing heat.

The Stepping Stone Inn was packed with travellers coming to and from the city. Many sat playing games in booths and drinking coffee. Others were upstairs sleeping off the heat of the day. It was quiet despite the crowd. There were twenty-six people spaced out around the room. Only seven were armed.

Rai took another draught of lukewarm ale. It was no Artonian brew but it did the job.

Haven't you put this off long enough? Fax asked.

"I'm not putting anything off," Rai said.

The barman stared at him. Rai tapped on his mug and the elderly man went off to find another bottle.

"I'm scouting," Rai said, quieter this time.

We've been sitting in this small desert town for three days now. So unless you are scouting out the bottom of every bottle in this place, I think we've seen all there is to see here, Fax said.

"You know," Rai said, "when I was growing up I never thought I'd leave Tansen. I didn't cross the threshold of those city walls until I was in my twenties."

Now I know you've had too much ale. What will the barman think when he returns to hear you opening up to that empty beer mug?

"I'm talking to you."

I'm not sure talking to your shadow is any better.

Rai sighed. Perhaps Fax was right. He was putting off entering Tansen and facing a past that he had never wanted to return to. But he couldn't spend the rest of his life cooped up in this inn drinking his days away.

Could he?

Scorn pressed in on his mind as Fax listened to his thoughts.

The barman stepped out from behind the bar as Rai said, "Okay. We'll leave tonight," to his beer mug. The old man froze and furrowed his brow.

"It'll be another three coins if you want to keep the mug," the bartender said.

Rai couldn't decide if handing the man the three coins for the mug that he just promised he'd leave with tonight or trying to find a way to explain himself was the weirder response. So he sat in silence as the barman refilled his drink and left to serve another customer. The more he drank the easier it was to forget that others couldn't hear Fax. Rai downed the ale in one go and stood.

The room spun and he gripped the bar to steady himself. "Maybe we should leave in the morning."

Rai crossed the last stretch of desert in the early morning light. Travellers swarmed the capital in a constant flow of aya and hyian. Trepidation spiked as they rode closer. This had once been his home. Shouldn't he feel a sense of belonging upon his return?

Their aya crested a sand dune and the Turi market came into view. The city walls were surrounded in a mile-long market of stalls and tarp shades. There was a story that centuries ago when taxes were first put into effect for merchants within the city, a trader named Turi set up a stall just outside the gates and this was the beginning of the outer market. Being outside of the city, Turi didn't pay any taxes and was able to sell his goods for less than his competition within the walls. Thousands passed every day and Turi soon became one of the wealthiest merchants in all of Tarris until the emperor changed the rules and taxed every merchant business, even those in small villages. And so the phrase, *'try to outsmart the rules and you'll get hit with the Turi tax,'* was born.

Rai slowed the aya as they entered the markets. The musk of perfumes mingled with spices and coffee in an intoxicating assault. Vendors shouted their wares. Buyers haggled. And pickpockets ran amok. Rai ignored the merchants that walked alongside him waving away necklaces and dishes of spices.

The sandstone city walls reached high into the sky. The grand gate was manned by a battalion of city guards. However, there was little in the way of checks and Rai had nothing of value on him. So after a swift search, he entered the city of Tansen.

Familiar city streets broke off between the uneven blocky buildings. Rai still remembered the night he had left. It had been late. The streets brimming with life and yet he had been numb to it. Numb to everything.

That night was when everything changed.

So what now? Fax asked as they continued to wander down the main thoroughfare.

"We need to set up a base of operations," Rai said. It was always the first thing he did when arriving in a city, and he knew just the place.

The Inep Pot coffeehouse lay deep within the city of Tansen. The coffeehouse and inn was only a couple streets over from the Atef Palace. A gleaming iron sign hung outside of a teapot with a crack in it. Rai smiled as he led the aya around back to the courtyard. He had spent so many afternoons and nights with the others in this place. Stable hands jumped into action and placed the aya in a pen with some water.

"If you could feed it three times a day instead of the two I'd be grateful." Rai tossed a coin to the boy. His eyes widened and he nodded.

Rai took a deep breath and then stepped into the Inep Pot. The scent of freshly brewed coffee swam in the air and a low buzz of conversation came from the common room. The back reading room was quiet with only one patron, who sat with a steaming mug. Most were likely settling in for their daily qed, a nap to sleep off the worst of the heat of the day.

The common room, however, was never quiet. The Inep Pot was

known far and wide as one of the finest establishments for coffee outside the palace walls. Long communal tables ran the length of the room with a narrow bar along the right wall where three people bustled around the glass tubes, steaming pots, and huge glass containers filled to the brim with coffee beans.

As they approached midday, the Inep Pot was only half filled. A rare sight in all the years Rai had spent here. He approached the bar towards the grumbling old man who hit a pot, squealed and then swore waving his hand about.

"They tend to get hot when on the flames," Rai said.

The man spun around. His brow was furrowed with bushy white eyebrows that covered most of his eyes. He was bald but a beard ran from his ears down to his lower chest. Rai had always envied Derin's beard. He was a short man only reaching Rai's chest, so Derin had set up wooden crates behind the bar so that he could reach the equipment.

Derin scowled at him, looking Rai up and down. He must have seemed a state after travelling for weeks on the sands. His long, tan cloak was more of a rag than the impressive piece he was gifted in the palace all those years ago.

"What can I do for you?" he asked.

Rai grinned. His old friend hadn't recognise him. "I'll take a room and a Derin special."

Derin's eyes widened. He leant over the top squinting at Rai. "It can't be. Akarai?" Derin leapt over the bar and clasped Rai's hand.

"It's good to see you old friend," Rai said.

"Mmm I'm not the only one getting old," Derin said. He stared at Rai a moment longer before turning to the other two behind the bar.

They were young and new. "Fre! Make two Derin specials and don't skimp on the spice this time."

The boy bowed and got to work as Derin led Rai over to a table at the far end of the room. Derin groaned as he sat down on the bench.

"Where have you been all these years?" Derin asked.

Rai wanted nothing more than to catch up and tell Derin about everything, but he didn't have the time and where would he start? It had been over five years since he last stepped foot in this coffeehouse and so much had changed. "Palace business," Rai said.

The old man nodded. He was sharp and saw through the half-truth but Derin never pushed. Rai sighed. He owed his friend more than that.

"Things got complicated," Rai said. "I will tell you all about it, but not today."

The boy, Fre, came over with two mugs. He slid them onto the table, bowed, and moved back behind the bar.

"Very well," Derin said. "What can I do for you?"

"I need to rent a room while I'm here, and I need you to look after my aya should I disappear again," Rai said.

Disappear? Why would we disappear? Fax asked.

Understanding filled Derin's eyes. "You don't know if you'll return."

Rai stayed silent.

The old man sucked on his teeth. "We'll take care of your aya and the room is yours as long as you need it."

He reached his hand across to Rai who shook it. "I can't thank you enough."

"You can thank me by coming back and telling me all about

your journeys," Derin said. "It gets dull around here without you bringing chaos wherever you go."

They picked up their mugs and took a draught. A Derin special was the only sweet coffee that Rai liked. Warmth blossomed with the first sip. This was the cosy familiarity he had hoped to find at the gates. He was a fool to think the buildings would spark such a reaction. It was the people of his past that evoked the joy and the dread. The memories that carried weight, both good and bad. But this coffee brought Rai back to the best memories when they frequented the Inep Pot, drank into the night, and distracted Derin from working.

Derin slammed the mug down and shouted, "Fre! I said don't skimp on the spices. This is as tasteless as a glass of water!"

Rai smiled. Derin hadn't changed a bit.

After dropping off some of his belongings in his room, Rai set off towards Atef Palace. The Sun Eye beat down on Rai as he approached the palace gates. Two armed guards stood at either side, eyeing him warily.

"No matter what happens, I don't want you to attack or show yourself," Rai whispered.

If this is as dangerous as you're making it out to be, I'm not going to let you get hurt, Fax said.

"It's not that type of dangerous." *I hope*, Rai thought. "Please Fax. Listen just this once."

The shade didn't answer.

"Only officials can pass into the palace," the guard said. The massive iron grate was closed but beside them was a doorway that led into the courtyard.

"Let Imayani know that Akarai has returned," Rai said.

The guards looked at one another before the senior told the younger guard to pass on the message. He came back several minutes later with four armed guards. They clutched their spears as they approached.

You clearly have quite the reputation here, Fax said.

Rai grunted as the guards rushed him. He didn't fight back as they forced him to his knees and stripped him of his weapons. Then they snapped shackles around his wrists and dragged him into the palace. Rai was grateful when the guards pulled him around the side of the palace to an entrance instead of making a scene in the Hall of Strain.

The iconic gold veins ran through the sandstone walls like a web of golden light. It was as beautiful as he remembered. They took the side passages and avoided the busier corridors but still servants peered as they passed. Rai knew where they were headed by the directions the guards chose.

Coming down a set of stairs, they stepped into a corridor with iron doors on either side. After passing the first couple, a guard threw open one of the doors and tossed Rai inside. The door slammed shut behind him and the shutter clanged closed throwing the cell into darkness.

Well. I guess this is better than execution, Fax said.

The guards hadn't uttered a word. No doubt it was Overseer Myain who instructed them to put him in a cell. Imayani probably wouldn't hear of his arrival until tonight or perhaps tomorrow morning. Unfortunately, Rai didn't have time to wait.

He had to warn them about the dark place.

I see you.

The words burned in his mind. The great presence in Ma-atan's temple. It was not unlike Fax the way he had felt it in his mind. It's recognition of him and of Nya. Like a great eye opening, it saw them. And its hunger…

Unlike Fax, this was too grand for Rai to comprehend. Its mind too wide. But he remembered that hunger. That feeling of *want*. Rai didn't know what it wanted but it would burn everything to the ground to get it and they had woken it. He doubted the Monarch of Yontar knew of the being on the other side of the tear. So he had to warn Imayani.

"Fax."

Fax cut the bolt and the cell door creaked open. Rai peered out but the guards had already left. He made his way back to the stairwell where a guard sat watch in a side room.

"I'm sorry about this," Rai said. Fax shot towards him and smacked him across the head, knocking the guard out cold. Rai stepped into the room and retrieved his weapons. The guard had been poking and prodding at his bow and its unusual colouring.

He didn't want to charge in with his weapons and look like a threat but this bow meant too much to Rai to leave behind. It was a reminder of all those he had let down. He slung it over his back and sheathed his daggers.

"Go ahead and let me know if there are any guards. I don't want to hurt anyone else unless I have to," Rai said. A black blur shot up the stairs and Rai followed.

Imayani's schedule will have changed, Rai thought creeping through the palace corridors. But there was one room she spent most of her time in. Right enough, as Rai got closer to the war room, more guards were posted on the intersections. He sent Fax around the corner and the shade screamed as if someone was being attacked. The guards piled into the corridor and Rai slipped by unnoticed.

At the far end of the corridor, huge stone doors led into the war room. They groaned open and Rai stepped back into a shadowed corner.

"She's a damn black sand-footed fool!" a stern faced woman said. She wore rich maroon robes and walked with her head held high.

"Shh, ma'am, the door is still open. The empress might hear you," her servant said.

"Good. She needs to know the mistake she's making!"

They marched out of sight. Rai walked to the doors as they were closing and slid through the gap before they shut behind him.

The war room was empty aside from a bulky stone table in the middle of the chamber and the person standing over it. A map of Tarris was engraved into the stone and small coloured pieces marked where the country's soldiers were placed. There were no chairs or seats in the war room, as the Tarrisians believed that war and battle was a matter for full attention and one shouldn't sit to make choices of life and death.

The balcony door along the far wall was open letting in a light breeze that played with Imayani's purple robe. She was hunched over the war room table reading some ledgers. Rai couldn't believe they left her unguarded. She was the *empress*.

Imayani glanced up. She had aged since Rai had last seen her. A hardness that hadn't been there before gleamed in her eyes. Her black hair was neat and pulled back with golden pins. Her robe was immaculately folded and creased. And yet Imayani appeared tired.

That tiredness fled when she looked at Rai. Surprise lit her face and some of the Imayani he used to know came back as her expression softened.

Rai got to one knee and bowed his head. When he rose Imayani was standing before him that stoic indifference back on her face.

"I thought you were dead," she said, voice flat.

"I'm sorry," Rai said. How could he explain? What could he say?

Imayani bit her lip. "I don't know whether I should slap you, hug you, or call for the guards."

"I will receive whatever punishment you see fit but I came back because there is something important I need to tell you."

Imayani waited.

"The tear," Rai started.

"Tysar told us all about it five years ago," Imayani said.

Relief flooded Rai at hearing his friend had made it back. "Yes but there's more."

Rai's shadow pooled around his feet and expanded.

"So much more."

3

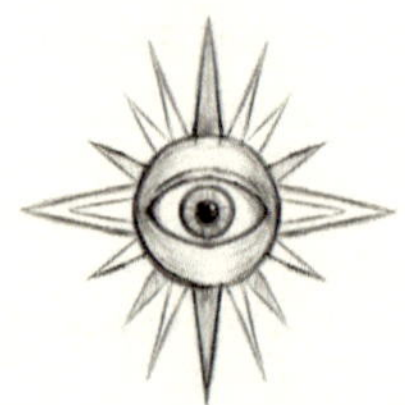

A Distinguished Guest

21 years ago.

News arrived at twilight. Upon receiving a letter, Maut-Eln fell into a frenzy, ensuring the orphanage was *'washed over with an aya's spit'*. At evening meal she looked visibly shaken and had the children clean the orphanage again, despite afternoon chores having already been completed. Whispers carried down the corridors, through the scrubbed bathrooms, and tidied bedrooms. A wealthy patron was coming to the Green Leaf Orphanage. What else would whip Maut-Eln into such a fervour?

Rai had grown numb to the orphanage around him and yet the tension and taut anticipation thrummed through the air at breakfast the following day.

Ping. Ping. Ping.

The rumbled excitement fell to silence as Maut-Eln tapped on a metal cup. The children all looked up from half-eaten meals to the mother of the orphanage. Her face was sunken, sleepless lines curling around her eyes spoke of a restless night.

Maut-Eln cleared her throat. "Today we have a special visitor coming to Green Leaf Orphanage."

The feast hall filled with sharp conversation. Maut-Eln tapped the metal cup for silence. "I need you to complete your morning chores with swift efficiency. The orphanage must be sparkling by midday." She glanced around at the children, concern furrowing more lines into her face.

"This is a very distinguished guest and I expect you all to be on your best behaviour. I don't want any fighting, shouting or screaming, or games that will have you rolling in the dirt," Maut-Eln said, and then mumbled something to herself as she glanced at Nib, who was coated in dust and sand from his 'scardrae burrowing' game.

Wealthy patrons had come before but they hadn't caused such a stir as this. *Something isn't right*, Rai thought.

There was hunger in the eyes of the children. A desire to be lifted from this life into one of luxury and comfort. Hope shone from the younger children like warmth from the Sun Eye itself, but some of the older children, like Rai, had the same resigned expression. It was unlikely the older kids would be adopted. Families wanted young children to mould. Blank slates that they could carve their hopes and dreams into.

Rai had given up on being adopted years ago. But that didn't matter. A couple more years and he would be able to leave the orphanage and get a job as a palace guard. They were given quarters in the palace and—

"Who is it?"

Rai wasn't sure who asked but the feast hall went quiet. Everyone faced Maut-Eln. She pinched her face as if displeased that she had to share the information.

"The emperor."

The stir in the orphanage erupted to hysteria. The emperor coming to the orphanage? Was he going to adopt someone? Morning chores were done swiftly, as if they were already trying to impress the emperor. Children danced around claiming that they were lost heirs or destined to be on the throne.

Rai washed dishes with two other boys. He dunked a plate into the mud-coloured water before passing it to Olu who dried, and then he passed it to Ips to put away. The water was warm and already needed changed after washing a quarter of the dishes. Rai tipped out the dirty water and set about heating more atop a flame.

The other two took the cue for a break. Olu groaned arching and stretched his back.

"This might be the last time I ever wash dishes," Ips said.

Rai had his back to the other boys but he could imagine Ips smug face. They were both a couple years older than Rai and kept to themselves.

Olu laughed. "The emperor wouldn't chose you if you were the last one here."

"He'll have to choose someone," Ips said.

"What makes you think he's here to adopt? It could be a check in. Nothing says *'I'm a good ruler'* like a trip to the orphanage," Olu said. Rai hadn't thought of that. Neither had most of the others, if the mad scramble coming from the rest of the orphanage was anything to go by.

"But didn't you hear?" Ips asked.

"Hear what?"

"Their baby died at child birth this week, which means he only has a daughter," Ips said.

The water started to bubble.

"Where did you hear that?"

"I heard the Mauts talking about it. The emperor doesn't have a male heir which means he's probably looking for one," Ips said.

"That's ridiculous. There's no way he would just adopt an heir from an orphanage," Olu said.

Rai lifted the basin of water and turned back to counter with the dirty dishes. Ips shrugged.

"It's too strange to be a coincidence."

At midday, they arrived. Maut-Eln had rules for patrons arriving. Each of the children had a place to be; a handful of the smartest children in the reading room, the most active playing in the courtyard, others helping prepare food. The children were each placed to reflect and highlight their strengths. That way patrons could easily pick out the child they wanted. Rai was sent to the courtyard with the rest of the active children. Maut-Eln instructed them not to move from their posts under any circumstance.

But this was the *emperor*.

Eyes peered over window ledges; heads stuck out from the side of the orphanage as everyone wanted to catch a glimpse of the emperor's arrival.

Rai peered around the corner of the building with three others who should have been pretend playing in the courtyard. The front of the orphanage was a walled stone garden with a handful of shrubs. Maut-Eln always said the walls were to keep intruders out but Rai couldn't help but see them as keeping him in.

A white and gold palanquin was carried onto the grounds by four palace guards. The ornate box was a gleaming white, trimmed in swirling gold patterns. Semi-transparent fabric flowed in the light breeze obscuring two darkened outlines shifting inside. Maut-Eln bowed, the other mauts matching the gesture. One of the guards pulled back the fabric.

"Here he comes," someone whispered. The emperor was said to be a stern man. And contrary to his age, he was supposedly fit and muscled. A mountain of a man. So the children were surprised when a young girl stepped out of the palanquin.

She looked to be around fourteen years old. Her caramel skin glowed in the sunlight and her black hair was tied up into a complex weave atop her head. The girl wore a white robe adorned with golden bracers around her wrist and a gold necklace. She was followed by an older man wearing a navy robe and the unmistakable nashk of an overseer. A nashk was a layered necklace that hung around an overseer's neck, with a row added for each year served. This nashk was gold and turquoise, the gold representing the highest rank an overseer could ascend to, and the turquoise indicating the man was in an advisory position. Rai was suddenly grateful that Maut-Sil made sure all the children knew the colours and what they represented.

"Who's that?" one of the others peeking around the corner asked.

"It must be the emperor's daughter."

"Why is she here?"

"Shh!"

The emperor's daughter dipped her head indicating the mauts could stand. Maut-Eln straightened. "Welcome to the Green Leaf Orphanage, Your Highness," she said. Maut-Eln showed no surprise that the emperor wasn't with them.

Looks like Ips was wrong, Rai thought. If the emperor was searching for an heir he wouldn't have sent his daughter and an overseer to find one. Maybe it *was* a check-in to make the emperor look good. His interest now waning, Rai realised he had been hoping to be pulled from this life too. He felt disgusted with himself to be so simple minded. No one was going to lift him out of his problems.

"Thank you," the emperor's daughter replied. "You have a beautiful courtyard."

The orphanage was once a rich manor, the memory of luxury lingering around its foundations. Shrubs ran in lines towards the building, and troughs of grubby water stretched down the length at their side. The mauts wouldn't let the children play out the front of the orphanage but Rai had seen others sneak around and dip their feet into the water. It pulled at the surface when they slid their feet in, as if a membranous skin of grime covered the pool.

Maut-Eln smiled and dipped her head.

"Can I give you a tour?"

The emperor's daughter nodded and was led into the orphanage, the overseer in tow. The children peeking around corners and peering through windows scattered, running to their designated positions. Rai and three others spaced out around the courtyard tossing the bevelled ball to one another.

The great tree threw a shifting shade over them making the midday heat more bearable. The others played with vigour, false smiles cut into their faces as if they had been playing all morning. The children stole glances at the orphanage, Maut-Eln's voice bounced around inside as she gave the emperor's daughter a tour.

"Why is the emperor's daughter here?" Uni whispered, catching the ball and passing it on.

"Probably to see if the orphanage is worth the emperor visiting," Kul said.

"Why would the emperor send his daughter? Surely he has people for this sort of thing." Uni paused. "What's her name again?"

"Imayan," Tiy replied. "She doesn't leave Atef Palace much."

"No wonder. There is nothing more disappointing for an emperor than having a daughter."

Maut-Eln's voice sharpened as she stepped out into the courtyard. "And here we have the symbol of our orphanage: the green leaf tree gifted to the orphanage by Fainin who was raised here and became a successful merchant," Maut-Eln said.

The emperor's daughter held a stoic practiced placidity, but part of that slipped when she saw the tree. Awe flickered across her face before falling back to her neutral smile. "It's beautiful," Imayan said.

Maut-Eln smiled, pleased to have impressed her. "The children often play in the courtyard after they complete their chores. Yil here spends most mornings running through drills with the practice swords. He's hoping to be a palace guard one day."

"An honourable profession," Imayan said.

Maut-Eln introduced the rest of them and then went on about the courtyards uses and history. Imayan nodded and asked polite questions about the small vegetable patch the children tended. The overseer never strayed far from her and he didn't mask his disinterest in the discussion. Instead, he stared at each of the children one by one, as if seeing into their souls and weighing their worth. Rai met his gaze. The overseer's dark brown eyes bore into him.

Smack.

The ball hit the side of Rai's head. A ringing pain shot through him as he rubbed his temple, eyes squeezed shut against throbbing. "Come on, Rai. At least pretend to pay attention," Yil hissed.

When Rai opened his eyes, Imayan and the overseer had walked on around the side of the building. But an uneasy feeling remained.

The excitement couldn't last forever, so when Imayan, the overseer, and Maut-Eln disappeared into her office for several hours, the buzz around the orphanage dimmed. The children were freed from their posts and went about their regular afternoon activities.

Rai was sitting in his nook in the roots of the great tree when he was summoned.

The musty smell of old parchment met Rai as he entered Maut-Eln's study. He had only visited the chamber a handful of times before and never for anything good. A circular table dominated the study with four chairs spaced around it. Scrolls lay scattered across its surface. They were the orphan's files, Rai realised upon seeing the names of the children scrawled at the top of each scroll. Rai's scroll lay unfurled and held by rock weights at each corner in front of Imayan and the overseer. They sat across from Maut-Eln who looked frazzled despite her trying to hold her composure.

Imayan and the overseer watched him in silence as Rai stepped into the study.

"Rai, come sit," Maut-Eln said, patting the chair beside her. She looked pleased to have someone on her side of the table, letting out a slow exhale as Rai sat. "Imayan and Overseer Lintou want to learn a little more about you."

Rai's heart hammered. What was this about? Why did they want to know about him? The other children's talk of lost heirs swirled in his mind but Rai could remember his mother, if only with glimpses and sounds in memory.

Lintou cleared his throat and sat forward. He was bald with a short neat beard, but lines creased his face like crumpled parchment. Rai couldn't place an age, he was like a scholar, ancient and yet a sharp lucidity spoke of an analytical awareness in his keen eyes. "We have a couple questions for you, Rai," Lintou said. "Answer honestly as we will know if you are lying."

All three stared at Rai. Was this about Kon? A wave of nauseousness roiled in his gut. Rai nodded.

"Where were you born?" Lintou asked.

Rai hesitated. It was a simple question but the seriousness of the situation was making it hard to think. "Here in Tansen."

"Have you ever left Tansen?" Lintou asked.

"No."

"Do you have many friends at the orphanage?"

Rai thought about lying but something in Lintou's eyes demanded truth. He felt Maut-Eln staring at him.

"No."

"What do you think of the emperor?"

"He leads Tarris and I follow." It was a phrase taught to all children of Tarris and seemed like a safe answer.

The corner of Lintou's mouth curled in amusement. "But how do you feel about his rule?"

"I…" Rai searched his mind but came up blank. "I don't know. I don't know enough about how he rules."

Rai's stomach dropped. Did he just say that to the daughter and adviser of the emperor? Rai dipped his head, cheeks flush. He could feel Maut-Eln's fury burning beside him.

Lintou stared at him a moment longer before nodding and then he leant back in his chair.

"We want to adopt Rai," Lintou said. "We will need all the paperwork on his past for a more thorough check and I want character references from the other mauts along with all of Rai's acquaintances: who he sits with in the feast hall, who he works with in groups, that sort of thing."

What is happening?

Rai stared at the overseer. He was going to throw up. Bile rode up the back of Rai's throat. He glanced at Maut-Eln but she was wide eyed, mouth agape and in as much shock as Rai.

"Along with classes and his scores," Lintou continued but Rai wasn't listening, couldn't listen. Rai felt frozen, like everything had stopped so that he could process that last statement.

I'm being adopted?

Imayan smiled at him.

4

Passing of the Nyfin

The coffee plumed in the filter parchment. The way it grew and spread when Nya added the hot water reminded her of a plant blooming. The coffee trickled into the pot and Nya waited for it to stop before topping the filter paper up with hot water. She stepped back to watch as the pot filled. Nya didn't particularly enjoy coffee but the scent was intoxicating.

Nya turned away from the coffee pot to face the common room of the Patched Cloak. Two tables were occupied but they were expecting more as the morning markets closed. The clatter of pots and pans rang from the kitchen, where Kit and Wenson were cooking breakfasts. Illy spoke to one of the tables. The occupants were Nuian like her and spoke in their language. While the Patched Cloak welcomed all, it had become a meeting point for Nuians in Tarris. There were so few of them and Illy had said it was rare to run into someone from her home country allowing the inn to act as a community centre letting Nuians meet one another.

Illy returned from the table, her brow scrunched.

"What is it?" Nya asked.

"They still haven't got their food," Illy said as she made her way to the kitchen.

"Let me," Nya said. She laid a hand on Illy's shoulder and gestured to the pot of coffee that had finished brewing. Illy nodded in understanding.

Nya came out from behind the bar and threw the door open to the kitchen. Sweet spices wafted from the room. Steam poured from pans as Wenson ran back and forth between them. He was shouting something in Nuian to Kit who stared blankly at a platter of diced meat in front of him.

"Sintela!" Wenson screamed at him. It was some Nuian word that Nya didn't understand.

Nya poked Kit and he startled, cowering away from her. His shoulders eased as he realised who it was.

"I think Wenson needs help," Nya said.

Kit glanced over to the man who was running between frothing pots, shouting what could only be Nuian curse words with how harsh they sounded.

"Damn it," Kit said and sped off.

Nya often found Kit spacing out. He had been that way since Ma-atan's temple when the deity tore his heart out before slamming it back into his chest. His heart hadn't started beating again and his skin had turned pale, but he was alive. Nya tried talking to him about it but he always changed the subject with a joke and when she pushed the point he would snap back and fall silent. She watched with concern as flames billowed from a pot.

The inn's door creaked as it swung open. Nya turned back to the common room as Lem stalked in carrying two crates of goods from the market.

"Where do you want them?" he groaned.

Nya swept in and took the top crate. She led him behind the bar where they stacked them in the corner. Lem gripped his lower back as he straightened.

"It's busy out there!"

"Oh yeah?" Nya asked as she inspected the goods. She would need to go through them before the rush.

"Yeah the festivities have already begun! Coloured streaks of fabric are hanging from windows. Street performers are singing and dancing in the street. It's hard to dance while carrying crates, you know?" Lem shook his finger. "But I managed."

Nya smiled. The Passing of the Nyfin was a rare event. Once every seven years the nyfin, a dragon-like creature with a long serpentine body, two great wings and many streamer-like strips cascading from its body would fly over before settling in the mountains to the north to sleep for another seven years. It was believed that the nyfin was once an entire race of creatures and this last remaining beast flew across the world in search for its lost kind. It called out as it made its journey, a mournful howl that haunted all who heard it. The last call of the nyfin. And so the Passing of the Nyfin became a festival across the world where people would shout back to the beast to show that it wasn't alone in the world.

Nya had missed the last festival because Mother had been going through a particularly hard time but she had heard its call and their answer. The Tarrisians all screamed at the sky to show their support of the great creature.

"It should fly over any day now," Nya said. After the nyfin passed, the Tarrisians celebrated for seven days ending with a parade through the city. Nya couldn't remember much about the last one other than it being bright and loud.

"Good. The rush of the nyfin's wind is unlike anything else." Lem closed his eyes and smiled reliving the memory of it.

"It does mean that it'll get busier in here though," Nya said, turning back to her notes. It looked like Lem got everything.

"I'll make sure the stables are spotless then." Lem bowed and marched out the back.

Nya leant over the bar. Illy had sat down with the Nuians and chatted animatedly. This was Nya's life now. It was a good life. Illy let her and Kit stay at the inn and fed them as well as paying them a little coin as payment for helping out. No more did Nya worry about the next meal. No more did she worry about getting beat by the guards or other gangs. It was comfortable. She still trained with Kit who had a little knowledge of sparring and she practiced with Bom testing their skills. The shade had become a quiet partner. They were settled and Nya rarely worried about accidentally lashing out at anyone anymore.

Nya thought this was what she needed.

But when the day darkened and she lay alone in her room, the hollowness remained. She tried to fill it with her friends and work but nothing abated the… nothingness. What was wrong with her? She had everything she wanted.

Well, not everything. Red splashes of memory brought her back to the attic. Brought her back to the look in Mother's lucid eyes when Nya speared through her with black tendrils. Mother came to her in nightmares most nights. Often having the voice of the dark presence from Ma-atan's temple.

I see you.

Nya shivered.

She just needed to focus on work. Eventually the dark nights would fade. She hoped.

Crash!

A rock shattered the shutters and skittered into the common room. Several patrons scrambled from their chairs and everyone stared at the bulky stone.

Illy stood and raised her hands in a calming motion saying something in Nuian. She picked up the rock and irritation flared across her face. Then she forced a smile and the customers sat back down. Illy placed the rock beneath the bar, out of sight. But not before Nya caught the Tarrisian inscription *'go home.'*

Nya felt sick. Not all Tarrisians were welcoming of this new haven for Nuians. There was a racist connotation that Nuians ate rocks because there was nothing else atop their mountain peaks, which was wrong. Illy had talked for hours with Nya about her homeland and the creatures and flora that covered the mountains. She had made many Nuian dishes for Nya and those who came to the inn. Illy said it didn't bother her but Nya could see it grated on the woman with the flashes of frustration whenever it was mentioned.

The door swung open and more customers piled into the inn and Illy put on a smile.

The Passing of the Nyfin came late that afternoon. Nya was sweeping the corridor upstairs when shouts came from the common room below.

"It's passing! The nyfin is on the horizon!"

"It'll be here any moment!"

Nya lifted her head and grinned. She tossed the broom to the side and ran to Kit's room. He said he was going for a qed but he couldn't miss this. Nya knocked and threw the door open. Kit slammed a book shut and glanced up wild eyed as if he had been caught stealing. He was sitting on the floor at the side of his bed. *Strange*, Nya thought.

"The nyfin is passing! Quickly, come on!" Nya said.

Kit cleared his throat, slid the book from his lap under his bed, and stood.

"Come on!" Nya said.

Together they ran down the corridor to the steps and piled out onto the Patched Cloak's rooftop. Outside was a buzz of chatter. Peering over the edge, Nya saw streets packed with people all staring into the sky. Illy leaned against the inn below with Wenson at her side. On the horizon, a white dot was outlined by the Sun Eye and it was growing.

"There!" Nya pointed.

"It's coming fast," Kit said. He sat on the edge of the roof, dangling his legs over the side. Nya made to sit beside him then patted her pockets. Oh no. She left them in the crates by the bar.

"I'll be one second!" Nya sprinted back into the inn, shot down the stairs, and into the empty common room. She skidded to a stop by the crates and pulled out the two shell whistles she asked Lem to get her at the market that morning. The cheers grew louder outside. Nya spun and threw herself up the stairs and back out onto the rooftop. She had made it. The nyfin was starting to take shape in the sky above. Nya could make out the waving body swimming like a fish in the sky.

Nya dropped down beside Kit and handed him one of the whistles. He looked at it and raised an eyebrow at her.

"These are for kids," he said.

"Well, this is the first year I've had one so shut up and use it."

In moments, the nyfin was nearly upon them. Its silver body gleamed in the dying orange light. Its iconic streamers whipped across its body catching the Sun Eye's rays in iridescent flashes. It was beautiful. The city below fell to an eerie quiet as it approached. Even the breeze stilled.

Then a torrent of wind tore through Yontar.

It almost blew Nya off the roof. She gripped the edge and shielded her face. The wind rumbled and shook streamers hanging from windows across the city. Nya squinted, looking up just as the nyfin passed above.

The nyfin howled. It was a powerful melodic sound that carried above the rattling of the wind. The crowds cheered and Nya lifted the shell whistle to her mouth and blew. A sharp serene note joined in the chorus of other whistles and melded with the whoops of the people in a cacophony of noise. Despite his earlier comment even Kit participated.

The nyfin passed overhead. The end of its body flicking with a crack. The beast howled again but this time it matched the tone of people. It was sad to think a creature so grand and beautiful was the last of its kind. It had to be thousands of years old. To wander so long and not give up hope was sad but also inspiring. Watching as it flew northward away from the city, Nya felt a well of elation.

If the nyfin could continue, then so could she.

The city quietened and the festivities began.

The Patched Cloak was a rush of people celebrating the passing. They revelled in the common room chatting and playing card games. Nya and Illy ran back and forth delivering coffees and teas as Kit and Wenson slaved away in the kitchen. Every time the door to the inn swung open the cries and laughter of the street poured inside. Nya had hoped to go out and explore some of the festivities and see some of the street performers that Lem had mentioned earlier but the inn was too busy and she couldn't leave Illy to deal with it alone.

The Patched Cloak only closed for a couple hours that night and it wasn't until late afternoon the next day that they had a lull in customers. Nya slumped onto a stool behind the bar and blew a strand of hair from her sweat covered face. Most had gone back to their homes or their rooms upstairs to sleep for qed. But they would all return after dark hour as the festivities often ran late into the night.

Illy slammed her arms onto the bar and grinned. "Well, that was something. That's the busiest the inn has been since we opened."

Nya blew out a breath and smiled back. It was contagious seeing how passionate Illy was about the inn despite its hardships.

"I'm going to close up the bar and kitchen for a couple of hours so we can rest before tonight," Illy said. She yawned. "I'm going to need some sleep if I have a chance of surviving another rush like that. You should do the same."

Nya nodded taking a deep draught from her waterskin.

"Will you go tell those two if I inform the customers?" Illy flicked her head towards the kitchen.

"I'll let them know."

"Thank you for today, Nya," Illy said. "I know it got hectic." She leant over the bar and lowered her voice to a conspiratorial whisper. "Now. You're young. You should be out there experiencing all the festival has to offer, but I would be a bad role model to tell you to go and enjoy it when I need your help tonight. However, I think your hard work deserves a reward." Illy pressed two coins onto the bar and slid them over to Nya. It was a week's salary.

"I can't," Nya said.

"When the inn does well, those who work here should reap the benefits. Take them. Just don't be late tonight and make sure you get *some* rest," Illy said.

Nya grinned and snatched the coins. "Thank you," she said and sprinted to the kitchen. Steam filled the air as the pair were deep at work. Their faces were scarlet and glimmering with sweat.

Nya told Kit that they had a couple of hours off and made enough gestures for Wenson to understand. They both blew out a breath and deflated against the countertop.

"I think it's cooler outside under the Sun Eye's glare than it is in here," Nya said fanning her face.

Kit grunted and ran his forearm over his forehead.

"If only we had some money to go out and buy some cool refreshments from the stalls." Nya let out an over exaggerated sigh and scratched her cheek with the two coins.

Kit's eyes went wide. "Where did you get those?"

Nya handed one to Kit. "They're from Illy as a thank you for today."

Kit studied the coin and bit it. "It's real," he said.

"Of course it's real," Nya said. "Want to go see the festival?"

"I don't know." Kit rolled his shoulders. "I'm pretty beat from cooking all day."

Nya rolled her eyes and shoved him. "Come on. We could die tomorrow. Let's go."

As soon as she said it, Nya regretted the words. Kit stiffened and the humour drained from his face. Death had become a sensitive topic since Ma-atan had ripped his heart out.

"I'm sorry I didn't mean it like that," Nya said.

"No, it's fine. You're right. We could." Kit looked at his hands. "Let's go see the festival."

You idiot, Nya thought cringing.

The crowd cheered as a street performer placed a blade against a brazier and flames ran up its length. The man was dressed in garish greens and blues. He spun the flaming sword around and Nya felt the heat from the fire as it whisked past her. Then he tossed the lit sword into the air. The crowd gasped as he flipped and caught it again. He flourished the blade and the audience screamed in approval.

All around, performers did death-defying stunts, sang and danced, and there was even a puppet show. People smiled and laughed and jostled one another. Even the city guards were joining in the fun.

It grew quieter as the Sun Eye rose higher. Usually at this time the streets would be empty. But still, people roamed the stalls. Nya inhaled. The baked goods and fresh coffee smelled delicious and some of the stands had themed drinks and nyfin memorabilia for sale.

"You're going to pull a muscle smiling like that," Kit said. Nya forced a frown before grinning again.

"Look, games!" Nya said. She took Kit's hand and pulled him through the throng to a stall.

The aim of the game was to throw small rings onto one of the pegs on the other side of the stand. The man behind the counter sat back against the wall and picked his teeth.

"Are you really wasting your money on this?" Kit whispered. "These things are rigged."

"Watch," Nya said. She slammed the coin down making the vendor startle from his stupor. "Three rings please!"

The vendor looked at her under his heavily eyelids. He clearly hadn't slept much. He grumbled something about kids having too much money and energy and slid the three rings across the counter.

The first pinged off one of the pegs. The second caught on a peg but flicked off with the momentum. Kit shook his head in dismay. Nya picked up the last ring making a show of turning it over and inspecting it. She closed her eyes and whispered a prayer under her breath before opening them and throwing the final ring. It flew through the air passing over the first peg but catching onto the second. However, much like her second toss there was too much power behind the throw and it was going to fly off. But just before it did, a black blur knocked the ring and it fell back landing perfectly onto the peg.

Nya held up her arms and cheered. The vendor blinked at the peg a couple times.

"I'll take the silver nyfin streamer please," Nya said.

The man groaned but handed her the streamer. It was a simple silver piece of fabric meant to represent one of the many streamers than hung from the nyfin's body. It was soft in her hand and Nya couldn't help but think that her mother would have loved to work with fabric such as this. All she had left of her was the half-patched blue cloak that she had worn every day since.

Turning away from the stand, Kit gripped Nya's wrist and pulled her into a quiet corner. He wore a stern expression as he glanced around to make sure they were alone.

"Nya, he saw your shade!" Kit said.

Nya waved a hand. "He was half asleep and saw nothing more than a black blur. Bom is too fast to be seen."

Bom sent a feeling of agreement.

"This isn't a game," Kit said. He was still holding onto her wrist, his grip tightening. "Just because you have more control over Bom doesn't mean you can start using it like this. It's still dangerous. What if you lashed out? You could have killed that vendor.

"You could have killed everyone in this street!" Kit shouted. Some people passing gave them a strange look. Nya looked at Kit's hand holding her wrist. He glanced at it, released it.

"Sorry. I didn't mean—" Kit stepped back holding his arms up.

Nya rubbed her wrist and watched Kit with concern as he fumbled over his words.

"It's okay," she said. "You're right. I shouldn't have used Bom like that. It was stupid."

Nya dropped the nyfin streamer and walked out into the throng. Kit reached for her and she slipped from his grip. He called after Nya but she ignored him, pushing deeper into the crowd.

5

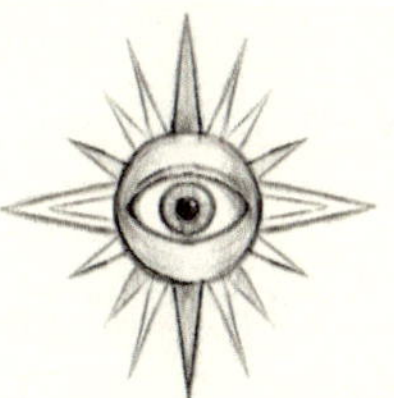

To Serve

21 years ago.

*H*ow long is too long to sit and look at your hands? Rai wondered interlacing his fingers. The horse-led carriage trundled through Tansen, the sounds of the city muted by its wooden walls. Horses were rare in Tarris. They couldn't walk across the desert so they were relegated to carting nobles around the cities, making them a rare sight.

Rai had never been in a carriage before but he was too rattled to enjoy the experience. He glanced up at Imayan who was reading. Overseer Lintou was to her left watching out the shuttered window. The last few days had been a whirlwind. After Imayan and Lintou left, Maut-Eln interrogated Rai on what they might want with him. The other children weren't any better, asking who his parents were and if he could put in a good word at the palace for them. Rai walked around in a daze that he still hadn't gotten over. He woke up the following day convinced it was a dream until Imayan and Overseer Lintou returned with the carriage.

Rai wanted to ask what he was doing here and what they wanted with him but the mauts taught them never to question superiors and one couldn't get more superior to the emperor's daughter and overseer.

"Do you like plants?"

Rai snapped his head up. Imayan peered over her book.

"Uh."

"What do you think of this one?" Imayan hopped over to sit beside Rai and slid the book into his lap. Sketched onto the page was a long stemmed flower with a bulbous yellow head, the tips of each petal a sun-burnt red.

"These are my favourite. They're called charah flowers," Imayan said. "They grow on high plateaus in the desert."

There was a sketch on the next page of a single charah flower poking out from between cracks in the rock high above the desert. The drawings were so detailed Rai thought he was looking through a window.

"Several grow together but they are so competitive that they all drain as much of the resources as they can, and grow tall as fast as they can. Normally only one survives and the rest are starved even if there are enough nutrients for all of them." Imayan's face scrunched as if it pained her to talk about it.

"Sad isn't it?"

Rai nodded, staring at the picture of the flower.

"They are also called the ravenous flower." Imayan flicked to the next page. "It's theorised that they only grow on high rock formations because they are closer to the Sun Eye, drinking in Ova's light. They can grow on the land but you won't find any unless someone brought them down from the plateaus. They have short lifespans gluttoning themselves on sunlight and whatever resources they can drain from the rocks and plant life around them until they have nothing left to live on. Then they wither and die."

Rai ran his finger over another set of images of the charah flower depicting it growing and then darkening and wilting. Detailed text covered the spaces between the pictures describing the stages of the flower's decay. It was sad that some flowers had to live such an unrelenting life when shrubs and bone trees survived for so long. Rai's mind fell to Kon. The boy he barely knew. Still he had seemed kind hearted while Zin was cruel and yet Kon was dead and Zin continued to live. *It's the way of the world*, the mauts would no doubt tell him.

"I have pictures of other flowers too," Imayan said, shaking Rai from his rumination.

Imayan flicked through the book, stopping at her favourite plants and telling Rai all about where they were located, what conditions they needed to grow, how big they could get. Rai had never been interested in plants but the passion burning in Imayan's eyes and flowing from her words kept him enraptured. Overseer Lintou glanced over once before turning back to his window with a sigh.

The rest of the journey passed quickly. Rai felt more at ease with Imayan chatting away than in the dreaded silence from before. The juddery ride smoothed out as they passed into the richer estates around the palace. Rai peered out the window as Atef Palace came into view.

Atef Palace was a sprawling manor of connected buildings and grand spires and arches. It looked more like a village than one building to Rai. He had seen pictures but nothing could capture its scale and detail. Stained glass windows stretched up the length of the spires. The taller centre building had a circular glass mosaic piece depicting a shattered tablet of stone held together in a glowing blue light. The symbol for Tansen. After the cataclysm at the old capital, Asuriya, Tarris was said to be a shattered country of warring clans, clamouring for power. This was until peace was restored with the Tablet of Convergence: a contract carved into the body of the world itself, a stone tablet, outlining a deal that each warring clan could hold a piece of what made Tarris great.

The monarch of Ossin got the river villages that fed the people with its rich farmlands. The monarch of Yontar got the city with the largest infantry. And the monarch of Rizu held the most active port in Tarris and gold flooded its streets from far off lands.

Tansen, however, became the new capital. Decisions for the Tarrisian people were made among the three monarchs and the emperor but the emperor had more stake in the voting.

The carriage trundled up to a gate that opened without them ever needing to stop. A guard on each side bowed as they passed and entered the grounds of Atef Palace. That niggling anxiety returned then as a curling in Rai's gut. They rode under an arch and into a grand courtyard. Before Rai could take in his surroundings, the door to the carriage swung open and Imayan hopped out ignoring the proffered hand from a palace guard. Lintou gestured for Rai to exit next.

The guard dropped his hand as Rai clambered out of the

carriage. The Sun Eye burned his vision to a blinding white. As his sight adjusted, Rai's breath caught. Standing around the courtyard were at least twenty guards spaced out and at salute. Huge gates hung open to their right, where a stable held lines of pens for horses, yarens, hyians, and other creatures Rai wasn't sure the name of. Stable hands were already tending to the horses that had pulled Rai from his old life and into whatever was next.

"Maut-Selus was looking for you, miss," a guard said to Imayan. He wore a jerkin and a sword hung from his side. Imayan looked chagrined rubbing the back of her neck and laughing uncomfortably.

"You told me Maut-Selus said it was okay for you to come pick up the boy," Lintou said stepping out of the carriage.

"I said she *'would'* think it's okay." Imayan grinned.

Lintou's eyebrow raised, disapproval furrowing his brow. "You better go and make up for anything you have missed. I will see Rai is settled in his quarters."

Quarters?

"But I—"

"Imayan," Lintou said.

Imayan deflated and nodded. "I will see you later. I can show you the gardens." And with that, Imayan ran off into the palace, two guards trying to keep pace with her.

It was quiet in the courtyard. Imayan's playful attitude had overwhelmed this otherwise uneasy atmosphere. Lintou stared at Rai and the guards stood like statues. Rai gulped.

"Come."

Overseer Lintou led Rai into Atef Palace. Pillars towered throughout the entrance chamber reaching into the rafters and the ceiling above. The pillars closest to the entrance had giant full body carvings coming to the same height as the great oak tree at the orphanage. They wore stern faces, arms up as if they were holding the ceiling aloft. Rai stumbled in, slack jawed and gazing upward at the grandness of it all.

"Hey!" a man in a navy cloak snapped when Rai bumped into him.

"Sorry," Rai said.

Skylights shone beams of amber light into the chamber. Palace guards marched through in twos, and scholars carried bundles of scroll work stalking further into the palace.

"Keep up," Lintou said.

"Who are they?" Rai asked gesturing to the statues carved into the pillars. Halfway through the chamber they stopped and the rest of the pillars were empty of design or ornamentation.

"This is the Hall of Strain. Every emperor that has ruled since the cataclysm is depicted on a pillar to represent how they held Tarris up for a time. It celebrates the burden of their rule as they are eternalised in the hall of the capital. You will know their names soon enough," Lintou responded.

Rai already knew many of the emperors of old but he thought better than correcting the overseer.

Then this will be Emperor Leondal one day, Rai thought looking at the first blank pillar.

Rai kept tight to Lintou's side afraid to fall into the ever-flowing currents of the palace. They passed out of the Hall of Strain and into a wide corridor.

"It's true," Rai mumbled under his breath.

The walls of the corridor were inlaid with golden threads weaving through the dark sandstone. Some said Atef Palace was a living thing and these were veins of gold. It wasn't any quieter here with servants, adorned with their dark red robes and spider web like gold designs matching the walls around them, speeding back and forth. Rai jogged to keep up with Lintou who didn't hesitate like he did. Lintou led Rai on a dizzying path through corridors, up staircases, and through enough doors that Rai would have no idea how to find his way back out of the palace if he needed to.

Panting, Rai crested the last flight of stairs into a quiet stretch where no servants or guards could be seen. They walked past several identical wooden doors before Lintou stopped before one and gestured to it. "Your quarters."

Rai reached for the handle but froze. He couldn't hold it in any longer. The mauts would scold him for questioning his superiors but they weren't here anymore. So he turned to Overseer Lintou and asked, "What am I here for?"

"To serve," Lintou said.

Something in Lintou's eyes stopped Rai from questioning further, so he pushed the door open.

Perhaps the grandness of the palace halls had built Rai's expectations too high, as when the door swung open, it revealed an unassuming room not unlike his in the orphanage. Two beds sat on either side of the narrow room with a chest at the foot of each. A single window let some light into the darkened room. It was how Rai imagined prison cells to look like.

A boy lay on one of the beds, hands clasped behind his head and legs crossed. He sat up when Rai entered.

"You have an hour until training," Overseer Lintou said. "Get changed." Lintou flicked fingers towards the folded clothes at the bottom of the empty bed then turned and left.

"What's your name, newbie?" The boy dipped his head in polite greeting.

"Rai." Rai matched the gesture. It was low enough to be polite but not low enough to show deference. The boy was of an age with Rai, his long brown hair falling to his shoulders in wavy creases.

"Tys."

A three letter name. So he was in the same standing as Rai. Rai lifted the garment at the bottom of his bed, letting it unfurl. It was a V-shaped neck dark brown robe and white loose trousers. The same outfit the boy in the other bed was wearing.

Rai dropped onto the bed and exhaled. It couldn't be long after midday but he was exhausted. He wanted nothing more than to fall back for qed.

"New recruit?" the boy asked.

"I don't know."

"They didn't tell you anything either, huh?"

Rai nodded. He wasn't sure if he was a recruit or not but Lintou expected something. *To serve.* To serve who? The emperor? Lintou? Imayan? And by what means? Was he being trained to become a palace guard?

"They picked me up from the orphanage this morning," Rai said.

"Orphanage? They picked me up from palace guard training. But it was strange," Tys said. "Had Overseer Kuji dig out my lineage scrolls for some reason."

"Overseer Lintou did the same with me," Rai said sitting up.

"Why do they care about our lineage? Do you think we're here to become palace guards?"

Tys shrugged. "It must be important if Overseer Lintou is involved. He works directly with the emperor."

"And Imayan," Rai said it offhandedly but Tys straightened.

"Imayan?"

"Yeah, Imayan was with Overseer Lintou when they picked me up." Rai could tell from Tys' face that she hadn't been there when he was brought to the palace.

"Did she say anything?"

Suddenly, Rai felt uncomfortable talking about this. "She talked about plants."

Tys stared at Rai a moment longer. "You better get changed. I'm sure they'll explain what's going on at training."

6

Simple

Rai told Empress Imayani everything. He told her about his trip through the tear, receiving Fax, and his five years of searching for the truth about shades ending with Kyan and the events at Ma-atan's temple. Rai left out Nya for now. If it became relevant he would mention her but Rai worried that Imayani would drag her to the capital if she knew Nya had a shade too.

It was therapeutic, pouring everything out. He hadn't realised that the secrets had become a burden weighing him down. And it was only as he voiced them that Rai realised the threat this posed to Tarris. If the monarch of Yontar had soldiers with shades he would become an unstoppable force. With the constant vying for the throne, it wasn't a stretch to see Kleran, the monarch of Yontar, marching on the capital, shade soldiers in tow. And then there was the presence in the dark place.

Imayani didn't give any indication of her thoughts as she listened. She leant against the war room table and didn't interrupt him. When he finished Rai slumped against the table and ran a hand through his hair.

"I know I should have returned before now," Rai said. "But when I left I didn't know…"

"I understand," Imayani said. She radiated confidence and Rai couldn't tell if it was a front. He used to be so good at distinguishing her reactions.

Imayani sighed. "Tysar told us of the pocket world. He and Genu were the only two to return."

"What of Ada?" Rai asked.

Imayani shrugged. "Genu was with him but lost him in the Thousand Floor Palace when they split up to avoid the guards. We think he's dead."

A piercing chill. Seven of them had entered the tear that night. There were so few left now.

"I confronted Kleran and he claimed the tear hadn't been open long and he had planned to declare it. Of course I couldn't claim any ties to your attack that night. But we both knew it was from me. I sent scholars over and they have collaborated with their research team. We've been kept in the loop since. Although they have never mentioned shades."

Fax was in the shape of a crow. The shade had gotten better at flying like one but it still couldn't simulate how they walked, so it glided over the table. Imayani watched it with unease. During his retelling of the events, Fax made an appearance and she had watched the shade with trepidation since.

"Then they are hiding the truth from you," Rai said.

"Maybe they haven't found any others? You said yourself that your shade told you it was unlikely they would find more hosts," Imayani said.

Shades are extremely picky, Fax said. It faced Rai. *I must be the exception.*

"There's a girl. She has one too," Rai said ignoring the slight.

"Why didn't you mention this before?"

"I promised to keep her safe."

"You promised me the same thing once." The words snapped back with a vitriol Rai hadn't expected.

An awkward silence came between them. They both had jumped into talking about Tarris and shades partly to avoid another conversation. One left unspoken of a past drenched in blood and lies. One neither wanted to revisit.

Imayani took a deep breath.

"I need a drink." She wandered to the side of the chamber and poured herself some amber liquid. She didn't offer Rai any.

"Nya was sent into the tear and returned with a shade. After they got out, the scholars waved a blade near those who had come from the pocket world. The girl thought they might have been looking for shades as her shade reacted to the blade," Rai said.

Imayani placed her drink on the table. "If that's the case and they know of these shades and are actively trying to find them, then we need to confront Kleran."

"Confront? I don't think he'll own up to this."

"He will. Like I said, we have been collaborating," Imayani said.

"Imayani, he could be planning an attack on the capital with shadowbound soldiers. He wouldn't own up to that."

"He won't be planning that. We have a truce."

"Imayani," Rai started.

"Akarai, we're engaged," Imayani said.

Rai stared at her. The marriage made sense from a political standpoint. Overseer Myain no doubt recommended the move.

"After most of the Seventh Sceptre died and I was left alone I didn't have a choice. A marriage to Kleran would bring peace to Tarris. None of the other monarchs could face us united. It would give Kleran the power he is striving for and the peace I am working towards."

Imayani furrowed her brow. "This is no doubt a misunderstanding. It's not likely that he knows about shades."

"I see," Rai said.

'I was left alone'. He had left her alone. Thinking about it from Imayani's perspective, Rai couldn't help but feel guilty.

If I had returned I would have only made it worse, he thought.

Imayani straightened and changed back to the regal ruler instead of the woman Rai once knew. "I'll look into this. Is there anything else?"

Rai opened his mouth then closed it again. There was one more thing she had to know about but he didn't know how best to approach it.

"In the tear. I think there's something in the tear. Like the shades but... bigger. There was a voice in my head and it came from the pocket world. It's only just become aware of us but we need to be careful," Rai said.

The empress fought to keep the disturbed look from her face.

Whether that was at the implication of this creature in the other world or the fact that Rai had owned up to hearing a voice in his head, he couldn't tell.

"Thank you. You're dismissed."

Rai could read Imayani's flat expression. She was deep in thought and still deciding what to do with him. That was understandable. He didn't even know what to do with himself. Rai turned to walk for the door.

"Tysar has his own quarters now but your old room should be empty," Imayani called.

Rai nodded without turning and left the war room. It was best not to tell her that he already had a room outside the palace.

It couldn't have been midday but Rai was exhausted. He wanted nothing more than to go back to the inn and collapse onto his bed, but he knew sleep wouldn't come. His mind was alight with memory, both bad and good. So Rai wandered the palace for a while. The familiar corridors sparking memories like embers from a fire. It seemed that every twist and turn in this place was ingrained with history. His history.

A long corridor spanned out in front of him and Rai vividly remembered running through here with Tysar, spears under arm, after Tysar had misplaced them the night before. They had been late to morning training and Overseer Rikai had them doing laps around the Eye for hours.

Once Rai had travelled far enough away from the war room he slumped onto an open window and gazed out at a small garden. Beside the massive garden at the centre of the palace there were these *scenes* as Imayani had called them, little courtyards filled with themed gardens. Some had stone sculptures, some water displays and others sprawling greenery. This one was a rock formation sitting in the middle of gravel. The gravel had been raked to create spirals and patterns around the rocks. Rai wondered if Imayani visited the palace gardens still. She had always loved them.

Well. At least you weren't hung, Fax said.

"Somehow, this is worse," Rai said.

There's nothing worse than being hung. It's a reminder that you can't fly and you die at the end.

"No. Hanging onto an edge wondering if the person above you will pull you up or stomp on your fingers is worse. The waiting is always worse. The hope and the dread and the bounding between the two."

"Akarai?" a voice asked.

Rai glanced up to see Mino. The short woman froze in the middle of the corridor staring at him. Her blonde hair was neatly woven into a bun on her head.

"It is you," she said.

Mino stepped up and slapped Rai. He didn't react. Then she bit her lip and pulled him into an embrace. "I thought you died."

"Me too," Rai said, hugging her back. "It's good to see you, Mino."

She sniffed and straightened, looking either way before taking his hand. "Come with me."

Mino led him to one of Imayani's sitting rooms where she met with nobles and other important guests. She closed the door and turned to face him.

"She grieved for you." The way Mino said it wasn't an accusation, merely a statement, but the words stung worse than any slap.

"Mino, you don't know the full story. It's complicated."

"I don't care why you left. I just wanted you to know that," she said. Mino walked over to the stand and poured two drinks. She handed one to Rai. He sniffed it and his head jerked back.

"I didn't know you drank," Rai said.

"It's a new thing," Mino said and took a long draught.

Look, she's like you, Fax said.

Shut up Fax, Rai thought back.

She swirled the glass and looked at Rai. "Does she know you're back?"

"I just spoke with her," Rai said.

"And?" Mino asked.

"And I'm still breathing."

"I don't know what went down between you two but you really hurt her, Akarai," Mino said.

"I would have hurt her more if I had come back," he said.

"I don't believe that."

"Because you don't know the whole story," Rai said.

"What is the whole story then?" Mino crossed her arms.

Rai stood rigid in the middle of the room. He played with the glass in his hand. "I can't, Mino. I wish I could but I can't."

Taking his hands, Mino dragged him across the room and shoved him into a chair. Then she sat across from him.

"I'm sorry, Mino. I can't tell you what happened. It's complicated."

"Whatever happened between you two must have been serious. Imayani refused to tell me too," Mino said. She raised an eyebrow at him and Rai looked away.

"I don't know what I expected, coming back here, but this wasn't it." Rai ran his hands over his face.

"Why *are* you back?"

"I was just asking myself that very question."

Mino sighed. Then she straightened her back, sniffed and met his gaze. "Okay. An easier question first. What made you come back now?"

"I wanted to help Tarris."

Mino raised an eyebrow.

"And Imayani," Rai admitted.

"And how can you do that?" Mino asked.

Rai sat back and thought for a moment. Daylight poured into the room in long streaks lighting dust motes floating through the chamber. *How can I help Tarris and Imayani?* The answer was obvious. What he had already been doing.

"By continuing my research into shades and being there for her."

"That sounds simple enough to me. You were always one to overcomplicate things." Mino took the glass from his hand and downed Rai's drink. "Sometimes you just need to break it down to its foundations." She dragged him up and led him to the door, patted him on the back, and then shoved him into the corridor. "It's only as complicated as you make it."

The door slammed shut.

I like her, Fax said.

"I don't," Rai muttered but Mino was right. He was ruminating on things he couldn't control. Whatever Imayani decided to do with the tear, with Kleran, and with him would come no matter what he did. But there was something he *could* do.

Rai stalked down the corridor and into his past.

7

Unchained

"Something is wrong. I just wish he would tell me what it is," Nya said.

"Maybe he just needs time to come to grips with what happened," Illy said. She sprinkled some spices over the coffee and then poured the water, letting it filter through to the pot below. The Patched Cloak was quiet in the early afternoon but the festivities still rang through the street outside.

Nya sat on the counter kicking her feet. "But I can't help him if he doesn't tell me what's wrong."

Illy blew out a breath. "Did you tell him what was wrong when you left with Kyan? You didn't want to talk about it but he stayed at your side anyway."

"Yeah, that's because he was always there. No matter how many times I pushed him away, he kept coming back," Nya said.

Illy raised an eyebrow.

"Oh."

"Just being with him can be enough," Illy said. "If he wants to tell you, he will. If not, then you can still support him by being there," Illy said.

She was a black sand-footed fool. When Nya needed help the most was when she pulled back from Kit. But Kit persevered.

Now he was doing the same and it was her turn to be at his side.

Nya leapt off the bar and hugged Illy. "You're the best."

Illy scoffed but hugged her back.

"Where is Kit?" Nya asked.

"In his room," Illy said. "Reading but he's fetching some supplies for me later. Maybe you could go with him?"

Thoughts whirled in Nya's mind. "I think Lem is going with him," Nya said. "But that's okay. I can still be there for him."

Illy smiled and nodded.

Nya scrubbed a table with her wet cloth. She felt the grain of the wood beneath her fingers as she pressed into the table. Nya doubted the patron had any coffee left to drink with how much they had spilled across the tabletop.

"We'll be back before you can say shefelog," Lem said, stepping out of the kitchen, Kit in tow. Illy had a confused look but thought better than asking Lem what he meant.

"Here's the list," Illy said and handed Lem a sheet of parchment with the supplies she needed for the afternoon rush.

Nya met Kit's eyes and smiled. He tore his gaze away and followed Lem out onto the street. He hadn't spoken to her since the game stall.

The second the door clanged shut, Nya jumped into motion. She ran to the bar and tossed the wet rag onto the counter and then headed for the stairs.

"Nya?" Illy asked.

"I'll be back in a minute!" she called taking the steps three at a time.

Nya tore down the hall and came to Kit's door. Breathing hard, she glanced back towards the stairwell. Then with a slow exhale, pushed the door open.

Kit's shutters were shut tight against the afternoon Sun Eye. A fetid stench rose from a pile of unwashed clothing. Nya turned her nose away and headed for the side of his bed. Kneeling, she reached under and felt around until her fingers landed on something. She pulled out a book. It was a navy leather tome with some sort of bird as a decorative sigil inlaid in gold. Flicking through the pages, Nya scanned the illustrations and passages of text. There were creatures of some kind in the drawings, but despite Kit teaching Nya how to read a couple words, she couldn't make out most of the text. She slung the book under her arm and marched back down to the common room.

"Good you're back. I need you to—" Illy faltered noticing the book under Nya's arm. "What's that?"

Nya slammed the book down on the bar. "I need you to tell me what this is about."

Concern wheedled its way onto Illy's face. "Nya where did you get this?"

"It's Kit's."

"Nya, I thought we said—"

"The reason I'm here is because Kit made sure he did everything in his power to help me. I have to do the same for him. Please, Illy." Nya held Illy's gaze and her face softened.

"Just a quick look and then you need to put it right back before they return," Illy said. She pulled the book over and opened it. Illy's expression darkened as she read.

"Illy what is it?"

"I…"

"Illy," Nya said.

Illy blinked and looked up from the book. "It's death rituals."

"Death rituals?"

"Yeah, it has details on different forms. Practices for communing with the dead, some that supposedly raise the dead, rituals that lengthen your life, and some death curses," Illy said, her voice cracking on that last phrase.

"That stuff isn't true though, right?" Nya asked.

"No, I don't think so. It's all made up. Witchcraft nonsense," Illy said. She pushed the book back to Nya. "Now go put it back." Illy shied away from the book even after admitting she didn't believe in its contents.

"But what would Kit want with this?"

Illy shrugged. "Something to do with what he went through at the temple I assume. Now, quickly. I don't want them coming back to us reading it."

Nya frowned at the book. She wanted to study it longer but Illy was right. So she grabbed the book and ran for the stairs.

The late crowd came in a flood of festivity. Illy had wedged the door open letting in the cool night air along with the cheers of the festival. Crowds huddled around the tables as storytellers wove tales of the great nyfin and the days when the skies were filled with their kind. Nya shoved through the throng, delivering drinks and snacks just to be dragged into dancing and games.

"Ah, our drinks," said a stout man who grinned with only one side of his mouth. He stood with four of his friends around the dart board discussing bets for the next round. Nya could smell the alcohol on his breath when she approached. Once this would have frightened her as so few were open with their drinking in Tarris. This was until she met Rai and learned that not all those who drank were bad people, despite what some Tarrisians had her believe.

"Tell you what, missy," the man said, taking the drinks from her. "I'll tip you a coin if you can score a kiren."

Nya looked at the board. A kiren was one of the hardest targets to hit. In the centre of the board was an amber circle that resembled a kiren's eye.

"Two coins," she said.

His friends cawed and howled laughing at the man's stunned face. He cleared his throat. "Two coins but you have to get it on the first try."

Nya smiled and nodded. She took the dart and stood where a line had been drawn onto the floor to indicate the correct distance from the board. She closed one eye and moved the dart back and forth lining up the shot. Bom filled her vision indicated the right angle and she threw the dart. It flew through the air and hit dead centre.

The man's friends cheered but he did not. He grumbled as he handed over the coins embarrassed by being bested by the waitress and wanting her gone. She clinked the coins into her belt and nodded before retreating to the bar.

"Good shot," Nya said. Bom rumbled in agreement. During the quiet moments of early afternoons she had been playing darts when Bom had first shown her that it could help direct her movements. The shade had incredible accuracy. Nya guessed that made sense for a being that could change its shape in an instant. The shade had to calculate angles and distances in fractions of seconds as it formed itself into different shapes.

On her way back to the bar, Nya noticed Kit talking to a customer. He spoke to a man in a grey cloak who was sipping on his tea. This wasn't out of the ordinary but the way Kit shot furtive glances around him implied that he didn't want to be seen. Nya slowed, clearing some empty mugs from a table and peering through a gap in the crowd.

The man was waving Kit away but Kit leant in and whispered something into his ear and then Kit pulled out a deran. He passed it to the man who grunted and pulled out a parcel wrapped in a rag. It was book shaped. Kit slid it under his cloak and stalked off towards the kitchen. Nya dropped to the ground and all but hid under the table as he passed.

Another book? He had become obsessed with reading recently. Was it more of the same death rituals? Nya wondered. "Bom, go see what he does with that book," Nya whispered and stood, brushing the dust off her robe.

The shade slipped through the crowd as a patch of shadow

towards the kitchen. Nya reached the bar just as Bom returned.

He stashed it in a cupboard, Bom said.

Nya nodded. "When it gets quiet, we should go have a look."

It was late into the early hours of the following day before the common room cleared. Tarrisians stumbled out onto the streets that had quietened to dull chatter compared to the roaring crowds it had been earlier. Nya waited until Illy was busy collecting the money and counting their earnings from the night to slip into the kitchen.

The lamps still burned despite the cooking pots having gone cold. Wenson and Kit were sifting through some of the stock in the basement in preparation for tomorrow's breakfast. This was her chance. Nya scuttled down the length of the kitchen.

"Which cupboard, Bom?"

The shade shot out and hovered as a black blotch in front of a corner cupboard. Nya dropped to her knees and pulled the door open. Spare pots filled the space but tucked down the side, almost imperceptible unless one knew what they were looking for, was the edge of a piece of cloth. Carefully, Nya slid the parcel from its hiding spot. It was certainly a book and it held some weight. Nya coughed waving away the dust and set about unwrapping the cloth.

The book was jet black. A splash of red, that Nya first thought was blood spatter, covered the front. She gasped when she realised what it was; the symbol for the Ghrobans. Not the street gang but the original cult. The street gang named themselves after the cult that went by the same name. In the old tongue it meant *"ones unchained"* referring to the Judging after death. They were said to kill and steal without restraint or fear of staining their souls until the emperor chased them from the city. The gang had taken up the mantle and name on a lower scale. They killed and stole but no more than other gangs in the Yontar.

What was Kit doing with *this*?

Nya's fingers trembled as she opened the cover. She only managed to look at a couple pages before slamming the book shut. Nya was grateful she couldn't read the words but the illustrations were enough to make her feel sick. It showed violent deaths and sketches of organs and innards.

Strange that what is inside you makes you feel so sick, Bom said.

"They make me feel sick because they should be inside. I shouldn't be able to see them," Nya said clenching her eyes shut. She could feel Bom think on those words. The shade was always so curious about human ways.

"Why would Kit want this? Death rituals, Ghroban tomes. It doesn't make sense," Nya said.

Maybe he wants to kill those who left him how he is? Bom said.

"The Decreed? They fell apart after Kyan died at the temple. Rai stayed to make sure no one else took up the reins," Nya said. Kit would have no way of finding the surviving members of the Decreed.

Nya stared at the book. She should confront him. Ask him what this was about, but she had to wait for the right moment when they were relaxed and he could open up about this. Nya needed to make it clear that she wouldn't think poorly of him, no matter what Kit was getting himself into.

Nya wrapped the book back up in the cloth and slid it back into place when the door to the kitchen swung open. Without Bom's warning, Nya would have been sitting on the floor when Kit trudged into the kitchen. Luckily she ducked behind a row of cupboards just in time.

Kit sighed. Nya listened to his footsteps that led him to the cupboard where the book was hidden. She steadied her breath, her back pressed against the cool wood of the cupboard. The cupboard door creaked opened and Nya listened to the sound of cloth unfurling from around the book. The click of pages being flicked. Then the book was slammed shut and Kit heaved and blew out a breath.

It was instinct that drove Nya to stand and walk over to Kit as he sat huddled in the corner, his face in his hands. He looked so… broken sitting there. She couldn't leave him any longer. Nya laid a hand on his shoulder and he startled, sliding the book behind his back.

"Nya?" Kit's eyes were red, a stark contrast to his now pale complexion.

"There's no point in hiding it," Nya said. "I saw the book."

Shock burst onto his face before settling into a scowl. Kit stood grinding his teeth. "What, are you stalking me now? Is that it?"

"No, I just saw you with the book and was curious," Nya said.

Kit turned his head away and laughed. "Curious enough to search it out and then hide when I come back?"

"You've been acting strange recently. So I wanted to help and—"

"Help?" He laughed again. It was a croaky forced laugh. "How can you help, Nya? I've had my heart torn out of my chest and now I'm some half dead thing! How are you going to help with that?"

Nya had never seen Kit this angry. It had bubbled to the surface so quickly, as if it had always been there waiting for the right moment to flare.

"I don't know I—"

"Have you got any idea what it's like to have died and return as a corpse? Of course not! No one does! Look at my skin, Nya." Delirium leaked into his tone as he gestured to his arms. His skin was ashen and pale. "We don't know if this means that I am still dying! I could topple over right now and just be dead! We don't know! We don't know anything about this!" Kit threw the book across the room. "There's nothing about this anywhere!"

He stared at her breathing hard.

"So that's why you've been looking at death rituals and the old Ghroban book?" Nya asked.

"I've searched every book on the topic and none of them mention the Judging being a thing that can happen to the living. Much less this." Kit reached out and pulled a knife from the counter and stabbed it straight through his hand. Nya screamed. He hissed, his face a frenzy of pain.

She stepped back as blood began to drip to the floor. It was darker than it should be, almost black. Kit tore the knife free and let it clatter to the ground. He breathed heavily, his shoulders rising and falling and then he lifted up his hand. The flow of blood slowed and then came to a stop. Then the gash across his palm began to *knit itself back together*. Nya watched in horror as moments later his hand was back to normal except for the dark coating of dried blood.

Kit slumped against the counter, deflated. "That really takes it out of me," he said.

Nya didn't know what to say. She just stared at her friend.

"I don't want to die, Nya," Kit said. His voice quiet. "But I think I'm already dead."

The softness in his voice hit Nya like a physical blow. It was more frightening than any shouting could be. She pulled him into an embrace. Kit went rigid in her arms. After a couple breaths his muscles eased into the hug.

"You're not dead." Nya said the words with a stone-like conviction. Whether to convince herself or Kit, she didn't know. But it didn't matter.

She *wouldn't* lose another that she loved. *Not again.*

8

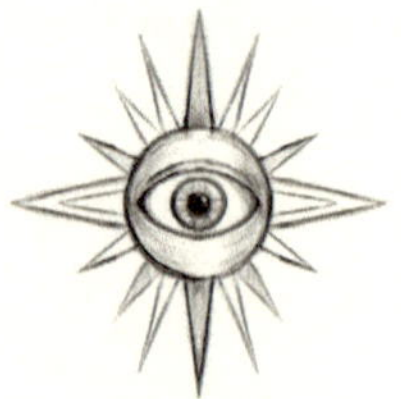

The Eye

21 years ago.

The heat was stifling. Each inhale burned Rai's nose and sweat trickled from his scalp.

"My name is Overseer Rikai. You're probably wondering what you're doing here." The overseer was a head taller than anyone else in the hall. He wore a short beard on his sharp jawline that slowly faded up to his shaved head. Thick muscle was taut all the way up his arm, as if he was constantly flexing. Around his neck, Rikai's nashk was silver with a band of red, placing him as an overseer of combat. Most combat overseers specialised in training combat or war room tactics and going by Rikai's build, Rai guessed he focused on the more direct applications of combat.

"You're here to be trained. Here to do as you are told. Here to serve." Overseer Rikai's voice boomed around the low-ceilinged circular room. They were on the third floor of Atef Palace deep within the expansive building. The glass dome above them framed the Sun Eye as it watched them with its burning glare. There were no windows, the walls were made of solid stone and the glass domed roof was seamless, making the room a sweltering oven of heat.

There were twenty children ages with Rai standing in a line, a mix of boys and girls but all in identical brown and white robes. They had only been in the glass room for a few minutes but some of the others had already started to sway under the Sun Eye's glare.

Overseer Rikai didn't pace but stood in the middle of the line looking at each of them. "Most of you will end up as city guards, a handful as palace guards, and maybe one or two of you *might* get the opportunity to go to the Verdin Temple to continue your training."

This caused a stir among the recruits. But none spoke. Rai doubted anyone knew each other but the mention of the Verdin Temple was enough to evoke an almost primal reaction from them. The Verdin Temple was where legends were created, warriors of untold ability. Only the best palace guards and honour guards to the emperor trained at the Verdin Guild. To be a part of the Verdin Guild was a dream for many.

Children dreamed of joining the Seventh Sceptre. A mythical crew of unstoppable assassins. But those were just stories. Men and woman dreamed of joining the Verdin Guild because it was *real*.

But the Verdin Guild wasn't somewhere one could apply to join. Members were handpicked by unknown means. Was this it? Was this the first stage of joining the Verdin Guild? Rai's back straightened and awareness sharpened despite the the heat.

One of the children collapsed.

"Or not," Rikai said. He clapped twice and two guards swept in from the hallway. Their eyes bulged at the heat as they entered the hall and dragged the passed out boy back into the corridor.

Overseer Rikai waited until the guards left and the door thudded shut. "You fail and that's you out. We do not accept weakness here." Rikai gestured to the hall around him. "Some of you may have already noticed that it's rather warm in this chamber. This is the Eye. Where Ova watches with its Sun Eye and judges your worth. To train in here is an honour. And to survive it is a privilege.

"Now, laps."

The recruits glanced at one another. Some of them were struggling to stay on their feet in the heat, to run was madness.

Overseer Rikai didn't snap at them. He waited and watched until one of the children, a boy with long blonde hair started jogging around the perimeter of the Eye. For a moment, Rai thought the others might leave but the promise of the Verdin Guild was too much. Slowly others joined the trail.

Rasping breaths and slapping footsteps bounced around the glass above them as the recruits circled the hall. Tys made to run alongside Rai but Rai picked up the pace making it clear that he wasn't here to make friends.

Already his vision was unsteady and his run was more of a forward stumble. His stomach swirled and Rai had to steady his breathing to stop himself from being sick.

It wasn't long before the first fell.

Overseer Rikai sat cross-legged in the middle of the chamber in a meditative posture. "When you pass him, make sure to trample over him," Rikai shouted. The boy who had fallen first tried to push himself up but his arms buckled. Two passed him giving him a wide berth.

"Any who don't step on the fallen will have to wear this." Overseer Rikai held up a leather jerkin. It was padded to stop daggers. Wearing that would add not only weight but another layer of warmth. Once a garment of protection, here it would be a death sentence.

A girl came up to the boy who lay panting on the ground. She looked at him and then to the jerkin. The boy grunted as she stomped on him. She cringed at the sound avoiding glancing down.

Time ticked on as they continued to run laps around the Eye. Rai's heart battered his chest. The room swirled around him. Tys was no longer behind him. Rai wasn't sure if he had pulled ahead or toppled to the ground and he didn't have the energy to check. He couldn't keep this up.

More fell and Rai ran over them as instructed. The guards eventually appeared and pulled out some of those who lay on the ground. A handful of them weren't moving.

Rai's body screamed at him to stop. His legs felt hollow. His heart beat with the ferocity of a galloping hyian. He was going to die. He had nothing left to give.

Dropping to his knees, the room shuddered, darkness pulling him in from the corners of his vision. Somehow, stopping was worse. A wave of nausea struck Rai like a blow to the head.

STAY UP.

He couldn't fall flat or they would run across him and he knew he wouldn't be able to rise again. Short, sharp inhales failed to fill his lungs and Rai couldn't catch his breath. He glanced over at Overseer Rikai who sat drinking a mug of water. What he wouldn't do for a single mouthful of water. He watched as the clear liquid trickled down the side of the mug.

Pain shot up Rai's leg. He squealed and glanced over his shoulder to see the long haired blonde boy, who was first to start running, dig his foot into Rai's leg. Overseer Rikai was watching and he didn't say a word as the boy kept running, a smirk on his face.

How could he smile? How could he keep running? How was this training them?

Rai wavered on his knees. He wanted nothing more than to fall flat and let unconsciousness take him from this Duat.

If he did, this would end.

He didn't want to be here and be a part of whatever this training was. Verdin Guild or not.

Overseer Rikai was staring at him. He was waiting for Rai to topple. There was no malice in the man's eyes, just an expectation of failure.

Rai held.

He wouldn't give the man the satisfaction of watching him fall. But he couldn't get back to his feet again, either. So he remained there on his knees until, eventually, Overseer Rikai stood.

"Training is done for today," Rikai said. Then he walked out without another word.

The last nine standing collapsed. The smell of vomit and sweat filled the air. Hissed breathing sounding more like dying animals than children. The door swung open letting in a cool breeze as the guards marched back into the Eye.

Rai dropped forward and consciousness fled.

-

The infirmary was filled with the other nine children who survived the test. What happened to the other eleven of the original twenty, Rai did not know. Doctors tutted and jogged back and forth topping up their water-skins. They were special water-skins with a nozzle that you had to suck on to drain the contents and they were filled with a strange tasting water solution. The doctor told Rai the nozzles were to ensure that he didn't drink too much too quickly and send his body into shock. So Rai laid back and sipped on the water-skin, watching the ongoings of the infirmary. Two of the other children were violently sick for hours. One rolled around holding his stomach. And one had yet to wake.

Tys was in a similar condition to Rai. Lying motionless but awake and seemingly okay. Despite not wanting to get too close to the boy, Rai was pleased to see that he had survived.

Eventually they were sent back to their rooms on strict instructions to rest and drink plenty water. Rai was set loose before Tys so he wandered out into the palace alone.

Still wobbly on his feet, Rai staggered down the corridor. Braziers threw warm light across the dark sandstone, glinting off the golden veins in the stone. A staircase spiralled upward. The doctor said their quarters were one floor up. Rai looked left and right but the palace was quiet.

He was in *Atef Palace*. The golden web snaked along the walls as it did in the drawings. But the sketches couldn't capture the magnetism that drew one's eye to the shining gold. Stepping back out into the corridor, he ran a hand over the line in the wall. It was smoother than the stone around it. And Rai could have sworn he felt a buzz on the tips of his finger as he touched the vein.

"Rai!"

Rai flinched. The whisper was cutting in the silence. Leaning around the corner was Imayan. She gestured for him to follow and then disappeared *down* the stairs. For a minute, Rai blinked thinking he had imagined her until he heard, "Come on, Rai!"

Rai ran to catch up, stopping at the staircase. His rooms were up a floor and the guards had made it clear that anyone found wandering would be beaten and tossed out the palace. But would that be so bad? He didn't want a repeat of today. And he was following Imayan. What harm could it do?

Rai took off down the steps. His legs felt like branches of bone trees, one step from snapping, but he was feeling better since the strange water concoction took effect. In the distance, he could hear Imayan running, her echoing footsteps the only sound filling the empty corridors. Rai leapt down the steps taking several at a time before stopping at a floor and listening at the next landing. A light giggle carried from further down so Rai continued. Arriving at the bottom floor, he saw Imayan at the far end of a long stretch of corridor.

"Come on!" she shouted.

"Imayan! I don't—"

Imayan ignored him and sprinted through a door, it swinging shut behind her. Rai growled in frustration chasing after her. Did she know what he had been through today? Was this a sick game to her?

Shoving the door open, Rai gasped as cool air rushed to meet him. The Moon Eye was high, staring down at the world with its cool glow. Around Rai, a sprawling garden sat in shadow and dark blues. Water ran under a stone walkway feeding down to a large pond surrounded by a varying shrubs and trees. But not bone trees with their dead white trunks. These were lush browns and greens. Rai had never seen wildlife like it.

He stalked out into the garden, mouth agape and running his hand across the arching branches that reached out over the path. The night had stolen some of the vividness of the colours and yet there was something beautiful and consistent in the more muted blues of dusk.

"Pretty, isn't it?" Imayan was sitting on a rock the size of Rai staring out over the pond. She hopped down at grinned at him. "Not far now." She took his hand and dragged him further into the garden. Rai was about to protest but this was the emperor's daughter. She could have him strung up and lashed to death if she wanted. So Rai let himself be led under the trees that swayed in the breeze. Moonlight filtered between the shifting canopy in dancing beams of light.

Imayan slowed and bent down pulling on Rai's hand to show he should do the same. Dropping beside her, Imayan pushed aside a leaf to reveal a patch of flowers.

"Charah flowers," Rai whispered. He recognised them from the sketches in Imayan's book. She nodded and grinned at him.

"But look, there's a whole patch of them living together," she said.

"I thought that…" Rai's voice trailed off trying to remember what wording Imayan had used about their vicious nature.

"They drain the resources and only one survives? Yes, well, that is unless you bring them down from the plateaus and settle them in a dark area. People see plants as decorations or as food but they're alive. They think, too." Imayan rubbed one of the yellow petals with burnt orange tips between her fingers. "They know that in dark times they're better grouped together so that they can spread and break through the canopy around them as one to get back to the light."

Imayan smiled caressing the flower. Her eyes were glazed, mind elsewhere.

"It's funny because it's the opposite with people. The dark separates us. We don't want to show weakness and we think we have to grow and push through the canopy around us alone. But even the most vicious plant knows that this is wrong. The dark separates us on purpose because one is easier to keep contained than many. But together"—she pointed to where several charah flowers were bunched together and poking through the leaves around them—"We're stronger." Imayan let the leafy branch fall back into place. "We can learn a lot from plants."

"Why are you showing me this?" Rai scrunched his brow.

Imayan sighed and stood, wandering onward through the garden. She looked disappointed. Was he missing something?

The stone path weaved among the thriving grounds. They were so engulfed in plant life that Rai no longer saw the palace that surrounded them. He felt like he could be out exploring some strange land. Red leaves hung from above. Rai poked one and it curled upward away from him.

"When I first saw you at the orphanage, you reminded me of a charah flower," Imayan said. "Cut off from those around you but striving for something more. I could see it in your eyes."

Rai watched Imayan's back as she walked ahead of him. She

glanced over her shoulder. "And you reminded me of myself."

They walked in silence as Rai thought over her words.

"Why am I here?" Rai asked.

"Because you're no one. You're of no consequence to anyone," Imayan said.

Rai stopped, feeling hurt. Taking a couple steps forward, Imayan spun around when she noticed he was no longer behind her.

"That's not what I meant," Imayan said, reading his face. "Come on, I want to show you something else."

Rai couldn't understand this girl. One minute she was showing him her favourite flowers and saying he was like her and the next she was saying that he wasn't of consequence.

Their steady breathing matched the whistling rustle of the plants in the breeze. Imayan leapt onto a rock and then over onto the other side of a stream.

It's so quiet, Rai thought. Shouldn't he be able to hear the city?

Rai hopped across stones placed in a stream as Imayan ran ahead and clambered up the side of a boulder. Jogging after her, Rai stood at the bottom of the huge stone. Her carefree smile came back then and she flicked her head gesturing for him to climb up. There were plenty hand and footholds in the craggy rock making for an easy climb. Rai reached for the top and a hand gripped his wrist as Imayan pulled him up the rest of the distance. She then walked a couple paces away and sat, letting her legs dangle over the side of the rock.

Past her, the garden settled between the now visible palace walls. From up here, Rai could see the entire palace gardens and it was beautiful. Firelight dotted the boundary of the greenery, contrasting the pale silver and blue moonlight and the shadow blanketing the stretch of untamed life. The Moon Eye reflected in the pond near where they had entered the garden. And there were patches of colour. Red plants blended with blue plants, purple hung over the white flower beds, and green life filled the empty spaces between.

"Come sit." Imayan patted the space beside her. Rai joined her overlooking what Rai could only describe as a painting. For something like this couldn't truly exist in Tarris.

"After my unborn brother died there was an attempt on my life," Imayan said. It took a moment for her words to register. "Someone was trying to wipe out my family."

Turning away from the garden, Rai stared at Imayan.

"You asked why you're here. That's why. My father wants to make sure my personal guards aren't secretly assassins for one of the other monarchs. He doesn't even let me wander alone anymore. Even tonight I had to sneak out of my chambers," Imayan said.

That's why they had checked Rai's lineage and past at the orphanage. It was to check that he had no ties to the other monarchs.

"When you said I was no one…"

"I meant someone unknown. Not attached to the political sphere," Imayan said. Suddenly, she looked older. She could only be a couple years older than him but that carefree joy was squashed under a strain of things Rai had no concept of. The weight of a world Rai didn't know existed. "My father cut me off from my friends. I have new servants. I don't recognise anyone around me. Then when I snuck out tonight and I saw you standing there… I don't know. I knew you."

She met Rai's eyes and smiled. "Sorry for dragging you out here."

Rai shook his head. "It's beautiful. I didn't know something like this existed in Tansen."

Imayan was alone like he was. Rai couldn't forget the feeling of the bonds to all those around him at the orphanage shattering and the emptiness that followed. She knew that pain, too.

Was that all he was here for? To be trained as a guard for the emperor's daughter? The brutality of the training left a sick feeling in his gut, his limbs felt weak, and he was yet to shake the headache that hadn't stopped ringing since he woke up in the infirmary. All this to serve Imayan?

"Why did you come to the orphanage?" Rai asked. He wasn't sure what made the question so important, but after hearing that she wasn't there when Tys was brought to the palace, he had to know.

Imayan's face scrunched up in confusion. "Because I heard of the great oak tree in the courtyard. We don't have one here. They're rare in Tarris."

Rai realised that he was hoping that he was *special*. He had hoped that he had been *chosen*. That it was more than chance that had brought him to Atef Palace. He wanted to believe that fate would pull him from the haze that he had been living in. But no. He wasn't special. He wasn't here for a grand purpose. He was here to serve. If the training didn't break him first.

It was foolish to think that he was special. He was an orphan with no great lineage or skills or prophecy like the heroes in the stories. And yet, that dream had perhaps been the only thing to get him out of bed in the morning. But now, it just felt silly. Childish.

He could run. Imayan wouldn't chase him if he got up and sprinted back into the palace to find an exit.

"Why keep going?" Rai whispered to himself. Imayan must have heard him. She must have thought he was talking to her.

"What else is there?" Imayan said.

Rai glanced at Imayan who was lost in her thoughts. He thought of the charah flowers bundled together in the dark trying to push through the overbearing plants around them. Imayan was special and she knew of the emptiness, she knew of the breaking of bonds, she knew what it was like to be alone, Rai could see it in her eyes.

She understood and she was the same.

What else is there?

Nothing. There was nothing out there. But here with her, Rai had someone who understood. And that was worth more than any life he could scavenge himself.

Words sat on the tip of Rai's tongue but he couldn't find the right ones to comfort Imayan. So instead he asked, "What's the weirdest plant in the garden?"

Imayan looked up, a smile creeping onto her face.

9

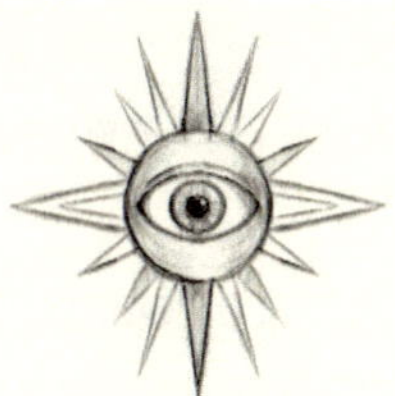

Taking Souls

21 years ago.

Crossing the threshold of the Eye, the stink and heat slammed into Rai. It was like stepping into another realm. The room felt alive, it had personality and memory. Rai could feel echoes of the struggle that had been endured here. He could see on the faces of the others that they felt it too. On entering, fear infected them like it too was part of the Eye.

Overseer Rikai didn't look surprised as he walked down the line that less than half had appeared for the second day of training. Only eight of the twenty had returned. Eleven hadn't passed the test in the Eye the day before and one refused to return from the infirmary. There was Tys, the blonde boy who stomped on Rai's leg, five others and Rai.

The heat from the Eye already drew beads of sweat on Rai's scalp. It itched but Rai didn't scratch it. The stink of sweat and vomit was ever-present in the Eye, as if it had seeped into the walls and floor. Overseer Rikai's bald head gleamed in the sunlight as he weighed each of them up.

"Laps," Rikai said, then walked to the centre of the room and sat. Dread settled onto the survivors. Their strong fronts crumbled and shoulders slumped.

They started jogging.

The blonde boy kicked off first keeping ahead of the others. Rai tried to keep his breath steady but the heat burned his throat and lungs and the panic was setting in. With a goal there was progress. If they were to run around the Eye ten times, Rai could measure that. He could see how far he had left. But with no goal or aim, they had no idea how long they had to run. They didn't have any indication of how to pace their running. The end was never in sight. And nothing drags fear out from the dark like the unknown.

Rai's heart rate was up. The more he tried to slow it, the faster it seemed to beat. The others weren't faring any better. A handful had slowed to a crawling pace and sweat ran down their scarlet faces. They wouldn't survive as long as yesterday and they all knew it.

Running in the Eye was unlike anything Rai had been through. His legs weren't tired in the way he felt when he had run around the track at the orphanage. Rai felt hollowed out like the Sun Eye had burnt the energy out of him. His body felt like it was fighting for survival, heart battering in his chest like a drum of war. He sucked in breath after breath but it was never enough. Glancing up at the Sun Eye, Rai wondered if Ova truly was testing them. Where else could this strain and weight come from than a God? It shone on the hall, glinting off the glass dome roof. Rai tried to shake off the dizziness.

The blonde boy passed him. He was breathing hard but kept a steady pace. *How?* Rai wondered floundering behind him. Rai's heart was beating too fast. His body wrenching with each pulse. He was sure he was going to have a heart attack. Slowing in an attempt to calm his heart, Tys ran past Rai too. He tried not to think about it. To keep looking forward. One step and then the next. The tromping footsteps and whistling breaths sounded far off in the blur of suffering. The heat burned the tips of his nostrils.

What was he doing?

This is foolish, Rai thought. Was he going to kill himself for the opportunity to serve the emperor's daughter? A voice screamed at him to stop. It screamed that this was a pointless venture. If he stopped, he could ease the pain. He could lie on the ground and wait to be dragged from this Duat-forsaken hall. Rai wanted nothing more than to give up.

He began to slow.

Another passed him.

What else is there?

Imayan's words broke his thoughts.

It was a throw away phrase and yet it tore through Rai like a razor, slicing through his haze with cool clarity. Under the burning gaze of the Sun Eye, reality struck him. What else *was* there? Back to the orphanage? Thrown out onto the street? He didn't *have* anything else. There was nothing else for him. He wasn't special. No one was going to save him. No one was going to lift him out of his pain.

He couldn't return to the orphanage. A numbness Rai wasn't aware he was harbouring ebbed for a moment and the rage he kept smothered deep within burned through the fog. Suppressed hate bubbled up for the other children at the orphanage and the mauts. He wouldn't return. There was nothing for him there.

So what else was there than to keep going?

Rai used that fire to fuel his limbs. He focused all that hate and pressed forward. Rai's breath didn't steady, his heart rate did not slow but he continued. He continued through the agony. For what else was there?

He couldn't live on the streets. Rai knew he wouldn't survive by himself. Physically he could feed and protect himself but what would be the point? He wouldn't have reason to.

Emptiness snapped at Rai's heels. He pushed harder.

When you have nothing to lose you have everything to give.

Others were waning while Rai sped up. The girl who had overtook him not a moment before stared as Rai jogged past. He passed Tys, who glanced at him, eyes wide. Tys slowed, defeated by Rai's persistence.

The blonde boy was ahead. He caught a glimpse of Rai and sped up. But he had pushed too hard too early and couldn't hold the pace and with the inevitability of one trying to outrun the sunrise, Rai caught him too.

No blood was drawn, but this was Rai's first kill. Part of the blonde boy died as he passed. Rai watched the light blink out in his eyes. And Rai breathed it in as if he were feeding on the boy's soul.

Rai wasn't special but he didn't have to be. He just had to take another step. He just had to not fall. He just had to keep going.

"Stop!"

Rai had forgotten where he was but the Overseer's voice shattered the illusion dragging him back to reality. When Rai stopped everything caught up with him and he turned to throw up at the side of the Eye. Down on his haunches he wretched until he had nothing left to bring up then collapsed onto his side.

The rest of the eight were on the ground too, breathing hard and staring at the Overseer and then to Rai. The Overseer met Rai's gaze. There was fire in Rikai's eyes and Rai thought he was about to be punished. Instead the Overseer said, "We break for a rest. Then we move onto the next part of your training."

Some of the others let out a harsh exhale that could have been a laugh. They had done it. They had passed the first test. But Rai didn't feel accomplished or relieved. This was how it was. He didn't have anything else so he would throw himself into the work, and become the best warrior Tarris had ever seen or die trying. With pain and suffering there could be no nothingness. There could be no emptiness. Pain was part of Rai now and no one could take it away from him.

He wouldn't let them take it from him.

The training under Overseer Rikai only got harder. The overseer put the trainees under the type of strain that stretches time itself. Gruelling endurance work callused their body and mind. Strength work tore their muscles to shreds pushing them past what they thought was possible.

Some were gravely injured. Others minds snapped. But Rai never broke. For he knew what waited for him if he did. Nothing. And that scared him more than any agony.

Rai spent more nights in the infirmary than with Tys in his quarters but when the next day came around, Rai rose again.

10

The True Nature of Darkness

*P**eople often mistake light and darkness for equals. They mistake them as two forces battling against one another. This isn't the case. Light is to be wielded. Light comes from a source, be it the glow of a flame or the glare of Ova's great Sun Eye.*

But darkness?

Darkness is something else entirely. It smothers the world. Consumes everything, everywhere, always. Yes, light can force it back for a time but darkness will always be there when it fades. It will always return. It was here long before the first light and it will consume everything again when the last light dwindles out.

This author seems like a cheery guy, Fax said. Rai sat back in his reading chair in the Nightraven, the Seventh Sceptre's hideout. The small library had an eclectic mix of tomes. Most of which were tied to combat and stealth but Rai remembered some of these had mentioned darkness being used as a tool. He read the books and scrolls years ago with the view that it was metaphorical but now he was looking upon the texts under a new light.

The library was a narrow stretch of shelves with a reading nook at the end. There were no windows in the Nightraven and even with the braziers lit and the lantern on the table in front of him, Rai had to squint to read the books. Perhaps it was his age. He had read for hours in that very chair in the past.

"I can't tell if this author is referring to shades or if this is all just philosophical nonsense." Rai flipped to the front page. There was no date but the book had to be hundreds of years old. It was called '*The True Nature of Darkness*'. A promising title but it seemed to think of dark as a deity. As if every shadowed corner was connected. The tome was damaged and missing pages. It wasn't a surprise given how frayed the binding was. However, it made it difficult to follow with its shattered narrative.

That excerpt was interesting but there were rambling passages that leaned more into the idea of the author being a raving fanatic.

The dark is always watching. It is more than a ruler, it is a God. One of the Seven and yet I believe it to be above the others, for it is omnipresent. It is the most feared among the aspects of our world. It is the unknown.

It is thought that we fear the dark for it can hold horrors we cannot see until it's too late. But I do not fear what the dark holds. My fear is for the dark itself.

Rai tossed the book onto the table and massaged his temples. He had been at this for hours. He needed sleep and food.

A noise came from the main chamber.

"Fax," Rai whispered. The shade shot off, coming back a moment later.

It's a man, Fax said. The shade visualized the man in Rai's head and he smiled.

Creeping through into the entry room, Rai watched as Tysar laid his weapons on the stone table and stretched. The main chamber was huge, with pillars lining either side of the room. The stone table was set upon a dais and behind it were seven weapon racks. The skylight shone a beam of pure sunlight onto the sigil inlaid into the ground. A swirling orb surrounded by seven swords. The sign of the Seventh Sceptre.

Tysar turned towards the doorframe Rai stood in and started.

"It can't be," Tysar said. For a moment, his friend just stared at him. Then Tysar smiled and marched over with his hand held out. Rai grasped his arm and they shook.

"I'm afraid so," Rai said, grinning back.

"What happened to you?" Tysar asked.

"It's a long story," Rai said.

"One I look forward to hearing," Tysar said. "We thought you died, Akarai." There was pain in his voice that both hurt and warmed Rai. At the time, he hadn't thought of how leaving would affect those around him.

"And I'm sorry for that. I will explain it all, I swear."

Tysar looked past Rai's shoulder to the library. "Doing some reading?"

"It helps clear my mind," Rai said. Tysar nodded. There was

something unusual in the way he carried himself. A reserved stand back attitude that made Rai think he was hiding something. *I've been gone for five years and assumed dead,* Rai reminded himself. Of course it was going to feel strange to be back. But it made him wary of telling Tysar the truth about his shade. Rai thought to Fax to stay hidden for now.

The silence strung out too long.

"How is Genu?" Rai asked.

"She had a hard time coming to grips with what happened that night, so she has been training at the Verdin Guild since.

"Akarai." Tysar looked pained. "We thought you had died and you know how tense things were when you left. So I was tasked with pulling together and leading a new Seventh Sceptre."

The realisation hit harder than Rai thought it would. It made sense, of course. Imayani needed the Seventh Sceptre and it had been over five years, but it still stung to come back and find himself replaced by his brother in arms. Was that why Tysar was acting strange?

Rai forced a smile and grabbed Tysar's shoulder. "I'm glad Imayani picked you. You were always the best among us."

Tysar grunted. He glanced up to the skylight. "We can talk later. I want to hear all that has happened but for now, I need to go. I just came to drop off my weapons before going to the meeting."

"Meeting?" Rai asked.

Tysar grimaced like he hadn't meant to say that. "Imayani called an emergency meeting. I have an idea what it's about now," he said gesturing to Rai. Tysar lifted his sword and slotted it into the weapon mount behind the table and headed towards the exit.

"I'll come with you," Rai said.

"I'm not sure that's a good idea." Rai ignored him walking past Tysar and through the door.

He clearly doesn't know that you don't do good ideas, Fax said.

They entered the war room to animated chatter. Imayani hadn't moved from the spot Rai left her in hours ago. Somehow she looked even more exasperated than that morning.

Overseer Myain was talking the way one would to a child. His condescending tone was targeted at a woman Rai didn't recognise on the other side of the table. She wore light travel clothes like she had just arrived at the capital. Further confirmed by the sand that was trawled through the war room leading directly to her. The girl looked to be in her early thirties with long black hair that was tucked into the cowl around her neck.

"No one is going to take something like this seriously. We officially moved the capital to Tansen!" Overseer Myain said.

"Tysar. Akarai," Imayani said. The other two looked up.

"What's he doing here? I put the deserter in a cell," Overseer Myain said.

"I let him out," Imayani lied.

"But—"

"Later. We have more important matters to discuss," Imayani said.

Overseer Myain looked like he might argue but instead he mumbled under his breath and turned back to the woman facing him. Rai and Tysar bowed before approaching the war room table.

"What's going on?" Tysar asked.

"The letters were true. The lost library of Nenelan has been found," the traveler said.

Imayani stared at Rai. He had sent word to her that the library had been found. It was coded in the way of the Seventh Sceptre so she must have guessed it was him or one of the other members of the seven who were thought to be dead. And now she knew.

"This is a good thing, no?" Tysar asked.

Overseer Myain laughed and Tysar scowled at the man.

"Yes, it is. We have access to the biggest fountain of knowledge perhaps in the world. And it's rare to have any records from before the cataclysm that took Asuriya but now we have an entire library of records. And it's… a lot," the woman said.

"I'm sorry, who are you?" Rai asked.

Imayani glared at him but the woman was straight faced and unperturbed by the question. "Yeru. I'm a scholar focused on pre-cataclysm history."

Rai nodded. So Imayani sent her and no doubt a battalion of guards and other scholars to check the validity of his letters and to study the library. He was glad she took his note seriously.

"The problem is that the library is massive and there are creatures we thought long dead roaming its corridors and some we don't have any record of at all. So it's extremely dangerous to delve into," Yeru said.

Tell me about it, Rai thought.

It had a peaceful quiet to it though, Fax said. That was certainly true.

"However, we gathered all the experts in the field from around Tarris to start excavation into the records and, well… we came across an interesting piece while we were studying books on Asuriya." Yeru pushed the open book to Rai. He felt Tysar shift uncomfortably. Yeru should have placed it in front of him rather than Rai.

He read the passage Yeru indicated. It contained generic phrases of how the ruling power worked in the old tongue. It was more of a dictatorship than Tarris was now but Rai didn't see anything to be concerned about. Then he saw a single line saying, *"The power of Tarris is forever tied to Asuriya and the Shroud Palace"*.

"Shroud Palace?" Rai asked.

"We believe this is the first instance we've found in thousands of years of the pre-cataclysm name for the Mad Palace," Yeru said.

The Mad Palace, or Shroud Palace, was the palace in Asuriya said to be made of the bones of a god.

"You're worried that the power hungry monarchs will hear of this and try to stake their claim of Tarris by returning to the old capital?" Rai asked.

Yeru gave him a curt nod.

"It's ludicrous! When the cataclysm came we made an *agreement* which means none of this is legally binding," Overseer Myain said.

"You know better than most that the monarchs don't care how legal their actions are. If they think they can turn people with this information, they *will* move on Asuriya," Tysar said.

Rai wasn't sure. A single line in an old text? That wasn't enough to act on.

"Look at the title page," Yeru said.

Rai flicked the cover over. *The Words of the Emperor: Volume 7.*

He stared at the title.

When the deal was made after the falling of the old capital, the monarchs swore to uphold Tarrisian values by remaining true to the three volumes of *The Words of the Emperor*. The only pieces of texts that survived the cataclysm. They had always known there were more as they had volumes two, three, and five. But the others were thought to have been lost.

An old text from the library stating such may have raised eyebrows but an official *The Words of the Emperor* lost volume would have them up in arms.

These were proclamations from the ancient emperor himself.

There was a moment of quiet as all stared at the title page and took in the implications of such a book existing. Myain turned away, shaking his head.

"We need to make sure the others don't find out about this," Rai said pushing the book back across the table.

Yeru and Imayani met eyes.

"They already know, don't they," Rai said.

"Like I said, we collected all of the experts in pre-cataclysm history once the report of the library was confirmed. This includes scholars and soldiers from Yontar and Ossin," Yeru said.

They all stared at the book. Tarris had been on the brink of civil war for hundreds of years and to think this one book was the thing that could light the fuse to an implosion was too much to wrap Rai's sleep deprived mind around.

"No one would risk the sickness. Even if they did claim rulership, they would be dead within the week," Tysar said.

There was murmurs of agreement.

"There's talk of the sickness not taking hold anymore," Rai said thinking back to Celabar. The Ear, his informant in the city, had told him there was talk that creatures were returning to the old capital.

And that people were mentioning that they were nearing a time when they could reclaim Asuriya.

"It's true," Overseer Myain said. "There have been no cases of the sickness in years and treasure hunters are flooding the streets with relics they claim to have found in Asuriya."

"It seems awfully convenient that this book turns up just as the sickness fades." Tysar crossed his arms.

"It's been fading for years," Yeru said. "We have records going back hundreds of years full of people testing the sickness and it trends downward. Because there is no way of testing for it, other than sending people into the capital to potentially die, there aren't a lot of teams researching it. However, there are some Ossin scholars said to be cooped up on the outskirts testing the sickness on animals. And I've seen some… questionable projects that have been shut down throughout the last hundred years with the same results. The blight that holds Asuriya *is* fading. We just don't know how quickly."

"Okay," Imayani finally spoke up. "We agree that something needs to be done if the sickness has indeed faded." There were grumbles of agreement, even from Overseer Myain. "But it might not be an issue if the sickness is still in effect. So we should send the Seventh Sceptre to check out this Ossin research post and see what they've found. Quietly." She glanced at Tysar. "We can't afford to show that this is concerning us. After, we can decide if anything needs to be done."

"Very good choice," Overseer Myain said with a smile.

Kiss ass, Fax said and Rai smiled. Tysar glanced at him. Smiling during this meeting was probably not the right response.

Tysar cleared his throat. "I'll gather the seven. We'll leave come first light of the Moon Eye's watch."

Imayani nodded.

"I'll come with you," Yeru said. Tysar was about to protest as Yeru held up her hand. "I'm familiar with studies and research readings. Without me, you may not be able to tell what any of it means."

Tysar didn't hide his distaste but he grunted in agreement.

"It's settled then," Imayani said.

"I'll go to," Rai said.

"No," Tysar and Imayani said at the same time.

"You're lucky you aren't locked up, *deserter*. You certainly aren't going on any more missions," Overseer Myain spat.

"I can be an invaluable asset." Rai looked at Imayani. Only she knew of Fax and his newfound abilities. "The sands around Asuriya have mutated blight-touched creatures from the sickness. Aside from the Deadlands Basin, it's the most dangerous stretch of land in Tarris. You could use all the help you can get."

Imayani held his gaze.

Everyone else squirmed in the silence.

"Leave us," she said.

"But—" Overseer Myain started.

"Now."

Tysar, Overseer Myain, and Yeru filtered out of the war room. Imayani didn't take her eyes off Rai the entire time. The door crashed shut and the silence returned.

"Akarai—"

"You know of my shade," Rai cut in. "I want to help."

Imayani slouched over the table. She looked so tired.

"This is too much, Akarai. It was easier when you were dead."

The words ran through him like a dagger to the gut. Her expression was soft and pitying.

"Imayani," Rai said.

"No. You can't just saunter back in here and expect everything to go back to how it was. I had planned to execute you if you came back that night," Imayani said. "I was so angry and confused and having you executed seemed like the only way to make it all stop. Then, when you didn't return and I thought you were dead, I realised that it only added to the grief. Killing you wasn't going to change anything. It wasn't going to make everything okay. It hurt. Losing you was like losing my father all over again. I have so few people who truly know me in this world." She blew out a breath. "Grief fades. Over time it loses some of its bite but it never leaves you completely. I have just started to heal, Akarai. But you being here. It's too much. It's opening old wounds."

There was a tremor in her voice that contradicted her placid face. She was always so good at hiding her emotions.

"I can't have you here."

Rai's heart hammered against his ribs. Her words swirled in his mind. "I swore to protect you," Rai said.

"And the best way you can do that is to go. Go to the Verdin Guild. You have always been an incredible fighter. Train with them. Teach them. And don't come back, Akarai. Please," Imayani said. She gulped, fighting back tears.

"I didn't mean to hurt you," Rai said.

"It doesn't matter what you meant. It happened and every time I see you my gut tightens as I'm slung back to that time in my life. I can't go back there."

"Neither can I," Rai said.

"Then start again. Just not here."

Rai searched for the words to change her mind. He *could* help. He *had* been helping. He had spent five years searching for the truth about shades to try and help. He had spent his entire life training to help.

In the end, it was for nothing. He saw that now. In truth, he had run away that night, afraid to come back and face Imayani. He told himself that he was continuing the mission. That he was out in the field studying the shades but that was a lie.

Only fools chase their own shadows.

"I'm sorry, Imayani," Rai said. Imayani turned away.

Rai bowed his head and walked out of the war room.

He didn't look back.

11

A Shaper Knife

Kit cupped his mug in his hands as if he were cold. Nya brought hers to her lips and grimaced at the taste. It wasn't bad but she could never get it to taste like when Illy made tea.

"I guess I'd never really thought about dying," Kit said, staring into his drink. "Living on the street, it always loomed above me, waiting for a moment of weakness. I didn't care. I didn't have anything to live for. But now..."

Kit screwed his face up as if he were in pain. "I have all this and all of you and I'm afraid I'll have it taken away from me."

Nya resonated with Kit's words. When you lived on the streets you held everything that was dear to you so tightly because it could be snatched away at any moment. Crumbs were shards of diamonds. A cut of meat a treasure to be awed at. Those feelings never left. Kit's fears made more sense to Nya now.

"Rai said you are going to be fine," Nya said. "Back in ancient times, the people wouldn't have used Ma-atan as a way to pass judgment on someone if they were going to die no matter the outcome."

The sound of Kit scratching his thumb against his cup filled the common room. It was late and all those staying at the Patched Cloak were up in their rooms, as was Wenson. Illy had been behind the bar when they stepped out of the kitchen but she sensed that they needed some time to talk and took to her chambers.

All the lanterns had been blown out apart from the lamp above their booth. It swung lazily in the breeze that rattled through the shutters.

"What is it?" Nya asked. She was getting better at telling when Kit was holding something back.

"Nya." Kit had a guilty look on his face. "I have done bad things in my life. Really bad things. I was convinced Ma-atan was going to kill me."

"You must have done some good too then," Nya said. She meant the words to be reassuring but Kit looked pained by them.

"Unless Kyan got it wrong. We clearly don't know much about the ancient times. Maybe Ma-atan doesn't judge you on your life. It could be something else that makes him choose life or death," Kit said.

He truly believed that he wasn't worthy of passing Ma-atan's Judgement. Nya could see it in his eyes. It made her question what she knew about him and what he had been like before they travelled to the dark place. Surviving on the streets put people in difficult situations. It was a hard life that drove them to do terrible things.

"Is that why you were searching through these books?" Nya asked. The Ghroban tome lay discarded at the bar. Neither of them wanted it close by.

"I was trying to find out what the Judging really is and what it meant for those that," Kit struggled to find the word, "survived."

"And?" Nya asked.

Kit met her eyes for the first time since they sat down. "I'm at a dead end." He dropped his head to the table. "I've asked all the bookshops for almost every book on the topic and now I'm moving onto things like that." Kit nodded to the bar.

"And?"

"And nothing relates to the Judging on living people. All the stories and rituals are based on after you die," Kit said.

"You said almost?" Nya asked.

Kit cocked an eyebrow.

"You said you asked the bookshops for *almost* every book on the topic."

Kit sighed. "Well, there is one book said to be from before the cataclysm to do with deities but some rich noble has it locked up in his private library."

"Have you tried asking them for it?"

Laughter bubbled out from Kit. He looked at Nya. "It's the Jeril family who have it."

Nya winced. The Jeril family were known for their greed. Nya didn't know what they did to become so rich but she had heard their name slip from many frustrated merchants.

"The Jerils?" a voice came from the darkness around them. "Nice folk."

"Lem?" Nya asked.

Lem sat up from one of the booths, his hair sticking up at odd angles.

"Were you sleeping?" Kit asked.

"Yeah, I bet a guy I could fall asleep faster than him." Lem looked around at the empty common room. "Did you see him? Did I win?"

Nya shook her head. "Did you say the Jeril family are nice people?"

Groaning, Lem pushed out of the booth and came round to sit with them. He budged Kit up as he slid into the booth. "Yeah," he said, with a toothy grin. It wasn't a surprise. Lem thought everyone was nice. "I feed their pets for them."

"You feed their *pets*?" Kit asked.

Lem inclined his head. "Nice animals."

"As in the kiren they have guarding their grounds?" Kit asked.

"Those are the ones. They got some screechers too though. They can be fussy eaters but seem to like me, so Erdui hired me to feed 'em for him. I'm the only one the beasts will let get close during feeding time," Lem said.

Kit and Nya's eyes met. She could see the same idea reflected back at her in Kit's gaze.

"Could you get us in?" Kit asked.

Lem shrugged. "I guess so. Why?"

The following day at the height of the Sun Eye's watch when most were sleeping, Nya and Kit sat atop a rooftop across from the Jeril's mansion. Deep within the city, the manor was a seven-story monolith with a sprawling garden at its feet. There was a small patch of vegetation at the back of the grounds but most of the space was made up of a stone garden with sculptures and gravel swept into swirling patterns and walkways leading through the ornate rock display.

"Lem said that is the outhouse for the kiren," Kit said pointing to a hut pressed against the huge wall surrounding the grounds. It was a simple, unassuming redbrick hut that housed the vicious beasts.

"One of the servants frees the beasts just before dark hour so they stalk the grounds attacking any who step foot in it," Kit said. Nya suppressed a smile as she watched him survey the garden his mind working through potential plans. It was amazing to see some life in her friend again. It had been too long since he had seemed himself. "And then in the morning, Lem comes and feeds them. But if Lem came early and fed them the night before then we might be able to sneak past them and into the mansion, find the book and get out."

"Sounds straightforward," Nya said.

Kit cringed. "Don't say that."

"Sorry." Nya grinned. They had talked about getting Bom to kill the kiren but this way they could sneak in and out undetected.

"We make our move the last night of the festival," Kit said.

"Why then?" Nya asked.

"The Jeril's will be out of the mansion," Kit said. "Everyone comes out to enjoy the last night of festivities. That means we just need to avoid any servants roaming the halls."

"This comes far too easily to you," Nya said.

"I worked with street gangs, Nya," Kit said with a shrug. "This isn't the first noble's manor I've ransacked."

Nya turned to look at the mansion. Just beyond it, the Thousand

Floor Palace loomed, filing the sky. Every time Nya looked upon the palace, she got a sinking feeling. It held nothing but painful memories for her. And to think that the tear was still in there and the dark place beyond it.

I see you.

Nya shivered. She couldn't shake the feeling of something breathing down her neck whenever she thought about the voice. Nya tore her gaze away from the palace.

"We won't go anywhere near it, I swear," Kit said laying a hand on her shoulder. She nodded to reassure him that she was fine.

"On the last night of the passing, we'll get that book," Nya said.

"Thank you, Nya," Kit said.

Shouting burst from the Patched Cloak. Those passing by peered inside before walking on. Nya and Kit looked to one another and rushed inside. Only a handful of tables were occupied. Most of the patrons sat in silence staring at Wenson who was shouting at a Tarrisian in Nuian. Nya didn't understand a word he said but Kit flinched.

The Tarrisian man was rotund and missing one of his front teeth. They approached and Kit went to calming Wenson. Illy stood nearby, her hands crossed over her chest.

"What's going on?" Nya asked.

"This man ordered a Nuian dish just to throw it on the floor and refuse to pay," Illy said.

"I said I wanted food, not this swill," the man said. At his feet, shards of a dish and a stew permeated outward. The tip of Dust's nose peeked out from under the table where she lapped up some stew. At least it hadn't completely gone to waste.

"Just because you don't like it doesn't mean you can break my dishes and not pay," Illy said.

The man stood and Illy took a step back. He was huge. Standing easily two heads above Wenson who was the tallest of the bunch. "If you serve Nuian filth, it'll be treated as Nuian filth. We don't eat that aya's stool here."

"You were given what you ordered," Nya said. "Pay for it and leave."

The Tarrisian man looked to Nya as if he just noticed her. "Spunky little one," he said. "I don't pay for swill." He made for the door but Nya stepped in front of him. The man grinned at her.

"Nya, let him pass," Illy said. "It's fine."

"Not until he pays," Nya said. His stare bore into her like a beast watching its prey.

"Nya," Illy said. The tone of her voice made it clear that she wanted Nya to move but how could she let him get away with this? To come into a Nuian run inn and order a Nuian dish to do this? It didn't make any sense.

Kit had sent Wenson to go get a brush because it looked like he was seconds away from hitting the rude customer. As Kit glanced over and saw Nya now facing down the man, he stiffened. He marched to Nya's side and tried to gently move her out the way.

"Come on, Nya," Kit said. "He's not worth it."

"Move along, little urchin," he said.

Nya let herself be pulled to the side. At that moment, Dust appeared at Nya's feet and ran at the man taking a bite out of his calf. He squealed and kicked out sending Dust flying across the common room. Fury and instinct surged in Nya and Bom blasted out a wave of shadow throwing the man over a table and into a crumpled heap.

Everyone went still. All eyes fell on Nya. The man groaned and heads turned to see him dragging himself to his feet.

"Sorcerer!" he screamed and fled from the inn. He continued to shout as he ran down the street.

Despite the man leaving, the tension did not. Bom let her know about the fearful glances from the other customers. But Nya didn't care. She ran over to Dust. The sand fox was already up when Nya reached her but she was favouring one leg over the other. Nya touched the leg and Dust yelped.

"Oh, Dust," Nya said.

Suddenly, Kit was at her side. "You need to go. Let Illy calm the customers down," Kit said.

"Dust is hurt," Nya said.

Kit bundled Dust in his arms and together they stalked up the stairwell. Behind them, Illy spoke words of reassurance and promised free drinks for all.

The heat from the Sun Eye stole Nya's breath away as they came out onto the Patched Cloak rooftop. Wenson and Kit had erected a shaded area with a tarp and cushions. Kit laid Dust on one of the cushions and dropped down beside her. He dipped his head to get a better look at Dust's leg.

"It's okay. I think she just sprained it," Kit said.

"How do you know?" Nya asked. She paced under the tarp. Nya was never one to favour being in the Sun Eye's gaze but ever since getting Bom she felt even more comfortable in the shade and dark.

"I've seen this before," Kit said. "She'll be back to normal in a week or so, I'm sure."

Kit rubbed Dust's stomach and the sand fox rolled over and purred. Nya blew out a breath of relief at seeing her so relaxed.

"Nya, come sit down." Kit patted the cushion beside him. She sat and pet Dust who had closed her eyes. "You should have let him pass."

"After that? He ordered a Nuian dish, Kit. It was his fault."

"I agree but you've made it worse for Illy now," Kit said.

"How?"

Kit sighed. "Why do you think he did that?"

"I don't know."

"Because he wanted a reaction," Kit said. "He doesn't like Nuians. He never planned to eat that dish."

Nya knew there had been some hostility towards the Patched Cloak because it was Nuian run, but she didn't think it would stir this kind of response. "But it doesn't affect him in any way."

"Some people don't have much going on in their lives," Kit said.

"I don't understand," Nya said. There weren't many foreigners in Tarris but Nya couldn't imagine why having Illy and Wenson here would bother anyone.

"Neither do I. It's easier to hate something than try to understand it," Kit said.

"Then he deserved what was done to him," Nya said.

"Sure, but now he's going to believe his assumptions are true," Kit said.

"You think he'll come back?" Nya asked. Bom stirred as if ready to chase him off again.

Kit shrugged. "I don't know."

"If he does, I'll be here to throw him around the common room again," Nya said.

Kit watched her and smiled. "In some ways you are a different person from the girl I met in that cell in the Thousand Floor Palace. But in others, you're the same stubborn girl who lived on the streets fighting to survive."

Darkness seeped outward from Nya's shadow. "But now I have Bom to back me up."

Some of that playfulness drained from Kit. "A sharper knife won't always end an argument. But it will always draw more blood."

PART 2

12

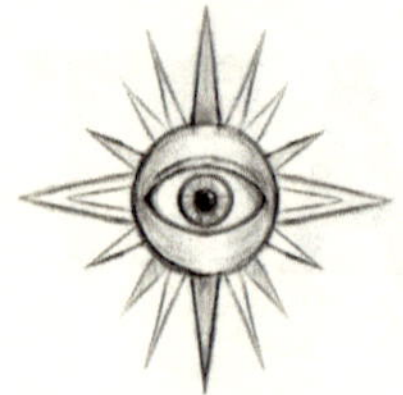

The Lie of Purpose

21 years ago.

Rai lunged, throwing himself up the climbing wall. The beating heat from the Sun Eye bore down on him as he crested the top of the wall and dropped down the other side. Landing hard on the dirt sent a dust cloud puffing up into Rai's face. Sweat dripped into his eyes but he ran on, wiping it away with the back of his hand. The others weren't far behind. He could hear their rasping breaths and almost feel them prickling the back of his neck.

The beam shook when Rai leapt onto it. He fought to keep his balance but his legs were weak. He had pushed too hard during the morning sparring sessions and with the added midday heat, his body was drained and giving up on him. Rai continued, his wobbling legs throwing him across the beam and off the other side. He collapsed into the dirt coughing and spluttering. The beam behind him shook as others clambered onto it. Rai stood and the world spun. The sudden dizziness almost toppled him. He forced his eyes shut until everything settled.

Everything in his periphery was a blur. Rai focused on the next obstacle trying to force focus back into his vision. A rope web spread upwards. Rai launched himself onto it.

A head-rattling scream almost knocked Rai off the second he grabbed the netting. He glanced up and three screechers hung from the ropes. The monkey-like creatures were long-limbed with dark brown fur and wore a vicious snarl. The screechers shot towards him. Rai climbed. He wasn't allowed to kill them and was instructed to incapacitate only. However, the beasts were given no such training. The ropes whipped with the screechers violent prowl. The first threw itself at Rai. Releasing one hand, Rai spun out the way and it fell past him crashing into the sand below.

Breathing hard, Rai bounded upward. The second screecher was more cautious. It clambered alongside him and wracked its claws across Rai's side. Rai screamed, one hand falling to the gash. The screecher swiped again but Rai was ready this time. He flourished his dagger, battering the swing in one motion. It howled and Rai had to force himself not to clutch his ears lest he fall from the web.

The third screecher would be atop him in seconds and he couldn't face two at once. A glance to check on the other screecher cost him as the one at his side sank its teeth into Rai's calf. He screamed and thrashed out with his blade. The pommel cracked the beast on the head and it went limp, falling to the dirt.

Rai turned his head just as the last screecher dove for him. It grabbed his face and Rai let go of the rope wall. For a moment he was falling, wrestling with the screecher mid-air, and the next, everything went black.

The stink of herbal roots made Rai's nose twitch. A musky earthy scent that was overlaid with strange oils. Rai knew where he was even before opening his eyes. He lay still for a moment, listening. Hushed words met groans and shuffling. The clatter of dishes and the slicing of roots cut through the harsh sounds. Rai opened his eyes to the infirmary roof. It was becoming the first thing he saw most mornings.

He tried to sit up, which sent shooting pains up his calf. *Oh yeah, the screechers,* Rai remembered glancing down at the bandages that had soaked through with blood.

Movement caught his eye and Rai startled. Sitting at his bedside was Imayan. It was the first time he had seen the emperor's daughter in weeks.

"Easy," Imayan said, not looking up from her book. "Maut Yojat said you shouldn't put any strain on that leg."

Rai glanced around. It was quiet in the infirmary. So what was the *emperor's daughter* doing here?

"Why are you here?" Rai asked.

Imayan looked at him over her book. She sighed and slammed it shut, setting it down beside her. "I came to check on you."

He didn't know what to say to that. After the night in the garden, he hadn't seen her. Not even in the palace corridors. Rai had looked for her but one did not stumble across the emperor's daughter. Rai had assumed Imayan went back to her duties and had forgotten about him.

"You shouldn't have hurt the screecher." Imayan crossed her

arms.

Rai scoffed. "They were trying to kill me."

"No, they were trying to knock you off the ropes."

"Were you watching?"

"I saw when you hit Ril over the head," Imayan said, scowling.

"You named it?" Rai asked.

"Of course I named him!" Imayan shouted.

One of the doctors stuck their head around the corner, a finger to his lips. His face paled when he noticed that he just scolded the emperor's daughter. The doctor smiled, nodded and disappeared back around the corner.

Imayan let her hands fall to her sides. "You can make it up to them by feeding them later. They're very receptive to meal time."

"I'm not..."

Imayan stared at him with a burning fury. It was probably best not to annoy her. He could feed some screechers. *As long as it isn't bits of me that they want,* he thought, feeling the pulsing heat in his calf.

Tapping her fingers on the table, Imayan watched Rai carefully. He felt uncomfortable under that gaze. "Why do you train so hard?" she asked.

The sudden change in her tone took Rai a moment to reorient to. "Because what else is there?"

Imayan smirked. Rai felt that smile melt some of the tension.

"When I said that I didn't mean you should keep running until you drop," Imayan said.

"I know."

Imayan sat forward. "Do you? I've only seen some of your

training but each time you push well past your limits. The doctors told me how often you end up in here."

Rai didn't met her eyes.

She blew out a breath.

"I was always searching for a purpose. My father rules Tarris and I thought I had to do something equally important." She stood and walked to the window, her back to Rai.

"I had to have a grand purpose. I spent so long searching. Reading about the great heroes of old and the legends that have been passed down through the generations and I realised something."

She turned to Rai. "They hadn't looked for a purpose. Most of them didn't really have a purpose. They had a direction. They improved themselves by spending time doing what they enjoyed and were good at. They took care of their loved ones and *themselves*." Imayan lingered on the word.

"They lived. They lived without some destined purpose. They just did what they thought was right."

The groaning and snoring from the others in the infirmary had fallen silent at some point.

"And you look like a man who will run around in circles until you drop dead. Directionless and lost. What is it you want?"

Those words should have stung but instead, they rang true. She was right. He had been throwing everything at training with little thought on why. What did he want? Rai didn't know. That was the problem.

Rai thought of Kon lying in a pool of his own blood. Even if Rai had been there, could he have stopped the other kids? No. It was why he wanted to become a palace guard in the first place. To help those who couldn't help themselves. To protect the vulnerable.

"I want to be strong enough to save those I care for," Rai said.

Imayan smiled at him. Heat flushed his cheeks as Rai thought she was laughing at him but he saw no malice in her eyes. She stepped up to his bedside.

"I need a personal guard. I was asked to pick from the more experienced candidates but word of your skill has already travelled among the ranks so I don't think there will be any push back if I offer you the position," Imayan said.

Rai stared at her.

"Well? Do you want to be my personal guard?"

Rai lay motionless. To serve one in the royal family was the highest rank a guard could ascend to. One he hadn't dreamed possible.

Rai hissed as he tried to get up. He should bow or something in a situation like this. Pain shot up his leg as he got out of bed. Imayan shouted at him to stop and told him not to move but he was already on his knee, head bowed.

"I'd be honoured," Rai said through clenched teeth.

13

Crossroads

R ai tugged down his cowl and took a drink from his waterskin. Wind whipped up the sand and Rai choked before pulling his cowl back over his face. He wore sand goggles to protect his eyes and they painted the dunes in bronze. The aya continued to tread through the deep sand.

Lovely day to start your travels, Fax said. *Truly a sign of good fortune.*

They had spent the morning gathering supplies for the long journey south. And then spent far too long saying goodbye to Derin at the Inep Pot, who demanded he come and visit more often. The old man had then supplied Rai with enough coffee to open his own coffeehouse.

The aya slowed as they approached the crossroads. High sand dunes stood like walls around them. Turning right would lead them south, towards their destination.

The trek to the Verdin Temple would be a long one. Because Rai refused to lose his aya, he would need to follow the Deadlands Basin all the way around the country until he could enter from the south, near Rizu. The journey would take months but it gave Rai time to reflect and prepare for his new life.

I can't have you here. Imayani's voice rattled through his mind.

He glanced left. It led deeper into the rocky paths of the Bandor Mountains, where Yeru, Tysar and the rest of the new seven were going to investigate the habitability of Asuriya. They would have left earlier that morning. He squinted into the blowing sand wondering that if he looked hard enough, he might see a plume of kicked-up dust from their passing, but there was nothing.

This is for the best, Rai thought. He didn't have a place in that world anymore. Rai whipped the reins and the aya marched onward.

So what, you're going to run off to the temple and train new recruits for the rest of your days? Fax asked.

The winds had settled enough for Rai to pull down his cowl. "It'll be a good life. You'll like it, Fax," Rai said. "You won't have to hide. And I'll continue my studies. They might have books that mention shades. Their library is expansive."

Fax shot out as a crow and flew in front of Rai's face.

What happened to your oath? What happened to saving Tarris? Fax said.

"They don't need us," Rai said, waving away the shade.

I know you don't believe that, Fax said. *You can hide the truth from yourself but I'm in that head of yours too, you know.*

Rai blew out an irritated breath. A retort sat on the tip of his tongue but Rai bit it before it was spoken. They may need him. It was a perilous journey traveling into the Bandor Mountains, but Tysar would see them safe and he was a good judge of character. Rai was sure the new seven would be prepared to face any threat that came their way.

"They don't want me," Rai said.

When has that ever stopped you?

That's your problem, Fax said, flapping in Rai's face. *You're wallowing in self-pity. From the moment we returned to the capital you've been looking for a reason to give up.*

"That's not true," Rai said.

Fax landed on the aya's platform.

"You don't understand. It's complicated."

It has passed. That's why you humans call it the past. So dumb you need to make the word mean two things so you remember, Fax said. *Since we arrived at Tansen you've become a different person. Where's the Rai who does what is right?*

Rai sighed. The bird was right. Something about returning to Tansen brought back parts of him he thought long dead. He wasn't that man anymore.

"Okay, you're right," Rai said. "But that doesn't mean we can march back to the capital and demand our place as part of the seven, Fax."

Good, Fax said. *Because you don't want to go back to the old you, right? You aren't Akarai any longer. What would Rai do in this situation?*

What would *Rai* do?

Imayani was wrong. Akarai hadn't survived that night. He was dead. Rai had taken his place. And Rai had come here because it was the right thing for Tarris. Turning his back on everything and running off to the temple was something Akarai would do but not Rai.

There are always crossroads. Their destinations shrouded in the unknown. But there is no stopping life's forward momentum. A path must be chosen.

Rai took a deep breath and pulled on the reins. The aya turned left, towards the Bandor Mountains.

Oh hi, Rai, Fax said. *I was wondering where you got off to.*

"Don't push it," Rai said. He flicked the reins and the aya sped up. "We're going to have to hurry if we want to catch up with Tysar. Once we enter the mountains, you'll need to scout ahead.

"And Fax." Rai hesitated. "Thank you."

Don't thank me. This just sounds a lot more exciting than training at a temple for the rest of my life, Fax said.

Rai grunted. "Exciting is one word for it."

His muscles eased and mind cleared as they moved closer to the mountains. Rai felt like he was waking up and coming back to himself. It didn't matter how many times he was knocked off his path. He would find it again. He would find himself again.

The sand became more uneven as they travelled north. Rocks broke from the golden sea, some as monolithic structures and others as nothing more than patches of stone to be marched over. The Bandor Mountains loomed on the horizon. They hadn't seen any signs of the seven but with the high winds, it was unlikely they would find any trace of them until they were upon them.

Dark hour came and went and still, they continued onward. The aya was skittish during dark hour but after Rai had killed a couple of creatures that tried to harm them, the aya's steps grew more confident.

The mountains rose around them as they travelled north. The passages among the rocky peaks hadn't been tread upon for thousands of years but the rocks still held man's mark. Pathways impossibly cut into the stone led through the mountains and they were wide enough for two aya to walk abreast. However, the aya slowed to a crawl with some of the sharp inclines.

It wasn't until dark hour the following day that they finally caught up with Tysar and the others. The aya tromped through the mountain passes as the first light of the Moon Eye broke from the horizon. Rai had seen the curling smoke and knew they were close.

However, as they passed around the bend no one was there. There was no camp. No seven.

The pass was silent.

To your left, Fax said.

With a burst of movement, Tysar dove from the rock wall and landed on the platform in a roll coming up with his sword level. Rai caught the blade with his dagger and knocked it away.

"Akarai?" Tysar said. His eyes bulged as they settled on Rai.

"I prefer Rai," Rai said.

"What are you doing here?" Tysar said. Movement came from the rock on the other side as more of the seven revealed themselves.

"I've come to help," Rai said.

"But you're no longer part of the seven, *Rai*," Tysar said.

"I'm here as a concerned citizen," Rai said.

"Rai this isn't a joke," Tysar said, sheathing his sword and calling the rest of the seven off with a gesture.

"And I am not treating it as such. But there is more at play here than you know," Rai said. Fax flooded the aya's platform in shadow. Tysar's eyes went wide.

"There could be threats that you're not aware of," Rai said. He was sure Imayani would have told Tysar about shades. She wouldn't have left him to walk into this without knowing about all the moving parts. Hopefully Tysar would see the benefit in having someone with his ability in the party. *Our ability,* Fax corrected.

"You'll need me. It'll be like old times."

Rai held out his arm. Tysar stared at it, conflicting emotions flickered across his face. "I'm not here to take back the seven," Rai said. "I just want to help."

Tysar met his gaze. He knew that if he denied Rai, he would follow them anyway. So the choice was either to try and incapacitate his old friend or allow him to tag along.

Tysar gripped his arm. "Like old times." There was a reluctance in the gesture but Tysar had to show the rest of the seven that he was in charge and allowed Rai to be there.

Despite having trekked all night without sleep, the party set off as the Moon Eye rose into the night sky. Rai had no intention of slowing them down so he could rest but part of him whispered that Tysar left early to put him off joining them.

Tysar promised they would have formal introductions when they stopped for breakfast but they had to move now while it was cool. The party was comprised of Tysar and six others that Rai didn't know, and Yeru the scholar that he met in the war room. They all rode hyians as they were lightweight and faster than aya. As they were single riders they were also more adaptable for the mountain passes. Still, Rai didn't envy them as he lay back atop the aya's platform in comparative luxury.

They had only been moving for an hour when Yeru pulled her hyian back to the aya's side.

"Do you think I could come up there with you? I can't do much reading on hyianback and I was told we weren't allowed to bring an aya," Yeru called up to him.

She had a book propped in front of her and gripped the reins with one hand.

"Sure. Come aboard," Rai said.

She tied her hyian's reins to the aya and clambered up the ladder. Then, tossed a book up before climbing back down to get her lantern. The book was old. A strange swirling sigil on the front.

Yeru came back up the ladder and Rai looked away, feigning disinterest.

"Thank you," she said. She wore the same outfit she had been wearing in the war room but it had been cleaned and pressed. Yeru lit the lantern and sat cross legged against the platform's side and started reading her book.

She had been one of the scholars who were studying the library of Nenelan. *I wonder if that's where she got the book.* It looked ancient with its weathered edges and faded design.

Yeru peered over her book, one eyebrow raised. Rai cleared his throat and looked away. Yeru closed the book and set it down in her lap.

"So you were the one who found the library?" Yeru asked.

Rai shook his head. "No. What makes you think that?"

"I could tell by the way Imayani looked at you."

She's perceptive, Fax said.

"I was with the person who found it," Rai said. "Is that book from the library?"

Yeru nodded. "I wish I was still there. I'm hoping to solve the mystery of the cataclysm. But this is important. Studying Tarrisian history will be a lot harder if Tarris is thrown into civil war."

Rai grunted.

"How did you find it? The library, I mean. We've been looking for it for hundreds of years." Yeru slid closer to Rai.

"Like I said, I didn't. The person who did is a lot smarter than me. His name was Kyan," Rai said. He hadn't spoken that name since he left Yontar. Rai couldn't shake the image of Kyan lying there and Ma-atan standing over him with his heart in the deity's fingers.

"What happened to him?" Yeru asked.

"He died chasing the truth."

"I'm so sorry," Yeru said, suddenly uncomfortable. "He sounds like an amazing individual and that's a worthy pursuit."

The night was calm and quiet. They were still in the lower mountains and the creatures scuttled away as they passed.

"What's the book about?" Rai asked.

"Oh, I don't really know." She hefted the tome and flicked through the pages. "I thought it was an account of the rulers pre-cataclysm. But it seems to be a religious text. It talks of a being called Kygian."

A cold wind wailed as if in response to the name. Rai shuddered with the sudden chill. Yeru glanced around and laughed uneasily.

"These ancient mountain passes are a little unsettling huh? Have you heard of the deity?"

"No, sorry," Rai said. He used to have extensive knowledge of the different deities as Maut-Fer was a big believer in leaving deitans, small dish offerings for the Gods, around the orphanage as offerings in hopes that they would look favourably upon them. But if deities were still out there, they cared not for the people. And after dealing with Ma-atan, Rai was beginning to think that what they thought of as deities were more likely to be incomprehensible forces of nature. Not the godlike beings that would care for those deemed worthy.

Yeru looked disappointed. "Me neither. I can't find any record of the deity. But the writer is fascinated by it. He writes about it like it was there with him. He has detailed worship practices and offerings he made to the deity. But it might be a mistranslation. These old books are in a dialect that is similar to the old tongue but not entirely the same, making it difficult to translate."

The scholar stared at the book like it might reveal the answers if she looked hard enough.

They trundled through the ancient mountain passes. The rest of the seven talked quietly and watched their surroundings. There was an eerie, otherworldly feel to the Bandor Mountains. *Probably because no one has walked these paths in thousands of years*, Rai thought. There was no reason to travel this way now that Asuriya had fallen. And these were dangerous passages through the mountains.

It was surreal to think that some of the last people to wander these mountains lived in a time before the cataclysm. A time when Asuriya was the capital. Was it more peaceful? It was undoubtedly different, but better? Unlikely. Where there are people there will be strain and hardship.

"What do you think the cataclysm was?" Rai asked. Yeru looked up from her book. "You said it was your area of study."

A grin spread across Yeru's face and she scuttled back to the side of the platform and climbed down to her hyian, returning with a leather satchel. She had a feral passion in her eyes.

I think you're going to regret asking that, Fax said. *It's like talking to Lem about boots.*

"The prevailing theory is that a battle transpired between a deity and the emperor at the time," Yeru said pulling out a small leather book. "How an emperor could fight a deity, I have no idea. I've never liked the theory. Can you imagine sending Imayani out to fight a god? No. Silly.

"However." Yeru opened the book and ran her finger over the text. "Here. Look." She handed the book over. It was in an ancient language but Rai picked up some of the words as being in the old tongue. Dates from a bygone time keeping system were scrawled into the margins. It had to be over a thousand years old.

"A journal?" Rai asked.

"Yes! We found it in the library of Nenelan," Yeru said. "It speaks of a rebellion *against* the emperor. In all of our interpretations until now, we thought a deity attacked the capital. But what if it wasn't a deity but a revolution? A band of Tarrisians trying to overthrow the emperor."

Rai grunted. It was what this journal seemed to imply. "What about the Mad Palace's explosion? And what caused the sickness and blight?"

Rai remembered riding on the outskirts of the city to find Ma-atan's temple. They had seen the Mad Palace and how it was frozen mid-explosion. Pieces of the palace floating in the air where a huge chunk of the stone had been shattered. Something needed to have caused that and the strange aura around the capital that made anyone who spent too long there sick.

"A weapon." Yeru grinned.

"A weapon?"

"Yes. Some ancient explosive perhaps?" Yeru said.

"Wouldn't we have found something like that?" Rai asked.

"Maybe. Maybe not. It could have been destroyed in the blast."

A weapon that could create the sickness and freeze a palace mid explosion? It was a terrifying thought. If a weapon like that truly existed then it should never have gotten into the hands of humans.

"Perhaps some pieces of our past should remain buried in the sand," Rai said.

14

The Red Wall

The Passing of the Nyfin always ended in one grand final night of celebration where everyone was out on the streets and a parade wound its way through the city. Coloured glass lanterns swung from aya's platforms as merchants marched down the street throwing nuts and dried fruits to the cheering crowd. Others stuck nyfin streamers onto their aya or hyian and sat upon its back blowing through their whistles and horns. Carts handed out free baked goods paid for by the monarch and nobles. It was the one time each year that the people were truly cared for.

It was late afternoon, the dying light of the Sun Eye faltering on the horizon. Nya and Kit sat atop the Patched Cloak inn and watched dark hour descend upon the city of Yontar. Customers crowded the rooftop, all huddled around a firepit sitting upon plush cushions. The last night of the Passing was one of Nya's favourite times of the year. It didn't matter who you were, you were fed, looked after, and pulled into the celebrations.

Wenson and Illy sat with some customers, deep in conversation. Nya stayed back from the crowd and Dust snored soundly beside her, having not moved all afternoon.

Ova's great Sun Eye passed from view and the world fell into darkness. For a moment, everything went black save for the few torches burning throughout the city. And then something magical happened. Lights started flaring across the city. Some were simple firelight whereas others illuminated planes of coloured glass painting the dark city in splotches of reds and greens and blues. The coloured lanterns and torches battered back the black in a show of defiance for the nyfin. It was not alone in the dark. They were here and they would light the night so it may continue its flight home.

It was beautiful, Nya thought gazing across Yontar. Like fallen stars burning bright throughout the city.

Bang. Bang. Bang.

Rhythmic impacts rang through the night. Suddenly another light flared to life near the palace, brighter than the rest. A model of the nyfin was held aloft by rows of servants. It was lit from the inside as they carried it through the gates of the palace. A shining white nyfin, several stories tall was carried through the streets. Acrobats and musicians danced at its feet smacking drums and singing. It was the '*Ballad of the Last*', a song about the nyfins final flight across the world before settling into the mountains to lay to rest. A haunting melody that was neither happy nor sad.

As the model nyfin passed overhead, more joined in the parade until half the city was singing along. Even those atop the Patched

Cloak sang and hummed and swayed to the song. Nya felt tears brimming. It was the only song her mother ever taught Nya to sing. On the last night of the Passing, Nya was grateful for the dark because it hid her tears.

They watched as the nyfin continued through the streets and out of view carrying its song with it.

Kit nudged Nya and flicked his head towards the stairs.

It was time to go.

Nya wiped the tears from her face. She had to be strong tonight. For Kit.

A problem that she hadn't considered with the plan was that, despite the festival bringing all the nobles out from their mansions, they still remained in the richer parts of the city. They didn't join in with the masses but stayed within their estates. And in a street full of nobles in their finest clothing, they couldn't hope to blend in. Kit had thought of this, however, and Nya loved his solution.

Nya stepped out of her room and twirled. The streamers spun about her silver costume, a nyfin design with ribbons hanging from her waist. Kit's door opened and Nya burst out laughing. He wore a nyfin costume too but his was red and orange with a mask that covered his head.

Kit sighed. "Get it all out now."

"You look ridiculous. I love it," Nya said. "How come I don't get a mask?"

Lifting the mask off his head, Kit shook his sweat slicked hair. "Because they're expensive. I'm only using mine so I'm not recognised."

"Do you really think you would be recognised?" Nya asked.

"It's possible. Like I said, I've ransacked a lot of noble manors and even worked with a few nobles, connecting them with gangs," Kit said.

"Nobles do that?" Nya couldn't believe it. She knew gangs backed certain merchants and establishments and that there was an entire world of politics on the streets of Yontar. But the nobles?

"They're just people, Nya. People with more power and connection means more ability to hurt others."

They made their way down the stairs and out the back of the inn where Lem was sitting on the courtyard wall watching the street's festivities. He leapt off the wall and greeted them, not mentioning their strange costumes. And soon they were headed towards the rich part of Yontar.

It was difficult to walk through the streets without being swept up in the atmosphere. The main parade had moved on but the partying had not. More song and dance broke out. A kindly vendor handed them a stick with some baked good hanging from the end. It tasted sweet with a crispy outside and soft centre.

There was no wall or fence indicating the richer part of town but that didn't make the threshold any less clear. It was sudden and abrupt. Homes started to have grounds around them. Perimeter fences and walls were erected around properties. The street productions changed, too. The costumes were more ornate and detailed. The music played by the musicians had a clearer tone. *There are less vendors though*, Nya noted. But she guessed the rich didn't care for the free food. Not like the people of the city proper.

No one gave them a second glance as they pushed through the crowd. Their costumes were cheaply made in comparison to those around them but they weren't questioned. It was a night of festivities after all.

They reached the Jeril manor as the Moon Eye surfaced for its watch. Lem led them around the back to a locked gate. Kit glanced around as Lem unlocked it and pushed it open. Lem had said the kiren would be running free because the Jeril family were out but they wouldn't attack them if he was with them. And right enough, after a couple steps into the darkened ground, growling came from the shadows.

"That's no way to speak to me!" Lem said.

The growling stopped and a three kiren passed out of the shadows. Kit and Nya froze. They were huge beasts with grey fur and taut muscled legs and shoulders. The kiren rose up to Nya's chest. Saliva dripped from their mouths as they approached. Lem leapt forward and ran his hand through the beast's fur.

"How are yah?" Lem asked. The kiren tilted his head towards Lem as he scratched behind its ear. "Told you they were friendly. See. Pet one!"

Nya reached out towards another and it snarled at her.

"Not Corm though. He can be a little grumpy before he's eaten," Lem said.

Nya decided not to pet any of the kiren.

Lem waved a piece of meat around and led the kiren over to the outhouse that they had seen several days before. Nya and Kit crept through the rock gardens watching the shuttered windows of the manor for movement. Lem had never been inside and had no knowledge of how many servants would be roaming its halls. But Kit had guessed a home that size could have upwards of ten. That was a lot of people to avoid.

With their backs against the home, they skulked around the building to find a side entrance. Nya walked up to it and Bom sliced through the bolt. She looked to Kit who nodded and Nya eased the door open. Peering inside, Nya was surprised to find a dirty, unfurnished room. Cloaks hung on the far wall and shoes were lined up beneath them. Kit snuck in behind her and scanned the room.

"This must be the servant's entrance," Kit said.

They moved to the corridor leading farther into the mansion. Braziers lit the inlaid stone walls. "Bom," Nya said. The shade moved ahead of them to warn them if they got near any servants. A courtyard opened up with a fountain bubbling in the centre, surrounded by stone benches. Nya gawked. Having a courtyard in one's home was a level of wealth Nya didn't know existed.

"Come on," Kit whispered.

They crept into a huge entry chamber, a grand brass door led out to the front of the manor, and a stairwell led up to the second floor.

Servant.

Bom returned in a rush taking Nya's breath away. She grabbed Kit and pulled him back into a shadowed corner by a stone sculpture. A woman sauntered past carrying fresh linen and she turned and walked up the staircase. As soon as she disappeared from sight, Nya released her breath and her grip of Kit.

"A little more warning would have been nice," Kit whispered.

Bom offered to skewer the boy's head and Nya sent the shade off ahead again. They took to the stairs, moving quickly, as they had nowhere to hide and didn't want to linger. At the top, a long corridor led in both directions lined with rooms. Kit pointed left.

Crash!

Nya and Kit looked at one another. What was that?

Rushed footsteps. They ducked into the nearest room and carefully eased the door so that it was open a crack. Two servants ran past.

"Could it have been Lem?" Nya asked.

"It sounded like the crash came from inside the house," Kit said.

They waited in the darkened room a while longer. Two more servants passed, all headed towards the back of the home. After everything went still, Nya and Kit headed the opposite direction. They checked every room they passed but none held the library. They came across no more servants, either.

An eerie quiet came over the mansion. Where once there was the distant scuffle of movement now there was silence.

"Do you think they have finished for the night?" Nya whispered.

"I wouldn't think so," Kit said.

After searching the entire west wing, it was clear that the library wasn't there. It had to be in the east wing where the crash came from. They skulked down the corridor. Nya hoped the silence meant there were no servants nearby. She lightened her footfalls and shivered against a sudden chill. Something felt off. But Nya couldn't put her finger on what.

The first couple of doors led to sitting rooms and a bed chamber. The fourth door however, was slightly ajar, torchlight wavering through the crack. Bom slid under the door.

It's the library, Bom said. *It's empty but the window has been shattered.*

"That's strange," Nya said.

"Maybe Lem did it to draw the servants outside?" Kit said. "It would explain why we haven't seen any in a while."

"We owe him a pipe of furthing leaves after this," Nya said.

They pushed the door open and slipped into the library. If Nya hadn't seen the lost library of Nenelan, this would have amazed her. It was the size of the Patched Cloak's common room. The walls were covered in shelves and two rows of shelving cut the room into segments. Kit rushed over and started moving down the aisles of books reading the spines.

Firelight flickered through the shelves. Nya walked around them to the far wall where a lantern was left on a table. A huge window let in silver moonlight, which illuminated what the firelight did not.

Nya frowned. Why would they leave this lantern here? Again the feeling that something was wrong flared in her mind. Bom felt it too and stirred uneasily.

Skulking along the back wall, Nya hissed as glass cut her foot. She glanced down and saw shards of glass scattered across the library floor. In the centre of the window, a ragged hole let in the chill night air. The hole was too large to have been a rock. What did Lem throw? There was nothing at her feet.

Nya peeked out of the window. The grounds were shrouded in darkness. No servants. No Lem. The hairs on the back of Nya's neck stood on end. There was a tearing sound.

"Nya!" Kit hissed and ran over slowing as he noticed the fragments of glass. "I found it!"

Nya stared at him wide-eyed and lifted her finger to her lips. A look of concern came over Kit's face as he fell silent. Together, they listened.

Snap.

A torn arm dropped between them with a meaty thud.

Nya brought her gaze up to the roof where leathery black wings shifted and the sheen of metal talons caught on the moonlight. A *husk* hung from the ceiling eating one of the servants. For a moment, she just stared in horror. How could that be here? Was she in one of her nightmares of the dark place? It made no sense.

Entrails fell from the husk's grip and Nya jumped back to avoid them as they splattered against the ground. She stepped back, bumping the table and knocking the lantern over. It rolled off the table and the glass box smashed. Flames rumbled as they spread across the floor.

The husk froze.

Its head spun to look at the fire and then to Nya and Kit.

Then, the husk shrieked.

It dove for Nya. Kit tackled her out of the way as the husk crashed into the spot she had been in not moments before. They rolled and came up to see the husk shaking itself off. Glass showering around it. The husk howled and lurched towards them.

Bom rose as a wall of shadow deflecting the beast as Nya and Kit ran for the door. Flames spread like spilled water running the length of the wooden shelves, igniting the library.

Nya felt the husk knock Bom to the side. She dragged Kit into the shelves to avoid a falling piece of burning shelving. The husk barrelled past them, screaming, its wings set ablaze. Shelves on either side were engulfed in the fire and Nya cowered between them as they ran down the length of the row. Something cracked from above and one of the walls collapsed forward crashing into a freestanding row of books. It knocked the shelf on their right over, which fell and caught on the left shelf. Books fell from above like meteors.

Nya shielded her face as burning books bounced off her. She squealed as the fire lapped at her skin. Bom, fuelled by Nya's pain, blasted a wave of darkness outward. It deflected the last of the falling books. The shelves creaked ominously.

Smoke filled Nya's lungs as she pulled her nyfin costume over her mouth. The world was burning. Fire covered everything. She felt the heat drying out her eyes.

A growl.

Nya spun to see the husk standing at the only opening in the blanket of flames. Kit patted at his arm which had caught on fire.

They were dead. There was no way out of this.

Kit seemed to come to the same realisation as he searched the billowing red around them. His face hardened when he met Nya's gaze. The husk had put out the flames on its wings and was about to charge.

"Get Bom to blast outward again!" Kit shouted over the rumble of the fire.

"But the shelves!" Nya said.

The husk shot towards them before Kit could answer. Bom blasted out in a black wave and the shelves collapsed onto them. Kit dove over Nya taking the brunt of the fire and debris. Bom recollected itself and held back the shelves as well as it could but Nya felt the strain the shade was under. The husk cried out as it was crushed under the flaming shelves.

Everything went still and Nya thought she might have died, but she could hear Kit's ragged breath above her. "Bom is about to give out," Nya said. Her voice was croaky and dry.

"Okay," Kit said. It sounded like all he could manage.

Bom's shield dissipated. The shelves groaned and then the fire fell upon them. Nya screamed as her skin burned. They pushed and tumbled out of the wreckage. Luckily the shelves had been alight long enough that the wood was weak and easy to break through.

Rolling around the floor, Nya put out the fire on her costume. She came to all fours and spat out globs of black, ashy saliva, retching at the sight.

Kit was in worse shape than her, his arms blackened and cracked by flames. He lay as a smoking pile of flesh looking like a corpse. Nya crawled over and shook him and he squealed at the pain. That was good. That meant he was alive. She couldn't check his breathing anymore as he didn't need to breathe after passing Ma-atan's Judging.

"Come on! We need to move!" Nya shouted. Panic held the pain at bay as the fire continued to spread. Kit's eyes rolled as he came to. He was in no condition to run. She had to think of a way to carry him. Maybe Bom could...

Nya watched as Kit's skin started to knit itself back together.

Beneath the rumble of the flames was a creaking.

Snap! Nya spun and stared as the burning shelves shifted. The husk was alive. Kit's body continued to heal as Nya heaved him to his feet. His eyes fluttered open.

"What's going on?" he asked.

"The hu—"

The husk burst from the curling flames sending out a deluge of sparks and embers. They ran from the library and slammed the door behind them. Nya and Kit held the door shut as the husk battered into it. The wood began to buckle.

"Bom!" Nya shouted.

The shade slid between the door and its frame and branched out as a spike jamming the door shut. Nya stepped back and the husk shoved against it but Bom's spear held. However, it wouldn't hold the husk in for long.

"Can you run?" Nya asked.

Kit looked miraculously better than he had moments ago. Cuts had closed. Burnt skin didn't look as crisp. He nodded.

Nya and Kit sprinted down the hallway and leapt down the staircase. They threw the front door open as the door to the library shattered. Bom slid back into Nya's shadow as they ran into the night.

They scrambled back through the garden to the side entrance. Lem was nowhere to be seen. Hopefully he had returned to the inn like he said he would. The gate clanged as Nya flung it shut behind them.

For a moment, everything was silent. Nya and Kit breathed hard, listening. They leant against the gate trying to catch their breaths.

Kiren started to growl.

There was a crack of bones snapping and the crunch of flesh. Other kiren whimpered.

Nya and Kit prepared to run into the streets when the gate burst open, skittering across the stone.

15

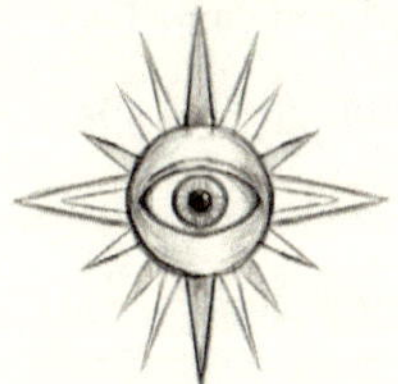

Perfectly Self-Defensible

16 years ago.

"Rai, you're doing it again," Tys said as the two circled each other in the training yard. Rai grinned. Tys claimed Rai had a predatory look when he was concentrating on a fight.

The sky was red, casting long black shadows. The crack of wooden spears and grunts of battle came from all around the courtyard. A fresh scent carried from the nearby garden doing little to mask the stench of sweat. Rai felt the sandy gravel scrape as he stepped over it. Drunk street fighters narrowed in on their attacker closing out the world. But warriors heard, felt, and saw everything. In war, awareness was the key to survival.

There, Rai thought spotting a moment of distraction as Tys glanced at one of the other fights. Within a breath, Rai covered the distance between them bringing his spear down hard. Tys brought his spear up to block but the force sent him reeling backward towards the edge of the sparring circle. He grunted and shoved Rai back.

"Maybe you should focus on our fight," Rai said.

"Yeah, yeah," Tys said, and charged.

Rai deflected Tys' jabbed spear with a sideways slash, then following the momentum brought his spear back around swinging for Tys' head. Tys ducked and came back up, spear first. Rai shifted his weight but not fast enough. The spear cut into his shoulder and knocked Rai off his feet. A cloud of dust spat up around him as Rai landed on his back, the air stolen from his lungs.

"Maybe you should hope that I'm not focused on our fight." Tys smiled.

With a growl, Rai pressed his hands behind his head and flung his body upright, spear coming down in a wide arc. Tys brought his spear up to defend but Rai's spear cracked over Tys' forearm and he hissed, dropping his spear. Rai spun his spear around clipping Tys' side as he reached for his spear and smacked the wooden shaft against Tys' calf, sweeping his legs from under him.

Tys lay on his back, coughing, his spear out of reach. Rai levelled his spear to Tys' neck.

"Okay, maybe I should have paid more attention to our fight," Tys said. Rai laughed and held out a hand, pulling Tys back to his feet.

Despite his best efforts, Rai had grown fond of Tys. It was hard not to when they shared a room and trained together. He had come from a middle-class family with dreams to join the palace guard before being plucked up and brought to Atef Palace to train under Overseer Rikai.

Rai wiped the sweat from his brow and flicked it to the ground. Around them two other fights were ongoing. Sen, a short boy with strength that belied his size, fought Genu, a girl who came from a wealthy family of aya dealers. She moved with the grace and unpredictability of falling leaf. It looked to be an even fight. Sen was strong but he struggled to catch Genu with more than a graze.

Past them, the blonde boy, Ada, who had stomped on Rai's leg on the first day of training, sparred with Overseer Rikai. He had apologised to Rai about that incident, claiming he just wanted to avoid wearing the jerkin. But Rai had seen the joy on his face, the quirk at the corner of his mouth. Ada remained polite and friendly but Rai didn't trust the boy.

The five of them were all that was left of the twenty that had been there on the first day in the Eye. Stress broke many of them and injuries took the rest. However, while training hadn't eased, how Overseer Rikai treated them had improved. He didn't make small talk but he did instruct them and point out ways to ease some of the harder training sessions.

Dark hour was almost upon them when Overseer Rikai dismissed them of practice. They had sparred through the worst of the heat again, now forfeiting the training grounds to the palace guards who came out to spar in the cooler temperatures.

The five chatted as they passed through the palace. Servants sped about them with platters of food now that most had their qed and were ready for their afternoon meals.

The high ceiling of the bathhouse was open to the darkening sky. The chamber was filled with seven different pools of varying sizes, temperatures and depths. Some were scented with oils, others nothing more than mucky tubs to wash off the worst of the dirt and grime.

Rai scrubbed off in one of the muck tubs and started to dry off when Tys beckoned him to come sit in one of the warmer pools. Sen sat with him and Ada was wandering about somewhere, while Genu had already left.

"I can't," Rai said, getting dressed.

"Running off to Imayan already?" Tys asked elbowing Sen who laughed.

"It's not like that. I'm her personal guard."

"Uh huh."

"Leave him alone," Ada said, wrapping an arm around Rai's shoulder sending a shiver down his spine. "It's his duty and he's taking it seriously." Ada smiled. With a pat on the back, he stalked across the bathhouse stepped into the hottest pool, pleasure easing onto his face. There was something almost reptilian about him that unsettled Rai.

"I'll catch you at training tomorrow," Rai said.

"Don't stay up too late," Tys replied.

Rai waved dismissively as he left the bathhouse. It *wasn't* like that. Even if it was uncommon to have a guard as young as Rai, this is what they were being trained for. Imayan couldn't remain unguarded until they finished their training. And it was more of a formality as Imayan rarely left Atef Palace and when she did, the emperor sent a company of soldiers to escort her as well as Rai.

Orange light chased away the dark and life burst into the corridors as the lamp lighters lit the braziers. They shone off the ever-present gold veins than ran down the length of the dark sandstone walls.

He had only been in Atef Palace for five years and yet it felt more like home than the orphanage ever had. Rai and Tys spent entire afternoons roaming its hallways and exploring the palace's vast reaches. Now Rai knew it like the back of his hand.

He made his way high into the palace, past guarded doors and into the forbidden corridors of the palace. Rai knocked on Imayan's quarters. Her door swung open in an instant. But on the other side was Mino, Imayan's servant.

"Where have… Rai? I don't know where she's gone." Mino blurted as she peered past Rai as if he were hiding Imayan from her. "She was there one minute and then gone the next. I was going to call the guards to shut the gates and sweep the palace and…" Her voice faded as she registered the smile on Rai's face. Mino scowled. She was a short woman. A little older than Imayan and she had long blonde hair that fell past her pinched face to her waist. She was newly appointed as Imayan's servant and still had to get used to her… unique ways.

"Don't look at me like that. If it were her father here at the door my head would be on a pike for losing her again."

"I'll go find her," Rai said.

"You better and tell her she needs to come back *now*. I'm not playing around this time," Mino said as Rai turned. She mumbled something about a spoiled noble as the door clicked shut.

There was only one place Imayan could be.

During the day the garden was a beautiful tapestry of colour, but Rai preferred it at night. At night, dusk painted the garden with midnight blue. What was once a garish mash of colours became a consistent flow of shades. The colours were still there, an echo of what they were during the day, but it was as if their essence had turned in for the night.

"Imayan!" Rai called.

There was rarely anyone in the palace gardens. Gardeners tended the plants in the early morning and occasionally the emperor brought guests out to roam its wild paths but no one spent as much time out there as Imayan.

Rai ducked under some leaves reaching out onto the path. He breathed in the fresh floral-scented air. It was the same smell that he could pick up from the nearby training grounds. The scent calmed him even in the heat of a fight.

A grunt came from Rai's left. Pushing a plant out the way, Rai foraged off the main path. It looked to be too dense to walk but after scraping through a bush, a space opened up. A great tree created a wide domed canopy over a stretch of hardened dirt. And standing at the tree's trunk was Imayan. The canopy was too thick for moonlight to reach them but the afterglow lit the space enough for Rai to make out her shadowed form picking something from the trunk.

"Imayan, you're going to give Mino a heart attack one of these days," Rai said.

"What do you think of this?" Imayan asked. She held some viscous goop that dripped from her hand.

"Indifference."

Imayan met his eyes with a disappointed expression. "It's called spor sap. It's quite common under the bark of these trees and it's really sticky."

The spor sap drooped from her hand.

"Like really sticky." Imayan grinned at Rai then leapt at the tree. Instinct prompted Rai to step forward at the sudden movement but Imayan clung to the tree and didn't slide.

"Now imagine a battalion with access to this," Imayan called down. "No wall could stop the spor sap army. No rocky plateau could impede their march to victory." With each word Imayan clambered up the tree trunk. Imayan got excited about a lot of plants and their properties but Rai had to admit that this was interesting.

"And my father says gardening is a waste of time. Wants me to train to fight." Imayan blew out a breath and dropped back to the ground. "Wait until he sees this," she said turning with a manic grin.

"Your father just wants to ensure that you have some self-defence," Rai said.

"I'm perfectly self-defensible." Imayan crossed her arms. "Try and attack me."

Rai raised an eyebrow. Imayan didn't move. With a sigh, Rai lunged forward preparing to sweep her off her feet but something caught. His leg wouldn't lift and his face slammed against the hard ground. Rai rolled over with a groan, holding his head. His hand came back bloody. Sitting up, he looked down and saw some of the spor sap stuck to the ground at his feet.

"See?" Imayan shrugged.

They made their way back into the palace. It was a hive of activity. Much like the rest of Tarris, people went about most of their business in the early hours of night. Rai didn't understand how it took so many people to run a country. What were they all doing? Surely the emperor made decisions and that was it. But important nobles busied themselves doing whatever it was that they did.

Anyone who passed made sure to bow deeply to Imayan despite her indifference to the show of respect. Rai had once mentioned that her disregard could be seen as disrespectful. She had laughed in his face.

Rai made for the bottom of the spiral steps that led towards Imayan's quarters but she grabbed his arm. "What?" he asked. Imayan's arms were rigid at her side, a habit that meant she was nervous.

"I don't want to go back yet," Imayan said.

"Imayan…"

"I know Mino worries but…" Imayan glanced over her shoulder then dropped her voice low. "I need to speak to you."

"Isn't that what we are doing now?" Rai asked. He had gotten so close to Imayan in recent years that he sometimes forgot that she was the emperor's daughter. If anyone had overheard him being sarcastic to her, he would be disciplined.

"Coffeehouse?"

Rai sighed. "Only for one. And I'm not being responsible for Mino's wrath when we get back."

Veering right, they marched away from the staircase and deeper into the palace. Atef Palace housed three different coffeehouses across its wide estate. One sat high in the palace with a two-storey glass pane wall overlooking Tansen. The second was in a grand hall narrow with tables laid out down its length and private balconies lining the walls on either side.

However, their coffeehouse was named Iluian Blend, which translated from the old tongue as 'blooming petals'. It was on the ground floor and opened out to the palace gardens. Some of the drinks even used plants plucked directly from the garden.

Rai led the way. They passed the entrance to the coffeehouse and turned a corner before passing into the servant's entrance. Inside was nothing more than a pantry with a cushioned bench where workers escaped to have their breaks. Bags of coffee and ingredients for the baked treats lined the shelves in a myriad of colours and smells.

Two workers sat on the bench but neither looked up. "I hope Imayan, the emperor's daughter does well this fine night, wherever she may be," Jyun said. She was the owner of the Iluian Blend. Skin the colour of coffee and eyes the colour of caramel.

"I hear she is well," Imayan replied. "I heard she was wondering how her palace coffeehouses and their respectable owners were doing."

"Well, she needn't worry. Coffee will always flow. And peace and conversation is a lucrative business." A mischievous grin spread across Jyun's face.

Imayan smiled back and they kept walking. After the attempt on Imayan's life, Emperor Leondal had banned Imayan from going out to the coffeehouses without a company of guards. He said that Mino could fetch her coffee whenever she wished for it, but he didn't understand that coffeehouses did not only sell coffee.

In a coffeehouse the very air was infused with the roast of the day. The firelight glowed, lighting the warm sandstone walls in shifting light. The buzz of conversation filled the space. Coffeehouses sold more than coffee. They sold respite.

And so Jyun and Imayan started this little game.

Imayan clambered up the ladder, Rai following. At the top,

wooden beams spread across the rafters above the Iluian Blend. They inched out, sliding across the beams until they reached one of the support pillars. Imayan leaned back against it and Rai could see her shoulders fall and muscles ease. This was somewhere special to her. Where her father and the responsibilities of her position couldn't find her.

Below, the coffeehouse was busy but no one looked up into the shadowed rafters.

"My father is planning something," Imayan said.

"He runs the country, Imayan. I'm sure he plans many things."

"No, I'm serious." Imayan sat up. "He won't tell me what, but he has hushed conversations. He's distracted at mealtime. Something is coming."

Knock, knock.

Rai looked over and Jyun had placed two steaming mugs at the top of the ladder. Creeping back over, Rai returned and handed one of the mugs to Imayan. As she took a sip, her brow eased.

"One of the monarchs?" Rai asked. The three monarchs constantly undermined one another and the emperor, destroying secret spy networks, burning farmland so soldiers couldn't base themselves close to their walls. Rai was shocked when Imayan told him of everything that happened beneath the noses of the Tarrisian people. They were all Tarrisian and working to serve Tarris and yet beneath the veil the country had been undergoing a war for centuries. The monarchs vied for power, wealth, and a chance at the throne. The assassins sent to kill Imayan were likely an attempt to wipe out the emperor's line so one of them could step in to rule.

Imayan shook her head. "I don't think so. He would tell me

about that. He thinks I should know these things in case there is another assassin."

There hadn't been another attempt on Imayan's life in years. In part due to the extra precautions put in place to keep her protected.

However, after the death of the emperor's unborn son, the monarchs were watching and waiting, biding their time to see what he would do next. If he were to take another wife and have a boy, they would no doubt shift their attention to the child. But equally, they listened for word of Imayan getting married. If she were to be with child the emperor could name that child heir to the throne.

"What is it then?"

"I don't know."

Rai sipped on his coffee. Jyun knew how he liked it, unadorned by spices and sweeteners. It was straightforward and strong, the raw taste of the coffee bean not smothered with any of the extras.

"It's a stressful job," Rai said. "Maybe he has been making some hard decisions recently." Despite being Imayan's personal guard, Rai had never met the emperor. He had been in the same room as the man a couple of times in his many years of service but he had never spoken to him directly.

"Maybe." Imayan went quiet, receding into her thoughts.

"Imayan."

She glanced up. "Sorry. I just… I feel like something is coming. Something big."

Rai reached out and laid a hand on her shin. "And if it does, we will face it."

Imayan's face softened and then she smiled.

16

The Bandor Mountains

Steep stone slopes walled Rai and the rest of the party into a wide trench. Wide enough that they could all ride alongside one another. Day was breaking, staining the rock in a deep red. Rai couldn't get over how quiet it was out here. The crackle of gravel beneath their feet reverberated around them but otherwise there was blissful silence.

They were deep in the mountain passes now. Rai had spotted a couple of packs of kiren but they didn't get too close. Not yet. But they would need to make sure the pack wasn't tailing them and waiting for nightfall.

Rai pulled up beside Tysar who had the map open. One of the seven, an older man called Bisu, spoke with him in hushed tones.

"Do we have the exact location for this Ossin base?" Rai asked.

"Yes and no. These mountains aren't mapped out as well as I had hoped. But we think we'll reach it in two days," Tysar said.

"We can't stray too far east lest we draw too close to Asuriya," Bisu said. His short, black hair speckled with grey and shaven face spoke of a man who liked to keep things simple. The faint green tinge to his jerkin placed him as part of the Verdin Guild. A warrior then. "But these old paths are leading us east. So we're trying to find another way over that." Bisu pointed to the ridge in the distance.

"You may have to free the aya," Tysar said. "We might have to scale some inclines."

Rai glanced down at his aya. Freeing an aya in the wild was one thing but leaving it alone in the Bandor Mountains was something else entirely. He had grown attached to the beast and he couldn't leave it to die out here.

We can't leave Yawn, Fax said. *I won't allow it!*

"Yawn?" Rai whispered.

Yeru gave him a funny look as she leant against the platform atop the aya. She had caught him talking to himself a couple of times now.

Yes. That's her name, Fax said.

"You named the aya?" Rai whispered.

Of course. I was thinking Zifildor but Yawn fits better since she yawns so much.

Rai blew out a breath.

The Sun Eye eased over the mountains and glared at them with its unrelenting heat. The party rode close to the rock wall where there was a slither of shade but they would need to find somewhere out of the heat to rest soon enough.

Turning a corner, the path opened up to a wide, circular area.

Standing at the far end of the opening was a kiren. The wolf-like creature stared at them with its glowing amber eyes. Its dark grey fur was matted and patchy, a long scar ripped across its side. It growled, baring its teeth.

The company didn't slow. "Loulu," Tysar said.

Loulu, a new member of the Seventh Sceptre, unslung her bow and loosed an arrow that bounced off the ground in front of the kiren. The beast didn't flee at the warning shots. It snapped at them as they piled into the open area. That had been enough to scare off anything that they had come across so far. But deep in the Bandor Mountains, creatures didn't see humans often which mean that some were brave enough to try and face them.

"It must be protecting its children," Bisu said.

Yeru inched towards the front of the platform. "Mmm no. Kiren aren't maternal like that. The strong get to grow old while the runts die young. A mother kiren can give birth over twenty times in her lifetime and on average only two or three children survive into adulthood."

"Fire another one," Tysar said.

Loulu loosed another arrow and it skittered dangerously close to hitting the beast. It didn't move.

"Why isn't it attacking?" Bisu asked.

The next arrow shot towards the beast. The kiren leapt out the way but didn't approach.

"It's a trap," Rai whispered. He remembered protecting Gamo village from a pack of kiren and they were smart and strategic. *This is a distraction*, Rai thought.

"In a circle!" Rai shouted.

As if sensing that they had figured it out, howls came from all around the basin and kiren popped up from the ridges. They were surrounded. The party pulled together as the pack began to climb down from the rocks.

The swish of weaponry coming from scabbards.

"Don't let them break our formation!" Tysar called. "Loulu shoot them down from the aya."

Loulu threw herself up the platform's ladder and stood with Yeru. Rai nodded to Yeru before leaping off the aya. Dirt splattered as he hit the ground.

The kiren charged.

One shrieked and launched itself at Rai. Even on all fours the beast came up to Rai's chest. Fax appeared like a shadowy wall and the kiren battered into it. Rai swept in and stabbed his dagger through the creature's head.

The others cried out as the kiren rushed them. Rai dove under a kiren that snapped for his head and Fax sliced it in two. Blood and entrails hit the dirt and the body followed. Rai was relieved to hear the roar of flame burst from one of the sevens' blades. They would have been doomed without diera weapons.

Tysar screamed and Rai spun to see a kiren chomp down on his leg. Rai threw a dagger but it bounced off the creature's hide. It's *too thick* hide.

"Fax!"

The shade shot over and sliced through the beast's neck. The blood gurgled and sprayed onto Tysar who gritted his teeth and shoved the kiren off him.

Rai turned back just as a kiren was inches away. They landed hard, knocking the wind from Rai's lungs. He gasped for breath holding the snapping kiren at bay with a dagger buried in its torso. But the beast didn't seem to notice as saliva dripped onto Rai's face from its gnashing mouth.

Rai twisted the blade and the kiren grunted. So it did feel. As the beast snapped, Rai saw its tongue. It had split into *two*. Rai's eyes went wide as the tongue shot out its mouth. Fax returned and speared straight through its skull. It gargled and fell still.

There's something strange about these kiren, Rai, Fax said.

"I noticed," Rai said, dragging himself to his feet.

A plume of flame chased back the oncoming pack. There had to be twenty kiren circling them. They regrouped by the aya. Three of the eight hyian had been torn to pieces by the kiren.

Tysar fell back against the aya, panting. "Rai that kiren had two sets of teeth," he said.

"Mine had two tongues," Rai said. "I think it's because we're near Asuriya. They say the wildlife has changed. Touched by the blight. I didn't think they meant this."

Tysar grimaced holding his leg. "We need to chase them off."

Back in Atef Palace, they had lessons on all the creatures that they might come across in Tarris and how best to fight them. For kiren, it was recommended that they try to scare off the pack. One of the best ways to do this was to kill the leader and the rest would scatter.

"I don't think they get scared," Rai said.

"It's that or die," Tysar said.

He was right. The others were in bad shape too. Two of the seven were pressed up against the aya unable to fight, the others defending them.

"There," Tysar said. He pointed up to the ridge where elders of the pack wandered and watched as the younger kiren fought and fed. Staying at the back of the pack, one kiren was larger than the rest. It was racked with scars and its tail broke into two halfway up its length. Nearby, kiren had their heads lowered in deference.

The leader.

Rai met eyes with the beast and saw intelligence there. Not the feral animosity of the younger kiren but experience and deep thought.

"Fax," Rai said.

The shade formed as a crow and flew over the circling kiren. There was no reason to hide Fax now. The leading kiren watched as Fax barrelled towards it. Then before Fax could slice open its neck, the kiren *bit* the shade out of the air.

Fax shrieked.

Its panic flared in Rai's mind like it was his own.

The kiren *caught* the shade. While Fax was made of tangible shadow and could be deflected in combat, he had never seen a beast catch the shade like this. Fax tried to keep the kiren's jaws open but they were forcing shut around the shade. Rai felt the teeth closing in around him. Panic swelled in his mind. His heart leapt up his throat.

Rai screamed and charged into the pack. He brought his daggers up and sliced at a kiren's face, blinding the beast. It howled and shook its head in pain. Rai didn't slow.

"Protect Rai!" Tysar shouted.

Rai unslung his bow and shot a diera arrow at his feet. The magnetic-like force of the diera arrow launched Rai into the air and he landed on a kiren thrusting his daggers into the beast's skull. It collapsed and Rai ran up the incline. Another kiren threw itself at him but an arrow hit the kiren's leg and it toppled over. Rai didn't need to glance back to know that Loulu was responsible.

Two of the other older kiren growled and moved towards Rai as he approached but the leader barked and they bowed back. The leader stepped towards Rai.

It had accepted his challenge.

Fax sent terror racing through Rai's mind. The shade was clasped down and unable to expand and cut through the beast as it wrapped around Fax's essence. How was that possible?

Rai and the kiren circled one another. Holding Fax in its mouth meant it couldn't chomp down on Rai but this kiren had claws the size of swords coming from its pawed feet. It would have no trouble skewering or slicing Rai open.

Rai twirled his daggers in his hands. He could have sworn the kiren was smiling at him. One hit from this beast would mean death. He had to make this quick.

With a blur of movement, the kiren crossed the distance, its paw swinging in a wide arc. Rai threw himself back and ran his daggers along the kiren's side. The beast grunted sliding to a stop. Then it shot towards him, its full weight hurtling at him with impossible speed for its size. Rai threw a dagger but the kiren ducked and it flew over his head.

Flicking his other dagger, a wave of flames arced out at the kiren but the leader charged through the fire unperturbed and dove at Rai. The kiren pinned him to the ground, its fur alight with flame. Rai could see the beast's skin bubbling and blackening underneath its fur. It was burning and it didn't care. The kiren's claws dug into

Rai's shoulders and he screamed. Warm blood bloomed between the kiren's paws.

"No!" Tysar shouted from below. There were more shouts and an arrow shot towards the leader but one of the other kiren dove in the way and took the arrow in the side. There was no interrupting a challenge for these beasts.

The flames curled and covered the kiren's body. These weren't the kiren Rai had seen in the desert. These weren't the kiren described in the bestiaries. These were blight-touched.

Rai shied away from the heat as the kiren dipped its head. It lifted a paw, ready to swipe at Rai's head and finish him off when the diera dagger he had tossed flew back to him. It ran up the length of the beast ripping a deep gash into its already scarred side before slicing through the beast's jaw. The kiren didn't seem to notice but now the bottom half of its mouth hung open and Fax was free.

In a blink, Fax speared upward through the kiren's head.

The other kiren stopped and stared at their dead leader. Fax stayed in the spear shape holding aloft the dead kiren as flames still burned across its flesh and fur. Rai lay on the ground breathing hard.

A kiren made its way towards Rai but another growled and the approaching creature stopped. The others were skulking away over the ridge and out of sight, heads dipped. Rai watched as, one by one, they disappeared from sight. Only after the last dropped behind the ridge did Rai roll from beneath the kiren and Fax let the burning carcass drop. He waited for a sarcastic comment from Fax. The shade stayed quiet.

They all agreed that staying in that open space was a mistake. So they marched an hour into the mountains where they found a small cave cut into the rock. Soon, a fire was crackling and wounds were being bandaged. The Seventh Sceptre had medical training so they were all equipped with basic knowledge and provisions to help one another.

After getting his shoulder cleaned and patched up, Rai helped Tysar wrap his leg. It wasn't as bad as he first thought and Tysar could walk on it, albeit slowly. Low chatter and the rumble of the fire bounced around the shallow cave.

Tysar glanced over at the others who were all resting or cleaning their weapons. "What is it?"

Rai raised an eyebrow.

"The shadow," Tysar said.

"Did Imayani not tell you?"

"She said something about it, but seeing the shadow in action is something else," Tysar replied.

"It's called a shade. I picked it up in the pocket world and now it lives in my shadow," Rai said. He expected Fax to hop out as a crow and introduce itself but the shade was shaken from its fight with the kiren and had curled up inside Rai, not answering his prodding.

Tysar nodded. Rai had expected more reluctance but his friend seemed to accept what he said. Tysar had been there. He had seen the other world with the ever-storming sky. After seeing that, anything could be possible.

"What can it do?" Tysar asked.

"It can form into tangible shapes like spikes and blades to fight."

"What about bigger shapes?" Tysar hissed as Rai tightened a bandage.

"There is a finite amount of its essence so the more the shadow spreads, the thinner it gets," Rai said. "I could fill this cave with a thin blanket of darkness but it wouldn't be particularly dense and I then couldn't create anything to defend myself with."

Tysar grunted. "You talk to it though, don't you? Yeru said she saw you whispering to yourself." Rai nodded. "What does it say?"

"Not much to begin with. It was like a child learning the ways of our world for the first year but it's a fast learner and it has a personality. Sometimes too much of a personality." Still, Fax did not stir. "It's not much use in figuring out what the pocket world really is though," Rai said.

"Can you control it?" Tysar asked.

Rai had grown close with Fax over the years and they had a bond but he didn't *control* Fax. It was a partnership. Rai couldn't see any situation where that would be a problem but it was true that he didn't have *complete* control over the shade.

This was a being that he had no knowledge of other than what it had told him. He thought of Kyan and how his shade had enabled him in his deranged ideas of justice. It seemed so far removed from what Fax was like. But Kyan had no doubt thought the same about his shade.

Rai felt Fax stir and silenced his thoughts. That was part of the problem: it was in his head. How could he trust his own mind?

This is ridiculous, Rai thought. *It's Fax.*

Of course he could trust Fax. He thought of the shade imitating a crow. It was hardly a strategic mastermind.

"I don't need to control it," Rai said, sharper than he meant to. He hated that Tysar's question got in his head.

"I didn't mean to question you," Tysar said lifting his hands.

"I know," Rai said. He finished wrapping Tysar's bandage and sat back. "That damn kiren spooked me and Fax, that's all."

Tysar gave Rai a questioning look.

"The shade. We've not come across anything that could fight back like that." Rai watched the flames whip back and forth. In the fire he could see the kiren's knowing eyes staring back at him. "It must be this place. This mutation caused by Asuriya."

"It'll only get worse from here," Tysar said. "These mountains are brimming with strange creatures."

"I didn't truly believe the stories until now."

"Me neither," Tysar said. He patted Rai's back. "But we'll push through. We always have."

Rai smiled. It was good seeing his old friend. Outside, the wind howled as the Sun Eye rose higher.

"Now, I want to know more about this shade," Tysar said. "How many men you think it could kill at once?"

17

A Shadow is Never Left

Nya screamed in warning as they ran through the estate. Their shouting was ignored, however, with the celebrations stilling ringing throughout the street. Most probably thought it was part of the show. They sprinted through a dance performance, knocking a woman over as they passed.

More screams.

The husk barrelled out onto the street barging through a cluster of people as it tried to take the sharp bend. A long gash ripped through its wing. The husk tried to fly but with a flick of its wing it howled in pain. Its eyes focused on Nya and Kit as it scrambled in their direction. Some of the crowd cheered thinking it was part of the performance.

It was chasing *them?* But why?

It senses me, Bom said.

"It's after us because of Bom!" Nya shouted.

"So much for losing it in the crowd!" Kit said. They ducked under a model nyfin and seconds later, the husk tore through it, the performers squealing as it passed.

"Can Bom fight it off?"

With the streets as busy as they were, Nya was worried about losing control in the panic and hurting someone. They needed to get somewhere with less people.

They shot through the city streets, the husk hounding their backs. Some people dove out the way but most were thrown to the ground. The husk didn't seem interested in the people around it, which was a stark contrast to the husks she remembered from the dark place who were undiscerning about those they killed.

They're simple creatures, Bom said. *Once something has their focus, they do not waver.*

But why is it after you? And how did it get here? Nya thought.

I am a remnant of home, Bom said. *Something familiar in this strange place. How it got here, I do not know.*

Finally, once they got out of the richer area of town, more alleyways opened up. Nya veered into one and kept running. Their footsteps echoed around them as they wound through the side streets. There was a crash and screaming, then the scrape of those silver talons raking across the stone of the alley walls.

They were deep into the empty alleyways when Nya motioned for them to stop. The festivities raging on as a muted beat with most people lingering in the main thoroughfares, collecting on the free food and entertainment. The scuffle of movement grew louder. Nya's heart beat faster as the husk approached. Kit stood at her side as they both stared at the dark opening of the alleyway.

The husk crested the corner and skittered to a stop. It roared and ran at them.

Bom flared as a black wave. It tossed the husk backwards and strained, holding the beast in place against the wall.

"Now!" Nya shouted.

Kit ran forward and ran his short sword through the husk's chest. Too-dark blood poured out the creature as it let out an ear-rattling shriek. Kit stabbed the husk over and over. The constant pressure of forcing the husk against the wall was becoming too much to hold for Bom. Nya released her grip and the husk crumpled to the ground. Kit jumped back pointing the sword at its body.

A moment passed with only Nya and Kit's wavering breathes sounding in the dark.

"Is it dead?" Kit asked.

Bom slithered over to it. The husk retched and Nya and Kit leapt back. It spluttered as a talon shot out from under its broken form and stabbed into the ground where Bom blackened the stone.

Bom howled in Nya's mind. She clutched at her ears but that made no difference when the screaming was in her head. Pain. Fear. Anger. They came in mixed flashes. Her stomach lurched and Nya dropped to her knees to throw up when the scream suddenly cut off.

The world was hazy. Bom was back in her shadow. Kit was dragging her onward through the side streets. Coming back to herself, Nya glanced back to see the bleeding husk galloping after them using its wings to propel itself forward. The sight spiked fear and she threw everything into moving forward and away from the nightmare at her heels.

What was *that*? Nya didn't have time to wonder.

Stone corridors whistled past. Some leading into darkness. Others back to the unsuspecting revelry on the main thoroughfare. Those flashes of sound and colour, so far removed from the dark alleys, looked like another world to Nya. She was back in the shadows only glimpsing the lively world that others lived in. It didn't matter what she had survived. It didn't matter that she bathed in that light for a short time. A shadow is never left. Never lost. And it always reclaims the light.

They burst out from the side street and through a crowd that was performing a show of Tok, the boy who killed a god. The performers shouted after them but neither Kit nor Nya turned.

"Nya, I need you to lead it around back," Kit said. "Can you do that?"

Nya shook her head still dizzy from the attack on Bom.

"Nya, can you do that?" Kit repeated.

They were near the Patched Cloak. The courtyard. She could do that. Nya nodded. Behind, the throng let out a confused mess of squeals. They didn't know what to make of the husk.

Kit dove inside as they passed the front of the inn. A quiet voice said that he had abandoned her. She silenced it before it took root but its words echoed in her mind. Nya skittered around the corner and down the quiet street to the courtyard. Hopping the fence, she saw the husk turn too quickly and topple over, crashing into the store next door.

There was a scream. There was a crunch. And then there was silence.

"Kit!" Nya called. She made it halfway across the courtyard

when the husk charged through the fence bending the metal and snapping the hinges.

Nya faced down the husk. The grotesque bat-like creature tilted its head and its neck snapped. It walked towards her on its back legs. The husk could almost be mistaken for a large human the way it walked and its proportions. It seemed to notice she was trapped in the courtyard and relished its walk over.

"Now!" Kit shouted.

Both Nya and the husk spun towards the top of the stable roof where Kit and Wenson shoved some kind of giant crate off the edge. The massive crate dropped, landing atop the husk. The husk battered into the side and the box lifted slightly. Kit and Wenson shouted as they leapt from the roof atop the crate. It cracked down and the husk shrieked.

Nya watched dumbfounded as the husk thrashed inside the box. Its talons ripped into the walls of the crate but didn't breach it.

Illy and Lem appeared, placing some heavy crates and barrels atop the husk's prison while Kit and Wenson hopped down. Kit stood back, hands on hips, panting.

"What is that *made* of?" Nya asked. She remembered how easily the husks tore through the scholars and guards in the dark place.

"It's elder oak from the east," Illy said. "It's used to transport dangerous animals."

"Why do you have one?" Nya asked. Her mind was still catching up. She was in shock and she knew it. But knowing that did little to settle her mind.

"All inns have one," Illy said.

"Protection in case you have some adventurous customers

appear with creatures they can't handle," Kit said, patting off the dust on his costume.

Nya swallowed glancing over to the crate. A husk. Here in Tarris. And it was captured behind their inn. Nya realised that she had been trying to convince herself that her time in the dark place was a nightmare. But there was no denying a nightmare when it sat outside your home.

"What do we do now?" Nya whispered.

Illy wrapped her arms around Nya and steered her towards the inn. "Now, we have a hot drink."

"Are you sure it's the same creature?" Illy asked.

"Yes." Both Nya and Kit said in unison.

With most outside enjoying the last night of the festivities, the Patched Cloak common room was quiet. Guards had come to the door asking if they had seen a wild animal said to be wreaking havoc across the city. Illy played dumb and sent them away.

Now, Nya, Kit, Illy, Wenson, and Lem sat huddled in a booth. Dust appeared after a time and lay sprawled in the centre of the table, then promptly started snoring.

"It's a husk. You can't mistake a creature like that," Kit said.

"I ain't seen anything like it, that's for sure," Lem said.

Illy cradled her mug. "So what if one of those things broke through?"

"If one can break through then so can others. We don't even know how it came to Tarris," Kit said.

"The tear," Nya said. The ethereal rip in the fabric of the world bore into her mind. The place where this all began. "It had to have come through the tear."

Kit grimaced. "The tear is in the middle of the palace. The husk would have to have killed a battalion worth of guards to have escaped from there. And even then, the palace is like a maze. The chances of it finding a way out and evading capture seems slim."

"Help," Wenson offered. His face was scrunched in concentration. His Tarrisian was getting better but it still wasn't great. He said something else to Illy in Nuian.

"Why would anyone would want to help the husk enter the city?" Illy asked.

Wenson shrugged and started petting Dust, who rolled over to let him rub her stomach.

"Whatever the reason, we have to stop it," Nya said.

Nya felt Kit's body go rigid at her side. "Nya, Rai said to stay out of anything like this and report it to him. He can send people to deal with this. What can we do?"

The room darkened. Shadows rose like smoke and held the firelight at bay. The others around the table shifted uncomfortably as Nya let the shadows reel back to normal size.

"What are the odds that *we* run across a husk out of everyone in the city?" Nya asked.

No one answered.

"I wanted this to be real," Nya said, gesturing to the inn around her. "But I can't live like this. The world won't let me. I don't know if fate or destiny exists but something has tied me to this whether I like it or not. And I don't plan on letting it hurt any of you."

The words tumbled out like they had been bubbling for some time. Nya had always known it would come to this. She was never meant for a normal life. Still, she was grateful for the respite it brought for a time.

"You don't need to go back to that. You can live whatever life you want," Illy said.

"But I can't," Nya said. "The husk was drawn to me. To Bom. This tear and the darkness it holds is drawn to us. I will not lead it back here, Illy. I won't let it hurt anyone else."

Kit had remained silent. Nya looked to him. He cleared his throat. "I swear I've spent every moment since meeting you chasing you into bad ideas. But you're right. We promised Rai not to get involved but that was before a damned husk appeared. We should send word to Rai anyway and then look into how the husk got here in the first place."

Wenson frowned and waved his arm around saying something in Nuian. Nya thought he might be trying to talk them out of it but Kit and Illy smiled.

"What did he say?" Nya asked.

"Help," Wenson said and pointed to himself.

"Me too," Illy said. "I don't care what you say, you're part of this family now and we don't abandon our own."

To hear Illy say that meant everything to Nya.

"Me four," Lem said.

"Four?" Kit asked.

"I'm sure Dust wants to help too," Lem said. They gazed at the sleeping sand fox whose chest rose and fell with the slow swell of sleep. Nya looked around the table and an immense feeling of gratitude bloomed inside.

"I can't ask that of you," Nya said.

"You're not. We're just helping in any way we can anyway," Kit said.

"It'll be dangerous," Nya said.

"Dust eats danger for breakfast," Kit said.

"I don't want to endanger the inn," Nya said.

"The Patched Cloak only exists because of you two. I was going to sell it," Illy said.

"Nya, we're in this together. I was there in the dark place too, and at Ma-atan's temple." Kit rubbed at his arms. "We're part of this."

Nya felt tears well and she smiled.

"Thank you."

Soon the Sun Eye would dispel the dark of night and the Passing of the Nyfin would end. So customers began to trawl in from the street for one last drink. As Illy and the others left to serve a customer a thought hit Nya.

"The book!" Nya said. She had forgotten about Kit's book. The reason why they went to the Jeril's manor in the first place. *It must have burned in the fire,* Nya thought back to the raging flames in the library. She glanced up to Kit.

The corner of his mouth curled and he pulled out a half-blackened tome. He placed the book on the table. It had been singed in the flames and blackened by ash. But it was in one piece. Kit tapped on the cover running his tongue over the inside of his mouth. Nya laid a hand on his shoulder and he tensed.

"It'll be okay. Whatever it says," Nya said.

Kit swallowed and opened the book.

He spent a couple moments skimming its contents before letting the book fall open on the table. A huge set of scales were illustrated on the page. The text was in an ancient language. Kit had shown her that if the text sprawled across the page with curls like that, then she needn't bother trying to read it because it was in the old tongue.

"Can you read it?" Nya asked.

Kit's finger slid over the page. "Only some words. I started learning when I realised all the modern texts on Ma-atan presumed it is a deity that lived in the space between life and death rather than a living breathing creature like we saw it."

Kit frowned.

"What?" Nya asked.

"This word means death," Kit said. He pointed to a strange shape that almost looked like a spiral. "But it's inverted. I read that they did certain perspective shifts to symbols to change their meaning."

Nya wasn't sure what he was saying. He almost sounded scholarly in how he spoke. It was a side of Kit she hadn't heard before and it made her again wonder about his past. But they swore not to delve into one another's past.

"So… deathless?" Kit said. He met Nya's gaze his frown deepening.

"As in you can't die?" Nya asked. That couldn't be. Could it?

"I don't know. I don't think so. If you slice my head off, I'm not going to recover from that," Kit said and after a moment added, "I think."

"What else does it say?" Nya asked.

"I'm not sure. I need to find someone who speaks the old tongue to translate this properly. It's no good making guesses on individual words," Kit said.

Nya could tell he wasn't telling her something. He wouldn't

meet her gaze and despite claiming that he couldn't read the text, Kit kept staring at the page.

"Deathless is a good start though, isn't it? It means you aren't going to die," Nya said.

Kit gave a noncommittal grunt. "It could mean many things. Death inverted doesn't mean life. They have a symbol for life. Undead is a better translation than alive."

They had heard stories of undead creatures. Foul things that had no recollection of their past lives. Some ate the living hoping they would consume their life force and be resurrected. Others spoke of human-like creatures with lives that reached far into the ages.

But all the stories had one thing in common. Despite the proclamation of undead and deathless, the stories always ended in blood.

18

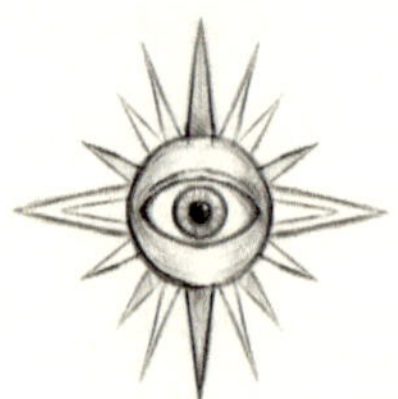

The Word of the Emperor

15 years ago.

The Word of the Emperor was a rare event. If there had been one in Rai's lifetime, he did not know of it. The emperor's Word usually travelled through Tarris by way of peddlers and sheets of parchment when Emperor Leondal wanted to address his people directly. So, to learn that Emperor Leondal planned to speak to his people from the pronouncement balcony caused quite the stir in Atef Palace, and no doubt the rest of Tarris. It could only mean something big was happening. Had war come to Tarris' shores? Had the emperor secured a new male heir to carry on his lineage?

A frenzied throng flowed down the palace corridors and Rai struggled to stay afloat in it. He shoved through and dove into the stairwell. Everyone was piling outside to get a good spot to see the pronouncement balcony. It had been a sudden announcement and the emperor planned to speak within the hour. Which added fuel to the rumours.

With most heading outside, the hallways grew quieter the further Rai delved into the palace. Voices dimmed and eventually fell silent. Rai rapped on Imayan's door. Mino didn't immediately throw it open as she usually did. He waited a moment longer but there was no answer.

He turned and stalked back down the flights of stairs rejoining the crowds. *She must be with her father*, Rai thought. Which was strange as Imayan said he was holding her at arm's length of late. Although he supposed, if something big was happening he would want her at his side.

The crowd was a roaring mass pressing into one another and pushing towards the pronouncement balcony. The Sun Eye beat down on them as if Ova itself was watching and waiting.

The balcony stuck out the front of Atef Palace with a large, busy courtyard beneath. Past that, the people mobbed the streets, filling every nook by the palace hoping to hear the emperor's Word. On either side of the balcony were two tubelike contraptions that slowly grew wider as they curled down towards the wall. When Rai had asked Tys about them, he said they were to enhance the emperor's voice and make it travel further. Tys then pointed out several large bowls attached to the palace walls claiming those too somehow carried his voice.

"Rai!" Tys stood with Sen, Genu, and Ada against the palace wall. It was the farthest point in the courtyard but if these sound deflectors were as good as Tys claimed, Rai guessed that didn't matter. He shoved through the rabble.

"Any idea what this is all about?" Tys asked when Rai reached him.

"No idea. I couldn't find Imayan to ask."

"You think she's involved?"

"I hope not. She said the emperor has been acting strangely of late," Rai said. Tys scrunched his brow and shrugged.

"Well, he certainly has everyone's attention."

The crowd grew, with late additions packing more bodies into the courtyard. Then a single light chime sounded over all.

Emperor Leondal, ruler of Tarris, stepped out onto the balcony. True to his reputation, he was a mountain of a man, towering over the guards around him. However, he was not muscular but gaunt. His thin limbs and light complexion told a tale of a life spent indoors rather than out on the training grounds. And yet, he didn't look any less regal for it. He wore a rich red cloak lined in gold and his thick hair fell to his shoulders in curls. He wore no crown like other rulers did, for no emperor since the cataclysm had worn a crown.

Behind him stood Imayan dressed in a loose flowing white robe and she wore a tired, false smile.

The emperor waved his hand and the crowd silenced. He cleared his throat. Rai glanced over his shoulder, it sounded like the emperor was right beside him. The voice carriers, Rai realised.

"People of Tarris," Emperor Leondal said. "I call you here today to make an announcement. There are some concerns about my lack of heir."

There was a stir in the crowd. Emperors didn't point out their weaknesses.

"However, this is fool's talk. This is the cowards trying to weaken the throne and it will not be tolerated."

He looked over the crowd as he let his words settle.

"But Tarris is stronger when the line of succession is clear. And because of this, I want to officially announce that Imayan will be my heir. She will be the first empress of Tarris."

Rai's stomach dropped as he saw the shift on Imayan's face. The inhale and widening of her eyes told Rai that she hadn't known. Not until this very second.

Imayan was going to be the first empress of Tarris.

The crowd bellowed in uproar and support alike. There hadn't been a female ruler in all of Tarrisian's recorded history. Snarls curled the faces of some of the nobles as they spat their complaints. They surged forward and Rai was knocked from side to side in the bustle. He shoved out creating a little space for himself. Tys pushed up to Rai's side and gave him a firm nod.

"Our line has never been stronger. Imayan will be a better ruler than even I. She will be the start of a new era and become a beacon among the rulers of Tarris." The voice carriers blasted Emperor Leondal's words over the uproar. The fervour of clashing voices left nothing distinguishable.

But one thing was clear.

Imayan would spend the rest of her life fighting against bias and backstabbing. Her father just put a bounty on his daughter's head. The other monarchs would see this as a weakness, his last resort. They had already been clamouring for the throne but now that it was being passed to the emperor's daughter? Assassins would be sharpening their blades.

"Rai." Tys nodded to the pronouncement balcony.

Imayan was gone.

Suddenly, every cloaked figure was an assassin. Every gleam of metal was a blade. He had to find her.

Rai pressed through the throng, his ears filled with piercing shouts, his body tossed back and forth in the undulating crowd. Tys helped clear his path before falling into the mob. Rai kicked and clawed his way back to the palace doors and tore down the corridor. The emperor's voice dimmed within the palace walls as he continued his speech. Rai threw himself up the stairwell and along towards the pronouncement balcony.

Guards stood at the end of the corridor leading to the balcony. "Halt!" one called as Rai slowed. The two guards crossed their spears blocking Rai's passage.

"I'm Imayan's personal guard," Rai said between breaths.

"No one gets close to the balcony while the Word of the Emperor still carries," the guard replied.

Beyond, Imayan stepped into the hallway, Mino in tow. "Imayan!" Rai called. She looked up.

"Let him pass," Imayan said. Her back was straight and voice carried the power of a ruler. The guards glanced at one another, torn between orders. "Did you not hear the Word?" she snapped. There was anger in her voice.

The guards lifted their spears and Rai marched towards Imayan. Her shoulders collapsed forward and she looked exhausted.

"Come on," Mino said, taking her arm and leading her into another room.

The lavish sitting chamber was for the emperor before he went out to share his Word. Plush chairs were placed sporadically around the room with squat tables that were only large enough to hold two drinks at their side. The shutters were half closed letting in a muted light and the discordant buzz of the city beyond. Imayan collapsed into one of the chairs and rubbed her head. Mino came to her side. "Can I get you anything?"

"Water please, Mino," Imayan said, and Mino sped off to sort her drink. "I don't want this." She said it so quietly, Rai wasn't sure if he was meant to hear it.

Stepping up to her side, Rai cleared his throat. Mino was on the far side of the room preparing her drink and the guards waited by the door. "Back when I was first brought here, I almost quit. Until the first night you showed me the garden and you said something. Do you remember what it was?"

Imayan glanced up, her brow furrowed. "Don't touch the yellow plant or you'll be itching for a week?"

Rai tilted his head to the side. "No. I asked why I should keep going and you said, *'what else is there?'*"

Imayan thought on this. "To run off and become a nomadic gardener tending the finest gardens across Tarris?"

"Imayan."

"I'm serious, Rai. I don't have what it takes to be an empress. The *first empress*." Imayan blew out a breath. "What is Father *thinking*? And to not tell me first. I can't do this."

Rai didn't know how to comfort her. He couldn't find the words to ease the strain. Rai placed his hand on Imayan's shoulder and gave it a light squeeze. Imayan met his gaze. She opened her mouth to talk when the door to the sitting room swung open. Emperor Leondal strode into the room with a retinue of guards and Overseer Lintou at his back.

"Well, that was as good a response as we could have hoped for," Overseer Lintou said. The Emperor glanced at Rai's hand on Imayan's shoulder as Rai ripped it away. The older man's gaze bore into him before falling onto his daughter. "It may have looked like everyone was against the idea but those with the loudest voices are not always the majority," Lintou continued.

"I want the room," Emperor Leondal said.

Everyone fell silent, then piled out of the sitting chamber. Rai nodded at Imayan before the door slammed shut and Imayan started screaming at her father.

The Inep Pot wasn't one of the coffeehouses on the palace grounds but Rai and the rest of his group liked to get out into the city occasionally. A raucous crowd filled their usual haunt. The news of the first empress had set the city alight. Heated arguments had broken into fights on the streets. Coffeehouses and night theatres were packed with those wanting to discuss the news.

"Here," Tys said and slid a steaming mug over to Rai as he sat down. Genu, Sen, and Ada all crowded around their corner of the coffeehouse nursing drinks of their own.

"Well, of all the things the Word could have brought this wasn't even a consideration I had," Sen said. "Did Imayan know?"

Rai shook his head staring into his cup.

"I can't imagine what it must have been like, having that sprung on you," Sen said.

"This changes everything for us too," Genu said. Sen and Ada nodded. They were being trained to be the emperor's daughter's private guard. Which meant they were now training to become the empress' guard. And that was a whole new world they would be stepping into.

"We're being trained to protect Imayan. This changes nothing," Tys said.

"It just makes our job a little harder," Ada said.

"We aren't being trained for an easy life," Rai said. "We do what we've always done. Tys is right, nothing has changed."

The others fell silent. They were sceptical. Understandably, Rai thought. They were still trainees. Despite being trained harder than any palace guard, they weren't the warriors they set out to be yet. Rai wasn't who he set out to be yet.

If an assassin came for Imayan, could he stop them? Rai didn't know and that terrified him. His hands tightened around his mug.

19

Anceint Paths Tread

The Sun Eye was nearing the edges of the Bandor Mountains. *We will need to find a cave soon,* Rai thought. It was one thing facing the kiren in the light of day but they didn't want to come across one at night. And few truly knew what roamed during dark hour in the mountains.

After the mutated kiren killed four of the company's hyian, they decided to find a path suitable for the aya so those whose hyian fell could ride atop the platform. Tysar and Bisu sat at the front of the platform with Rai, maps sprawled out as they looked out over the Bandor Mountains. Yeru leant against the platform near the rear with Loulu, who had her bow laid across her lap should they come across anything else. The rest of the seven spread out around the aya on the remaining hyian, two at the front and two at the back watching for any signs of movement.

"There should be a main thoroughfare coming up soon where we can loop back and travel west," Bisu was saying. He was a navigator and had studied the pieces of ancient maps they had for this journey. "The maps spoke of a well-traversed passage leading through the mountains from Ossin to Asuriya, where many merchants and travellers moved between the two cities instead of circling out into the desert."

Tysar nodded, staring at the map.

"We still have some light but if we find a cave, we should stop until the Moon Eye begins its watch. I don't want to be stuck out in the open during dark hour," Rai said looking at the sky.

"I agree," Bisu said.

"We continue on for now," Tysar said.

"But watch for caves," Rai added.

Tysar cleared his throat. "Would you go inform the others please, Bisu?"

Bisu stood and stretched before making his way across the platform. Rai started gathering up the maps.

Tysar waited until Bisu was out of ear shot before turning to Rai. "Rai, a word? The seven isn't yours anymore."

Rai paused. "What?"

"I command the Seventh Sceptre now, Rai. I allowed you to come along, but you need to remember that. It's not yours anymore."

"It was never *mine*, Tysar, and I'm not trying to take the seven from you. It was merely a suggestion." Rai straightened.

A cold threat lingered in his old friend's eyes. "You took command when we were fighting the kiren and you've just done it again with Bisu."

"You were injured and I was trying to keep us alive."

"Just keep it in mind, that's all. I command the seven and they need to know who is leading this mission." Tysar stalked off after Bisu.

"What was that about?" Rai muttered.

Sounds like he's feeling threatened by you, Fax said.

Threatened? Rai wasn't trying to take back the seven. He might have gotten carried away giving out commands to the others but it felt natural. And more importantly, it kept them alive.

I thought I might feel jealous when I met your old friends, Fax said. *I was looking forward to it. I've never felt jealous before. But I think Mino is the only one who doesn't have it out for you.*

Rai watched as Tysar talked with Bisu pointing to the mountain peaks.

They rode on through the dying light. Rai found himself talking with Yeru, the scholar. Perhaps it was because she too was an outsider amongst the Seventh Sceptre. She talked about some of what they found in the lost library of Nenelan and her theories about how the library was lost. The people had little use for it as they rebuilt their homes and set about founding a new ruling power, she guessed. And it was forgotten. How something as grand as the library could be forgotten was beyond Rai. It made him question what else laid buried in the sand of their past.

The scouting pair shouted from the front of the party. They were atop a ridge backed by the sinking Sun Eye.

They had found it.

Yeru gaped as they crested the side and peered into the channel. The ancient thoroughfare was a massive trench between two ridges.

It was huge, stretching out in either direction disappearing into the horizon. They rode down into the flatland staring around in awe. Rocks skittered down in front of them as they slid down the ridge. The sound of the clattering stones echoing in every direction. It was as if the ancients had painstakingly carved out this trough through the mountains themselves. It couldn't be natural, Rai thought. They could easily have fit twenty aya abreast.

Some wild hyian were eating the corpse of a creature but fled once the party entered the thoroughfare. Lizards clambered up the rock walls away from them and two molluskans slithered back into their spiral shells. The natural world had claimed this once well-travelled, ancient path.

Yeru stuttered and spun around trying to see all of the thoroughfare at once. "This is incredible."

"I've never seen anything like it," Bisu said.

Rai, Fax said perched on his shoulder as a crow, *have they not been looking at the rock that has surrounded us for days now?*

"This is different," Yeru said. She still looked uncomfortable with the shade and faced Rai rather than Fax when she spoke. "Look at how the rock walls are shaped. This is no normal erosion. This is a man-made path cut into the mountains. How such a feat is possible, I don't know."

Yeru stroked the rock reverently, scoffed, and then took notes.

Fax put on its best impression of Yeru's voice and said, *Yep, definitely still stone.*

Yeru put her face up to the stone inspecting it closely.

Now for a taste test, Fax added.

Rai hoped Fax only let him hear that.

The seven spread out in a defensive position to keep watch. Rai had to give it to Tysar, the new Seventh Sceptre were well trained. It must have taken years of drilling to have this level of structure and ease in which they worked together. Rai missed that. The feeling of a team at his back. People he could trust with his life. He knew he should have felt like that with Tysar and this seven but it wasn't the same as being part of it. He was on his own now. Well almost.

"Overseer Myain's spies said the Ossin research base was attached to this main pathway," Tysar said. "So I guess we start walking that way." He pointed west. "I want Shol and Jrenu to scout ahead. I don't doubt that the Ossins will have lookouts out here, and I don't want us to be spotted."

Two of the seven rode off down the trench and the rest followed. They pressed on down the thoroughfare for hours and soon the Moon Eye was right above them watching with its crystalline glow. Yeru sat near Rai on the aya scribbling furiously. It was amusing to see the sweat beaded on her brow and her tongue peek out in concentration. While fighting off creatures was Rai's battle, the search for the truth was hers. And right now, Yeru was at war.

"What're you writing?" Rai asked.

"Everything," Yeru said not glancing up. "We knew there must have been passage through the mountains connecting Ossin to Asuriya. We have records of merchants crossing the distance in record time so they couldn't have been circling around the mountains. But this." She lifted her head and smiled. "It's unlike anything we imagined."

"Did the Ossin scholars not share that they found this thoroughfare? If their base is right off it, they must have known about it," Rai said.

"Yes but I didn't think it would be like this. They skipped over some of the… grander details," Yeru said.

From the outside, Tarris was a unified country but with monarchs constantly undermining one another, Rai wasn't surprised to hear that even the scholars did what they could to get the upper hand over the other cities. Skipping over details and only sharing vague findings was its own battle.

"How does an ancient civilization create something that we can't even *fathom*? We don't even know where to begin with something like this. It would take thousands of years using modern methods to create a passage through mountains this size," Yeru said.

Rai looked around the channel. To some, this was a worn path of old but to someone like Yeru this was a marvel. And she was right. To carve a path through the mountains like this was impossible. What had it been like in those days, when Tarris was under one rule and worked together?

Rai tried to imagine how it had once been. When thousands of travellers moved back and forth along this main thoroughfare. They had no doubt thought this was always going to be a well trodden path.

But time takes all.

Shol and Jrenu returned at a gallop. "It's up ahead. We don't see any lookouts but smoke rises from the stone. They must be in a cave," Shol said.

"Pick up the pace. We attack tonight."

Rai lay peeking over a rock escarpment. Below, warm light

poured from a cave entrance and further up the rocky mountain, smoke poured from an opening. During the day this would have been impossible to spot but at night the orange glow was like a beacon in the dark.

"Shol, Jrenu, and Loulu go around back and see if there's another entrance. Yeru, Rai, Bisu, and I will go in the front," Tysar said. He had asked the other two of the seven to hold back and look after the aya and hyian. Rai thought he might have asked him to stay back but Tysar wasn't petty, not when it came to the mission. He would put Rai's skill in combat over his personal grievances. At least, for now.

Shol, Jrenu, and Loulu shot off into the night. Tysar waited a moment before leading the others towards the cave entrance. They leant against the outer wall and listened. Nothing but the crackle of fire could be heard from inside. Tysar motioned that he and Bisu would enter first and Rai and Yeru were to follow. Unsheathing his sword, Tysar crept into the cave.

Inside was less a cave and more a tunnel system. Winding tunnels broke off in all directions. A lit brazier flickered at the intersection but gave no indication on which opening to take. Without slowing, Tysar picked a tunnel and moved through it. They continued through the unmarked tunnel until voices echoed from further within. Tysar lifted a hand and they froze. He gestured to Bisu to follow but Rai and Yeru to wait and they disappeared around the bend. Rai was about to send Fax ahead too but decided it was safer to keep the shade with him and Yeru in case anything were to happen.

Yeru's breathing was fast and ragged. She clutched too tightly to her short sword. Rai gave her a comforting nod and took a deep breath. Yeru mimicked the deep breath and her breathing settled.

The signal came as a bird call and Rai and Yeru marched through the tunnel. The tunnel opened to a larger space with stalactites hanging from above. Tysar was dragging an unconscious man to the side of the chamber where a woman in Ossin colours lay knocked out. Bisu was peering into a tunnel on the far wall.

Hammocks hung from the ceiling. Four in total. "There must be more further in," Rai said. Crates of supplies were stacked in a corner. Rai stepped up and inspected the goods. There was enough here to last four people for months.

"Given how dangerous it was to get here, it makes sense that they come stocked," Yeru said, reading his expression.

This chamber seemed to be living quarters so they moved on down the far tunnel. The tunnels were smooth and not quite tall enough for Rai to walk upright.

It was a burrowyrm nest, Rai realised. The massive worms hollowed out structures by eating the rock and leaving tunnels branching throughout. It was rare for them to be so close to the surface but this was undoubtedly once a burrowyrm nest. However, given that the scholars had been here for some time, the burrowyrms must have moved on.

A low gargling growl came from the dark ahead. They slowed noticing that the braziers were placed further apart until they suddenly ended, the tunnel becoming an inky black hole. Bisu pulled out a torch from his pack and lit it on a brazier before they continued into the dark.

Rai could tell by the way their footsteps echoed that the space opened up again. Why would they not keep this part lit?

There are things ahead, Fax said. *I see movement.*

The others looked at Rai. "What things, Fax?"

I thought they might be human but now I'm not sure.

With that worrying note, they crept silently into the space. The growling stopped as they entered, their torches lighting the grates of a cell. Inching forward, Bisu held the torch aloft trying to see what was inside.

A feral creature launched itself at the bars of the cage and screamed. Everyone jumped back as the beast howled at them.

"Shut that thing up!" Tysar said.

The creature was the size of a small child but its skin was wrinkled and hair patchy and white. It had a human-like naked body aside from its hands which had three fingers on one and four on the other. The creature snarled baring pointed teeth. Its too human eyes feral and wide. Yeru stepped towards the bars.

"Don't get too close," Rai said.

The creature clung to the bars and heaved.

"A new species, perhaps?" Yeru mused.

"Come on. We don't have time for this. If there are others, they will have heard that," Tysar said.

They skulked through the darkened cavern. There were two other creatures in the cages. One wasn't moving. Fax was convinced it was dead. The other looked like a mutated sand fox. It had four ears and snapped at them as they passed.

This place is a horror, Rai thought. He thought of Dust and how this sand fox could have been brought up like her. Healthy and well. He wanted nothing more than to free the creatures but they could warn the other Ossins of their presence if the screaming hadn't already.

A burning light framed an opening in a wreath of flame. Tysar gestured for silence and they moved towards the light. Tysar's eyes went wide as he peeked around the corner.

"No!" He ran into the room.

Rai knew what he would find before he turned the corner. The heat by the entrance prickled his skin. Flames engulfed the room. Scrolls and meaty tomes were piled up and set alight. Acrid smoke filled the air. The scholars must have heard the creature in the cages and had set about destroying their research. It was extreme, but it spoke of the importance of their findings.

Rai rushed in and started kicking at some of the books, trying to put the fire out. It was too late to save it all but if they could recover some of the research they might be able to find the answers they were looking for. Yeru joined him, coughing and spluttering, her hand covering her mouth, as she stomped on another book.

"Bisu go see if you can catch the scholars!" Tysar shouted over the roar of flames. The man bowed and ran off.

The fire was spreading too fast. It ran like water across the ground and up the walls. Rai pulled his cowl up as he choked on the smoke. He pulled out a half burnt book from the wreckage but the heat was becoming too much to bear.

"We need to go!" Rai called. Tysar had some scraps under his arm when he inclined his head. Yeru didn't respond. Whether she had heard him or not was unclear so Rai tugged at her arm and they pulled back to the room with the cells.

Rai coughed and spat ash dragging in the fresh air.

"Damn it!" Tysar said and kicked a rock that went skittering through the chamber. "How did they get it burning so quickly?"

He was right. They couldn't set a fire that size in the time since the creature screamed. They must have had scouts after all.

"We might get some answers still," Rai said. He dropped his tome and burnt scrolls onto the stack Tysar put down.

He turned to see Yeru reading a scroll her eyes wide and unbelieving.

"What is it?" Rai asked. Yeru didn't respond. "Yeru?"

She glanced up. "They've been experimenting for hundreds of years."

"That's hardly a surprise. There have always been scholars studying Asuriya," Rai said. He approached Yeru to see the scroll she was holding.

"Not like this."

The scroll was covered in notes and illustrations. They were of mutated creatures, not unlike some of what they had come across getting there. Rai didn't see why Yeru was so concerned until he read the descriptions. These weren't creatures they had found. These were illustrations of what happened when the scholars dropped caged animals close to the capital for years and let the infection change them.

Yeru pointed to the bottom of the scroll where a familiar creature was illustrated in detail. It was the same one that was in the cell. Beside it, the text read:

Conversely, as it shortens the lifespans of some creatures, Helf is the ultimate antithesis. Records show he is over two hundred years old. Placed in one of the first batches he is the only one to survive. However, his unusually long lifespan brings into question everything we thought we knew about the blight. It doesn't seem to have a singular effect, but many. What causes this change is unclear…

The bottom of the page was burnt but scrawled across it was:

Classification: Human.

Rai looked up to the cages and then to Yeru. That thing had once been a *human?* Rai's stomach roiled. Together they walked over to the creature they saw when entering the chamber. It jumped squealing at all the noise and smoke piling into the room.

"Helf?" Yeru asked.

The creature stopped and glanced at Yeru, recognition in its eyes.

"Sun Eye scorch me. It is human," Yeru said. She reached for the lock but Rai grabbed her wrist.

"It's been infected and caged for hundreds of years," Rai said. "It was once human but letting it out now would only harm it."

"But the fire."

Rai reached for his dagger.

"No," Yeru said. Her voice was pleading.

Fax offered to kill it but Rai wanted to do this. It deserved to die by a human's hand. Yeru closed her eyes, tears rolling down her cheeks. Unlatching the lock, Helf launched itself, himself, at the door but with one precise swipe Rai cut it down. Blood spattered the empty cell and Rai could have sworn he saw gratitude in those eyes just as they closed. He was probably fooling himself.

There was a moment of silence.

"We need to get out of here," Tysar said from behind. He

had scooped up the recovered tomes and scrolls. The smoke was billowing into the chamber and flames would follow. Rai nodded and they made their way back through the tunnels.

Black smoke poured from the cave entrance as they charged back out into the night. Rai sucked in the air trying to clear the taste of smoke from his mouth.

"Tysar!" Bisu shouted.

Tysar, Yeru, and Rai circled the formation to find Bisu and the others standing on the edge of the trench.

Bisu turned and bowed. "They had a secret exit. We didn't see them until it was too late."

In the distance, two figures rode hyian down the thoroughfare and back towards Ossin. They rode at a gallop. There was no way they could catch up to them now.

Tysar sighed and rubbed his eyes. Soot clung to his hair and clothing.

"Let's hope there's enough in those books that this mission wasn't a complete waste," Tysar said.

20

The Final Song

Kit leant against a merchant's shop watching the store across the street. The midday heat was cooling and most were still asleep. Kit caught a drop of sweat with his sleeve. The coarse fabric was harsh on his skin. Under the crook of his left arm was *The Tome of the Ancients,* tightly wrapped in nondescript cloth.

Old Jirma stepped out from his shop and strained to reach the open sign, eventually spinning it around. The short, weathered man hardly needed old in his name. It was clear just by looking at him. But that was what everyone knew him by. He took a moment to shuffle his dark navy robe back into place then waddled back into the store. Kit glanced around the empty street and marched over to enter the bookshop.

The Broken Binding was the grandest seller of tomes in all of Tarris. It was two floors of back to back shelves lined with books, some thought lost to time. Old Jirma was its sole keeper having been given it from his father, and him from his father before him. But after Jirma's wife, Shel, died and they had no children, Jirma had brought on two *'Keepers of the Knowledge'* as he liked to call them, or lackeys, as Kit came to find a more accurate title. Still, the old man took Kit in at a time when the street would have devoured him and he never forgot that.

The musty smell of dust-covered books threw Kit back to that time in his life. He moved through the shelves where books were stack haphazardly. Some stuck out forcing Kit to duck under them. He pushed through to the back of the store where Jirma was in the midst of settling himself into his chair, a meaty book at his side. He glanced up as Kit approached.

"Kit?" Jirma asked.

"I got the book," Kit said. He placed it onto the counter and began unfurling the material but Jirma slammed a hand down atop it.

"Kit," Jirma said, urgency in his tone. "Where did you get this? I heard of a fire at the Jeril family home and prayed it wasn't you."

"It wasn't," Kit said. "I swear." In a way, he wasn't lying. Kit hadn't caused the fire in the home.

Jirma wiggled his nose and held Kit's gaze.

"The fire wasn't me," Kit said blowing out a breath.

"What have I said about stealing?" Jirma said.

"Only steal when they don't offer a fair price?"

Jirma cuffed Kit's ear. He probably deserved that. Jirma rubbed his forehead. After a moment he straightened again. "Well, you have it now. And it's not like the Jeril's will miss it. What does it say?"

Kit had returned to the old man seeking comfort and familiarity after the events at Ma-atan's temple. He opened up about the Judging and how his heart no longer beat. And Old Jirma did what he did best. He brewed tea and sat with Kit. Listening. Kit then begged the old man to help him find the truth. If anyone in Tarris could, it would be Jirma.

They scoured through the books together for answers until it was clear that they needed to find older books. Books like the *Tome of the Ancients*.

Pulling the rag free, Kit slid the book over to Jirma. "It's in the old tongue, maybe an even older dialect, I can't read all of it. Only words."

That piqued the old man's interest. He ran a hand over the leather cover, feeling the grooves of the sigil. Then he flicked over the front cover and began reading. "You're right. It has some of the old tongue but this is older than that. What those foolish Jerils were doing with such a book, I have no idea. Probably little more than a decoration."

"Lucky they don't have it anymore," Kit said.

Jirma raised an eyebrow and Kit glanced down. "Few would be able to decipher it."

"Can you?" Kit asked.

Jirma scratched his beard. "With time. I will need to pull some old texts and sit with it. Care for some tea?"

Open books surrounded Jirma as he spun around, taking notes with the *Tome of the Ancients* in his lap. Kit smiled as the old man muttered to himself. It was like some kind of ritual. Then Kit grimaced remembering the last ritual he had been in.

"So what is it you hope to find?" Jirma asked.

The question confused Kit. He had told Jirma that he wanted to learn more about Ma-atan and his new… condition.

"To understand," Kit said.

"Understand what?"

"Understand what's happening to me," Kit said. He glanced down at his hands. "I can't keep living with the idea I could die at any moment."

Jirma looked up from his book and humphed before going back to his notes. "Did I ever tell you how Shel died?"

Kit shook his head. The old man had barely mentioned his wife. Kit only knew her name because of what he had heard on the street.

"Of course I didn't." He sighed. "Come sit." Jirma gestured to a nearby chair and Kit moved closer.

"I hadn't long taken the Broken Binding from my father. He set off to a quiet village on the river, near Ossin, to retire with my mother. He was wary going so far and said how much work this place was to run. He didn't think I had it in me." Jirma tutted. "They left and within the year, Shel started getting tired earlier at night. She wore out quicker and quicker. Soon, she found it difficult to help around the shop."

Jirma dipped his head and fell silent for several moments. "I'd burn this whole place down for another day with her."

He went quiet again. Kit felt like he was intruding on a private moment and didn't dare speak or move. He just watched as Jirma's eyes glazed over.

"She didn't tell me. She… she went to the doctor and learned that she had a wasting disease. And she didn't tell me. Worried I would act different around her. Of course I would have acted differently. I would've done more to help. I would have…" He cleared his throat. "She knew I had the shop and what it meant to me. Didn't want it to fall to the wayside as I was barely keeping it afloat at the time. Damn woman knew I wouldn't have left her side if I knew the truth." Jirma rubbed his face to mask wiping away a tear.

"The morning she died was different. She must have known it would be her last. She pulled me back to bed, asked if I would take the day off. I shook her off as we had some bigwig noble that I can't even remember the name of now coming to pick up a book. She was dead by the time I got back that night."

Kit sat stunned. He had known Jirma for most of his life and he had never opened up about any of this. He could feel the pain in the old man's words. Feel it seep through the words like a stain.

"I should have known. When I left, she hummed a song. The same song she always sang at the end of a year. I wondered as I left why she was humming that song as it wasn't the right time, but I never questioned it. I sometimes hear a street performer sing it now. I always stop. It may be a sad song but it should be sung, nevertheless. It was her song and now it's mine," Jirma said. The old man stared at the book in his lap, not meeting Kit's gaze.

"Whatever we find in this book, you do not fear death." The words were a command. "It is the living you should fear for. It's so easy to lose what and who is important. Shel thought the most important thing to me was the shop, so she let me follow my passion. She was wrong. *She* was the most important thing to me. And I'll never forgive myself for letting her think otherwise."

They sat in silence as Kit thought about what he had said. But he didn't understand. How could Shel have allowed Jirma to leave if she knew she was going to die? She knew she was going to face the huge black expanse of nothingness. The idea of dropping into an endless darkness. Everything being nothing. Forever falling through the unknown.

The emptiness.

Kit clutched at his chest. It felt like a hand was squeezing his lungs.

He couldn't breathe.

Kit lurched forward gasping for air. He was dimly aware that Jirma was at his side but everything was abuzz. Sucking in air didn't fill his lungs. This was it. He was going to die. A hand clasped his shoulder. Kit felt the warmth ease into him. After a few moments, the feeling started to pass. Slowly but surely he began to breathe again.

Jirma watched him with a worried look.

"I'm okay," Kit said, taking long, steady breaths.

"No, you're not, boy. But you will be," Jirma said. "Drink this." He handed Kit a mug of something hot. Kit sipped on it as Jirma went back to work. "You're going to be okay. I promise."

The Sun Eye was flaring a deep red as dark hour approached before they spoke again. The silence and the tea brought a calm back to Kit's mind. However, a rising panic began to flare again when Jirma closed the books around him and turned to Kit with a grim expression.

"It's still rough but I think I have the jist of the passage," Jirma said. He came to sit beside Kit and opened his notebook.

The Judging is more than a test of one's heart and mind. It is a promise for a better life. Those with corrupt hearts and a force of chaos will perish. But those who have promise in their heart and minds are given the gift of the deathless. Their bodies remain frozen in time, unmarred by times passing. Damage is reverted back to the moment of their ascendance. Death is no longer a promise but a lie. Bound to death, it stalks the deathless like a killer in wait. It will steal breath and life, drinking it in, all the while growing stronger.

Kit stared at the words rereading them, his hands tight around the notebook. "I'm not going to die?"

"Not from old age," Jirma said. "But I don't know about that last part. The translation there is rough."

Blowing out a breath, Kit felt a weight shift from his soul. He wasn't going to die. Not yet.

"This idea of your body being frozen in time indicates you can be killed," Jirma said, pointing to the line. "If you're fatally wounded."

"I don't understand. Why would Ma-atan do this?"

"Those who have promise in their heart and minds are given the gift of the deathless," Jirma recited. "The deity must have thought you have more to give this world."

After taking time to wander the city, Kit returned to the Patched Cloak. He had spent dark hour with Jirma tidying up the shop and preparing it for the nightly rush. The Moon Eye was high in the sky and torches danced outside of homes and shops. Hanging lanterns crackled under the murmur of those venturing out into the night.

The Patched Cloak joined the waking city. Its shutters alight with fiery oranges, echoes of the life inside. As Kit approached, he heard shouting. At first, he thought it was some drunk customers but as he got closer, the voices became clearer.

"You ain't welcome here. It's time you learn that." It was the half-wit gruff that had caused a scene a couple days ago. Pio was his name. After he was chased out of the inn, Kit had worried he might return and checked with his connections on the street. The man was easy to find.

Pio was a simple man. He had been recently fired from the city guard for being too rough with the prisoners. And Kit had seen firsthand how rough the guards got on a daily basis, so to be fired because of his brutality meant it was likely that Pio had killed someone. Now, the man wandered the Night Theatres getting drunk and starting fights. He had clearly lost his way. Kit almost felt bad for him. Almost.

Kit crept up to the window and peered inside. Right enough, the same bulky man had returned with three others of similar size and temperament. One picked up a metal tankard and tried to smash it against the ground. It bounced and skittered out of view with little more than a scratch.

Same level of intelligence too, Kit thought.

Illy stood in the centre of the room hands on her hips, Wenson at her side. Customers rushed out the back. "We aren't doing any harm," Illy said.

The gruff guy swiped along the bar and bottles shattered on the stone. "Oh, but you did. You set up here taking up space in a perfectly good Tarrisian establishment." Kit was impressed that he knew what 'establishment' meant.

He searched around for Nya but she was nowhere to be seen.

She must be out getting supplies with Lem, Kit thought. They often set out to restock before the night rush. That meant it was only Illy and Wenson.

And me, Kit thought.

If a deity thought he had more to give, perhaps this was it.

Wenson threw a punch but it was sloppy. One of the henchmen stepped in and caught the blow following it with a fist to Wenson's gut. He groaned and was sent reeling.

I'm coming, Kit thought as he ran from the window and around the back of the inn. Careening past some guards, Kit slowed. It was a sign that the street life was still a part of him that going to get the city guard wasn't his first thought. But since they were nearby…

"Hey!" Kit shouted. The guards looked him up and down. "There are some guys fighting in that inn."

"The Nuian one?" the guard asked.

Kit nodded and the guard relaxed and shrugged. "It's what those mountain dwellers do. Less air up there, you see."

"No, no, it's some Tarrisians trashing the place." Kit pulled on the guard's sleeve as he turned to leave.

The guard threw him off, disgust lining his face. "Doesn't mean the Nuians didn't start it. The nephew is a blood den regular, kid. Just stay away from it."

"Wenson hasn't taken any blood in months," Kit snapped.

The guard raised an eyebrow at his tone and then grunted, stalking off down the street. Kit watched them go. He wanted to scream coward but bit his tongue. He knew from his street days that the city guards were a mixed bunch. They were people, in the end. And most people didn't want to face confrontation. Not all the city guards were cowards but he didn't have time to search another out.

Kit leapt over the gate into the courtyard and skidded to a stop. A figure sat above the container that held the husk. The man glanced up, the glow of the Moon Eye shining off his bald head.

"You have a husk in here," Bas said.

Bas had been one of the Doomed Others. He had come with Kit and Nya into the dark place and had been one of the few survivors of the journey.

"Bas?"

Bas jumped down sending out a puff of dirt. "Where did you find it?" he asked. He wore a white loose fitting robe. His face was neutral. But this was the most he had ever spoken to Kit. How had he tracked them here?

Now wasn't the time to ask questions.

"Bas I need your help," Kit said. "There are people inside the inn who are going to get hurt. I'll tell you everything you want to know but I need you to help."

He looked over his shoulder, towards the inn, and nodded. Kit couldn't believe his luck. Bas was an Urdahl. A great stoic warrior. And Kit had seen him fight. He was someone you wanted on your side.

"Good because when this plan blows up in my face, I'll need someone like you to put it back together again," Kit said.

"Pio! Come out here, you coward!" Kit yelled into the common room of the Patched Cloak. He scuttled back into the courtyard leaving the door wide open.

Eventually, Pio and his three companions stepped out, shoving

Illy and Wenson ahead of them. Both looked bruised and beaten but were alive.

A vein pulsed on Pio's forehead as he rolled his shoulders. "Who are you, boy?"

"I am Kit. Just a Tarrisian street kid."

"Who are you to call me a coward, Kit the street kid?" Pio said.

Kit shrugged. "Anyone with eyes can see that you're a coward. I mean, you claim Nuians are weak but then outnumber them when you attack."

Pio sneered at Kit. "I'll show you a coward."

"You already have," Kit said. "And well, it's rather amusing. The good thing about being a street kid is how many *connections* you have. Lots of people to tell of your cowardice."

That vein that ran along Pio's forehead bulged. That was exactly what Kit was hoping for. He was a man floundering after losing his job and the truth was there was only one place a fired city guard could go to get work. The gangs. Gangs hired the worst sort from any background. However, there was one type of person they didn't hire: cowards.

Pio didn't know Kit directly. But Kit often found a straight back and confident voice was enough to show someone you were serious. And Pio had too much to lose with plenty of witnesses who saw him and his thugs at the inn.

"I offer you a deal," Kit said.

"I'm listening."

"Face me, one on one," Kit said. Illy cried out and one of the thugs smacked her across the face. "If I win, you let them go and never come back here. If you win, I'll tell everyone you singlehandedly chased twenty Nuians out of town."

Pio sucked on his teeth weighing Kit's offer. It all came down to whether Pio thought he could beat up a little street kid. In the end, it didn't matter what Kit bet. Pio wouldn't care about others hearing that he forced twenty Nuians out of town, but this was his chance to kill Kit and solve his problem right now.

This was where Kit's previous work of connecting gangs, merchants, and nobles came in handy. He often had to act and had gotten good at it. His shoulders sagged and his knees were bent to make him look small and weak. When he spoke he strained his voice as if it was taking everything he had just to face the man. Kit doubted he would win in a fight against Pio but he had to make sure Pio was certain of it.

"Stupid kid," Pio muttered. "I'll make sure not to knock all your teeth out so you can tell my story."

Kit suppressed a grin as Pio approached. He trudged towards Kit shifting his bulky weight between his feet with exaggerated steps and a half smile.

Kit waited until he was almost upon him.

"There is one thing you don't know about Nuians though," Kit said. Pio frowned. "They keep some strange pets."

Pio crossed the mark that Kit and Bas agreed upon. Far enough from the others and close enough to the cage that the husk would set its sight on Pio first. Bas yanked the lever and the cage lifted from the ground.

The husk shot out with a feral shriek.

Pio saw the beast the second before it tore through his throat. He didn't even have time to show his surprise. The husk gluttoned on the gore pouring from the man's neck. The others' eyes grew wide at the terrifying bat-like creature eating the remains of their friend. Kit had assumed the beast would be hungry after being trapped in there for so long. And with Nya nowhere near, Pio would have to do.

Illy elbowed her captor in the face and he flew back, cracking his head against the wall. The man holding Wenson cried out when Wenson flicked his head back, smashing the man in the nose. The last one scattered, sprinting back into the inn.

The husk was beginning to slow with its eating.

"Anytime now, Bas," Kit said.

The husk looked up at Kit. Bas was moving the mechanical arm that they had connected to the cage after capturing the husk. It groaned and rust crackled as the arm moved out over the courtyard. It was going too slowly.

"Bas!" Kit said.

The husk lunged at Kit. He squeezed his eyes shut.

Crack.

Opening his eyes, Kit watched as a black shape deflected the husk and sent it reeling backwards across the courtyard. Bas loosed the mechanism and the cage crashed down atop the husk. It squealed and rattled at the bars.

Kit fell to the ground and blew out a breath as Nya walked into the courtyard with Lem, both laden with crates of supplies.

"What happened here?" she asked.

21

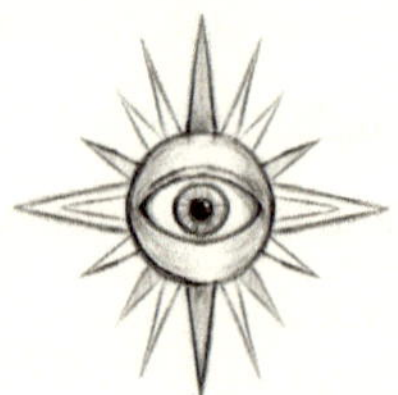

A Swish of Silver in the Black

15 years ago.

Rai watched as Imayan's days were filled with a new type of training. She shadowed her father as he talked with his advisers and visiting nobles. Nights were spent under the tutelage of Overseer Lintou as Imayan learned about the different noble families in play and where their loyalties lay. Rai stayed at her side as often as he could but Overseer Rikai had increased the volume of their training in response to the news. However, even worked ragged during his morning training sessions Rai always made sure to return to Imayan's side when he could. The emperor placed Imayan under constant guard but Rai felt more at ease being there. And he could sense that she did, too. Or perhaps he was just seeing what he wanted to be so.

The Moon Eye lit Overseer Lintou's study in a sheen of pale light. It was austere for an overseer of Lintou's status but Rai had learned that he didn't spend much time in his rooms. The single bookshelf that covered the back wall was home to stacks of parchment, curled scrolls, and only a couple books. Most of it was Overseer Lintou's private works. Occasionally, he brought a scroll over for Imayan to study. They contained records of business dealings between the emperor and nobles, as well as personal notes on anyone of note in higher society.

Being at Imayan's side, Rai learned a lot about how Tarris was run. He learned more about the hidden battle amongst the monarchs and emperor and how a series of seemingly random events told a tale of a secret war that raged on under the noses of the people.

A well-known merchant may turn up dead in Ossin slowing down shipments of perishable foods to other cities, forcing the other monarchs and emperor to make new trade deals with less favourable terms.

A pass caved in, blocking trade routes, forcing supplies to travel through the other cities to offload their goods.

And from what Rai gathered, it had only gotten worse since the emperor named Imayan as his heir.

Imayan leaned across a desk, writing on a piece of parchment, her forehead scrunched like the arching dunes of the desert. Flickering candlelight danced across her face.

"Well?" Overseer Lintou asked.

"Don't rush me," Imayan said.

Overseer Lintou paced behind her. "You won't always have the luxury of time."

"Here." Imayan shoved the parchment at Lintou. He took it and continued to pace as he read. Rai stood at the door, leaning against the wall. Outside, two armed guards stood watch. A wordless thrum of conversation abated the quiet of the study.

"These are getting better but you've left out the mention of a timescale. Without that, the other monarch could claim to be working on the repairs until we're all dust," Lintou said laying the parchment back on the desk.

"If I was sending important letters as an empress, I would have you read over them anyway," Imayan said.

"Yes but you have to know the skills behind it. It's almost impossible to catch everything but if you can ensure the main points are included and irrefutable, I'm freed up to look for the smaller details," Overseer Lintou replied. "And I might not always be there. For prompt decisions you may need to reply swiftly or miss a window of opportunity. Again."

Imayan groaned and dropped her head against the desk. They had been studying for hours and the night grew late. Rai could see Imayan struggling to keep her eyes open.

"It's a lot like sparring, is it not, Rai?"

Rai startled, straightening. In all of his time guarding Imayan, Overseer Lintou hadn't ever acknowledged him, much less included him in the discussion. Rai cleared his throat. "Sure."

"It's a combat of words. Arguments are fists that one can repost or counter." Lintou walked to the window and stared out over the gardens. Imayan shrugged at Rai. "Pacing and looking for openings is key, whilst keeping up a guard with a constant barrage of words leaves no openings for your opponent."

"Although words won't spill your guts on the sand," Rai said. He regretted it as soon as the words slipped out.

Lintou spun, his eyebrow arched. "Don't they? What puts the sword in one's hand? What leads to wars and death? The swords are merely the reapers of destruction, not the causes of it."

Moonlight bathed the edges of Lintou's shape throwing him into shadow.

"If you slip up during a fight you may die. If an emperor or *empress* fails, thousands die. Words are the *only things* that spill guts on the sand. They're shaper than any blade. They command armies. To believe words have no power is to deny more deaths than there are grains of sand in the desert."

Silence shrouded the study. Lintou was right, Rai didn't understand. The implications of what Imayan was training to become was hard to wrap his head around. He should have stayed quiet.

Quiet.

It was quiet now.

Overseer Lintou opened his mouth to talk but Rai raised a finger to his lips. A scowl formed on Lintou's face and he was about to snap back when Rai pressed his ear against the door. Silence. The guards were no longer chatting.

Bad sign.

With an ear-shattering crack, the door flew off its hinges. Rai dove out the way as three figures entered the room. One was a human in a dark brown jerkin and a wrap around their face. The other two were duons. Short tan-haired bipedal creatures with two pointed horns on their heads. Duons were not unlike goats with long faces but they were vicious creatures and their claws closer resembled long pointed nails than hooves.

The closest duon screamed and charged at Rai. Unsheathing his daggers, Rai rolled out the way as the duons horns embedded itself in the wall.

"Get the girl," the obscured woman said. The other duon charged at Imayan. Overseer Lintou sidestepped in front of Imayan and brandished a black short sword. He waved it in small circles and an impossible gust of wind threw the charging duon against the far wall.

What was that?

Rai didn't have time to wonder as the duon beside him finally tore his horns free and howled. Pushing to his feet, Rai met the duon before it could build momentum and run at him again. Those horns could skewer through metal plating if he let the duon pick up enough speed. Rai drove his blade for the beast's heart but with a single flick of his head, he was tossed across the room.

He slid along the desk splintering the wood before falling down the back. Imayan's petrified eyes stared down at him. "Are you okay?" she asked helping him up. Rai hissed holding his side. It didn't feel like anything was broken.

Overseer Lintou was holding back the duon and woman with his blade that seemed to cast the wind itself. Rai was supposed to be the guard but Overseer Lintou, an adviser, was faring better than he was. The other duon growled. Rai shook his head. He needed to focus. This wasn't like fighting another human. He had to think outside the box.

"Imayan stand over there," Rai said, gesturing to the corner.

The duon stalked back and forth readying to charge. Lessons with Overseer Rikai came to mind: *The headlong sprint of a duon is a death sentence for those in its way but once thrown into the charge they cannot change course.*

The duon charged. It ripped through the desk splitting it in half letting out a bone-rattling scream as it approached. Rai waited until there was no doubt the creature couldn't veer off course and then lunged forward narrowly missing its wide horns. The duon continued headfirst into the bookcase, stabbing through the shelf and into wall behind. Spinning, Rai moved to finish the beast off but it was waving its clawed hands wildly. Rai swiped his dagger along the duon's arm. It squealed and pulled it into its chest as Rai thrust the other blade into the creature's guts. The duon hissed and screamed bringing its other claw around to tear up Rai's forearm.

Pain screamed up Rai's arm. He twisted the blade in the beast's gut and the duon went still. Dropping back, Rai saw that his forearm was a mess of sinewy flesh. He was losing a lot of blood. Already, the room felt airy and light.

"Rai? Rai! Duat be damned," Imayan said. She disappeared and Rai took a moment to orient himself before she returned with a torn piece of cloth. With trembling fingers, she placed it over his ripped up forearm. Together, they wrapped it around and Imayan tied it so it would stay in place.

Rai held his arm tight to his chest to help staunch the blood and used his other hand to pull himself to his feet. Lintou was pinning the duon against the wall with his blade, approaching to kill the creature. He was doing a great job holding the beast at bay but where was… Rai saw too late as the cowled woman leapt over the chair to the overseer's back and rammed a dagger into his side.

"LINTOU!" Imayan screamed.

His eyes bulged as he glanced down at the blade. The wind dissipated dropping the duon to the ground.

"A stubborn old thing aren't you? But not so strong without your diera blade," the rasping female voice said. She twisted the sword.

Imayan made to surge forward towards him but Rai grabbed her. Whoever this assassin was, she knew what she was doing. With the angle of the blade, Rai knew that the man was dead.

Lintou took a sharp intake of breath. He then looked to Rai. His eyes said what he could not. *Protect her.*

Lintou head-butted the woman and used the space to toss his short sword. It shot past Rai and pierced the bookshelf where the dead duon hung. Rai stared at it and noticed the holes in the wall lead to darkness. They weren't merely dents in the stone but punctures through the rock. It should have been solid stone. There was no room next to this one that Rai knew of. Rai dragged Imayan towards the bookshelf and yanked on the dead duon, who collapsed in a heap, and sure enough one of the gaps led into a dark passageway. Lintou had been pointing him this way. It was a squeeze but they might just fit through. Imayan hadn't taken her eyes from Overseer Lintou.

"Imayan," Rai said clutching his forearm to his chest.

"We need to help him," she said.

"We can't. Come on," Rai said.

The last duon shook its head as if disorientated and screamed.

"Imayan, now!"

Defeat softened Imayan's hard features. She knew that they would die unless they fled now. Lintou was wrestling with the woman but he was dying and couldn't hold her off for long. Imayan ducked into the hole and disappeared into the black. Rai followed, groaning as he struggled to fit through. Just before he pulled his head through Rai saw Lintou's short sword stuck in the wall beside him. He wrenched it free before pulling himself all the way through.

A diera blade, the woman had said. Magical weapons said to once have been wielded by Gods. Rai hadn't thought they truly existed. *It couldn't be, could it?* He turned the sword over in his hands.

Lintou had called the wind itself with this sword.

A candle burned on a desk, lighting the small chamber hidden behind Overseer Lintou's bookshelf. It contained chests and more bookshelves covered in scrolls. At the back of the chamber a tunnel branched off into darkness.

Crack.

The duon's horn widened the hole. It screamed in frustration, its amber eyes stared at them with fiery hatred. It pulled back, ready to charge at the wall again. It wouldn't be long before it broke through.

Rai and Imayan ran down the tunnel. Imayan jogged forward, her rasping breath carrying further into the black. Rai swayed, struggling to keep pace with her. He had lost too much blood and his vision swam.

"Are you okay?" Imayan asked noticing him falling behind.

"Yeah just keep going," Rai said.

Eventually, the first brazier appeared bringing light back to the tunnel. The added light caused the tunnel to spin and Rai fell against the wall. Imayan skirted to a stop and glanced back.

"Rai?"

"Just keep going. I'll catch up."

She came to his side and clutched his arm to help support him. Her hand came back wet and red and Imayan realised that her makeshift bandage was soaked through. Worry creased her face. In the distance, the crash of shattering wood echoed down to them. He wasn't going to make it but he could slow down the beast to let Imayan get away.

"Go."

"Here. Give me that." She took Lintou's blade and brought his arm around her neck supporting some of his weight. Rai didn't have the strength to fight. They stumbled on down the tunnel as the screams of the wild duon grew ever closer.

"This isn't going to work. Go and I'll slow it down," Rai said.

Imayan gripped his arm harder, towing him along. "I won't lose anyone else tonight."

The patter of hooves rang from the dark.

Imayan glanced to Rai.

She knew that they wouldn't make it. The duon was too fast and who knew how long this tunnel was or where it would take them.

"Give me a minute," Rai said. The roiling in his stomach threatened to make him throw up. Imayan eased him against the wall and he slid down to seating. "Please, Imayan, I can't go any farther. You need to go without me."

Imayan hefted the black short sword as if testing its weight, and then pointed it down the corridor. "You aren't leaving me yet. I'll need you in the years to come. Other than Overseer Lintou and Mino, you've been the only constant in all this mess and I will not have you dying until I say you can die."

They were nice words but Rai saw the tremble in her arm as she pointed the sword. She had barely trained in sword-play.

"Please. Before it's too late. Run," Rai said. He wanted to scream the words but they came out soft with no force behind them.

The echoing footsteps of the duon silenced.

"It's here," Imayan whispered.

Panic cut through the pain. It brought clarity and Rai's instincts kicked in. "Spin the blade," Rai said.

Imayan glanced at him but she had seen Lintou too, and nodded in understanding. She twirled the sword in her grip. The duon's ear-piercing scream reverberated from the dark and then it appeared in a headlong charge right for Imayan. It got closer and the blade wasn't reacting to Imayan's movements. The duon would be upon them on seconds. Icy fear clawed at Rai freezing him to the spot. He couldn't do anything. He was going to let Imayan die.

The blade sputtered out a light breeze.

The duon was upon her.

Then, a torrent of air burst out of the blade and blasted down the tunnel ripping the duon from its feet. It battered against the walls of the tunnel with a sickening crack. The duon landed hard and slid to the ground. Imayan stopped spinning the blade. She was breathing heavily staring at the unmoving duon. Blood began to pool under its head.

"Is it…"

"I think so," Rai said.

The black sword clattered to the ground.

Voices carried from down the tunnel. At first Rai thought it might have been the woman but then he heard the unmistakable clash of metal swords clicking against plated armour.

"Imayan!" a voice called. It was Overseer Rikai.

"We're here!" Imayan called.

Saferooms were placed around Atef Palace for emergencies such as these, and Imayan and Rai had been deposited in one of them as the guards searched for the cowled assassin. A medic, after surveying Imayan, patched up Rai's arm with tight bandages.

The chamber was similar to a sitting room but it held two beds on the far wall and a separate sleeping chamber for Imayan. There was a pantry's worth of food in the cupboards and no windows. The single entrance was locked, bolted, and reinforced with metal bars so that even an aya couldn't stomp it down.

Rai sat on the edge of one of the beds. The medic said the light-headedness would pass but he needed plenty of rest. There were four armed guards in the room with him and Imayan, but Rai refused to sleep until he knew the threat had passed.

"Here, eat," Imayan said, handing him some sweet bread.

Rai took it with a grateful nod. "I should be the one helping you, yet here you are, taking care of me."

"I'd be dead if it weren't for you and… Lintou," Imayan said. She sat beside him on the bed and stared at her feet. "He'd be alive if it weren't for me."

"Overseer Lintou would have given his life a hundred times to save yours," Rai said. "This wasn't your fault."

"If I hadn't been there, Lintou would still be alive. That makes it my fault."

"If Ova shut its Moon Eye throwing us into darkness, the assassin might not have been able to find you. Ifs and possibilities are for storytellers. You couldn't have known they would come for you tonight. None of us could have known," Rai said.

"However, I'd be interested to know how an assassin and two duon were able to sneak so far into the palace undetected," Rai whispered watching the other guards roam by the door.

Imayan said nothing, eyes glazing over as she was lost in thought. "Imayan." Rai swayed bumping into her. "Are you okay?"

"He's just gone," Imayan said. "He's always just been there but now he just… won't be."

There was a sequence of knocks tapped against the door and one of the guards glanced through the peephole before a stern voice came from the other side, "Is Imayan safe? Let me in."

Emperor Leondal.

The locks snapped and the door flung open to the emperor rushing in. He glanced over the room before stalking towards Imayan, a company of guards in tow. He dropped to his hands and knees and held his daughter's face. "Imayan are you hurt?"

"I'm fine but Lintou…" Imayan's voice cracked and Emperor Leondal pulled her into an embrace.

"It's okay. Everything is going to be okay," the emperor said.

Rai felt like he was intruding on a private moment. This was made worse when Leondal noticed and scowled at him.

"We'll hunt this woman down, I promise you," he said.

Emperor Leondal straightened and faced the guards. "I want every corner of the palace searched until we find this assassin." Two of the guards bowed and sped off out the room. "And you," Leondal said to Rai. "You're dismissed. There are plenty guards here now."

With the company the emperor brought, there were now twelve guards in the saferoom. Rai didn't want to leave, but there was no denying the emperor.

"Wait, no. He saved my life. I want him to stay," Imayan said laying a hand on Rai's shoulder as he was about to stand.

The emperor cleared his throat. "Very well. Lock the door. We have much to discuss."

22

Death at the Dinner Table

Yeru had spent the entire ride back to Tansen scouring through the remnants of scrolls and books that they recovered from the Ossin research base. Rai had woken several times during their short breaks to find her sitting by the fire, reading, her eyes dry and begging for sleep.

By the time they reached the capital, Yeru was certain of two things. First, the Ossin scholars had been taking part in illegal experiments on animals and humans by caging them and leaving them near Asuriya to study the effects of the sickness. Second, that most of the horrific mutations were hundreds of years old. Leading Yeru to believe that the sickness was fading. Not only that but some of the records seemed to conclude that, while humans may find some effects from the sickness, it wasn't likely to shorten their lifespan a noticeable degree. They may grow sick towards the end, but they would still live to around the average life expectancy of any Tarrisian.

Yeru sat back on the aya's platform after explaining her findings to Rai, Tysar, Bisu, and Loulu. They had set up the tarp to shelter themselves from the Sun Eye's glare.

"If this is true, then we may be able to recover the old capital," Bisu said.

No one looked excited about the revelation.

"It also means we may have just set off a race to retake Asuriya and perhaps the rulership over all of Tarris," Yeru said.

If the Ossin monarch believed the old capital was habitable again and heard about the ancient volume declaring it the seat of the ruler of Tarris, then she might move to take control of Asuriya and rally the people to respect the oath that they swore. The oath that said the breaking of the emperor's power among the monarchs would once again be reforged at the capital under one ruling power.

The rest of the ride back to Tansen was quiet. It felt like the calm before a storm. And perhaps the last reprieve any of them would have for some time.

Rai didn't go with Yeru and the seven to share their findings with the empress. He was no longer welcome within the palace that much was clear. And he didn't know how to approach Imayani after disobeying her orders to travel to the Verdin Guild. Instead, he directed the aya towards the Inep Pot coffeehouse. There, he would be welcome.

Rai opened the door from the courtyard and a sweet aroma wafted out. He almost fell into its comfort and familiarity. Derin was behind the coffee bar as always running back and forth between his strange piped machines that spat out steam and sputtered into the busy coffeehouse floor.

His old friend gave him one look before turning back to his machines. Minutes later, he slid a mug across to Rai and smiled. Rai inclined his head in thanks and Derin turned back to the queue that Rai had skipped.

Rai felt the gazes from those in wait but was too tired to care. The steam from the machines blasted out in a hot wave and Rai ran a hand through his sweat drenched hair. He would need to bathe after this. They had been on the road too long and he needed a good wash.

Given that no one is sitting near us, I think that may be a good idea, Fax said.

Rai glanced around and noticed that was indeed the case. Despite the fact the coffeehouse was packed with people, the stools on either side of him were empty. He smiled and sipped at his drink.

It wasn't his usual coffee. This was *cold. A cold coffee?* Rai wondered lifting the mug. But this wasn't a normal coffee, either. There were spices and… was that milk?

Derin was watching him with a grin. Rai nodded appreciatively. It was refreshing after being out in the heat of the desert.

Rai wondered how Imayani was taking the news. She had been through a lot as an empress already and now it looked like the civil war that had been threatening for hundreds of years was coming to pass. Like a pot atop a flame, it was beginning to boil.

Hey, did you hear that? Fax said.

Fax filtered Rai's focus on a conversation happening a couple tables over. While they couldn't directly share senses, if they were both hearing or seeing the same thing, Fax could focus it in Rai's mind.

"How did you miss it? They arrived just after the Passing of the Nyfin," a woman said.

"That's probably how. I spent most of the festival in the Night Theatres. Wonder what he's doing at the capital?" a man asked.

"I heard they plan on marrying," the woman whispered.

Rai stood, the stool clattering to the ground. That could only mean one person. The Monarch of Yontar, Kleran had come to Tansen. Did he know about the research base? About Asuriya?

And you say I need to work on not attracting attention, Fax said.

People at a nearby table stared at Rai. He cleared his throat and picked up the stool. Finishing off his drink, Rai slid a deran to the waiter as Derin was occupied making drinks. Then, Rai made his way upstairs to his room. He needed to bathe and change. Welcome or not, he was visiting Atef Palace tonight.

Aren't we banished from the palace? Fax said.

The Moon Eye lit the city in silver, contrasting the fiery light of the city torches. City goers revelled in the crisp cool reprieve from the heat of day. Some sat slouched on tables sipping on teas and coffees watching the world pass. While others marched with the conviction of those with business to attend to.

"*Banished* is a strong word," Rai whispered. "We were asked to go somewhere and we didn't."

I'm not sure Imayani will see it like that, Fax said. They walked down the main thoroughfare towards the palace. Here, the scent of cooking meat and spices rode the wind from the many eateries.

236

Shuffled movement came from the dark alleyways between buildings. It was a child. Younger than Nya and Kit. Rai only saw her for a second before she skulked back into the shadows but her frail form and ragged clothing labelled her as a street kid. There were so many like her. While the monarchs fought for riches and power they missed the starving and the sickly sprawled out at their feet, searching for scraps.

"Banished or not. What did you say to me at those crossroads?" Rai asked.

You're wallowing in self-pity and the moment we returned to the capital you've been looking for a reason to give up?

"No, Fax. The other thing."

It has passed. That's why you humans call it the past?

Rai ignored the shade. "You asked me, what happened to your oath? What happened to saving Tarris? That was what I set out to do that day. And the only place I can do that is in the palace. It has taken me a long time to realise that words spill more blood than a sword ever can. But they can save lives, too."

You think this Kleran is planning to take the throne from Imayani?

"I think he'll use this threat to his advantage," Rai said.

The guards waved him by recognising him after the stir Rai made on his return. And Rai noted how full the stables were as he passed. Inside, the palace was flocked with servants running back and forth. Asking a servant about the uproar, Rai learned that the monarch had brought a larger company than expected and they were struggling to keep to the demands of such a sizeable group.

It didn't take long to figure out where Imayani and the others had cooped up. Rai followed the stream of servants carrying trays of coffee and tea and slabs of cooked meats and platters of smaller dishes. Guards stood watch at the end of a corridor leading to the main dining room. Rai pulled back around the corner before the guards spotted him.

So are we just going to charge in there? Fax asked.

Rai didn't know. He hadn't thought this far ahead. As he considered ways to sneak into the dining room, Yeru appeared dressed in a fine gown. Her eyes widened when she saw him. The beige gown was made of a light satin material that fell to her ankles. She looked like a different woman from the Yeru that wore the dusty travel clothes.

"Rai? What're you doing here?" Yeru asked.

Rai raised a finger to his lips and gestured to the guards around the corner. He hadn't spent a long time with the scholar but he knew her curiosity would win over. They passed down the sandstone corridor out of earshot from the guards.

"I need you to get me into the dining room," Rai said.

To Yeru's credit she didn't gasp or look surprised. "I'm not sure that's a good idea."

"You know I'm here to do what's right. That's why I caught up with you and the seven," Rai said. Yeru raised an eyebrow. "Let me help, Yeru. You saw what I can do. I'm guessing Imayani didn't react well to the findings."

Yeru shook her head. "She wanted to consult with Overseer Myain and Monarch Kleran. That's why we're here tonight. To discuss what they have decided to do."

"There's no harm in me sitting in, then," Rai said. "Without me, Yeru…"

"Okay, okay." Yeru acquiesced. "You can't go in like that, though." Yeru studied Rai as if deciding how best to present him.

Rai looked down at his ragged tan cloak and light travel jerkin. "What's wrong with this?"

Yeru sighed. "Come with me."

Not ten minutes later, they returned to the dining room, Rai sporting a scarlet dress jacket with a white undershirt. How Yeru was able to source the outfit so quickly, Rai wasn't sure. He pulled on the shirt that clung to his shoulders.

Dashing, Fax said.

"Stop pulling," Yeru scolded him like a child.

The boots were too tight but Rai bit his tongue. The guards waved them in without a second glance. He knew she was right to dress him like this but that didn't mean he had to like it.

Yeru worried that they would only have places set for those who were asked to attend but Rai knew she needn't worry.

Yeru gaped. The high ceiling reached deep into the palace. Huge glass mosaic windows were shaped as eyes letting the light from the Moon Eye shine directly into the chamber. Servants bustled up and down the immense table. The far side already had places set. However, as soon as Rai entered the room, waiters shot off without a word and returned with cutlery and an extra bowl and mug.

Pulling out a chair, Rai bowed letting Yeru sit. She looked as uncomfortable as he felt but it was best to play the part and remember the etiquette he learnt in this very palace.

The shuffle of the many servants' footsteps across the cool stone floor was all that could be heard echoing into the rafters above. Despite there being fifteen servants wandering around, they sat in an almost eerie silence before the others started arriving.

Imayani and Mino entered the dining hall from a different door than Rai and Yeru. Rai met Imayani's gaze and saw the shock fill her eyes before being hidden behind a hard façade. Mino didn't have that same skill and approached the table looking like she saw an aya sitting there sipping on a mug of tea.

After a prompt from Imayani, Mino pulled out her chair at the head of the table and then fell into the servant's position behind Imayani.

"Rai, I thought we discussed your departure," Imayani said, settling into her chair.

Rai glanced over to Yeru who was trying not to meet his eyes. Had they not told her that Rai had helped them retrieve the scholar's research? He turned back to Imayani, cursing to himself. Rai opened his mouth to respond when the doors to the dining hall opened again and Tysar and Overseer Myain entered the room. They wore dress jackets, making Rai glad that Yeru had found him his. He would have stuck out even more without it.

"Good evening, Empress." Overseer Myain bowed. As he rose, his face puckered at the sight of Rai. "What is he doing here?"

"I asked him here," Tysar said and sat across from Rai. "I wanted his advice on how the seven could help with this."

Rai was caught off guard at the lie but he dipped his head in acknowledgment. Tysar's words seemed to placate the room, Imayani shifting her attention to speak to the servants.

Hadn't Tysar wanted rid of you? Fax asked.

He hadn't wanted Rai to take the seven back. Perhaps after making it clear that he truly did want to help, Tysar didn't feel the need to hold him at arm's length.

The doors to the dining hall swung open one final time and in stepped the monarch of Yontar. Kleran was a typical pampered noble. His ink black hair was swept across his head as if an aya had licked it. He wore a black dress jacket with gold stitching atop a grey undershirt. The way he walked into the room with two servants at his back made it seem like he expected an applause.

"Kleran, thank you for coming. Please, come sit," Imayani said.

Kleran sauntered up the length of the hall whispering pleasantries along the way and sat at the seat closest to Imayani. "Thank you for your hospitality," he said. "I seem to be the last to arrive and I apologise."

"No apologies needed," Imayani said. "We just sat down. Now, let us eat."

Imayani clapped twice and the servants piled out through the doors as if they had been standing there in wait. It was a trick her father had used. When they had an important guest over to dine, he would clap and a flood of food and servants would arrive.

Platters were scattered across the table. The air was pungent with the scent of spices and fresh herbs. Cuts of meat glistened under the light of the torches. Fresh vegetables were paired with colourful pastes of yellow and red. And freshly brewed teas steamed from ornate golden teapots.

They made quick introductions as they picked at the food. It was customary, in Tarris, to have a meal before any serious conversations were had, so they talked about the food and the weather. It felt forced under the weight of what they were here to discuss. Rai was a believer in tradition and culture but there was a point where some traditions became constrictions rather than celebrations of their past.

Servants started to clear the plates and Rai caught sight of the guards standing at the edges of the hall. Rai had once been in their place and how he envied them now.

"We have brought you all here as Monarch Kleran and I have been discussing our approach to the recent revelation that Asuriya might once again be habitable," Imayani said. The conversations fizzled out as everyone faced the empress.

Imayani and Kleran discussing alone? Fax asked.

Myain looked perturbed that he hadn't been privy to such conversations. "Empress, if I may be so bold, why wasn't I brought into the decisions?"

"That's what we're doing now, Overseer Myain," Imayani said. "I had some ideas but I wanted to check with Kleran before offering them as options."

The straight-backed noble nodded, a smile lining his lips. Kleran waited a heartbeat and announced, "We plan to retake the old capital."

No one moved for several moments as the news was digested. "Ossin are likely to already be moving on Asuriya. We could perhaps reach the old capital before them with a small force but we need to *claim and hold* Asuriya and we can't do that with a small force. But with a battalion leaving from Yontar's garrison, we have a chance of beating them there," Imayani said.

Overseer Myain stammered some half-formed words. "Is it wise, Empress, to use another monarch's forces?"

The Overseer was careful with his wording but it was clear that he worried that Kleran might then seize Asuriya as his own.

"I will arrange for some soldiers to follow us and further fortify Asuriya after we've taken it. But they won't arrive until long after any battle may occur," Imayani said. What she said was right. It was a long ride from Tansen to Asuriya. A lengthy journey that would take weeks for a battle ready company. However, Yontar was a lot closer and sending troops from there could mean that they would reach the capital before Ossin's forces. Now that Rai had seen the passage through the Bandor Mountains, he knew that it would be close. However, the mountain passes were treacherous and brimming with strange creatures, which would slow the Ossin army.

"I've already sent word and my men are readying themselves for battle." Kleran leant over the table, clasping his hands. His jovial attitude was grating on Rai. "We will meet them on the road to the old capital."

"We also plan to be married. Tonight," Imayani said.

Rai's stomach fell. Tysar straightened. Yeru's eyes grew wide. Myain spluttered the mouthful of tea he had sipped.

"By marrying I can ensure my safety as it allows Kleran the same power as I," Imayani said. "We had planned this anyway. We're just bringing up the date."

Overseer Myain went off on a tirade of tradition and how this is not how things were done. Rai zoned out. This wouldn't ensure Imayani's safety as Kleran would be on equal footing with her. He may still decide to be rid of her but this did take out some of the urgency once they reached Asuriya. Kleran wouldn't need to kill her right away.

Imayani had once told Rai that she wanted to marry one day. She wanted to escape the royal life once her father had a male heir and settle down somewhere where she could care for her garden and have a quiet life. It was never going to happen. Not after she became empress. But this felt like another arrow piercing a dying version of Imayani.

"Do you plan to bring the Seventh Sceptre?" Tysar asked over Myain continuing his complaints.

"No," Imayani said. "I need to make sure that Tansen is protected. I will go myself with Kleran."

Overseer Myain scoffed. "Empress, I do not think this wise. Your place is here, where you can run the operations."

"I can't claim the capital if I am not there, Myain."

"I will go with you," Rai said.

Imayani surveyed Rai a moment before nodding. Overseer Myain threw his hands up. "This is foolish," he said, all pretence of hierarchy thrown aside in his frustration. "He shouldn't even be here!"

"I will come too," Tysar said. "The Seventh Sceptre can hold Tansen without me. The true battle will be for Asuriya."

Imayani nodded. "Very well."

The chances of another monarch trying to take Tansen while she was gone was slim, but Imayani was right to leave part of the seven and most of her garrison in the city to defend its walls. However, this meant that they were relying on Monarch Kleran and his garrison. Rai watched as the man took in the conversation with the interest of a general. Yontar had the largest garrison in all of Tarris. It had once been the home to all of Tarris' forces until the cataclysm. Kleran was a direct descendant from the war general that was said to have led the country's forces before the cataclysm. And many said that prowess for military strategy had been passed down through the generations. That made Kleran a useful ally and a dangerous enemy.

Which one are you? Rai wondered.

"What if the records were falsified or wrong and the sickness is still there? You will all die!" Myain said.

"It's unlikely given the depth of the scholar's notes and how they burned them hoping we wouldn't see the results," Yeru said.

"It is a risk we must take," Imayani said when Myain screwed his face up to Yeru's response. "We risk plunging Tarris into civil war if we don't take the capital."

The Monarch of Ossin, Haduan, was hoping to call upon the ancient law they now battled over. Whether the people would accept this was up for debate, but one thing was clear: the Tarrisian people would splinter. Sects that followed the old ways would flock to the capital. Those who trusted in their empress would stand against that. And others would turn to other monarchs that may stake claim to the throne.

It didn't matter if the people would accept the Ossin monarch as their ruler. Haduan taking Asuriya would light the fuse and the whole of Tarris was the bomb.

Time stretched in the silence. Overseer Myain blew out a breath seemingly coming to the same conclusion as Rai. There was no other choice.

"We will have to move fast," Tysar said.

"We leave at dawn," Imayani said.

One by one, those around the table nodded.

I didn't see any cracks in his expression, Fax said in Rai's mind. He had asked the shade to watch Kleran for any indication of subterfuge.

A twitch or a half smile. Nothing. Rai still didn't trust the man. He had no doubt that Kleran would try to kill Imayani and claim her throne.

But Rai would be there. At the first sight of silver, there would be a flash of darkness.

23

Essence

Nya wondered if she would ever get used to the sight of death. Bas and Kit dragged Pio's dead body into the stables to not attract attention. The Patched Cloak never truly closed. With guests coming and going, they couldn't simply shut off the courtyard. However, there were times when they closed the bar.

After the early night rush there was a slow and steady decline of customers until Illy shut the services completely a couple hours before dark hour. The monotony of the routine helped settle their nerves after Pio's attack. Kit had caught Nya up to date but he was as shaken as the rest of them. Wenson had fallen silent and went about cleaning the smashed glass whilst Illy fell into character and served drinks with a smile.

The bald man, Bas, who Nya hadn't seen since the dark place, helped Kit and Lem carry supplies into the basement. She still wasn't sure why he was here.

It's no coincidence, Bom said.

"What makes you say that?" Nya asked under her breath as she went about making another batch of drinks.

He watches you when you aren't looking his way, Bom said. *He senses me.*

"He's just a man," Nya said. Bom didn't respond. Kit had said Bas was looking into the cage containing the husk when he arrived back at the inn. "Do you think he can sense the husk?" Bom stayed silent. The shade often did that if it didn't know the answer to Nya's questions.

Bas returned and picked up another crate before descending back into the basement. Nya knew she didn't need to be wary of him. The Urdahl had saved her life in the dark place. But Nya agreed with Bom. This was no coincidence.

Nya fought the urge to usher the last customer out the door. She stood behind the bar with bated breath as an older gentleman sipped his drink. Kit, Lem, and Bas already sat in a booth talking is hushed tones.

Finally, once the man paid and left, Nya made her way over and slid into the booth. The others went silent.

"How did you know where to find us?" Nya asked while staring at Bas.

The Urdahl gave no indication that the question bothered him. His placid gaze remained as neutral as it always did. Nya waited.

She was about to repeat her question when Bas said, "I can sense the dark place. It has an essence." The words were slow and methodical, as if he put thought into every one. "I see it on you."

"How?" Nya asked.

"Only Urdahl can know our ways," Bas said.

"Will others be able to see me?" Nya asked. The thought was concerning and she felt Bom bristle at the idea. She could only imagine what uses monarchs could find for her. They'd turn her into a weapon. It reminded Nya of the black blade that the scholars raised to the survivors of the dark place, and how it burned as it drew close. Perhaps they already knew how to locate shades.

"I don't think so," Bas said.

Nya squinted at the man. Could she trust him?

The idea made her skin crawl. Bas could watch her and track her. The skittish Nya that was in the Sand Rat gang itched to run. The old her screamed to get away from this. Fleeing into the cover of the alleys was always an option on the streets. But everything was so much more complicated now.

"Can you stop interrogating our friend please, Nya?" Kit said. "He helped save the inn."

Nya sat back but asked Bom to keep an eye on Bas.

Kit sighed. "Thank you. Bas was telling us that he can see a darkness coming from the palace. He broke in to investigate and got arrested. That's why he was in the cells with us when we went to the dark place. But recently he's been seeing—"

"Trails," Bas said. "The same darkness is trawled throughout the city. I followed it and it led here."

"Our bat-boy has been leaking invisible goo," Lem said.

"The husk?" Nya asked.

Bas nodded. "Not goo, though. It's an essence. Not something that can be touched or removed. But it fades with time," Bas said.

The Urdahl barely spoke a word when they were part of the Doomed Others. Nya had learned that the Urdahl only spoke what they thought was of the upmost importance. *So he must think this darkness and the husks are a threat.*

"Tell them what you told me," Kit said.

Bas took a moment. Whether he was thinking of what to say or this was his way to deal with discomfort, Nya wasn't sure. "There were other trails."

Nya's eyes went wide. "More trails?"

"Which means there might be more husks," Kit said.

Suddenly the stories of lost people and strange beasts roaming the dark corners of the city took a new darker light.

"It's worse than we thought," Kit said. "If other husks are already in the city. We need to close that tear and soon."

Bom flared with worry and Nya felt the shade curl in her gut. "The husks can sense Bom," Nya said.

Kit nodded like he had already made that connection.

"They would overrun the city," Nya said. "And it would be my fault."

"We don't know if they are coming through for you or if they were coming through anyway and are just drawn to you. That husk in the library didn't know we were there until you were directly beneath it," Kit said.

He was right. They must only be able to sense Bom when they are near. However, that still put her loved ones in danger if many were already in the city.

"What was it Bom said?" Kit asked.

"That they sense a piece of home in the shade," Nya said.

"So they wouldn't be leaving home to seek it out," Kit said. "And you said yourself, they would need help to escape the Thousand Floor Palace. The tear isn't exactly by a big window."

Nya nodded. Someone had to be letting the husks loose in the city. Or at least bringing them through the tear.

"I said Bas could help us," Kit said. "He is a great fighter and he has already infiltrated the palace once."

"He got caught last time," Nya said.

"I will not fail a second time," Bas said. He spoke in short sharp words.

"And we have no hope of getting into the palace without him," Kit added.

Lem had stopped listening and was petting Dust who sat on his lap.

Nya blew out a breath. "Okay. But we can't just go charging in. If someone really is helping the husks get out, we need to find out who. It must be someone in the palace who has access to the other world."

"And we need to figure out how to close the tear," Kit said. "There's no point in breaking into the palace if we can't close it."

"There's only one person who will know all this," Nya said.

Kit ran a hand through his hair. "I'll ask my connections on the street to track him down."

"Who?" Bas asked.

"The scholar running the research project, Mirt," Nya said.

Mirt had been the one in charge of the tear and the research team looking into the dark place. Nya remembered his awkward demeanour as he introduced himself to the group that he sent into the tear to die.

With a yawn, the group decided that they needed to sleep. Illy offered Bas one of the spare rooms and after the eventful night they disbanded. As Kit made for the stairs to their rooms, Nya grabbed his wrist and pulled him aside.

"How did the translation go?" She had begun to ask earlier but with a firm shake of the head, it was clear Kit didn't want to talk about it with the others.

"We couldn't translate it all." Kit squirmed under her gaze. "But it doesn't look like I'm going to die from it. I think I should be okay."

"That's what you wanted to hear, right?" Nya asked.

Kit nodded but grimaced.

"Is something else bothering you?" Nya asked.

"No, no, no, it's fine. I don't know. I just— I don't know." Kit looked like he was about to say something and then shook his head. "I think I just need some rest. Goodnight."

He slipped out of her grip and continued up the stairs. Dust brushed against Nya's leg. She knelt and pet the sand fox who leant into the attention.

"Nothing stays the same, does it?" she whispered.

The next few days were a rush. Bas helped around the inn and then joined in the planning after closing. Despite months having passed, his recollection of the Thousand Floor Palace was impressive. They bought parchment and ink from the markets and Bas got to work marking a path to the chamber that held the tear.

At the same time, Kit reached out to his connections on the street to help track down the scholar, Mirt. They didn't have much to go on other than his appearance and where he worked, but Kit seemed hopeful that they would turn up something eventually. Wenson had gone unusually quiet and Nya caught him more than once swinging the broom around as if it were a sword. Nya could tell he was frustrated that he wasn't of more help with the intrusion from Pio. She tried to reassure him but he waved off any reassurances.

Nya distracted herself by filling her days with work around the inn. Her nights were haunted by nightmares of husks swarming the city and killing everyone she knew. They ripped into the Patched Cloak and slaughtered Illy and Wenson. Then the husks burst out to the courtyard where Kit and Lem were cleaning out the stables. Nya could only watch from the rooftop as her friends screamed for her help. She woke up covered in sweat and unable to fall back asleep even with Dust nuzzling against her.

Still it was better than the emptiness. It was better than the hollow feeling that had held her nights before. Husks were a threat. It made sense that she feared them and feared what they might do. The inexplicable nothingness that filled her before didn't make sense. She was surrounded by those who loved her and she had a future here. So then, why couldn't she shake the pit that swallowed her every night?

Nya felt *better* with the threat of death. She felt better with the nightmares because they made sense. There had to be something wrong with her. Maybe she wasn't meant for a life of joy. Maybe she wasn't meant to stop.

The darkness stalked her and she had to keep running, for when she slowed, it bled over her and drowned her in the black.

The waiting felt like standing still. Nya could feel the dark breathing down her neck. So when Kit finally brought back news, Nya was ready.

The night crowds flowed through the streets of Yontar. Kit led the way through the throng of people to a quieter section of the city. Nya had rarely entered this part of Yontar, as most of it was full of middle earner's housing. When she lived on the streets, there had been little reason to pass this way. Even the thoroughfares quietened as they continued onward.

"He stays in the palace and rarely comes out anymore, but he does live in the city," Kit was saying. "Occasionally he comes home in the middle of the night to stay for a couple hours before returning to the palace. It's one of the reasons the gangs found out where he lived so quickly after I asked. They were keeping an eye on the unusual behaviour in their territory."

The homes here were mainly two storey buildings broken by monolithic five or six storey apartments that were rented out. An off-duty city guard strode past them eyeing them warily. Dust growled at the guard until Nya told her off.

"We shouldn't be out in the open like this," Nya whispered.

"It's fine." Kit waved a hand dismissively. "Some of the street gangs run out of streets like this because no one questions them in a middle-class area. Anyway, here we are."

Kit gestured to one of the six storey towers. It was a simple blocky building with a rickety staircase zigzagging up the side.

"He lives on the fourth floor," Kit said.

They climbed the metal staircase. It was little more than a frame of what should have been there. It groaned and rattled as they made their way up to the fourth floor. Once at the door, Kit knelt and started working on the lock.

"How long does this usually take?" Nya asked. The street remained still with the sounds of the city distant and muted. She would have felt more at ease if there had been some life to the dead street.

"Not long," Kit said.

"Why would anyone want to live in a lifeless street like this?" Nya asked.

"Easier to come and go undetected." His pick snapped and Kit sighed, reaching for another at his belt. Dust was watching with interest, snapping as the pick past her.

"Mirt is a scholar. Why would he need to go undetected?"

"He's working on a secret project that leads to another world with living shadows and bat-like creatures."

Nya supposed, but this felt excessive.

"Do you think he's the one freeing the husks?" Nya asked.

"He could be," Kit said. "That's what we're here to find out."

The lock snapped again but this time Kit yipped and turned with a grin. The door swung open to darkness.

"Dust, *stay and watch*," Nya said putting a commanding tone into her voice. The sand fox trotted to the edge of the landing and lay down, watching the street.

Nya brought in the brazier from the landing and lit the lamps by the door.

"It looks like someone threw up a bookshop," Kit said.

Parchment lay scattered in piles. Some were pinned up, lines drawn across the wall to connect them with other scraps. The musty scent of mildew hung in the air. It was a single room apartment with a cot in the corner. More pages were piled on the cot, the sheets crumpled as if Mirt hadn't slept in it for some time.

"They weren't kidding when they said he doesn't stay here," Nya said.

Kit ran his finger over a page. "These will be his notes."

"What do they say?" Nya asked coming to his side.

"I barely understand half of it," Kit said.

"Is it coded?"

"No, it's just… nonsense. He talks about the great one. It reads more like it was written by a cult fanatic rather than a scholar." Kit continued to read so Nya set out to explore more of the apartment. Not that there was much more to see. Moving further into the apartment brought a stench of rot. Nya spotted the source, a half-eaten meal discarded under an open scroll. She gagged stepping back.

As she did, something caught her eye. An illustration of the black blade that Mirt had waved in front of the Doomed Others after they returned from the dark place. Fear stole her breath away. Bom bloomed outward ready to fight an unseen foe. Nya settled her breathing and convinced Bom that they were safe. It was just a sketch.

"Kit," Nya said.

He came over and saw what she was pointing at. Lifting the scroll, Kit furrowed his brow.

"This is more legible," Kit said. "I think it's an older note. It seems we are standing in the middle of the notes of a man descending into madness."

"What does it say about the blade?" Nya asked. She felt Bom flare at the sketched blade. It remembered the burning it felt as the dagger drew near.

"It describes the material and an opening in the bottom and…" Kit's face went pale.

"What is it?"

Kit swallowed. *"I fear to activate the blade as it could open another rend in reality,"* Kit read. *"Whether it would lead to the same dark place or another is up for speculation among the research team. While I would take it out into the desert and attempt to open another tear, it has been decided that we won't activate the blade until we know more about the pocket world. We do not know what the other side holds or what might live in this dark realm."*

"The blade created the tear?" Nya asked.

Silence rung as they let that settle in. What kind of dagger opens rifts in reality? Where did they get such a weapon? What, then, is the dark place?

"Keep reading," Nya said.

The look on Kit's face implied that he didn't want to but he lifted the parchment. Dust skittered into the room and snorted. Nya and Kit looked at one another. She would only have come in if… Kit ran to the shuttered window and peaked through the slats.

"Sands suffocate us. It's Mirt," Kit said.

"I thought you said he wasn't due to return tonight!" Nya said.

"He doesn't stay on a schedule," Kit said.

"Clearly," Nya said as they made for the door.

The scholar was reading from a notebook as he wandered down the street towards his building. Kit eased the door closed as Nya took for the stairs, Dust at her feet. They made it down to the third floor when it was clear that Mirt would reach the steps before they could make it all the way down.

"He'll recognise us," Nya said. Kit gestured to the edge of the railing.

"We're three floors up!" Nya said.

"Rai can do that floating down thing with Fax! Can't you do the same with Bom?" Kit asked.

The stairwell shook as Mirt started his ascent. There was a feeling of discomfort from Bom. They hadn't tried anything like that yet. And now there wasn't enough time to take them down one by one. They needed to hide.

Nya projected an idea to Bom, who reluctantly acquiesced. Bom flowed out of her as a sheet of black. It flapped in the wind like fabric and blew over the edge, clinging onto the railing. Not waiting for Kit's reaction, Nya scooped up Dust and climbed over the railing and dangled over the drop below. Kit did the same. There they hung behind Bom who acted as a black cloak.

They waited with bated breath as Mirt wound his way up the staircase passing them without a second glance.

Nya and Kit didn't move until they heard Mirt's door slam shut. They pulled themselves onto the landing and Nya let out a shaky breath.

Kit nodded. "That was clever. A cloak of darkness."

Nya's lips drew to a line. She had been practicing a blanket of darkness to obscure her passage but they were far from perfecting it. Bom found it difficult blending into the shadows around it. Often they were too dark or too light a patch of shadow. So if anyone were to look directly at them, it would be obvious that something was there. But she wasn't going to admit that to Kit now.

"We were lucky. Come on."

They scuttled down the steps and ran into the nearest side street. Nya couldn't stop thinking about the black blade. It had *created* the tear. Could it then close it, too? She felt push back from Bom. The shade didn't like the idea of the tear closing. Nya guessed it made sense. The dark place was the shade's home but she couldn't leave it open for husks to pass through.

Do you want to go home? Nya asked.

Bom sent a negative impression.

So why do you care if I close the tear? Nya wondered. Then it clicked. *What would happen to you if I closed the tear?*

The shade didn't respond but Nya felt its curiosity. It didn't know.

Ever since Ma-atan's temple, Nya felt a connection to the dark place. Like she could feel it stirring.

I see you.

Nya avoided thinking about the voice that came from the dark place. But she had a connection to that other realm. She could feel it if she focused. And something was there alive in the darkness.

They had to close the tear before it was too late.

24

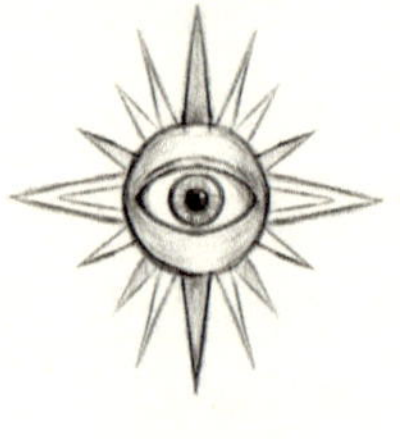

Duty

15 years ago.

"Theben? The Monarch of Rizu?" Tys asked. Steam filled the bathhouse as Rai and Tys soaked in the tub. Rai breathed in the burning oaky scent and listened to the soothing sound of gargling water. Shifting, he felt a twinge in his leg from the day's training.

Rai had waited until the others left to tell Tys about the assassination attempt the night before. After arriving well into the night back to their quarters, Tys had a lot of questions about where he had been, but the emperor wanted to keep the situation quiet. They couldn't show weakness. They couldn't show how close they were to killing the heir to the throne.

"They believe so," Rai said. "The woman was with two duon."

Tys breathed out. Duon were found all over Tarris but in the city of Rizu, duon were used in the fighting pits for entertainment.

If anyone had access to duon trained for combat it would be the Monarch of Rizu.

"You don't think it was Theban, though, do you?" Tys asked.

Rai shook his head.

"You think that would be too obvious. Theban wouldn't be stupid enough to send duon for the assassination attempt. That would implicate him," Tys said.

Rai nodded. This was why he came to Tys. He saw through the nonsense.

"Did you say that?" Tys asked.

"Of course, but I was brushed aside. Most of them don't even believe I'm Imayan's personal guard." Rai sighed. "The faster we finish training and get our official positions, the better."

Tys snorted. "You're not joking. We train harder and longer than any of those palace guards but because they have a uniform they look down their noses at us. Just wait until we have our honour guard armour."

They sat for a while, letting their sore muscles soak in the hot water. It was a couple of hours until afternoon training and Rai knew if he wanted to be able to move tomorrow morning he had to let the knot in his calf ease.

"What're you going to do?" Tys asked.

"The only thing I can do," Rai said. "Keep Imayan safe."

An hour later, the two left the bathhouse. Dried and dressed, they walked through the corridors of Atef Palace. The hushed hallways of midday were a stark contrast to the rush of morning or late afternoon. Sunlight broke the corridors in strips of light unmarred by hurrying scholars and servants. Their footsteps sent ringing echoes through the quiet. It was peaceful.

Tys threw the door to their quarters open and tossed his sword onto his bed. "Want to drop by the coffeehouse? We still have some time before training."

"No time for that, I'm afraid," Genu said.

Rai spun to find her leaning against their door frame. "Overseer Rikai sent me to find you two. He wants a word," she said and turned and stalked off.

Rai and Tys met eyes. Overseer Rikai didn't make small talk, he didn't congratulate, he scolded.

Silence from the man was a compliment.

"This doesn't sound good," Tys said.

They met in one of the training halls high in the palace. Weapons were mounted on one of the walls. A long beam ran across the hall above them, a ladder on each side. Rikai often had them duelling atop the beam. The first to hit the hard ground lost.

Tys, Genu, Ada, Sen, and Rai stood in a line not unlike the one they stood in on that first day in the Eye. Rai and Tys wore fresh robes but Genu and Ada had their training gear on. Sen looked like he had been woken from a nap, his brown hair poking out in all directions.

"I know training isn't for a while yet but I was told this couldn't wait," Overseer Rikai said. He was more tense than usual. His back was straighter, face harder. "While you were to have another couple of years of training, it's been decided to move along with the next stage of your training early."

Overseer Rikai hesitated but they had learnt not to interrupt him.

"You are to leave for the Verdin Temple this evening."

Silence.

Everything froze. Rai's head scrambled to make sense of what Overseer Rikai had said. The others were equally perplexed.

"The Verdin Temple?" Sen asked.

"That's what I said, is it not?" Overseer Rikai said.

Training at the Verdin Temple had always been the goal but to have it handed to them when it should have been years away felt… wrong.

"I don't understand. Are we ready?" Genu asked.

Overseer Rikai wouldn't meet her gaze. "As ready as time will allow for. You're to pack your things and leave before dark hour."

Tys opened his mouth then closed it again before saying, "Excuse me for saying, Overseer Rikai, but this feels very sudden."

"That's because it is."

Excitement fought confusion as worry crawled up Rai's throat.

"I am proud of you five and I am sure you will make great members of the Verdin Guild and return stronger than you left. It saddens me that we do not have longer together."

Overseer Rikai's face twitched. *Is Rikai getting emotional?*

"But I have trained you to the best of my ability. You've grown from frail little children into warriors. It is an honour to even be *considered* for the Verdin Guild so take this as such. If you survive the guild, you will return as something different. Greater than a warrior. Greater than what most believe possible. Now, go pack and say your goodbyes. Training is cancelled. You leave tonight," Overseer Rikai said.

"Go now."

Ada ran off. Genu stepped forward to speak to Overseer Rikai.

Everything was a whirl. Tys, Sen and Rai stood together in their thoughts.

Rai waited for the others to leave before approaching Overseer Rikai. Slowly one by one the others drifted out the hall to prepare. Tys nodded at Rai as he left. They would catch up later.

"Overseer Rikai?" Rai asked.

Rikai looked distracted as he scratched his chin.

"Overseer?" Rai repeated and the man glanced up.

"What is it?"

"What about Imayan? I have duties here," Rai said.

His face softened then. "Imayan will be safe. The emperor has increased the company of guards protecting her."

This was always what was going to happen. However, Rai was supposed to have longer. Frustration and anger roiled in his gut. He wasn't ready to leave. Rai could see the hesitation in Overseer Rikai. They hadn't earned their places in the Verdin Guild. No. This had to be because of the assassination attempt.

With a firm nod, Rai spun on his heels to leave.

"Rai," the Overseer said. Rai turned. Rikai took a moment. "Be careful with Imayan. We all have our duties and becoming the first empress comes with certain responsibilities and a requirement to emanate strength. I don't want to see a good soldier taken away from where he's meant to be."

Rai thought on the Overseer's words. He wasn't sure what they meant but there was a warning in there to tread carefully, that much was clear. Rai nodded and left the hall.

The five of them saddled up their hyians as the Sun Eye dipped, painting the world red. There were no goodbyes. No one came to see them off. Tys, Genu, Ada, Sen, and Rai were alone in the palace courtyard leading their hyians to the gate. It was opened without a word and they set off into the night.

They rode in silence through the quiet streets of Tansen. Most were indoors for the oncoming dark hour but a handful of cloaked figures scuttled down alleyways, none getting too close.

I wish I could have at least said goodbye, Rai thought.

Immediately after leaving the hall, Rai went to Imayan's quarters where Mino told him she had been whisked off on last minute official duty with the emperor. He guessed it didn't matter. He was a guard and this was always how it was meant to go. Did guards even say goodbye? Still, he would have liked to have seen her before he left.

The city gates groaned as the great metal teeth rose revealing the open desert. A grating breeze of sand blew through the opening as the dunes greeted them. As they rode out onto the sand, Rai glanced back at Tansen, the only home he had ever known. Tys fell back to ride alongside him.

"It's only until we complete the training. We'll return to Tansen better than we left," Tys said. He left out the possibility that they didn't complete the training. Rumours of the Verdin Temple said those unable to keep up with the gruelling schedule were killed. They knew too much and the Verdin Guild did not share their secrets.

"I know."

Dark hour hounded their backs as they ran through the last of the light. By the time they reached the Waypoint, the sand had turned solid and black beneath their feet. The tall mudbrick hut was nestled by an outcropping of rock. Rai and Tys entered to check for bandits while the others led the hyian into the stables. As they were so close to the capital, the Waypoint was in better condition than most. A fire pit sat in the middle of the space, a circular stone bench cut into the rock floor. And another room branched off from the main chamber containing twelve cots.

Rai started on the fire while the others prepared the food. Sen soon had a pot of stew boiling over the flames and passed out bowls to each of them. It was rich and flavourful. The meat and vegetables cooked to perfection. They had brought basic provisions but this meal spoke of seasoning outwith the simple pack they had brought.

"This is a damn good stew, Sen," Tys said.

Scratching the back of his neck, Sen shrugged. "My parents were cooks. They wouldn't let me get away with not knowing how to make a stew."

"My parents were blood dealers," Ada said. They all stared at him. "What? I thought we were sharing."

"Can I see the map?" Genu asked.

Rai pulled the map from his belt pocket and unfolded it. He passed it to Ada, who passed it to Genu. "It's a straight line south until we hit the edge of the Deadlands Basin. The map says there is a hidden path into the basin from this side."

Overseer Rikai had given them the map with the route already plotted out for them.

"Is it true that there are monsters that roam the Deadlands Basin?" Sen asked settling down with his bowl of stew.

Genu nodded. "It's too dangerous to traverse. That's why they hid the Verdin Temple there. Some believe there is rare ore in the rock around the basin but, well… The people who ventured into the basin in search of the ore are why it's called the Deadlands Basin."

"Part of the test of the Verdin Guild is getting to the temple itself," Rai said.

They were quiet, ruminating on the stories that surrounded the basin. Monsters were known to appear across the deserts of Tarris during dark hour and some believed the Deadlands Basin was where they roamed the rest of the time. Sand serpents that swam through the sand as if it were water. Bouldons, massive rock creatures that disguised themselves as boulders and crushed any who came close. Beetles that buried beneath traveller's skin and ate them from the inside out. The stories were never ending and fueled by the fact that scholars estimated that they only knew about a quarter of the creatures that roamed the Deadlands.

"Well, better rest up." Ada stood. "And I was worried about getting bored."

Finishing their meals, the others settled onto cots to catch some shut eye. Soon only Tys and Rai were left around the fire.

"This was very sudden, wasn't it," Tys said, breaking the silence.

"With the attempt on Imayan's life, I think they want us to be ready," Rai replied.

Tys stayed quiet.

"What?" Rai asked.

A conflicted look crossed his face. "I was just thinking about what you told me about that," Tys said. "The way the emperor tried to get rid of you but Imayan asked for you to stay. What did she say when you left?"

"She wasn't there. Taken away on some official business in the city," Rai said.

Tys bit his lip.

"Tys," Rai said.

"You're usually the strategist," Tys said.

Then it clicked.

"You think the emperor wanted me out the way. You think he sent us early and took Imayan out for the day so she couldn't object."

"It's possible. If he thought you were getting too close to his daughter—"

"It isn't like that," Rai said.

"If he *thought* that, then sending you off early to the Verdin Temple would be an easy fix," Tys said.

A sudden wave of anger flooded Rai. Would the emperor really want him out the way when he was the one keeping his daughter safe? Emperor Leondal's cautious glare lingered in Rai's mind. He thought of how frustrated Imayan had become about constantly being separated from those around her on her father's orders. The black sand-footed fool was upset because Rai was there for Imayan more than he was.

"Easy, Rai," Tys said.

Rai realised he was gripping the bowl of stew so tight his knuckles went white. "I need to go back." Rai made to stand but Tys leaned over and pushed against Rai's chest forcing him back down.

"And do what? Disobey the emperor's Word? Follow Imayan around like a lost sand fox? Don't be foolish, Rai. You are level headed in everything apart from when Imayan is involved."

Rai exhaled. He was right. He had sworn to himself not to make any more bonds and yet he felt the thread connecting himself to Imayan even now. It was taut and threatening to snap. Rai couldn't go through that again.

"I know it's hard and maybe something was possible when she was just the emperor's daughter but she's going to be the *empress*, Rai. She can't be with her personal guard." Tys leaned over and squeezed Rai's shoulder.

It isn't like that. The words tasted sour on his tongue. What once came so easy to him now felt false and unspeakable.

"We're soldiers," Tys said. "I still remember that second day in the Eye. Something changed in you then. The boy I met in our room was gone and Rai the soldier was all that was left. We need you to be that soldier. The others wouldn't say it, but they look up to you. You were always the immovable rock in our group. The unspoken leader. If we are to survive the Verdin Guild, sands allowing we even get there, we need you, Rai."

Rai gulped back what felt like a stone in his throat. He was a solider. That's what he was here for. Disconnected and unemotional. An immovable rock. The others needed him. Imayan needed him. It was his duty to protect those who couldn't protect themselves.

Flashes of the duons attacking Lintou in his study made Rai realise he had been thinking about Imayan at the time. He had wondered how to keep the beasts away from her. If he had been more *focused*, if he had been *stronger*, could he have saved Lintou? Could he have not gotten hurt and gotten them all out unharmed? That was supposed to be his job.

Tys was right. He had to focus. The bond that stretched across the desert, snaking over the cresting dunes and into the capital of Tarris to Imayan slackened. He couldn't disconnect it. Not truly. But he could do this. He could focus on his duty. His duty as a soldier.

25

War in the Shadows

Empress Imayani and Monarch Kleran were married that night. It was a small affair with those who had been at dinner as the audience and an official to witness the marriage. Royal weddings usually took place in the palace gardens but when Mino offered to send servants to the garden to prepare the dais, Imayani snapped that she would prefer the ceremony take place in the grand hall. Mino and Rai shared a knowing glance. Imayani saw the gardens as a special place and she didn't want it associated to this marriage of convenience.

The ceremony had little fanfare as they planned to announce the marriage to the people upon returning from Asuriya. Kleran promised grand celebrations. But for now, they needed to rest and prepare.

At first light, they rode for war.

To catch Kleran's forces, they would need to be fast. Imayani had arranged the palace's strongest hyian for their party. And they kept the company small. *Too small*, Rai thought watching the four guards saddle their hyian. A simple bandit party would be a threat if it weren't for him and Fax.

The party consisted of four guards, Imayani, Mino, Kleran, Kleran's servant; a skinny man called Utop, Yeru, Tysar and Rai. They dressed in travel clothes and carried no sigil implying royalty as they couldn't risk garnering too much attention along the way.

The hiss of buckles tightening caught Rai's attention. He spun to see Tysar at his side attaching a pack to his hyian.

"They're more than guards. They're part of her new honour guard," Tysar said. He always had the strange ability of knowing what Rai was thinking.

"Still, four of the finest guards stand little chance against a bandit party of twenty," Rai said.

"That's why we're here." Tysar smiled.

"Thank you for covering for me at the feast last night," Rai said. They led their hyian towards the stable entrance and out into the courtyard. The Sun Eye teetered on the horizon.

"I've been covering you for most of my life. Why stop now? And anyway, it was true. We will need all the help we can get."

They rode hard across the desert, rarely stopping for rest or meals. The guards surrounded them in a cart formation, two at the front and two at the back. Within them, Rai rode with Tysar and Yeru. The scholar talked little and spent most of the time reading. And in front of them, Imayani travelled alongside Mino, Kleran, and

Utop.

I see upon the sands something the colour of... Fax started.

"Don't," Rai said under his breath.

You're no fun, Rai, Fax said.

Tysar glanced up, thinking he spoke to him. "What do you think of this marriage?" he asked.

Rai hadn't missed that his friend watched him during the ceremony the night before. Was he expecting a reaction?

"It is a smart move for some short term safety," Rai said.

The warm desert winds blew through them. Coarse sand bit into exposed flesh so they each had their cowls up and sand goggles on.

Tysar grunted. "I'll give you that, but I don't like the idea of the empress being indebted to Kleran."

He watched Rai for a response. What did he want him to say? That he thought Imayani shouldn't marry the monarch? Yeru pretended not to be listening but Fax confirmed that she had been staring at the same page for the last several minutes.

"We all do what we must. We have duties that outweigh what any of us might want. Trade-offs, deals, and compromises are what hold the world together. Kleran has gained the power he strove for and Imayani has an army that can reach Asuriya in time. For now, that's all that matters," Rai said.

Tysar nodded and faced the desert, satisfied with his answer. Yeru turned the page of her book.

Do you really believe that? Fax asked. The shade was genuinely curious. It could sense Rai's emotions but not always the cause of them.

Yes. But what I believe isn't always how I feel, Rai thought. *It takes discipline to act on what you know to be right, instead of what you wish to be right.*

Despite their haste, none of the party wanted to continue across the black sands of night when creatures roamed. So they travelled onward until they found an empty Waypoint to spend the night in. The four guards swept the interior to ensure that they were alone in the mudbrick building.

As the stretch of desert between Tansen and Yontar was frequented by merchants and travellers, this was a well-kept two storey Waypoint with a stock of provisions, from bedding to some food supplies.

The common room had an empty fire pit in the centre. The door must have blown open as sand lay scattered throughout the space.

"I want a guard on each of the two doors," Tysar said. "You two can rest and then switch out in a couple of hours." He pointed to two of the four guards.

Imayani, Mino, and Yeru retired to a room upstairs and Kleran and his servant turned in for the night in one of the first floor rooms. They had to make use of the short time that they did stop to sleep. That left Rai and Tysar around a crackling fire sipping on steaming drinks while the cool night took hold around them. *Just like old times,* Rai thought. Some time passed in silence as the shuffling in the rooms stilled.

"I still dream of that night," Tysar said. He sat back, eyes closed and feet warming by the fire. "I've always wondered if I could have done more. If we had found you faster."

Rai dreamt of it too. The night they went to the dark realm beyond the tear.

"You can't think like that. It's done. We do what we can with what we know. You can't ask for more than that," Rai said.

Tysar leaned forward. "But we can learn from it, right? You always said a mistake was only ever a mistake when done twice. I don't know what's coming but we will face more bloodshed and strife before this is all over."

Rai didn't speak, sensing Tysar wanted to say something. "This war in the shadows has gone on for hundreds of years. So many have died as these monarchs vie for power. But now it's being pulled out into the light. After we take Asuriya that could be it. The end to the fighting. Or it might not. People will always find reason to draw a blade. Perhaps we weren't meant to rule," Tysar said.

Rai must have twitched as Tysar's face darkened. "I don't like him either. Kleran's arrogant, set in his ways, and uncompromising. But he is also smart and wants the best for Tarris. I truly believe that."

"If he doesn't stab Imayani in the back and try to take the throne for himself," Rai whispered.

Tysar shook his head. "He isn't like that. He would rather rule a united Tarris than one suspicious that he had killed Imayani."

"You seem to know him awfully well," Rai said.

"You don't think I sent spies and looked into him as soon as Imayani mentioned the marriage? I had spies tracking him for months. He is all that you think he is: a stubborn noble who knows little of how life truly is for the Tarrisian people but he is also a man who paid to reinforce the Waypoints near his city. He reduced tariffs for small merchant businesses. Kleran cares about Tarris and its people."

"Why do you keep bringing him up?" Rai asked. It was the same out in the desert, as if Tysar was trying to get a rise from him.

"I just… I know once you may have felt differently about Imayani," Tysar said. Rai opened his mouth to speak but Tysar lifted a hand. "I'm not making any presumptions. I'm here to protect both of them and I want to make sure you aren't planning to hurt Kleran, that's all."

Rai blew out a breath. Of course it had crossed his mind. He could kill the Yontar monarch without anyone knowing. *But Imayani would know*, a voice said. And the chances of his army helping Imayani reclaim Asuriya after he turned up dead were slim.

They both leant close to the flames. This conversation was treasonous and they were under the same roof as the empress and a monarch. Even a drunken passing comment in a Night Theatre could have someone tossed in a cell. And here they were talking about Rai assassinating one of the monarchs. "If he doesn't press any threat to Imayani, I have no intention of hurting the man," Rai said.

Tysar weighed him up trying to judge if he was lying. Rai stared back, unflinching.

"Okay." Tysar sighed and pulled back. "I'm sorry, Rai. I didn't mean to throw accusations at you. I'm on your side, old friend. I just wanted to check that we were on the same page."

The most frustrating part was that Tysar was right to ask. It *had* crossed Rai's mind. But it wasn't what was right for Tarris. If they join in marriage, Tarris would be all the stronger for it. He wouldn't draw a weapon on the monarch unprovoked. He wouldn't endanger the country because Imayani wasn't meant to be with Kleran. They all had their duties and he was a soldier.

"It's okay, I understand—"

Fax usually used words rather than impressions, as the shade had grown a liking to acting more human in the years since their bonding. So when Fax returned in a flurry of impressions, Rai knew something was wrong.

Tysar froze, mirroring Rai's stillness. "What is it?" Tysar asked.

"The guards at the door are dead," Rai said.

Tysar sprang to his feet but Rai waved him to still. "Poisoned," Rai said.

"I'll go check on the empress," Tysar said.

"No. Help me barricade the doors." Rai stood and made for a wooden bench in the corner.

"What if they're already inside?" Tysar asked.

"There's no one here. But outside Fax has spotted assassins dressed in black surrounding the Waypoint." Rai crept towards the door.

Tysar's eyes went wide. "How did they find us?"

"It could have been anyone," Rai said. He stuck his head out the door to see the guard lying dead against the Waypoint. A half-eaten roll lay at his side. Rai pushed the door shut and pressed the bench against it. "The servants who saw us last night or this morning. It could have been someone on the road that spotted us. It doesn't matter. We need to control the entrances."

They piled up furniture by either door while Fax woke Imayani, Mino, and Yeru, informing them on what was going on. The monarch still didn't know about the shade and Rai wanted to keep it that way. So Tysar woke him and brought him upstairs to Imayani's room.

They all gathered around a single lantern, the light doing little more than giving shape to the others in the room. Moonlight shone through the window. Mino made to look out but Tysar pulled her back and shook his head. Rai stood against the window frame peering out across the black sand. Tysar matched him on the other side standing like a sentry.

"What about the other guards?" Kleran asked.

"Dead too," Rai said.

"They were poisoned," Tysar said.

That elicited some gasps from the dark.

"I don't understand. We ate and drank what they did," Imayani said.

"It was probably given to them before we left the city," Rai said. "Guards often share coffees or snacks on watch. Whoever did this has been careful and didn't want us to know that they were here until it was too late."

"Like being stuck in a Waypoint in the middle of the desert at night," Mino muttered under her breath.

There, Fax said. The shade directed Rai's eyesight and right enough, he saw a line of slightly lighter dark moved across the black dunes. *I count four*, Rai thought.

Another four on the other side, Fax said.

"There's eight assassins surrounding the building," Rai said. Tysar's gaze snapped up to meet his. He knew as Rai did that these assassins would be well trained to have pulled off a stunt like this. None of the others had combat training, which meant this was all up to Rai and Tysar.

"I'll get the other side," Tysar said and jogged off through the building.

Rai unslung his bow. *I'm trusting you to adjust my aim*, Rai thought to Fax. It was too dark for Rai to see the assassins against the black sand but Fax could. Nocking the arrow, flames burst up the length of the shaft. Rai loosed it before the assassins could glance up and the arrow zipped out the window. A scream broke the night as the first fell.

The ruse was up and the other three rushed the building before Rai could take aim again. Rai hoped Tysar was quick enough to kill one on the other side of the building before the cry of pain alerted them. He felt a surge of adrenaline as he ran out to the landing where the stairs led back down to the common room and stables. He wasn't meant for politicking. He wasn't meant to be sitting around dinner tables or discussing shadowy machinations. This. The buzz of the fight, daggers in hand. This was what Rai was made for. It's what he had trained for.

"I got one," Tysar said.

"That leaves six." Rai took for the stairs. "Take the back door by the stables."

They passed down the steps and into the darkened ground floor. Rai had extinguished the fire and lanterns leaving it in deep shadow. He moved for the door. Fax spread through the shadows of the room further darkening the space and Rai stood in the centre staring at the barricaded door.

The embers from the dying fire shone in his eyes. He stared at the door, waiting for it to be thrown open. Then, the slaughter would begin. But the door did not move. It was only when the scream came from upstairs that Rai realised his mistake.

Fool! He shouted at himself barrelling back up the stairs. They would have tried the doors and upon realising they were blocked taken to scaling the building. Rai would have done the same.

Stepping out onto the second floor landing, Rai threw his dagger. The door was open just enough for the dagger to slip through. Rai threw the door open. He concentrated on the blood on his wrist and spun his hand around. The dagger matched the motion, arcing to the right and slashing one of the assassins. Their body hit the floor as Fax cut through the shadows, collapsing two of the others' lungs.

Rai glanced around the room. No one was hurt. On closer inspection, Rai noted that Kleran had a sword out and had been in combat against one of the assassins. His breathing was ragged but he had remained unharmed. Rai hadn't expected the monarch to know how to fight.

That's three of the six, Rai thought as Fax withdrew its spikes letting the corpses fall to the ground. The sounds of fighting echoed around the Waypoint. Rai spun and stalked through the building. He peered out the window on the far side to see Tysar engaged in a fight with two of the other assassins. The third was scaling the building.

Rai dropped out of the second storey window landing atop the climbing assassin and knocking him from the wall. The assassin's bones crunched when they hit the black sand. They did not stir.

With a grunt, Tysar drove his sword through a felled assassin's shoulder. He screamed and thrashed but Tysar didn't give him the chance to get back up. The other was lying on the sand, gasping for air, a slit across his throat draining him of blood. His panicked eyes met Rai's before Fax cut into his skull putting the assassin out of his misery.

"Who sent you?" Tysar asked the last remaining assassin.

The assassin spat at him and Tysar leant on the sword causing the assassin to scream and buck.

"I do not fear the Judging," the assassin said after his screaming subsided.

"That's good," Tysar said. "It should be the living you fear." Tysar spun a dagger in his other hand and drove it into the man's thigh dragging it up a couple inches towards his waist. His shriek carried across the desert. A shrill sound that would haunt most men and woman.

"Easy, Tysar," Rai said. He glanced about the desert but neither him nor Fax could see anything else. "We don't want to draw attention to ourselves."

Tysar grunted and yanked the blade from the man's leg, eliciting more screams. Dropping to his haunches, Rai met the assassin's gaze. Fax swirled through Rai's shadow making it convulse and shift like disturbed water. Lucidity flooded the man's face as he watched in horror.

"Who sent you?" Rai asked.

The assassin didn't respond and Fax started to leak out as black tendrils.

"Haduan!" the assassin shouted. So it was the Monarch of Ossin that sent the assassins. "He has spies everywhere. He knew about Kleran's forces leaving Yontar and that Kleran was at the capital. Please! It's all I know."

Rai let Fax continue to spread outward. The man's eyes widened. "Are there more of you?" Rai asked.

The man screwed his face up conflicted on speaking. Fax touched the assassin and he squealed. "Yes! There are more. I don't know how many. He put a bounty on the empress and Kleran's head! I swear that's it! That's all I know!"

Rai stood as Fax receded into his shadow.

"What are you?" The assassin's voice was weak and dry.

"The darkness."

Fax jutted out and split the man's skull in two.

"Get the others. We're leaving."

26

The Shadow Wall

"**B**ut it's at least a couple hours until the Sun Eye begins its watch," Kleran said.

Tysar was readying the hyian as Rai corralled the others down the stairs. The once peaceful quiet of the Waypoint had sharpened to an edge. What was once a tranquil quiet became a held breath.

"We don't have time to wait until sunrise," Rai said. "There could be more assassins moving on us right now. The Ossin monarch knows our plan. If he can kill us out in the desert, reaching the capital won't matter."

"Haduan knows?" Imayani asked. Her eyes were wide. Any semblance of serenity shattered, laying in shards amongst the corpses of the guards and assassins. Imayani had assassins come for her before. But never like this. Never in the open where she was undefended.

"We need to toss any food and drinks we haven't already tried," Rai said. "We don't know what else could have been poisoned." Rai balled his fist. He hated feeling so out of his depth.

"What will we eat and drink?" Mino asked as they made their way through to the stables. The hyian shifted and shook their coats sensing that something was wrong.

"We should reach the camp in a week. We can live off what we have opened already if we ration it," Rai said. "Quickly. We can talk more come daybreak. We need to ride fast."

"Can't you just kill any assassins that come for us like you did these ones?" Kleran asked.

"I don't think you understand. We're only two men." Rai gestured to Tysar who threw the stable doors open. "If Haduan learns that eight assassins weren't enough, he'll send eighty."

"If he kills us, he's won before any battle has even begun," Imayani said.

That knowledge put fiery coals beneath their feet. They set about readying the hyian and soon they were riding the black dunes of night.

The company pushed hard. It would tire the hyians quickly but all agreed that they needed to create some distance between them and the Waypoint. Rai led them with Tysar at the back. He hadn't wanted to fall into a leading position but it had happened so quickly and naturally. Rai felt a tug of guilt for taking Tysar's role. *None of that matters*, Rai reminded himself. They just needed to survive this.

The hyian were skittish running upon the hard black sand. They were used to the soft sand of day. Few were foolish enough to travel on the black dunes. The others had been hardened to the situation but Rai felt their unease and Fax noted how often they scanned the horizon in search of assassins and that which roams the desert at night. They hadn't been riding for an hour when the first was spotted.

"Hey, I think I saw someone standing on that dune!" Kleran called over the rush of movement.

Black sand phantoms.

"Ignore it," Rai shouted back. "Do not look at its face!"

Even knowing the ways of the black sand phantoms, one could easily be convinced they saw someone they knew, usually someone who had died. A voice would draw travellers nearer and it would transform into its true self. No one who had seen a black sand phantom's true form had survived. They knew so little about them. Some said they were mindless remnants of a god. Torn from the true body and left to wander the black sands of night. They never appeared during the day but roamed through the night and seemed to grow in number and strength during the dark hours.

A wisp of shadow trailed across the path and a cloak figure formed in the darkness. An impression against the black sand. It took all Rai's will not to pull on the reins. He blinked and the figure was gone. For a moment, it had looked like…

He shook his head.

No, it couldn't have been.

"Don't slow down!" Rai shouted. "They're black sand phantoms!"

As he said the words, doubt flickered in his mind. What if they weren't? What if it *was* Kon he had seen? Should he not stop and check? Rai started to slow and Imayani came to ride alongside him.

"Rai look at me," she said. Her voice sounded distant as he saw Kon in the distance. "Rai, I need you here." The desperation in her tone pulled Rai out of the trance and he glanced over. She nodded drawing her lips to a line.

"Thank you," Rai said coming back to himself.

Wordless whispers lashed at them like the wind. The phantoms drew individuals out and several times another in the company had to rein them back in. No one spoke of what the whispers said or what they saw. The black dunes rose around them, creating a valley of sand. The hyians began to flag and they had to let up on their pace in fear of being stranded out there with injured mounts.

The sky darkened as the Moon Eye completed its watch throwing them into dark hour. They lit lanterns and held them aloft, warding back the darkness. Riding in silence, the party searched for another glimpse of the black sand phantoms or anything else hiding in the dark.

"I meant what I said," Imayani said. Rai startled at her voice. He was so focused on ignoring the phantom's whispers and feeling for Fax, who flew ahead to ensure that there were no threats, that he almost missed Imayani's words.

"I do need you here," Imayani said. "If you hadn't come then we would all have died in that Waypoint. So thank you."

Rai inclined his head, unsure what to say.

"It's my father I hear in the whispers," Imayani said. Her eyes had glazed over. "He tells me that I've failed him and our line."

"That's the phantoms. You've been a great ruler. Especially during these difficult times," Rai said.

"Have I, though? Wouldn't a great ruler have prevented Tarris from falling upon difficult times? I was never meant for this."

"Difficult times come to all. It's what you do about it that separates one who merely sits on a throne and a ruler," Rai said.

A smile tugged at the side of Imayani's lip. "You've changed in the last five years. Older. Wiser," Imayani said.

"Wiser comparative to then, perhaps," Rai said. "Things ended poorly between us and I understand I can never earn back your trust but know that I will continue to protect you and do what's best for Tarris."

There was a pause.

"You know, when you left for the Verdin Guild, I followed," Imayani said.

Rai turned to face her.

"My father sent guards to find me. I had barely made it beyond the walls. But I wanted to bring you back. I was under no illusion that my father had sent you away with no plans to have you return."

A flood of melancholy hit Rai. He had known it was her father who wanted rid of him but to hear that Imayani had tried to bring him back unravelled a deep-seated concern Rai didn't know he had been holding. Chasing after him showed true concern. He had worried that she hadn't truly cared about him leaving. He was lesser. A soldier. Not someone who would matter to the daughter of the emperor. But he had.

Rai opened his mouth to speak when Mino's shrill tone ripped through the moment.

"Rai!"

They both spun around to see that a lantern from the party had separated from the rest trailing off into the dark. Tysar had fallen behind and he was off his hyian, lantern held aloft.

And he was approaching a cloaked figure.

Rai galloped back towards him. As he approached, the firelight lit his friend's face. He was transfixed, tears running down his cheeks.

Leaping from his hyian, Rai tossed his own lantern at the phantom. Tysar lifted a hand and reached out. It was inches from the phantom when Rai's lantern burst. In a flash of flame and light, the phantom let out a hiss and dispersed into shadow. Rai grabbed Tysar and pulled him back and they both toppled to the sand. The darkness that had once been the phantom swirled and coalesced.

"Rai?" Tysar said looking about, dazed.

Pushing to his feet, Rai felt Fax start to fly back from scouting ahead but the shade was far off and it could be a minute or more before it reached him. Plenty of time for a phantom to kill them all.

The dark started to take shape. Contorted faces swam in the black like impressions pressed against fabric. Rai recognised some of them: Kon. Zin. Sen. And others that he had killed. The faces looked pained and yet wore crooked smiles.

A squeal came from Imayani. Rai turned to see the dark reaching around them like a wall. It was blocking them in and moving too fast to outrun.

"Group together!" Rai called.

They pulled together as the pulsing black wall drew ever closer. Setting the lanterns around them in a ring of light did little to dissuade the dark. Rai nocked an arrow. It lit as he pulled back the bow string. He loosed. The flaming arrow plunged into the black and disappeared. The phantom was unphased and continued to close around them until they were walled in.

"Try the lanterns!" Imayani said.

Tysar waved his lantern around. That, too, made no difference, so Tysar held it out to the shadows edge and thrust it into the black wall. There was a grinding sound.

An extinguished and crushed up lantern launched back into their encased circle. Mino squealed jumping out of the way as it bounded to a stop.

"Now what?" Kleran asked. "What say you, scholar?"

Yeru stood stunned. "I… I don't know. I've never seen anything like this."

With a rush of energy, Rai felt Fax return.

Can you fight it? Rai asked.

Fax flicked out as a whip but the shade just passed through the dark shroud. Then taking the shape of a crow, Fax dove into the black.

There's something in here. Like a heart made of darkness, but every time I get close, I'm pushed back, Fax said.

Fax sent an impression of where the heart was located.

"There!" Rai pointed. "Focus our efforts there. The phantom has a heart. On my mark!"

Imayani, Mino, Yeru, and Kleran waved torches around in a vain attempt to slow the enclosing space. Tysar filled his sword with a blood vial at his hip and it burst into flames. Then he nodded to Rai.

"Now!" Rai loosed.

The arrow tore through the air becoming enveloped by the wall, followed by the thrown lanterns. At the same time, Tysar stabbed his flaming blade deep into the black. The darkness rippled. They all pulled back into a circle as the wall of shadow thrummed and spat out arcs of darkness.

It ceased moving. Kleran grinned, picking up one of the

remaining lanterns.

Fax, did we get it?

The shade sent back panic.

The wall of shadow was studying them. Fax felt it prod through the shadows as if realising the shade was something new. It had merely been playing with its food before. The knowledge came through like the phantom was in Rai's head.

The others cheered thinking it was all over. Imayani's smile faded when she looked to Rai.

The wall rushed towards them.

Fax tore through the shadows creating a dome around the company. Someone screamed as they tumbled in this too-small dome of protection.

"What's happening?!" someone shouted. Rai was too focused to respond. He felt Fax strain as it held back the phantom. The darkness would crush them soon. They were going to die. Rai couldn't think straight with Fax pulsing in his head.

Think, Rai. Think! Rai thought. But there was nothing amid the swirling frenzy of terror.

"How long has it been dark hour?" Tysar asked Kleran.

The Monarch stuttered. "What?"

"You're a numbers guy," Tysar said.

"The hour should almost be up," Kleran said.

Rai tried to take in what they were saying but his mind was awash with the battle between Fax and the phantom. It was communicating with Fax through impressions, much like the shade had done early on before it learned to use language.

And one thing was clear in its communications. The wall was

not trying to consume them anymore. It was trying to consume Fax.

The phantom believed they were the same. It had been dormant but it remembered. Remember being one.

Rai's head throbbed as he attempted to perceive the conversation between the two. They couldn't be the same. His shade was from the dark place not Tarris. Flashes of pain erupted in his mind as Fax fought back the encroaching dark.

Blearily, Rai realised he was on the ground. When had he fallen? The others were around him. All he could feel was the fight of the shadows. And Fax was losing. The phantom was breaking through and it would consume his shade and then the company.

Then he felt it. A searing burning pain flared across his mind. The phantom buzzed and thrashed and then it pulled back and fled. Rai watched through Fax's impressions of the world as the phantom slithered into the softening sands and the Sun Eye glared from the horizon.

The light had burned it away. Every muscle relaxed as relief blossomed within Rai.

And he drifted into unconsciousness.

27

The Dark That Lives

Everything was set. They had a plan to break into the Thousand Floor Palace. Bas mapped out a route and had several contingencies for their passage through the palace to the tear. Once there, with the help of Bom, they would steal the black blade and figure out how to close the rend. A lot could go wrong with a plan like this but Nya was sure they could make it work.

Kit had stolen the page about the black dagger from Mirt's apartment which contained passages on ways to close the tear. They were all theoretical, as the scholar claimed he didn't want to risk not being able to open another tear into the pocket world. However, Mirt seemed quite confident in his theories.

Bas had spent weeks tracking the palace's patrols before getting arrested and being sent to the dark place with the Doomed Others and said the best window to gain entry was in a couple days, which was plenty time to gather supplies and prepare.

Nya perused the morning markets. The tarps strung across the street beat back some of the blazing heat but sweat still ran down the side of her face. She caught a drip with the back of her hand and blew out a breath. The old woman behind the stall grinned at her.

"I have hats that will hide you from the Sun Eye's gaze," she said, rummaging around under the stall. She pulled out the most hideous hat Nya had ever seen. It was wide brimmed with a tall dome shape.

"No, thank you," Nya said.

"I'll give you it for a coin?" the old woman offered.

Nya wouldn't have taken it if the woman were to offer *her* a coin for it. She shook her head and kept walking. Bas was at the next stall bartering over a length of rope that they needed for one of the backup plans in case they couldn't close the tear and had to escape. Nya had never seen an Urdahl barter before. He was unflinching. The stoic hard gaze broke through the vendor and Bas walked away with the rope for half the price Nya would have expected.

"I should have had you get all the supplies," Nya said, coming to his side.

"What else is on the list?" Bas asked.

Nya unrolled the piece of parchment as they walked with the flow of the crowd. "A spice crate to pick up for Illy but we have everything we need for the plan."

They made for the aya traders at the edge of the market. There, travelling merchants set up their bulk stock of crates that large businesses like inns bought.

Pushing through the crowd, Nya would have missed Bas suddenly stopping if Bom hadn't told her. He was staring at something. She followed his gaze but couldn't see what he was looking at. Already other market goers jostled and complained about him blocking the path.

"What is it?" Nya asked.

"The essence," Bas said.

Nya frowned.

He noticed her confusion and added, "The essence that clings to the husks and you."

Nya spun. "Here? Is there another husk?" She scanned the street but Nya couldn't see anything and she heard no screams. Bom bloomed outward and returned without finding anything, either.

"I don't know. It's a block over," Bas said. "It doesn't look very big."

"We should go and check it out," Nya said.

Had it tracked her to the market? Hundreds of people wandered this street. How many would die because a husk had followed her here? She remembered how close they had come to dying in the nobles' library when they fought the last husk. But Bas was a talented fighter and she wouldn't let anymore die for her.

Bas glanced at her.

"We can take one, and you said it was small," Nya said.

He hesitated but inclined his head and they set off toward the essence. Bas weaved between the people with ease and Nya had to shove through the crowd as to not lose him. They veered around a corner and Bas slowed at the edge of a market square.

"What is it?" Nya asked.

"It's over there," Bas said. He pointed through the crowd. The people continued to go about the market. Too calm, Nya thought.

If a husk was truly on the other side of this square, people would be screaming and running away. Unless someone had captured it?

They barrelled through the throng, eliciting some curses. Pushing through the bulk of the people, they came out onto a busy thoroughfare. Bas skidded to a stop staring up the street.

"It's him," Bas said, gesturing to a man in palace guard garb. "He's producing the same dark essence as the husk and you."

"He must have gone through the tear," Nya said. Her resolve solidified. "Let's follow him."

They stalked up the street following the man at a distance. He walked with the purposeful gait of someone going somewhere. The man didn't hesitate at turns or slow to look at goods. *He's not headed for the palace*, Nya thought. That was in the other direction. Was the guard headed home for the afternoon?

If so, there might be more notes to check out, Nya thought.

The image of a shocked and impressed Kit came to mind. He wasn't the only one who could learn things on the street.

They tracked the man for several blocks before he turned off the main street and down an alley. Nya sent Bom ahead to follow. Just as Nya turned the corner with Bas, Bom sent a too late panicked warning. Standing in the mouth of the alley was the man, a grin lined his face. Bom lay as a patch of black on the dirt as another shade *pinned Bom down* with spikes of shadow.

"Well," the man said.

Bas didn't let him finish. He launched himself at the man, his fist aimed right for the man's head. The palace guard's shade battered the arm away and the guard swept in with his boot cracking against Bas' face. The Urdahl staggered, his shock clear as blood dripped from his burst nose. This was the first time Nya had seen true emotion on Bas' face.

The palace guard's smile widened. It was almost demonic, the way it stretched across his face. Two tendrils burst from the shade and pinned Bas to the wall. One ripped through his side and the other caught his arm. Bas hissed as blood began to pour from the wounds.

Nya pulled her concealed dagger from her waist and screamed, leaping forward. The palace guard backhanded her and she fell, reeling. He approached Bas. A well of panic filled Nya and fuelled Bom, who thrashed beneath the guard's shade. But even with part of it holding Bas, the shade held Bom down without issue. Nya ran at the palace guard and this time he turned and disarmed her in one swipe. A thin cut ran up Nya's forearm. His sword moved too quickly. She hadn't even seen it touch her.

"They didn't mention how impatient you were," the guard said. "I'm going to have a little fun with your friend here and then we can go."

His sword flashed out and cracked Nya across the face before his words could register. It all happened so quickly. As she fell to the ground and consciousness fled her, Nya heard Bas start to scream.

Nya woke to the sound of crunching meat. The hard ground sent a chill through her and her head thumped and pulsed. Clutching her temples, Nya sat up noting her surroundings. She was in a cell. Bom buzzed in her mind but it blended into her fuzzy thoughts.

A guard sat across the room eating at a table. Memories came flooding back of the alleyway. Nya lurched for the bars.

"What have you done with Bas?" she shouted.

The guard finished tearing the meat from the bone and then let the bone drop to the plate. It wasn't the same guard from the alley. The one with the shade.

Wait.

Someone else had a shade. The realisation rang in her mind.

Nya rattled the bars and the guard glanced up. "What did you do with him?"

"You came in alone," the guard said. He was tall. Dark hair drooped from his black cap and he had the beginnings of a beard fuzzing his face.

Nya reached out with Bom and cut the lock to the cell.

"I wouldn't do that if I were you," the guard said. Nya ignored him and shoved the door open. Then she kicked the entrance to the cell room door open and sprinted out into the sandstone corridor. Nya looked over her shoulder as she ran but the guard didn't follow. Glancing back almost caused Nya to topple over but she regained her footing and kept moving. Battering into the next door, it flew open into a busy room. Scholars froze to stare at her.

Mirt stood at a table.

"Nya," he said. Surprise lined his face.

Bom burst from Nya in a shroud of shadow ready to explode. Mirt stepped towards her hands held aloft in a calming gesture.

"We don't want to hurt you," Mirt said.

"What did you do to my friend?" If she found where they were keeping him, Nya could break them both out. Bom flared a warning in her mind. The other shade was here.

The chamber darkened.

"Adani, don't," Mirt said. His eyes darted back and forth.

"It's been a while since I've had worthy prey," the guard, Adani's, voice whispered in her ear. Nya turned but there was only darkness. An undulating smog of shadow floated behind her.

Nya screamed and Bom erupted outward forcing back the smothering black. It fled like dark to a flame. Nya saw a door and in the crack of darkness and ran.

She burst out into a palace corridor. Already her lungs burned. Nya attempted to straighten her thoughts but it was like trying to count while someone was screaming in your ear.

All the corridors looked the same. She veered around a corner to find the same simple sandstone walls around her. Braziers roared and shook as she passed. Nya threw herself down corridor after corridor. Eventually, she slowed and pressed against the wall struggling to draw breath. Her head pivoted to look back. The corridor was empty.

"Bom, how did that shade hold you down?" Nya asked.

It is strong, Bom said and Nya felt the fear in its voice. *And I did not see it coming. It has been in your world longer than me.*

So they couldn't fight it. They had to escape then. They had to—

He's here.

Nya's breath caught. How could he catch up so quickly? This Adani hadn't been chasing them. Bom had checked. She looked down the corridor. It was still, the flames within the braziers the only movement. The crackle of the fire the only sound. But she felt the presence through Bom.

Black shadow oozed from the palace wall like a slime. Nya couldn't move.

Nya, run.

It dripped down and pooled at her feet.

Nya!

Within it, the face of the palace guard, Adani, Mirt had called him, started to form from the darkness of his shade. It was as if he could travel through shadows themselves.

Run!

He was smiling.

Nya sprinted down the corridor. As she ran, the walls started to leak shadow too and his voice soft and near echoed around her.

"You can't run from the shadow at your feet. You can't run from the darkness in your mind. The sooner you see this, the sooner you can stop. The sooner you can rest."

Cold prickled Nya's neck as if someone were breathing on it. Braving a glance over her shoulder, Nya saw the hallway being devoured by the darkness. This wasn't like the Ahmune in the Library of Nenelan. It was a tangible black wave. Thick and opaque. Conjured by her mind or by Adani, Nya couldn't tell.

"I can sense it in you. You already know that it's part of you," Adani said. "Like it's part of me."

She wanted to scream into the dark but Nya didn't have enough air to manage more than a gasp.

"We're the same. Not meant for a normal life. I know you felt it while you played server at that inn. You had everything you thought you ever wanted."

Nya tripped and skidded across the stone scraping her knees.

"Stop!" she screamed to the pulsating wave. It did stop, then. Inches away from her.

"But it wasn't enough."

Adani took form from the shadow and stepped out in front of her.

"You should have been happy at the inn," Adani said. "You had people who loved you. You had a roof over your head and food in your belly and yet darkness remained."

"How do you know all this?" Nya asked.

"Because I'm the same. I tried to find my place in this world. I had everything I ever wanted but the darkness would not dissipate." Adani stalked back and forth mumbling the words more to himself than to Nya. Suddenly, he faced her and smiled.

"That's because it doesn't dissipate, Nya. So why fight it? We are the dark now."

His words resonated stronger than she cared to admit. After defeating Ma-atan and returning to the Patched Cloak, everything was supposed to be fine. Everything was supposed to get better. But it didn't. Kit had withdrawn. She had found no purpose in her life. And the darkness had followed her. It was there for her. It would always find her. Nya thought she could escape it but it wasn't possible to run from your own shadow.

It was part of her.

"What do you want from me?" Nya asked.

Adani smiled. "We were searching for you."

"Why?"

"*It* wants you to come to back the pocket world."

"The dark place in the tear?" Nya felt a shiver creep up her spine. The place with the ever-storming sky and monsters hiding in the dark. She vowed never to go back.

"Yes. It asked for you specifically."

"What asked for me?" Everything seemed to freeze in that moment as she waited. Nya knew the answer but she needed to hear it.

"The Dark that lives there."

28

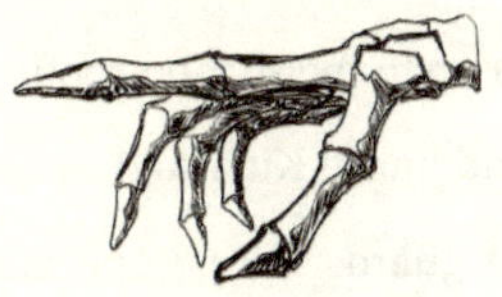

Death Lurks

Kit knew something was wrong. He paced behind the bar while Wenson swept the inn's common room. Light chatter came from across the room, where Illy served a customer draped in a cloak.

"They're taking too long," Kit said.

Wenson grumbled. He knew what Kit was saying even if he didn't understand the words. "They've been gone for hours. They should be back with the supplies by now."

The kitchen had long gone cold for the afternoon, leaving only the smell of spiced coffee and tea permeating the air. Wenson scraped the sand towards the back door. He paused at the end of the bar and leant on the broom, eyeing Kit.

"They fine," he said.

"They no fine," Kit said in the same clipped tone. "I should go out and look for them."

Just then, the door to the inn swung open. Two guards entered carrying a beaten, bleeding Bas. His skin was pale and his tunic shredded where several bloody wounds leaked onto the floor. The entire common room froze and stared as blood began to pool.

"He said he stayed here," the first guard said.

Kit and Wenson rushed over to help carry Bas to a booth while Illy sent the customers up to the shaded rooftop seating.

"Where did you find him?" Kit asked.

Worry creased the guards' faces. The first one shrugged and said, "Laying in an alley, half dead."

"What alley?" Kit snapped.

"Off the east market square, near the palace," the other guard said.

"Was there a girl with him?" Kit asked.

The guard shook his head. Bas was dipping in and out of consciousness.

"Bas, where is Nya?" he asked.

Clarity sharpened the Urdahl's gaze but it faded as quickly as it appeared.

"Bas! Nya?" Kit shouted.

"Hey, hey, hey," Wenson said, pulling Kit back.

Bas spluttered, spitting out blood as he managed one word.

"Taken."

Illy spoke with the guards and sent them away, teas in hand as thanks, while Wenson ran off to fetch bandages. Kit was no doctor but went about cleaning Bas' wounds with his mind elsewhere. He had patched up enough gang members to know what to do before the doctor got here.

Taken? It didn't make sense. Who would take Nya? If the palace had caught onto their infiltration plan then the whole inn would have been swarmed with guards. Bas mumbled shade in his stupor. Was this something to do with Bom? No one knew about the shade apart from those at the inn and Rai.

Had the palace somehow found out about Nya's shade and taken her?

A hand fell onto Kit's shoulder tearing him from his thoughts. He glanced up to Wenson who watched him with concern. Kit saw that he had wrapped Bas' cut far too many times. Kit sighed and started to unravel the bandage.

The cuts were deep. Not the glancing cuts of a blade, they were more like the piercing stab wounds of a spear. But they were too wide to be the spears that the palace guards used. Still, Kit guessed Bas would heal in time. It almost seemed purposeful in the way he had been stabbed to miss all his main organs.

Kit hadn't been there but he couldn't help but think this was his fault.

Bound to death, it stalks the deathless like a killer in wait.

That was what the *Tome of the Ancients* had said. Was this what it meant? Was he bound to death and where he had been spared, now others would pay the price?

It was the next day before Bas was able to tell them what had happened. The doctor arrived that night and put an ointment on his wounds to ward off infection as well as a draught to help with the pain and let Bas sleep. He woke the next day more panicked than

Kit had ever seen him as he told the story of the palace guard with the shade.

Illy, Wenson, Lem, Bas and Kit argued for some time about what to do. Illy and Bas were the voices of reason, wanting to find out more information before trying anything. While Kit and Wenson wanted to storm the palace. But that was foolish and, in their hearts, they knew that.

Kit reached out to his connections on the street but no one knew anything about a missing girl or a strange palace guard with a moving shadow. It was rare that his connections came back with *nothing*. Not even a whisper. Which led Kit to believe that they were keeping their mouths shut. That meant that there were some powerful people behind this. Silence spills secrets as well as words do.

Bas was out of bed and helping around the inn the following day despite Illy's protesting. At night Kit and Bas looked over their plans to get into the palace but they all required Nya and Bom. Without the shade, infiltrating the palace was impossible. Kit slammed his fists on the table, startling Dust. He apologised and pet the sand fox.

Kit found himself wandering the late afternoon streets. Walking cleared his head and right now, that was what he needed. He needed to *think*.

Yontar was beginning to wake from qed. Shutters rattled open, letting in the blaring light of the Sun Eye. The cool breeze carried the smells and sounds of sizzling meat being prepared for afternoon meals.

Mirt and the scholars had to be involved. A palace guard with a shade meant they had continued to send others into the tear. Bas had told them that they had followed the guard because the Urdahl could see some connection between him and the dark place. However, Bas said he could only see the trail if he was close. And yet he said the tear was always in his sight, like a black cloud around the palace. He wouldn't elaborate how he gained the ability to see such things, claiming it was '*of the Urdahl*' and would remain so.

Leaning on a street corner, Kit stared at the monolithic Thousand Floor Palace. It rose high as a testament to what the Tarrisians could do. Few knew of the horrors it hid. Even fewer knew of the horrors it let roam the city. They had heard little of other husks appearing around the city. That was reassuring in a way. But it brought more questions than answers. However, one thing was certain. Nya was right. They needed to close that gateway into the dark realm.

Kit was sure he wouldn't need to convince the others to help rescue Nya. But wouldn't he be leading them to their deaths? Without Nya and her shade, it was hopeless.

Death. The black void.

Even after Jirma translated the book, Kit couldn't shake the panic he felt when he thought about dying. If Ma-atan was a creature from ancient times and not the deity they thought it was, then was the afterlife, the Reed Fields of Aru and Duat, all a lie too? He hadn't voiced his worry to the others for it seemed silly, but Kit couldn't shake this immobilizing fear of the nothing that could follow.

He dreamt of falling through a black expanse and there was nothing to grab onto. There was nothing to see or feel but somehow, he knew he was falling. And that he would continue to fall through the nothing until the end of days.

"Are you alright, son?"

An elderly merchant had ducked down to Kit's eyeline. Only then did he realise that he was clutching his chest, breathing hard. He no longer had to breath but that didn't stop his body from mimicking the action like muscle memory.

Sweat beaded his brow and his stomach lurched as the world spun. He cleared his throat but couldn't manage anything other than a curt nod to the concerned merchant. Glancing around, he saw others staring at him. He had to get away.

Kit took off through the narrow streets where tall buildings obscured the palace from his vision. He attempted to quiet his thoughts but they were a whirl of half-formed ideas and worries. Kit had been so in his thoughts that it took him several minutes of walking behind Lem before he noticed who he had been trailing.

Lem had left the inn early that morning stating that it was his friend, Sleeping Siv's birthday. Kit had never seen this supposed friend and for a while, Kit thought Siv was imaginary. The invisible friend that hid Lem's boots that he likely just misplaced.

However, Lem carried a single flower. A strange gift, but a gift, nevertheless. Kit tailed Lem. It had been some time since he had to follow someone unnoticed, however, it wasn't a skill that one forgot. Staying in the shadowed eaves, Kit moved silently through the streets. It gave him something to focus on. Something to calm his mind.

Lem didn't have his familiar spring in his step and warning bells rang in Kit's mind. Something was off about the old man.

They wound through the streets, leading to the eastern part of the city. Lem unlocked and slipped into a private gated garden. After waiting several moments, Kit threw himself over the metal fencing. Inside was a rock garden with a small patch of greenery on the far side. An algae-skinned pond caught the sunlight as Kit crept around a rock sculpture. Private gardens weren't common in the city. Often they were used for…

Lem sat under a tree beside a grave. And on the grave was a boot.

He leant over and whispered to the grave as he placed the flower inside the boot which had been filled with dirt.

Kit's heart sank and he suddenly felt foolish. This was an intimate moment and here he was, creeping around in the shrubbery. He turned to go and a branch snapped underfoot. Kit closed his eyes and groaned as Lem called out, "Who's there?"

Stepping out from his hiding spot, Kit held his hands up in a placating gesture. "I'm sorry, Lem. I saw you walking and you were in here before I caught up with you."

The old man smiled. "Come then. I'll introduce you to Sleeping Siv."

Kit made his way over and sat beside Lem in the shade of the tree. The breeze shifted the branches, crackling in the calm and beams of light filtered through the leaves. Lem didn't speak but took a deep breath with his eyes closed.

"I really am sorry, Lem. I—"

"There is no need to apologise," Lem said. "This is Siv. He's my best friend." He gestured to the grave. "We used to be thieves in a gang, you know. He could steal the boots from your feet and the hat from the head, all the while making you stare at your elbow." He laughed.

Kit glanced over to the boot. It was Lem's. The one he had been missing for a week now. Kit didn't know what to say. Lem must have noticed as he laid a hand on Kit's shoulder and smiled at him.

"There is no reason to be sad. Death is the end for us all."

Kit swallowed. Why was everyone talking about dying? First with Jirma and his wife, and now Lem. Bas was hurt and Nya could be dead for all Kit knew.

Bound to death, it stalks the deathless like a killer in wait. Had Kit been led here? Since becoming deathless it seemed to be everywhere he turned. It crept in the shadows and danced in the sunlight. The inevitable end breathing down his neck.

"Doesn't it scare you?" Kit's voice came out small. He felt a fool for asking. And Lem, of all people. Not to mention that Kit asked while Lem was mourning his best friend on his birthday. Kit couldn't meet his gaze.

"Yes," Lem said. Kit glanced up. "I'd be a black sand-footed fool not to. We don't know when it'll happen. We don't know what follows. Will we end up in a bootless land? Will there be something after?"

The sounds of the city were muted by the garden walls and Kit felt like he and Lem were alone in the world. Scardrae burrowed out the sand and scuttled across the garden. Linsips, thin-bodied flies that had flesh-coloured mushroom tops sheltering them from the Sun Eye, buzzed in the air. For a place of death, it was a lively garden.

"And the unknown will always be scary. It's why we fear the dark. It's why we fear the future. It's why we fear losing someone. Because we can't imagine what life will be like without them," Lem said. He closed his eyes then listening to the stir of the wind on the water and the scratching of some unseen animal in the bushes. Kit envied him. It had been so long since he just *was*. He was always locked in his head thinking of days gone and days to come.

"But you're so relaxed," Kit said.

Lem opened his eyes and Kit didn't recognise the depth and wisdom on the old man's face. He was so different from the jovial frolicker that Kit thought he knew.

"Do you still fear the dark?" Lem asked.

"Not since I was a kid," Kit said.

"And why is that?"

Kit thought for a long while. He was going to say that he learned that it didn't hide monsters after all, but that wasn't true. Even before the dark place, Kit knew of the horrors in the dark. Of the gangs that fought wars in the shadows. Of the desperation that clawed at some street dwellers souls until they would no longer see others as people but as a means of money and food and blood.

So why did he no longer fear the dark? Surely knowing what was hiding in it made it worse?

"I don't know," Kit said.

"Because you strode into the dark. You've seen what it holds and it has lost its power over you."

"But we can't know what's after death," Kit said.

"No but that doesn't matter. Much like striding into the dark, much like getting up and starting a new day, we are always moving into the unknown. Whatever it is, we'll face it when it comes," Lem said.

"What if there's nothing to face after you die, Lem? What if everything is an endless black that you fall through alone?"

"Alone?" Lem asked. Kit looked up from his hands. Lem smiled and gestured to his boot. "You're never alone. People are like boots. We're all paired. Connected. Does it matter that this boot is across the city from the other?" He pointed to Sleeping Siv's grave. "No. We still consider it a pair of boots. It will always be paired. You can't unpair boots just like you can't break the connection between people. It just is."

Kit thought about visiting Jirma after not seeing the old man in years and how he didn't hesitate to help Kit learn about being deathless. He thought of Bas who he had met in a cell and how he had jumped to help Kit capture the husk. Of Illy and Wenson who had become his friends. And Lem who Kit had underestimated.

And Nya who had saved his life countless times. Who he went to Duat and back with. Who stood with him as they faced down a God. And who had been there when he needed her.

"So I just march on?"

"Yes. Good things will happen. Bad things will happen. But things will happen. Life will be lived. Boots will be walked in. Boots will be lost. Boots will be found again."

What was Kit doing? He had been wallowing in worry and closing off from the others. Fear had stolen his mind and shrouded it in darkness while the others had been fighting for Tarris.

And now Nya had been kidnapped.

Was he too late? No. He was Kit. He had some of the biggest gangs in Yontar wrapped around his finger. He had rich merchants on their knees. And he Duat-damned wasn't going to sit about and let his friends fight without him.

Death could stalk him. Death could hound at his heels. But he wouldn't let it reach those he loved.

"Thank you, Lem," Kit said, after a while of sitting in silence. "I know what I need to do now."

"And what is that?" Lem asked.

"I'm going to die."

29

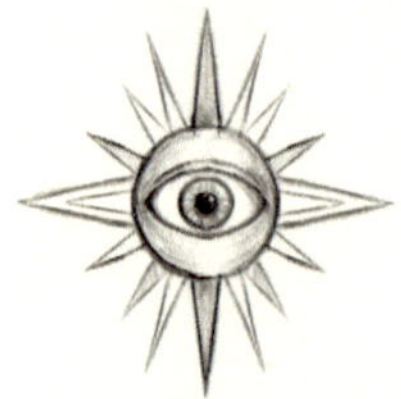

A Path of Stone and Water

15 years ago.

They rose before the Sun Eye bled light onto the sand. The hyians were packed and saddled and they took off across the unforgiving desert. The ride south moved them farther from the well-traversed parts of the desert. Some parties skirted the Deadlands Basin travelling from Yontar to Ossin but most passed through Tansen to restock. This meant the further south they got, the more decrepit and damaged the Waypoints became. One had been raided by some wild beasts. The door lay flat and sand piled in the corners. The cots were torn to shreds and the cupboards ripped open, the rations missing. Probably kiren, Rai guessed.

They didn't stay long.

Dunes rose and fell as a sea of sand. The serene tan and golden sheet was unmarred by life. The heat was wearying but the quiet and the separation from society brought a stillness Rai didn't know that he needed.

It wasn't long after midday and they all wrapped themselves in tan cloaks to keep the Sun Eye off. Most wouldn't ride during the worst of the heat but they were training to join the Verdin Guild. Resting and hiding from the heat would be a sign of weakness and Rai had no doubt they would be timing how long it took the party to reach the temple.

They made good progress moving south and soon rocks started to break the sand as they approached the Deadland Basin's rim. Escarpments rose in patches of stone creating some shelter from the burning gaze of the Sun Eye. Stone, Sun Eye, and sand blended and moulded the landscape around them as the company moved into the mountainous passes. There was an eerie feeling to the stone path. Rai kept telling himself that it was the change from the open desert, where one could see for miles to the enclosed pathways with limited vision, but he couldn't make himself believe it. More than once he was sure voices carried on the wind. Unnatural breezes picked up and fell away coming from different directions. The others must have felt it too as the chatter had faded and they searched the surrounding stone.

"Why do you think all these monsters are said to live in the basin?" Sen asked. He could never linger in silence long and always voiced his concerns. Rai couldn't blame him. The Deadlands Basin was the most treacherous stretch of desert in Tarris. No one travelled there but everyone heard the rumours of the monsters that lived there.

"Don't you know the story of how the Deadlands Basin came to be?" Genu asked.

"I assumed it just… *be*," Sen said.

Genu shook her head.

"In ages past, when the Shapers roamed the land, there were creatures that some believe are no more than myth and legend. One of these was the Bandor," Genu said, her voice echoing through the mountain pass.

"The Mountain Eater," Tys said. He rode alongside Rai but had slowed to listen to the story. Genu followed, preferring to ride alone and Sen and Ada trailed behind her.

"One and the same," Genu said. "Made from stone that fell from the sky, Otar the rock Aspect breathed life into that boulder and the Bandor took its first breath. Little did Otar know that the beast would have a taste for stone. It ate entire mountains and grew with each stone it consumed, flattening the land turning Tarris into the desert we live in today. Otar took notice as the Bandor travelled northward towards where Otar made his home in the mountains of Nuia, although it was not named that then.

"Perturbed by Bandor's efforts, Otar pleaded for the Bandor to stop its ravenous journey north before it entered his territory. But the Bandor fell further into a frenzy with each rock it ate and ignored the Aspect."

Sen cleared his throat. "But Otar is an *Aspect*. Why didn't he just crush the Bandor?"

"The Bandor was created with the Aspect's breath. He could do no harm to the Bandor and any mountain Otar rose to slow the beast only fuelled it. So Otar went to the local people and promised the power of rock and earth to the one who killed the Bandor. Many tried and failed, the Bandor slaughtering thousands leaving a trail of blood through the sand. But finally, the Bandor was slain by a warrior named Fieren, a Nuian woman who was said to have a blade as sharp as the wind that cut into the beast's heart.

"However, during the fight, the Bandor was already the size of a mountain and slammed its fists down, breaking the earth and rock. This shattered the land with cracks working their way deep into the planet, freeing the many monsters who lived underground, and creating the Deadlands Basin," Genu said. "With the Bandor killed, Otar was grateful and bestowed the power of stone onto Fieren, who then became known as the Queen of Wind and Stone and ruled in the north for a time. Then Otar entombed the Bandor's body in the mountains around the basin, to forever mock the beast and remind all that *stone doesn't forget.*"

A breeze blew through the party as if the wind itself remembered the tale. An uneasy silence returned to the company. Tys grinned and flicked his head back gesturing for Rai to look. Sen had sped up and rode near Genu's back not taking his eyes from the ridges above them, as if he expected the Bandor to rip through the rock at any moment. Unperturbed, Ada played with a lizard.

Stone that fell from the sky, the Aspects, and creatures that lived under the sand. Rai couldn't imagine the world in ages past. There was no way to know what of their stories were true and what of them were nothing more than that. Stories. What truly mattered was that the Deadlands Basin was dangerous and filled with unknown monsters and threats. If they were to make it to the Verdin Temple they would have to tread carefully.

Paths wound through the rising rock in an unfathomable pattern. Even with the map on Rai's lap, they had to double back many times to find the true path marked out for them.

"It'll be dark soon," Tys said.

Rai sighed looking up from his map. "They made this difficult to follow to ensure we'd spend a night in the mountains."

Tys nodded as though he had thought the same. It was part of the test.

They set up camp in a cramped hollow in the rock face. It was at an intersection of three paths allowing them to see a good distance in each direction. The stone around them was bulbous and Tys had clambered up to find a ridge that they could climb to. That gave them plenty of escape options if anything were to bother them during dark hour. They fell into their familiar roles. Genu set up the fire, Sen prepared the food, while Ada, Tys, and Rai scouted the area to ensure they hadn't camped out by a nest and then set up the cracklers.

Cracklers were strips of the crackler plant's stem that snapped when one stood on them. They were often placed around camps to warn travellers of any beasts that may be approaching in the black.

Dark hour descended and blurred the hard lines of the mountains into an indistinguishable black shroud. Embers spat and crackled, lighting the faces of the party in reds and blacks.

"We must be close," Genu said passing the map to Sen.

"Yeah, I think we should reach the hidden path into the basin by dawn," Rai said. He had taken on the mantle of leader but only fools believed that they were infallible. So Rai made sure everyone got to see the map and voice their opinion. A true leader listened to those who follow, for all voices carry the same weight. One may dress in gold and rich fabrics but all words are unadorned and equal.

They each looked at the map but it was vague at best. A small sigil marked where they should enter the Deadlands Basin. From this northern side, it was a sheer drop down into the basin. However, Overseer Rikai said there was a hidden passage. It was likely to be a ledge that curled downward but Rikai refused to expand on the map and its cryptic notes.

We will find out soon enough, Rai thought.

"This path should lead us to the passage." Tys gestured to the path leading further into the mountains. Sen nodded and offered the map to Ada who shook his head, instead focused on the lizard's tail he twirled around his finger.

"And then we just need to face whatever is in the basin," Sen said. Rai took the map from Sen and folded it up.

Worry creased their faces. Making decisions during their travels came naturally to Rai but reassuring the others was always a struggle. He knew how important it was for leaders to bolster those who followed them but Rai could never find the right words.

The fire crackled.

He thought of everything that had brought them here and Rai cleared his throat. He could do this.

"Twenty of us stood in the Eye that day. Only we four have survived. We've been beaten, broken, and bloody ever since. But we stayed and rose again and again." Rai looked at them each in turn. "Because we knew this was the path we were meant for. It doesn't matter what is on the path because we will overcome it. People don't strive to become rulers, they strive to rule. They do not strive for power, they strive to become powerful. Being on the path is the destiny.

"We continue because what else is there?"

It wasn't the rousing speech he had hoped for. It wouldn't be written in the records of the Tansen Archive but it didn't need to be. They were here at the precipice of the most treacherous stretch of desert in all of Tarris and the meaning and emotion behind the words were more important than the words themselves. The fire reflected in their eyes and that wasn't the only thing that was burning.

Crack.

Silence grabbed Rai by the throat.

He strained his hearing, searching the quiet. *Crack.* It was unmistakable this time. Something had set off their cracklers. The others had noticed too, their eyes going wide. Slowly and silently they crept to the edge of the hollow.

"It came from the right," Tys whispered stepping up to Rai's side. Moving away from the fire to shroud themselves in shadow, Rai and the others drew their weapons. Rai stared down one of the paths. He searched for shape or movement but the blackness was a wall. The fire snapped against the dull beating of the wind. A swish of motion, as Rai heard one of the others sheathing their weapons again. Rai turned and shook his head.

Crack.

They all spun. It had come from the opposite direction, from where they had entered the mountain passes. Again Rai peered into the shadow for any sign of life. Nothing.

Another crack came from further down the path and they all turned again.

"Fan out," Rai said. Ada, Genu, and Sen faced one way and Rai and Tys faced the other. A grating rock scraping on rock rumbled in the unseen dark. Rai realised he was squeezing his dagger. He loosened his grip. *Focus*, Rai thought breathing out.

A feral shriek struck them like a blow, blasting in from the path leading from the desert. It almost knocked Rai over in a flurry of wind.

"What in Duat was that?" Sen asked.

"Dwellsand," Genu whispered.

In the mountain passes? Impossible.

Crack, crack, crack.

The third and final path was set alight with noise. The trampling of what sounded like many creatures set off their trap. And they were coming fast.

"Move!" Rai shouted. There was too much happening that they couldn't see. Rai hoped the others had listened when he said not to unpack their hyians.

Unlatching the rope, Rai leapt into his hyian's saddle and snapped the reins sending him hurling into the black. The others galloped ahead and Rai made a quick count of the shadowed outlines to ensure they were all accounted for. *All here.* The creature screeched at their back. Whatever it was it was huge and catching up with them.

They passed the path leading left off into the mountains as a pack of duon charged from the opening. That was what the trampling was, Rai realised. The duon barrelled into the party. Tys was launched from his saddle. Whipping a dagger out, Rai cut a duon sending it screaming and skittering away. He grabbed Tys as he passed, slowing and helping lift him onto the back of his hyian. The others were still moving among the stampede of duon, swept away in its chaos.

The duons bumped and harried their hyian but they weren't outright hostile towards them. "They are running!" Rai said. Tys stared at him. Whatever creature was behind them was chasing the pack of duon. And Rai doubted it would discriminate on meat.

Their hyian struggled against the pack, whinnying and bucking. Swinging his blade, Tys created some space but the duon were delirious with herd mentality and terrified of whatever hunted them in the dark.

A duon squealed from behind. Then a nauseating crack of bones and slosh of gore silenced the scream. Whatever was at their back was almost upon them.

Rai met Tys' gaze and whipped the reins. The others were lost to the dark. Rai knew he couldn't worry about them. He had to focus on getting him and Tys out of this.

The herd blew through intersections without so much as a glance down the other paths. Rai and Tys had to hug tight against the hyian to avoid being pulled off by the force at which they veered around corners. The feral grunts and howls of the duon shook the rock.

In the jostling, a duon got too close and trampled their hyian's leg. *Snap.* The hyian howled and bucked Rai and Tys from its back. For a moment, Rai was weightless then, scrambling for anything, he clutched at a duon's horns. If he fell under the herd he would be as good as dead. Losing its balance, their hyian toppled and was crushed under the duon's charge. A sickening splutter came from their feet but Rai didn't look down. Pulling himself onto the duon's back, Rai spotted Tys similarly hanging from another duon. Luckily the duon were more focused on escaping the monster at their heels than their newly found weight.

He blew out a breath of relief. It was short lived as the pack in front started to disappear. Rai squinted. Where had they gone? No, they hadn't disappeared. They dipped out of sight. *The edge of the basin,* Rai realised. The duon were charging over the edge.

Panic surged and bile rose up Rai's throat. He searched for something to grab hold of but there was nothing. The duon were a tightly packed landslide toppling over into the basin. They burst out from the mountain passes to an open area and Rai's suspicions were confirmed. Just ahead, the ground fell away and the large expanse of desert known as the Deadlands Basin stretched into the distance. The Moon Eye peered from the horizon bringing an ethereal glow to the black sands. With the added light, Rai could see the herd was thinner than he thought. They had been corralled through the passes, not letting them spread out.

"Tys!" Rai shouted. Tys fought to stay on his duon, who shook and flicked his head about. "The basin!"

Tys' breath caught. They needed to get out of this headlong charge. The duons might be able to survive the drop but they certainly wouldn't.

Rai lunged. A duon sprinted beneath him knocking his legs and changing his trajectory. Cracking his head off a duon's horn, Rai slid under the herd. A cloud of dust filled Rai's lungs. He choked, eyes bulging. A duon's hoof landed a hairs breadth from his head. A jolt of terror brought clarity to the chaos. Watching the oncoming hooves, Rai barrel rolled. A leg came down hard on his foot and he felt the bone shatter. Rai screamed and lurched out the way of another two duon.

The pack was thinning closer to the back and Rai dragged himself out of the direct line of the charge. Pain rang up Rai's leg. Glancing down, his boot was torn and his foot was at a wrong angle. He hissed lying back.

"Sands suffocate me, Rai," Tys said, coming to his side.

Duons continued to pile over the edge and the grinding noise grew louder.

"We need to move," Rai said.

"You won't be moving far with that foot," Tys said.

"Whatever is chasing them is coming, Tys. If we stay, we die," Rai said between gasps of pain.

Tys' lips drew to a line, his face grim but determined. "This is going to hurt," Tys said as he ducked under Rai's shoulder and eased him up. Rai bit his tongue as fiery tendrils ran up his leg. He came to standing, leaning on his good foot and Tys.

"Come on," Tys said. He made for the mountain passes supporting Rai as he hopped, when Rai hesitated. "What?" Tys asked.

The grinding rock sound had stopped.

A duon ran for the basin. A gooey appendage shot from the mountain pass, wrapped around its leg, and dragged the duon back into the dark. The duon squealed and kicked as it disappeared and, with a crack, silence consumed its screams.

Rai flicked his head towards another mountain pass and they hobbled as quietly as they could away from the opening. A swish of movement. They spun around but the open space was empty. The duons having all thrown themselves into the Deadlands Basin. The ground softened and Rai glanced down. It was night so the black sand should be hard as rock. The mucky ground quivered.

"Tys!" Rai shouted but it was too late. The Dwellsand ran over their feet as an ooze and yanked them into the air. In less than a breath, they hung upside down suspended staring upon a monstrosity of the black sand.

The Dwellsand looked to be made of sand and rock but its body was soft and pudgy to the touch. One great eye opened. It had no iris and was made of the same texture and colour as its body. The viscous goop spread across the ground beneath them. Dwellsands often hid in the sand to catch unsuspecting travellers during the night and burrowed deep to sleep during the day. But here, where few travelled, this Dwellsand must have gotten a taste for duon in the mountain passes.

A gaping maw opened among the rock beneath them and the oozing hold around Rai's ankle loosened. Agony rung from his shattered foot making it had to concentrate.

An arrow bounced off the beast's body.

The Dwellsand tightened its grip again and Rai looked up to see Sen sitting high on the rocks another arrow nocked. Ada leapt from nowhere shearing through the leg that held Tys and together they dropped away from the open maw. The tap of footsteps made Rai glance up to where Genu launched herself from a ledge, dagger in hand.

Unsheathing his daggers, Rai tucked his head in so when he was cut free, his legs fell first. Embedding his dagger into the beast, Rai dropped tearing the Dwellsand open as he slowed his decent. Still, on landing, his leg crumpled beneath him but Genu was already there helping him up.

The Dwellsand roared, a gargling, stony sound. Its rocky eye darted back and forth between them.

"Take Rai to shelter while we distract it!" Sen shouted. He loosed another arrow that stuck in the beast's head. Genu led Rai away while the others took turns attacking the Dwellsand.

Once they were a safe distance, Rai pulled out of Genu's grip and sat. "Go back and help them," Rai said. Genu nodded and ran back into the fray. He hated not being able to help. But Rai knew he would only slow them.

Arrows littered the Dwellsand's body and Tys and Ada had cut off huge chunks of the creature. However, the Dwellsand was unphased, regrowing and healing quicker than they could hack off bits of its body. Frustration bubbled up from Rai's gut. He should be helping. Not sitting there, nothing more than a burden.

They each attacked from different directions forcing the creature to constantly spin around. However, the Dwellsand was catching onto their plan and faced Sen, sending a slick spike straight through Sen's gut.

Rai's heart dropped as Sen toppled off his perch high in the rocks and hit the ground with a crack. The Dwellsand turned slowly, the sound of rock grinding on rock. Rai couldn't take his eyes from Sen's lifeless body. He had failed him like he failed the rest. Despite the endless hours of training, he still wasn't enough.

The others continued to fight but with less of them now the Dwellsand was finding it easier to focus on them individually. They were all going to die. Rai had to do something. He stared at his mangled foot. He wanted to scream.

Deep breaths. Find the still sands of first light. It was Overseer Rikai's voice.

Rai inspected his surroundings. There had to be something. That's when he saw the sigil that marked the passage on their map, carved into a rock. The hidden pathway of stone. Rai crawled towards it. He couldn't see any openings. Peering over the edge, Rai felt another wave of nausea. A thin ledge wove its way down the rock face and into the basin.

Glancing back at the fight, Genu was cutting Tys free from the Dwellsand's grasp. Rai had to distract the creature. Rai slid a hand into the sheath at the back of his belt and pulled out Overseer Lintou's short sword. Imayan slipped him it in the chaos after the assassination attempt. A diera blade. He would have never believed them to be true if he hadn't seen Lintou use it. Imayan had told him it had limited use. So Rai had sworn to only use it in life and death situations. This seemed as good a time as any.

Rai whipped the blade around in the same motion Lintou did. Wind was drawn to the blade and circled it, expanding and stretching, growing stronger. With a flick, a blast of wind hit the Dwellsand in the eye. Its whole upper body bent backwards as it squealed.

"Here! I found the passage!" Rai shouted. The others looked in confused awe as a torrent of wind held the Dwellsand at bay.

"Come on!"

They finally came back to themselves and ran towards Rai. Sen's corpse lay off to the side.

Rai felt the wind waning. Tys was the first to spot the passage and gestured for Genu and Ada to go first. They crept onto the thin ledge, Genu breathing hard and doing all in her power not to look down.

The torrent spat and spluttered before dying out, then Tys grabbed Rai and helped him onto the path of stone. It was large enough for Rai to shuffle along. But glancing down he saw it grew narrower towards the middle of the wall.

The Dwellsand roared.

One problem at a time.

They started their descent into the Deadlands Basin.

30

A Path of Wind and Flame

15 years ago.

Wind pressed against them as they weaved their way down the rock and towards the black sand of the Deadlands Basin. Little could be heard over the roaring wind. Tys had bandaged Rai's foot up but he couldn't put any weight on it. He moved along seated and using his hands to shuffle himself on. The cool serrated rock sliced his hands bloody. But that was nothing compared to the pain of losing Sen. No one had spoken up. The silence a scream of mourning among the party.

How could this keep happening?

If Rai hadn't spoken to Kon back in the orphanage, Zin wouldn't have attacked him in the bathroom. If Rai was stronger he could have saved Overseer Lintou. If Rai hadn't needed saving, Sen would still be with them.

The weight of dragging his broken foot was nothing compared

to the weight of his failures. Imayan was lucky to have gotten rid of him when she did. He would have failed her too.

Coming to a corner, Rai lifted his legs up and slid down. He dug his hands into the rock as the ledge thinned past the point of being able to shimmy along. This was it then. Tys had stopped at his back.

"Go on," Rai shouted over the wind. "I can't go any further."

Genu and Ada turned back at the shouting.

"I won't go on without you, Rai," Tys said.

"You must. I will just slow you down," Rai said.

Tys' face twitched, conflicted. Rai nodded and acceptance settled in Tys' eyes. He made to inch past when Genu shouted, "No! I won't go on without Rai. I won't lose anyone else."

Tys stilled. Leading the way, Ada looked unperturbed by the whole situation.

"Genu, there's no way for me to continue. I won't have you all dying for me and my mistakes," Rai said. Genu grimaced and blew out a frustrated exhale. She knew he was right. They were about halfway down the rock. A fall from this height was sure to kill them several times over and with the wind and crumbling rock of the stone path, no one would be able to take Rai's weight and clamber the rest of the way down.

"What about your magic wind blade thing?" Ada said.

They all looked to Ada as he picked his teeth. He froze realising they were staring at him. "What?"

"He can't fly with it, Ada," Tys said.

"No, but if he can make a stream of wind strong enough to slow his fall…" Ada waved a hand about as if the rest was obvious.

Words caught in Tys' throat and he glanced at Rai. Rai rolled the blade in his hand. Was it possible? The others assumed he knew how to use it but distracting the Dwellsand was the first time he had ever used a diera blade. He had kept it as a reminder of Lintou and how he needed to become stronger to protect those he cared for.

"Well?" Genu asked.

"I don't know," Rai said.

But what were his options? Stay on this cliff face until he starved to death or grew too weak to hold on and fell from it?

The black blade had a texture not unlike obsidian. Rai ran his finger down the length of the pommel. There he felt a ridge. On closer inspection, Rai realised there was a latch hidden in the pommel. Rai pulled at it and a small opening appeared. Inside, Rai could see… blood?

There was so much he didn't understand. But Rai wasn't done until he was robbed of his last breath. He silenced the wind and the others chattering, and listened to his breathing, finding still in the chaos.

Rai nodded. A thread of hope was all he needed.

The immediate problem was summoning the wind fast enough to catch his fall. If it took as long as it did with the Dwellsand, Rai might as well throw himself off the cliff now. But after a couple practice shots, he found he could create the wind faster.

Is it fast enough, though? Rai wondered. He didn't want to practice too much as he was unsure if there was a fuel source or if the diera blade needed a cool down period. Imayan had only said that their abilities had limited use and not to waste it.

Before he could talk himself out of it, Rai moved to the edge of the cliff.

He sat forward staring down at the black sand below. Vertigo hit him bringing a rise of nausea. Closing his eyes, he blew out a breath.

Rai turned to Tys and the others. "Keep Imayan safe."

"Are you sure about this?" Tys asked. "We can find another way."

Rai shook his head.

He threw himself from the rock plummeting towards the Deadlands Basin.

It all happened so fast. The sand reached out for him with incredible speed. Wind buffeted Rai as he fell. He twirled the blade. Nothing. The sand grew closer. Rai screamed spinning the blade. It wasn't working. He was going to die.

A torrent of wind blasted downward.

Rai felt himself slow. The wind strengthened and he slowed further until the death spiral became an uncontrolled fall. He landed hard. His foot flared in agony and he screamed again clutching his leg. He wouldn't be walking on it anytime soon. As the pain settled elation flooded him. He'd survived.

Lying on his back, Rai looked up at the rock and searched out Tys, Genu, and Ada. They were nothing more than specs.

Rai laughed through the tears.

The others took some time to catch up. Enough for Rai to regain control of himself so they didn't find a squealing, cry-laughing bundle lying on the sand.

"You black sand-footed fool. I can't believe that worked." Tys jogged up to him, grinning.

"What, that? That was nothing," Rai said, delirium leaking into his tone.

Genu dropped beside him and gave him a hug. Rai coughed at

the pincer grip. Even Ada nodded appreciatively like he had been curious to see if his idea would have worked. Rai returned the gesture. He still felt uneasy around the man but without him Rai would be sitting high upon the rock alone right now.

"This is it, then," Tys said. "The Deadlands Basin."

They stared over the open desert. Black dunes crested and fell under the silvery glow of the Moon Eye. Despite its reputation, the serene flow of the dunes was beautiful. Rai could see no threat of creature and heard no sound other than the light breeze and steady breathing of the others. According to the map the Verdin Temple wasn't far from here. But traversing the desert at night and with a broken foot would be no easy task. It had begun to numb with tingling sensations whenever he shifted his weight. Rai didn't think that was a good sign.

"Do we wait out the night here?" Genu asked.

They were relatively safe against the cliff with only one direction monsters could approach from. And day would lessen the amount of creatures roaming the sand. Bolstered by the fall, Rai shook his head.

"We go now," Rai said. He traced the arc of the solid sand with his finger. "I have an idea."

After the duon's charge, they had lost most of their gear. Together they had two bedrolls and enough food to last half a day. Rai's foot throbbed but Genu had found some paroot, a painkiller that eased the agony.

Tying together the bedrolls, Tys and Ada used their belts as strips on the underside to act as runners. Rai could tell by the others that they were just humouring him but he wouldn't allow himself to be a burden any longer. He had to try something. They tightened the last of the ropes and belts and sat back looking upon the makeshift sled.

Tys supported Rai as they climbed to the top of a sand dune, Genu and Ada dragging Rai's contraption. They climbed onto it. It was just large enough for the four of them to sit close together on. Rai took a moment watching over the desert before he started spinning the diera blade. Tys tightened his grip.

A gust of wind blasted from the end of the blade and they were sent skittering down the dune. They bumped and rattled over the hard sand. Their sled bunched and Genu had to hold onto it to keep it from folding in on itself, but it was working.

Coming to the bottom of a dune, Rai glanced up. It worked well rolling down a dune but was it strong enough to travel up dunes, too? He flicked his wrist, strengthening the wind and they shot upward. Using the diera blade was becoming easier after feeling out how it reacted to his movements. They crested the dune and launched into the air. Ada howled in delight and they thudded back down onto the sand, barrelling on into the night.

Raucous laughter poured out from Ada as he sat at the front arms outstretched. Genu snickered shaking her head and even Tys was smiling. They flew across the dunes faster than they would have with their hyian, riding the sands like waves. The hiss of the wind rattled over the rumble of their sled grinding against the hard sand.

At this pace, they would make it to the Verdin Temple in no time.

Something moved on the horizon. Tys noticed it too. It vanished as they blasted off the side of a dune. A dark grey hide rose into sight just to dip below a lip of sand again.

"Eyes up!" Tys shouted.

The smiles were wiped from their faces as they searched the horizon. It was ever shifting and, at the speed they were going, rose and fell in the blink of an eye. A black blur burst from behind a dune. It had six legs and a long snake-like body. Its hide was rough and plated, scraggly thin hairs breaking off in bunches. The cylindrical face had no eyes and only a circular mouth in the centre of it lined with fangs.

"What in Duat is that?" Genu shouted.

"I don't know but its fast," Tys said.

He was right. The creature was keeping pace a couple of dunes over.

"Ada hold this," Genu said gesturing to the sled she was stretched out on. Ada did as asked and Genu unslung her bow from her back. They had all trained with a variety of weapons but Sen had always been the best archer. *But he is dead now,* Rai reminded himself.

Genu loosed an arrow. It hit the beast in the side of its body. The creature squealed and disappeared behind a dune.

"Good shot," Rai said and Genu nodded.

Six more of the strange black creatures crested the horizon. Rai's heart sank. Surprise flared on Genu's face. The beasts bounded towards them. Genu nocked an arrow as Ada shouted, "More on this side!"

Another four charged them from the left.

"Rai, can we go faster?" Tys asked. Part of their training had been learning the habits and patterns of the various creatures that inhabited the desert. But these were unknown. These were some of the Deadlands Basin's monsters. Rai doubted anyone knew of their weaknesses.

Twirling the diera blade faster, they picked up the pace. Tys hurled his throwing knives and Genu loosed arrow after arrow. With the increased speed their sled was starting to fray. It curled at the edges and the rumble of friction changed to a sharper noise that Rai didn't like the sound of. Ada did his best to hold down what he could but the sled wasn't going to last.

"There's too many!" Genu shouted. More had appeared. A pack of around forty surrounded them running at either side. They moved in formation closing in with the occasional beast rushing in to attack.

Tys growled in frustration throwing down his empty pouch of knives and unsheathed his sword. "They're coming!"

One of the black creatures leapt.

Tys swung his sword decapitating the beast. Its head thumped down on their sled. Its death didn't put off the others as two more jumped at them. One landed on Tys who fell onto his back. He held it aloft with his sword. The creature's mouth widened and squealed. Rows of teeth rippled in anticipation and drool dripped in viscous clumps. Rai kicked out with his good leg knocking the creature off him.

Ada screamed as the other bit into his thigh. Spinning, Genu battered the beast with her bow, knocking it off the sled. A bloody patch of ripped up flesh glinted in the moonlight on Ada's thigh but he didn't let the sled fold. He knew that would mean the death of them.

Genu's distraction allowed the pack on her side to dive onto the sled. She cracked one across the face with her bow while sliding her dagger into her other hand swiping wide and slicing through another's hide.

A silhouetted black point marred the perfect silver glow of the Moon Eye. Rai squinted. It was the unmistakable sweeping roof of a temple. A wave of relief came over Rai.

The Verdin Temple.

"Hold on!" Rai whipped the blade again unleashing a quick flurry of wind. Rai ducked as the sudden jerk forward tossed several of the creatures off.

Finding her feet again, Genu went back to loosing arrows at any that got too close. Tys shook off one of the beasts he had been wrestling with.

The Verdin Temple grew, details of the legendary place becoming clearer as it did. Even in the dim light of the Moon Eye, Rai could make out its stark emerald colour. The temple sat upon a rock. A pillar among the flat sand dunes. It seemed to glow in the moonlight beckoning them onward.

Groaning, Ada grimaced as his thigh oozed and festered. It looked to be infected. He hissed and reached for his thigh.

The front of the sled folded and buckled.

It caught on the hard sand and threw the back of the sled into the air, catapulting the party across the dunes.

Rai hit the sand and rolled to a stop. His foot pulsated pain up his leg and he let out a howl. Steadying his breath, he sat up, scanning his surroundings to make sure those things weren't near. The others were scattered around nearby. Ada clutched his thigh, his face a rictus of pain but otherwise the others seemed to be okay.

The pack of long, black creatures bounded towards them.

"Regroup!" Rai shouted shuffling towards the others. Tys ran and helped drag Ada and together with Genu they stood together facing down the oncoming charge. Glancing over his shoulder, Rai looked longingly at the Verdin Temple. They were so close but there was no way they could outrun these things.

The company looked at one another. Their faces were hard. Death was calling but they wouldn't come willingly. They unsheathed swords and daggers. Rai stood leaning on Tys. The flood of creatures piled down the dunes and Rai blew out a breath, tightening his grip around his dagger.

Suddenly, a plume of flames arced from behind them smashing into the front line of the creature's charge. The beasts squealed and tossed back and forth on the sand trying to extinguish the flames. Rai spun and stared as a man and a woman approached. They wore matching leather jerkins trimmed with verdant green. The man flicked his sword and another raging wave of fire scorched the black sand. Some of the creatures were burnt to a crisp. Others turned and ran but a few continued their stampede towards them. The woman loosed an arrow. It looked to be headed straight for Tys who ducked. However, before the arrow reached him it veered *around them*. The arrow swam through the air cutting through a beast's head just to swivel around and cut down another, finally it wove through the last of the creatures until their bodies littered the sands.

The skittering scrape of the fleeing survivors was all that could be heard until even that fell to silence.

The strangers approached. The man had a flat, square face topped with brown hair that grew up more than it did out. Long black hair fell to the woman's elbows. Her features were soft with pudgy rosy cheeks. Tys twirled his blade but Rai shook his head. They could only be from one place.

"You certainly know how to make an entrance," the man said.

"Our friend has been bitten," Rai said.

They looked to Ada whose eyes were rolling back into his head. The wound had gotten worse. Pus bubbled and dark purple lines snaked outward from the gash.

"A hexil got him?" the woman asked.

"Is that what those things are called?" Tys asked.

The man bent down to inspect Ada's wound. Genu glanced at Rai who nodded and she leant back letting the man in. "That's what we call them," he said. "This is bad. We need to get him to Joku, fast. Grab his arms. We'll have to carry him."

The woman introduced herself as Eril and led them across the desert. Her words were short and sharp with a twang that was not Tarrisian but Rai couldn't tell where she was from. Tys supported Rai and Genu and the man, Quar, carried Ada.

They drew near to the pillar of stone that held aloft the Verdin Temple. It was a sheer cliff, not unlike those that served as the edges of the basin. However, they were in no state to do any more climbing. Eril didn't slow, leading them up to the rock face where a crack led into a cavern. Inside firelight filled the space, lighting the rocks in warm flickering oranges. A cage like contraption lay at the back of the cavern with a chain disappearing upward.

"Everyone on," Eril said then wandered off to the side. "Yor. Wake up!"

A flustered old man popped his head up from behind the rock. His grey hair stuck out and his beard looked to be coming out from his large nose.

"Yeah, yeah," he tutted. His back snapped and creaked as he

made his way over to a metal bar. Tys helped Rai onto the platform and sat him down. Everything had become hazy as the adrenaline wore off.

"Everyone on?" Yor called.

Eril nodded and the old man yanked down on the bar, launching the cage upward. It shook and swung in the dark but Eril and Quar didn't seem concerned. Darkness consumed them. The rattle of metal was the only indicator that Rai hadn't collapsed from exhaustion. Now in the cool after the battle, his limbs felt heavy and mind sluggish. Light burst into the cage as they crossed the threshold. As Rai's eyes adjusted, the cage shuddered to a stop.

A path stretched out in front of them. Long one storey buildings lined the path and in the distance towering over all was the temple. The three tiers each had an ornate stone balcony surrounding it, which narrowed with each floor, and it shone a brilliant verdant in the moonlight.

"Welcome to the Verdin Temple," Quar said as the gate to the platform creaked open.

Andrew Watson

PART 3

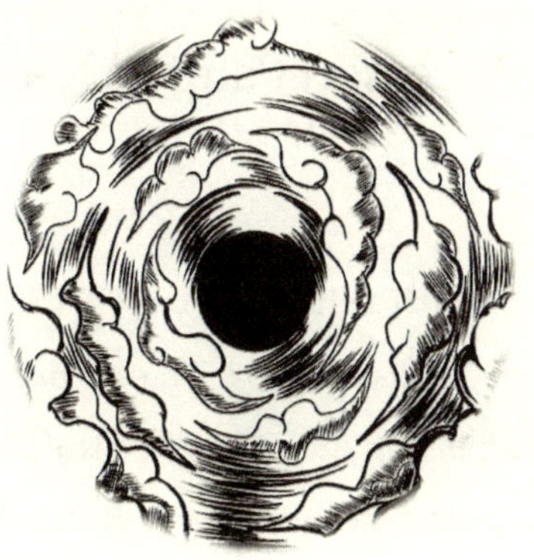

31

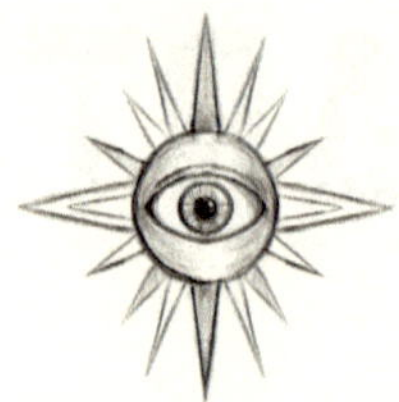

A Lesson Painted Red

15 years ago.

A single beam of light shone onto Rai as he stood amidst the dark. Rai listened to his breath rise and fall. A slight creak to his right. Spinning, Rai swiped his sword in a wide arc. The mudball burst on impact, raining him in dirt. Another shot from the opposite side. Rai leant back as it barrelled past his face.

Pop. Pop. Pop.

Three fired towards him from different angles. Rai jumped, spinning so one flew under him, another passing inches above him. The third hurling through his open legs. He landed on the thin beam suspended in the black. Shooting pains ran up his leg from his foot. It could hold his weight now. However, it was still healing from getting caught in that duon stampede.

A sweeping metal arm swung for Rai's legs. Rai leapt over it as another two mudballs flew at him. His sword cut through the first as he leant out of the way of the other. Two arms at different heights shot out of the dark. Rai made to dive between them when a click came from behind him. Sliding between the two arms, Rai spun to face the noise. Two mudballs connected by a chain twirled towards him. Landing, Rai knew he wouldn't have enough time to leap out the way so he brought up his sword. The chain connected and the mudballs cracked Rai on the side of the head. He tossed the sword and chain away.

Disorientated, Rai shook his head. A mudball he missed in his respite caught him in the side. He hissed. Did that crack a rib? Two more mudballs shot at him. He didn't have his sword to break them now so instead he jumped out of the way. His foot met the beam at a wrong angle and he squealed, his leg crumpling beneath him. Just as he made to stand, a metal arm came into the light and threw him from the beam.

Rai landed in a heap on the padded floor. He spluttered, catching his breath as the shutters opened bringing light back to the room.

"You should let your foot heal before training," Quar said. "You would have landed that jump if it wasn't injured."

The hall was filled with slingshot contraptions that would launch the mudballs from all angles. Ropes held aloft the beam that swung in the middle of the hall. The roof was made from shutters which could throw the space into darkness leaving only a single stream of light shining onto the beam. The Verdin Guild called it the Hall of Night. A little dramatic, Rai thought.

Quar pulled Rai to his feet.

"It's getting better," Rai said.

"Your awareness wavered the second you landed on that foot.

It's clearly still painful," Quar said. "I respect the work ethic but an unsharpened sword will draw less blood no matter how many times it is swung."

Rai grimaced but nodded. Throwing an arm around Rai's shoulder, Quar laughed. "Come on. I have someone who wants to meet you."

Shielding his eyes from the Sun Eye, they walked out of the Hall of Night and onto the temple grounds. From afar, the pillar of rock that homed the Verdin Temple didn't look wide but atop it housed many different buildings and training grounds. A main pathway led down the centre of the plateau. It led from the lift they rode up in to the Verdin Temple itself. The temple glinted an even more brilliant verdant during the day.

Others nodded and waved, wishing Rai and Quar a good morning. They had only been there a week or so but their party had been treated like family. They were given living quarters and doctors had set about patching up their wounds. Rai couldn't believe how quickly his foot had healed. And while the doctor, Joku, said it would be at least a month until it would be back to normal, he could already walk on it.

The laid-back nature of the Verdin Guild still flummoxed Rai. When he had asked if there were initiations to become a member Quar laughed in his face.

"No, no, nothing like that. If you were selected to be sent here and survived the journey you're immediately part of the Verdin Guild," Quar had said.

Rai couldn't believe it was that easy. Not that the journey here was easy but he expected… *more* from the legendary guild. Although they hadn't officially started training, so Rai expected the hard part was yet to come.

"You have had the same perplexed look on your face since you got here." Quar laughed.

Verdin warriors sparred on the training grounds around them. The familiar clack of wooden training swords settling some of Rai's unease.

"I guess I never thought I'd be here," Rai said.

The dusty path crunched under their feet as they continued towards the temple. A warrior with speed unlike anything Rai had seen before whipped his training partner from his feet. They laughed and he helped his partner back up before falling back into a fighting stance. There was a level of companionship here that Rai had never experienced. He had thought it would be brutal training from barking overseers like Rikai. But he had yet to see anyone get shouted at or even a sense of hierarchy among the warriors.

"Are there overseers here that lead the training?" Rai asked.

"Not like you've had up to now. We have masters who often train classes in their expertise but how we train is more communal. We spar with other warriors of all skill levels. There are things to learn from fighting warriors of all levels of experience and walks of life. If you always train with those your better, you look for skill where there may not be any. Likewise if you only fight with those your equal or lesser, you can stagnate. Variation is key," Quar said. "Look there."

He pointed to an elderly woman who was squaring off against a girl. She bounced on her feet while the older warrior was still as a statue. The girl unleashed a flurry of blows, moving around the old woman, trying to break her guard, but the elderly woman parried and deflected the blows with ease. It was becoming clear that the younger woman was flagging, her energy sapping with her constant motion. Once her moves were sluggish, she left openings and in the blink of an eye, the older woman cracked her sword across the younger girl's arm. Quar grinned.

"And why are there three different styles of jerkin? Is that tied to your skill level?" Rai asked.

Everyone in in the Verdin Guild wore the same dark green jerkin but some were trimmed in a forest green while others were emerald. Some weren't trimmed at all.

"Perceptive." Quar nodded. "But no, it isn't a reference to ones skill. Those who wear the darker green edges are Verdani and those who have the lighter green trim are Verdin warriors."

"What's the difference?"

"Verdani are trained as hammers and swords. They are the fire and stone. Whereas the Verdin are the bows and daggers, the water and wind. At the Verdin Guild we believe there are two true fighting styles and a warrior should lean into what comes naturally to them. Those who are stronger usually chose the path of fire and stone. Those who are lighter on their feet chose water and wind. We all train together but if war was to come to Tarris we would have a strategic advantage knowing our warriors strengths and weaknesses."

Rai nodded. "And those without either haven't chosen yet."

Quar grinned. "Exactly. The initiates are wanderers who have yet to pick their path."

Rai wondered what path would call to him. He was fast on his feet but brute force and resilience was what got him here. Having trained with all weapons under Overseer Rikai's tutelage, he wasn't adept at any in particular. Although he preferred daggers.

"I can see the thoughts in your head," Quar said, bumping into him. "Do not worry, your path will become clear with time."

Nothing had ever been clear in Rai's life. He had stood at many forks in the road since the orphanage and none were the obvious choice. In his mind there were only grey paths that couldn't be right or wrong. They each led onward and could not be left. So he chose and walked on. In the end, they all led to the same destination.

Ash and eternity.

Coming up to the temple, Rai thought Quar would show him inside for the first time but he turned off the path and led Rai into a circular building just off to the side of the Verdin Temple. Shoving the door open, it ground against the stone floor. Lanterns and braziers lit the interior in splotches of orange. In the centre of the room was a step that led into a dirt fighting pit surrounded by a stone bannister. On the outside of the pit, the room was a mess of tables and shelves filled with weapons and strange objects.

Metal clanking sounded from the far side of the building.

"Shesmu, I brought him," Quar shouted and the clanking stopped.

A six-letter name? Rai thought. Who was this man? Quar said they had no leaders, but to have a six-letter name meant a direct connection to the emperor.

"Come in, come in," a gravelly voice said from the dark.

"I have training but I'll catch up with you later," Quar said. He patted Rai on the shoulder and gave him a reassuring nod and shove forward. Then turned and left. Exhaling, Rai walked deeper into the strange domed building.

Rai supressed a shiver. It was cool in here. Almost cold. Shesmu stood at a long workbench covered in tools Rai didn't recognise. At the back was a shelf of vials containing a variety of liquids. Shesmu looked to be in his sixties and his sleeveless shirt revealed faded old wounds painting a vivid past in red and steel. Scars covered his face and arms, masked only by long white hair that fell to his chest.

"Please sit," Shesmu said. He gestured to a couple of chairs surrounding a small table in the corner. Rai walked over and slumped down into one. After a moment, Shesmu sat across from him. He studied Rai, mulling over something. Rai sat up straighter, reminding himself that the man had a six-letter name. He had to show respect.

"That was some creative use of your diera blade," the man finally said. "Ada told me when I visited the infirmary. It does, however, raise the question of where a trainee got hold of such a weapon."

Shesmu sat forward. His body was relaxed but there was a hardness to his words that had Rai feeling uneasy. Suddenly he didn't want to tell the old man where he had retrieved the blade. But he couldn't be caught lying to someone of his stature, either.

"An overseer died and I was given it," Rai said. An undetailed truth could be as useful as any lie.

"Overseer Lintou?" Shesmu asked.

Surprise must have shown on Rai's face as Shesmu nodded and blew out a breath, the hardness dissipating. "I was sad to hear of his passing. He was a great man."

"He was."

"What do you know of diera blades?"

Shifting in his chair, Rai cleared his throat. He had been trained to avoid sharing ignorance and it made him uncomfortable to be so out of his depth. "I wasn't even sure they existed until I saw Overseer Lintou use his."

Shesmu burst out laughing, startling Rai. "Yes. We've worked hard to give them their air of mystery. Keeping them secret would be impossible. We wouldn't want that, anyway. Having a legendary item with the reputation of diera blades is almost as powerful as the weapons themselves. Come."

Shesmu stepped into the fighting pit in the middle of the room beckoning Rai to follow.

"Let's see Lintou's blade," he said. Shesmu held out a hand expectantly. Rai unsheathed the short sword and handed it to him. He grinned running a finger down the length of the blade.

"What have you been using of late old friend?" Shesmu murmured and flicked the blade. A lash of wind blasted across the space. Dust plumed and bottles rattled. "Vulmure blood."

So he had been right. The red inside the blade was blood.

"Diera blades are made from diera ore," Shesmu said, wandering off back to his workbench. As Rai stepped up behind him, Shesmu turned and tossed him a lump of black rock. "It is a rare ore that is only found in Tarris. Do you know what diera means in the old tongue?"

Rai shook his head rolling the ore around his hand. It looked and felt like any other rock but it was as black as the dunes at night.

"It means *'living'*. They called it the living rock," Shesmu said.

How could a rock be alive? Shesmu snatched the ore back and made sure Rai was watching as he unlatched the end of Lintou's blade and emptied the contents into a vial. The blood had congealed and dripped slowly. There wasn't much blood left, filling the vial only a quarter of the way up. He slid the vial into a holder at the side of his desk then waved his hand over the cabinet above, filled with vials of different colours.

"Pick one."

Rai pointed to a reddish-purple vial and Shesmu grinned. "Good choice." He pulled the vial out and emptied the liquid into Lintou's blade, and they both made their way back into the pit.

"Now, diera got this name because it can replicate the biological properties of some creatures using their blood. Not all, mind you. We still haven't worked out what the difference is between blood that works and the blood that doesn't yet. Most blood doesn't have any effect with diera. We've tried thousands of creatures' blood and only forty or so have activated diera ore."

Shesmu placed a drop of blood on his finger and rubbed it into the back of his hand. "Stand over there." Rai stood on the far side of the pit.

Shesmu then threw the blade right at Rai.

It shot towards him. Rai's breath caught. His nerves flared in warning but it was coming too fast. At the last second, Shesmu flicked the wrist with blood on it and the blade veered off course and embedded itself into the shelving outside the pit.

Stunned, Rai started at the blade as it twanged, slowly falling still.

"The blood that you chose is better for throwing daggers or even diera arrows. But it allows me to control the trajectory of the weapon while it is in the air. It's not complete control but I can nudge it in different directions."

Rai wanted to berate the old man but awe blossomed in his chest. To think such a thing was possible. He remembered when Eril, the woman who had saved them outside the temple, fired an arrow that moved unnaturally among the hexil. "Eril used this," Rai said.

Shesmu nodded walking over and yanking the short sword free. "It's likely she used refin blood. Like I said, it works best with arrows or throwing daggers. Refins have an incredible ability to know where the rest of the pack is at all times. We think they use a form of silent communication that works like pulses through the air. And when diera comes in contact with their blood you can use a drop on your hand to nudge the projectile that contains the rest of the blood. We think this is because it's using this invisible pulse to connect with the rest of the blood. But it takes years of practice to use it like Eril does."

Tales of ancient Verdin warriors who could control arrows with their mind no longer were ludicrous stories but skills.

Skills that *Rai could learn*.

"Why don't all Tarrisian soldiers have these?" Rai asked. Assassination attempts would be rendered impossible if the palace guard had such weapons.

Shesmu laughed. "Well for one, we don't have much diera ore. It's rare and only appears in small deposits. It takes some time to find enough to forge even one weapon. Secondly, I wouldn't entrust these weapons to just anyone, which is why I was suspicious of where you found this. But I had heard of the incident with the assassination attempt on Imayan."

Shock rang through Rai and he glanced up. That was supposed

to be kept quiet. Only a handful knew about the attempt on Imayan's life. "Who are you really and why are you telling me all this?" Rai asked.

Shesmu gestured to his clothing. It wasn't the same jerkin everyone else wore. "They call me the Master of Blood. It's a fancy made up title to say, I study diera ore and its properties then train the Verdin Guild on how to use them. Diera weapons are no secret here." He held his hands out. "I'm not revealing anything to you that everyone else here doesn't already know. Even the other monarchs know of it. They just don't know where we source it from. That is a secret between me and the emperor."

Rai's mind was reeling. This is what he was looking for: a way to become stronger. To step into battle ensured that he would win and protect those he cared for.

"Will you teach me?" Rai asked, fighting to keep the desperation from his tone.

Shesmu grinned and threw him Lintou's blade.

Rai caught it.

32

Copse of Corpses

Golden sand flowed like water beneath Rai. He coughed out a cloud of dust and wiped it from his eyes. His senses reorienting, Rai realised he was laid across his hyian. Fax reached out to check if he was okay and Rai waved the shade off as he pulled himself up into the saddle.

"A drink?" Imayani asked. She rode at his side, waterskin outstretched. He nodded his thanks as he threw back the water and surveyed the scene.

Rai remembered burning. The black sand phantom. His eyes widened and head swivelled.

"Everyone's here and unhurt thanks to you," Imayani said and right enough, Kleran led the company and Tysar held up the rear with Yeru. Mino was at Imayani's side, pouting.

Rai relaxed and took another swig of water. "What happened?"

"The Sun Eye burnt away the black sand phantom," Mino said.

"*After* you and your shade held it at bay." Imayani gave her friend a scolding look.

That must have been the burning sensation. He had been too wrapped up in the phantom's mind. They had always been described as mindless creatures but it seemed to *awaken* after coming in contact with Fax.

It remembered, Fax said.

Remembered what?

Its past life. Being something more. Something greater. I think, in a way, it's like me.

Like you? Rai asked.

We connected. If I wasn't bonded with you, I think it would have consumed me, Fax said.

You won't let me become like that will you, Rai?

When talking through Rai's mind words held impressions like a voice did inflections and Rai could sense the shade's fear of becoming a mindless creature like the black sand phantom.

"Is everything okay?" Imayani asked.

Rai straightened, realising he was scowling. "Yes, sorry. I guess I must have hit my head. How long have I been out?"

"Three days," Imayani said.

"Three days?" Rai's mind whirled. How could he have been unconscious for three days?

The phantom put strain on your mind, Fax said. *I've been watching them for you.*

"We've been fine," Imayani said with placating hands held up.

"Were there any other attacks?" Rai asked.

"No. We've been riding hard and only stopped a couple of times," Imayani said.

Rai rubbed his face.

"Rai, I'm truly grateful for your help but we aren't completely reliant on you," Imayani said amusement lining her tone.

"I know. I just…"

It's all I know how to do. The thought was silly but Rai couldn't shake it. He had spent his life guarding Imayani, trying to do good by Tarris. And the thought that he could have lost everything while he was unconscious, leaving the empress and a monarch to fend for themselves without guards gripped his chest.

It was a line of thinking Rai had been ignoring. Who was he if he wasn't the man who returned to Tansen to save it? If he wasn't the man who turned at the crossroads and rode into danger to help the Seventh Sceptre. If he wasn't the man who could protect the current rulers.

Who was he if he wasn't the hero?

Without the constant threats to Tarris, who was he?

He liked to think of himself as the hero who turned back to help but really he returned because he had nowhere else to go.

"Do you know why I sent you away?" Imayani asked.

Rai glanced up. She had pulled her hyian closer and Mino had fallen back to talk with Tysar and Yeru.

"It was too painful to see me," Rai said remembering her words.

"That was true," Imayani said. "But there was another reason. I was so angry when I saw that you still lived. But with time that faded. I remembered a better time when I showed you the gardens. This stubborn boy who refused to give up." She smiled and Rai couldn't help but smile back. "I imagined a life for you. A wife. A house. I wanted that for you.

"I thought you might have had that. That if I sent you away you might be able to have a normal life. It was a way out."

"But the Verdin Guild?" Rai asked. She had sent him to the Verdin Guild.

"You could have disappeared again. I had *hoped* you would disappear again," Imayani said. "I'm trapped in this life but you aren't."

They rode in silence as Rai thought on her words. Imayani had created an out for him. A way to live a simple life, like Elder Kalt and Syl in Gamo village.

Rai had that opportunity the night he abandoned his post at the Seventh Sceptre. But he had spent the last five years hunting for the truth about the shades and the dark place beyond. He had never truly left. In his mind he was fulfilling the mission Imayani had sent him on all those years ago.

There was nothing for him in simplicity. Like a young adult learning the ways of the world, once he had learned the truth, there was no returning to innocence. He bore the weight of knowing and strove to protect those who lived unknowingly within the war of shadows.

Rai didn't know how to put these thoughts into words. He didn't know how to explain it to Imayani.

"Given the choice, I wouldn't be anywhere else," he finally said.

Imayani smiled at him. But it wasn't a thankful smile. It was a sad, pitying thing. Frail and false. It did little to settle Rai's mind. He had to explain that he had to be here.

"You once told me charah flowers never truly lived. That they spent their lives striving to live. You were wrong. Maybe the charah flowers fight for life is living. What is a life without fight? What is a life without seeing what you're truly capable of? Growth is living. Striving is living. Perhaps what we thought was pointless effort was the reward itself. The strain of showing the world that you are alive, you are living and death will have to put up a fight to take it from you." Rai thought back to the choice he made in Atef Palace, when Overseer Rikai had them doing laps in the Eye. And again at the crossroads where he could have fallen back into obscurity. He had chosen a life of suffering for it was better than a life without. Pain is inevitable. How one reacts to it is a choice each must make.

Her eyes were distant and face thoughtful. "I can't believe you still remember that."

Rai was about to respond when Mino called, "Hey, look!"

Ahead was a grove of bone trees. Sheltered by tall rock formations on either side, the alabaster trees grew in a copse. It was rare seeing more than three or four together, much less an entire grove of them. They reached towards the sky like withered hands flayed of skin and flesh.

The party passed beneath them. Branches reached over them like an arch, fracturing the light from the Sun Eye. A lone bone tree was a bad omen among the Tarrisians. But a group was rare and seen as a sign of good luck.

"I've never seen so many together," Mino mused.

"Sheltered in between these rocks will make it easier for them to survive," Yeru said. They had all grouped together as they made their way through the grove.

"Bone trees are sometimes referred to as dead reaches," Imayani said. Rai caught a glint in her eye. A remnant of the old her that loved plant life. "Some believe they are the Unjudged dead who are to forever linger in this world. And that these are their hands reaching up to Ova the World Turner begging to be released."

"Foolish superstition," Kleran said.

Imayani scowled at the back of the man's head. This was the first time Rai had heard Imayani mention flora since his return.

"I had once thought Ma-atan was little more than a superstition," Rai said.

Kleran blew out a breath.

"I've always wondered what bone trees live off," Rai said.

Imayani glanced over to him but she saw through his stilted attempt to have her talk about her old love. However, that didn't stop her from answering his question.

"They have roots like all trees that sap what they can from deep within the sand. They can delve for miles in search of water or some sort of mineral deposit," she said. "Contrary to popular belief they aren't dead plants. They live like any other plant. They grow and survive by any means they can. Resilient and beautiful."

The flickering light of the Sun Eye flashed over Imayani's face as she looked over the copse of bone trees in wonder.

Only Imayani could be surrounded in death and call it beautiful. But when one lived a life like hers, death had to be beautiful or it would consume her.

33

An Unwelcome Return

Nya peered out from the cave mouth upon the place that haunted her nightmares. The sky stormed in grey waves of cloud and the pale light blanketed the black rock landscape of the dark place. Bom thrummed with the energy of the place. It was different than being here the first time. With the shade's perception, she could feel an underlying buzz. An energy coursing through the air. It beckoned her forward.

Bom wasn't pleased about being back, which surprised Nya. She had assumed the creature thought of this place as its home. But as she searched through the shade's impressions, this place carried another connotation.

Prison.

"Come on." A guard set a hand on Nya's shoulder, bringing her back to the moment. Taking a shaky breath, she followed the party down the slope of black scree.

The company consisted of four guards, a scholar, Mirt, Adani, and Nya. She had been given a pack of supplies and a change of clothes before they set off. Her palace garb matched the others with a red tunic under a thick leather jerkin. Still, she wore her half-patched blue cloak that her mother had never finished, draped over her shoulders. All the gear was heavier than Nya was used to and she was sure she would feel the strain if they were to be walking for any length of time.

While never said outright, the threat for Nya's cooperation was there. Mirt had explained that they had planned to come and get her and that they knew of the Patched Cloak and those who worked there. Illy, Wenson, Bas, Kit and even Lem. His words had been sharp and they might as well have been a knife to their throats. However, he promised that Bas was alive despite Nya's lingering memories of Adani using his shade to tear into him.

After seeing what Adani could do, Nya had no thoughts of being able to save her friends. He was too strong. All she could do was go along with their plan.

For now.

Her machinations had begun to take shape in her mind in the last day since she had woken in the palace. Nya glanced up to see Adani watching her. But she had to be careful and time her move.

"Brave to face up to that one," a guard said. Nya tore her eyes away from Adani and brought them to the guard at her side. It was the same one who had been in her cell when she woke. He walked with a straight back and eyes forward, a palace guard through and through. His dark hair was tucked into a black cap. "Best to avoid him if you want to survive this."

"I'm not afraid of him," Nya said.

"You should be."

Mirt marched on ahead talking with his scholar and waved dramatically over the landscape. The other three guards surrounded them watching the sky, listening for the beating of black wings. Nya, too, searched the sky. Memories of the husks appearing as a black wave sent a shiver up her spine.

"You've been here before," Blackcap said.

Nya tried to hide her apprehension but nodded.

"You've seen them? The husks?"

"Yes," Nya said. Phantom pains of the creature's claws tearing into her back.

The guard inclined his head. "Keep your eyes to the sky, girl. Mirt promises that the tear will protect us but if you see movement, run."

"The tear will protect us?" Nya asked.

Blackcap cleared his throat. "Apparently so. Mirt talked to it."

"Mirt talked to *the tear*?" Nya asked.

I see you.

The voice that came from this place. The connection and feeling of reawakening Nya had felt in the temple of Ma-atan clutched at her lungs.

"I wouldn't have believed it either. Not sure if I do, but I've seen what Adani can do and it is not of our world," Blackcap said.

"What did it say?" Nya asked.

The guard shrugged. "Mirt only talks to Captain Ewyna about it. But even that's rare. Mostly he mumbles to himself or to a voice none of the rest of us can hear."

The voice she heard in Ma-atan's temple was from here. She felt it through Bom and through this place. That connection closed off when Nya had regained control of her shade and her emotions. But if she quested out, Nya could feel it stirring just beyond her perception.

Why was it speaking with Mirt? Nya wondered. She felt Blackcap staring at her.

"You're being awfully open with your prisoner," Nya said.

His deep-set eyes were as dark as the stone around them. "You're no prisoner and I'm no guard. Not since we crossed the threshold into this Duat-damned realm. Now we're just people trying to do a job and get home alive."

There was no hint of a lie in his expression. Nya doubted he wanted to be there any more than she did.

"And I don't like our chances," he added under his breath.

When Nya had first come to this dark realm, fear had stained her sight. Rocks took shape as monsters. Movement flickered in the corner of her vision. But as the company made their way through these dead lands, Nya did not feel that same fear that once held her in a stranglehold. With Bom's strength and awareness she had become more confident, which let her survey the landscape with a more discerning eye.

What once she saw as random rock formations, Nya now found shape and structure. The cave with the tear was part of a mound of black stone that towered above the rest. But as they moved down the scree, rock walls corralled them on either side in an almost purposeful grid-like layout.

There couldn't be people here. They would have seen them. Nya ran her hand across the rock wall. The glass-like texture undulated and ridged like the sand dunes. So did the husks or something else create these structures? Or was she looking for patterns where there weren't any?

Mirt and the scholar laughed, their voices echoing through the landscape. Nya cringed and glanced upward. The other guards were doing the same. How could Mirt strut through this place so brazen when the scholar knew what it held? Was he that confident about their safety after speaking to the voice?

They marched on through the day and although the sky never dimmed, growling stomachs and sore legs required them to stop. Nestling into a small cavern, the guards set about lighting a fire. And despite Nya's wariness, they hadn't come across any husks or living creatures yet.

Nya watched as Mirt settled down by the fire talking animatedly to his scholar friend. Blackcap had said Mirt spoke to the tear and that it would keep the husks away but was that possible?

She had spoken to the darkness here, too. After connecting with it, Nya somehow knew it. Knew it was here and felt its… grandness. It ruled this domain. But did it truly have the power to hold back all the creatures here?

Bom, I need to know what you know about the voice, Nya thought. It had curled into a ball and hid every time she brought up the topic. Even now she felt the shade's fear.

I do not know.

Come on. You must know something. You were born here, Nya

thought.

I… I was only truly born when I bonded with you.

What?

Before then, things are murky. I was not as I am now.

Rai had said something similar happened with Fax. He said his shade became more human-like and able to understand more the longer they were bonded. Nya hadn't been bonded to Bom for long but already what was once a creature of essence had now formed a personality of sorts. When they were first together it did little more than feed off her emotions but now she could feel its emotions too. As if it were becoming its own creature.

It rules this place, Bom said. She could feel the shade straining through memories. *And it can see from the darkness.*

A shiver crawled up Nya's spine as she stole glances at the darkened corners of the cave. They were still and empty.

It is trapped here.

Nya's eyes went wide. *The voice is trapped in the dark place?*

And it wants out.

Nya yelped as someone touched her side. She turned to see Blackcap holding out a strip of meat.

"Are you okay?" He furrowed his brow. The others around the fire looked her way. Adani was grinning. "You look a little pale. Come by the fire."

"I'm fine," Nya said.

"You need to eat if you want to survive this," the guard replied quieter.

Nya snatched the meat from his hand and ambled over to the fire. Rations were passed out and Adani set to boiling a pot over the fire to brew tea.

"We rest here for the night," Adani said.

"Does this place even have night?" one of the guards asked. Outside, that pale light still illuminated the dark landscape.

"It does," Mirt said. "Whether time works differently here or if this light is not of Ova the World Turner, we do not know. But it does get dark. Days just last a lot longer here."

"One day is about equal to seven days Tarrisian time," the other scholar added.

Nya squinted at Mirt as he tore off a piece of his meat strip. She needed answers. "You said the dark asked for me. What is this darkness?"

Mirt went rigid. His food halfway to his mouth. Nya noted the unease that crept into the other guards' faces. This was clearly not a topic they wanted to discuss. The only one who hadn't reacted to her question was Adani, who continued to make tea.

"It is an ancient deity beyond our understanding," Mirt said.

"And what does it want with us?" Nya asked.

"It wants back what you stole from it," Mirt said. Nya scowled, not understanding. "The shade, Nya. Why do you think we were looking for you?"

Nya felt Bom's conflicting feelings. There was a wave of shock and then a questioning as it searched its memories once more. Part of it screamed to turn and run, while the other half of it wanted to return to this deity.

"What does it want with my shade? And what is it offering you in return?"

Mirt licked his lips and grinned. "It promised us answers. Once we're in its good favour, we can ask it questions about how the world works. What this place is." Mirt sat forward, fervour burning in his eyes. "We will singlehandedly progress our understanding of everything overnight. Tarris will become the place of knowledge in the world once more.

"Already the tear has told us much. We have many misunderstandings on how this world works. How do you think Adani overpowered you so easily?"

Adani continued to brew his tea but Nya noted the beginning of a smile curling at the side of the man's mouth.

"It speaks to me because I opened myself to it," Adani said. "The sooner you see that you are part of the darkness, the sooner you can be free, Nya."

A sudden chill came over the cave. Nya's breath caught and then it was there.

It was as if a great overbearing presence was standing over her. She felt it calling from the shadows of the cave. Clawing fingers dug into her mind. The dark used no words but it spoke and Nya saw through eyes that weren't her own. She flew over the landscape from where they hid. Over the rocky surface, past the scree-covered expanse to a place of pure shadow.

It looked to be a city of black stone. Dark rock walls rose around more structures made of the same black glass-like rock. And in the centre of the city of stone was a black shroud. Nya squinted through this new sight but she couldn't break the thick darkness and see what was inside.

A patch stirred in the black. A purple eye. It looked at Nya.

Nya inhaled sharply and looked around her. The familiar cave walls lit by the pale light of the entrance. The faces of the guards and scholars. She was back in the cave. Her heart raced in her chest. Adani had a similar shocked face. Was he shown the same?

Bom reached out to the Dark. Nya dragged the shade back into herself shutting it off from the beckoning presence. She was breathing hard, eyes darting between the shadows, searching for movement. Adani grinned at her as the others continued talking. And just like that the presence was gone.

"Did it show you?" Adani asked.

Nya glared at him over the fire.

"That's where we are headed. The Black City."

Nya did not sleep. Some of the guards took turns napping by the fire. However, Nya couldn't sleep. Not after that. Not after seeing that darkness. It was so much grander than she had imagined. Much like in Ma-atan's temple, when the dark connected with her, Bom fell into an almost trance-like state. The shade was inexplicably drawn to the Dark and it was dragging her along with it. The pull was stronger now that they were in the dark place and Nya had no doubt the closer they got to the black stone city, the harder it would be to break its connection.

Nya rolled over, facing the fire. Past it, the sky was still light. Mirt and the other scholar, who Nya learned was called Novi, and two of the guards lay sleeping around the fire. While Blackcap, the guard who had taken a liking to Nya, stood watch at the cave entrance. Adani was nowhere to be seen.

Drool dribbled down Mirt's face as he let out long deep breaths. Nya hadn't planned to make her move so soon but she couldn't risk getting any closer to the darkness. That vision had scared her more than any nightmare of this place. She couldn't unsee that purple eye staring at her. Nya eased herself up from the bundled blankets and pushed up to her haunches.

Bom, let me know if any of them stir, Nya thought and Bom reached out through the shadows watching the others.

Creeping around the flames, Nya couldn't take her eyes off the pack that Mirt clutched in his slumber. He hadn't let it leave his sight since they left Tarris. Nya's heart hammered as she approached and slid her hands around the pack. Nya tugged on it lightly but Mirt's grasp was firm. There was no way she could remove it without waking the scholar. So instead, she worked at the knots and pulled the flap back.

Mirt stirred and Nya stilled.

He let out a long exhale and moved onto his back. The movement threw open the top of the pack and the black dagger fell out. Nya's breath caught as she dove for the dagger, snatching it before it could clatter to the ground. Bom hissed and pulled back into the depths of her shadow. The dagger felt hot in her grip. It wasn't a normal heat but one that burned her from the inside out. Nya stifled a scream and the impulse to toss it away. She felt the fear pulsing from her shade.

Bom! Calm! I have it, Nya thought. *It can't be used against us.*

Bom reacted slowly and Nya stood frozen, afraid to move as the shade unfurled in her gut and the heat eased. Nya could feel the shade's instinctual terror regarding the dagger. It was like a human seeing a wild kiren with its pointed teeth, snouted face and long wolf-like features. One doesn't need to see a kiren tear something apart to know it is a predator.

The heat subsided.

Nya felt lightheaded. She took a moment to steady her racing heart, then straightened and slid the dagger into her belt, pulling her tunic over the pommel.

Nya made her way to the cave entrance and nodded to the guard as she passed. He glanced up over his book.

"Where are you going?" he asked.

"Taking a leak," she said, not slowing.

The guard made a noise as if to say something.

"You said I wasn't a prisoner. Surely I can go to the bathroom in peace? Where would I run off to?" Nya raised an eyebrow.

He let out a strained sigh but nodded. "Okay but be quick."

Nya turned and made her way around the side of the rock formation and out of sight. She felt bad for the guard. He had been kind to her when he hadn't needed to be and she was abusing that kindness. But what choice did she have?

Nya broke out into a run. They had walked for most of the day so she had a lot of ground to cover to make it back to the tear. And while she couldn't run the whole way, she wanted to create as much distance from her and the party as quickly as possible. It wouldn't be long until the guard would come looking for her.

The dagger rubbed at her side. Elation and fear fuelled her limbs as Nya sprinted over the scree of dark rocks. Kit, Bas, Wenson, Illy and she had planned to sneak into the palace, steal the dagger, and close the tear. Now Nya could do that without endangering the others and trap those who may be able to reopen the tear inside this dark place.

This might be the only chance she got.

Soon her pace waned and she slowed. Nya glanced back but no one was on her tail.

"It's okay. We won't need to face that thing, Bom," Nya said. Although the words were to comfort herself as much as the shade. "Once we close the tear, this'll be over. The husks will stop coming through. The darkness won't be able to take you. And we'll be free."

The crunch of stones at her feet was almost inaudible under the rumble of the storm in the sky. Clouds roared and swirled. This was a realm of violence. Everything was hard and sharp enough to cut. Even the rocks dug into Nya's feet. She could see why Bom thought of this place as a prison.

A thought came to Nya.

"Prison."

Bom stirred.

"You think of this place as a prison?"

Yes.

"So you're not from here?"

No.

"Then where are you from?"

Home, Bom said. It sent images of Tarris.

"You mean that's become your home?" Nya asked.

Bom strained through its thoughts. Coming to this dark place seemed to have opened its mind and the shade was able to delve deeper into its memories.

No, Bom said. *Tarris is home.*

Nya stopped walking.

"You were from Tarris?"

The shade sent more flashes of memory to Nya. It was undoubtedly

Tarris but not as she knew it. It was *dark*, like a sandstorm blocked out the Sun Eye. And the buildings looked different. If these were memories, it had been a long time since Bom was in Tarris. And if it considered the dark place as a prison, perhaps it had been locked in here?

Nya's mind was reeling. She didn't know how long she had stood there staring blankly as she searched through Bom and her thoughts.

They were so deep in thought that Nya barely noticed the rocks shifting under her feet.

34

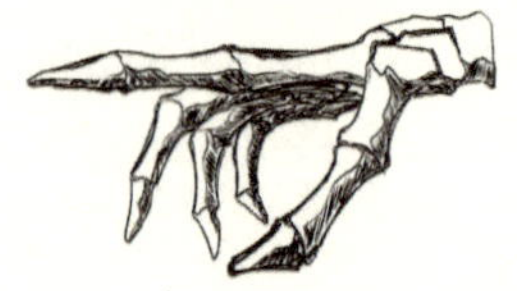

A Gift in the Ashes

Kit had made a living using his weaknesses as strengths. He was small and wiry for his age so he wasn't much of a fighter. On the street, that meant death for most. But not Kit. Being small meant he could sneak into places others couldn't. Because he was non-threatening he made the perfect liaison between merchants and the gangs of Yontar.

This is no different, Kit told himself.

The Sun Eye shone bright as Kit walked down the thoroughfare. It was late morning and most were finishing up their errands to get out of the worst of the heat. The Thousand Floor Palace loomed above, the palace wall protecting it from people like him. The problem with walls was that most had gates. And soon enough he would be carried through like an emperor of old.

He caught sight of Bas and Wenson wandering towards him

from the opposite direction. Bas was healing slowly but the Urdahl refused to wait any longer. Every second they wasted here was a second Nya was alone and held captive.

Kit couldn't believe the Urdahl's strength. After cleaning and binding his wounds, Kit thought he would be in bed for days. But here he was. Ready to take part in Kit's plan. Of course Kit had heard that the *Silencers of Thought* had the ability to quieten pain. But he hadn't *believed* it.

Kit slowed his pace so that he would meet Bas in front of the palace gates. Two guards stood at the gate and more were upon the wall. Most Tarrisians gave the gate a wide berth as any who got close fell under the scrutiny of the guards. He glanced up at the palace.

We're coming, Nya.

Kit bumped into Bas. Bas stopped and stared at Kit.

"Watch where you're going! I didn't realise you silenced all thought!" Kit shouted and then shoved Bas. Wenson scowled at Kit. The Urdahl kept his face still but shoved Kit back. Kit tripped and sent up a plume of dust. Damn, he was strong.

"Now you've done it," Kit said. He pushed up and charged at Bas. The guards started shouting for them to stop just as Kit threw the first punch. It cracked Bas across the nose and blood gushed from the wound. The Urdahl wiped his nose and then unslung the two broken hafts of his spear as Kit fell into a fighting stance.

Despite being broken, the spear hafts were sharp.

Suddenly, Kit wasn't so sure about this.

Bas lunged. Kit dove to the side and brought his fist back around as one of Bas' spear ends pierced his side. Kit's eyes bulged and his arm dropped to his side. He gasped clutching at the wound. There was no blood. Hopefully the guards wouldn't question the strange phenomenon. Kit swayed as Wenson swept in and held him. Then Bas came in close and stabbed him again in his shoulder. Pain ran hot spreading over him like a fever.

"Was that necessary?" Kit pulled in a ragged breath.

"The first was a grazing wound. They would know you couldn't die from it," Bas whispered. "This collapsed your lung."

Good to know, Kit thought and collapsed. He closed his eyes and heard the guards swarm them. They demanded Bas and Wenson drop their weapons. One ran to Kit's side and inspected his wounds before checking his pulse.

"He's dead," the guard said.

It was a fair, if wrong, assumption that the boy lying with two spear ends sticking from him that had no heartbeat was dead. For a while, Kit stayed still as the guards conferred.

Come on, Kit thought. *You can't leave us out here.*

Arms pulled him up and dropped him into a sling. Someone yanked out the two spear ends and Kit did everything in his power not to scream at the pain. There was clanging of a metal mechanism and then they were moving again. They had made it past the gates.

And we're in. Carried in like an emperor of old. Kind of.

Kit was jostled as they carried him into the palace. He had only seen this once before when a beggar died outside the palace walls. They brought the corpse in and took it to the infirmary before, Kit assumed, disposing of the body.

Guards scolded the Urdahl with discriminatory slurs. Kit did all he could to bite his tongue but was glad Bas wasn't far from him. Eventually their voices passed out of hearing and Kit tried to track what turns the guards took him so he could find his way back to Bas and Wenson. They carried Kit down a flight of stairs and through some long corridors until they came to a door. It clattered open and Kit was tossed inside. He landed on something soft. The smell made Kit's eyes water and he suppressed a gag.

A door slammed shut and everything was still. After a few moments, Kit cracked an eye open to darkness. This wasn't the infirmary. Kit sat up, heaving. The smell was turning his stomach. Maybe this was where they left the dead when the infirmary was full.

A latch slid open and Kit collapsed into the position he was left in. Even with his eyes closed he could see a light appear before the latch slammed shut.

Kit opened his eyes to fire.

He squealed rolling and patting an ember than singed the edge of his clothing. The fire lit the room in a red light. It was a circular chamber that rose high towards an unseeable roof. Kit had never seen a room like it. He glanced down. The soft ground he thought might have been bedding was a pile of corpses. He screamed and scrambled up but his hand pushed through a decaying rib cage.

This was too much. Kit threw up. He steadied himself and wiped his hand clean as the fire expanded.

This chamber was for burning the dead.

"Hey! Help! I'm not dead!" Kit shouted. He had to get out. He couldn't die. He couldn't die. Not yet. His hands started to shake uncontrollably. He ran to the edge of the room and battered on the wall but it was no use. The fire was spreading too quickly. Panic seized his chest as death entombed him.

The door was just out of reach so Kit started to clamber up the uneven stone wall. Under him, the fire crackled and roared covering the floor of the chamber. If he fell back now he would die a long and painful death. Kit knew he could regenerate but there was a limit. He would live through the fire burning away his skin. It was only when it had burnt through his vital organs that he would die.

His arms shook as he climbed.

"Come on, Kit," Kit said. "Get a hold of yourself."

He reached the door and tried the handle. Locked. He banged against it shouting as loud as he could. The heat was becoming unbearable as the fire fed on the dead. The door cracked open and a young guard stared down at him. Kit couldn't imagine how he looked. Half dead, burnt clothing, hanging from the door of a room of burning corpses.

Kit yanked himself up and into the corridor breathing hard. He looked at his hand that still trembled.

"Who are you and what are you doing in there?" the guard's voice came out as a high squeak.

Kit slowed his breathing and watched as his trembling hand stilled. Never in all his years of running scams did he panic in a life and death situation. Even after his talk with Lem, he felt the unbridled fear of death. He would need to get that under control.

"Hey!" the guard said. He didn't come any closer to Kit.

Exhaling, Kit glanced up at the young guard. "Sorry to scare you. I'm Kit." He then kicked out and the guard grunted as he tumbled back. Kit turned to run but then saw the young guard trip on his own feet towards the open door.

Kit leapt after the boy, hand out. Their fingers touched and a sudden rush of cold took Kit's breath away. Energy flowed from the guard and up Kit's arm with a tingling numbing sensation. The guard screamed looking at his hand. His skin peeled and flaked, black with decay.

The boy screamed as he fell into the fire. The rush of energy passed as quickly as it came but all of Kit's aches and pains had vanished. He looked down to see that his two wounds had completely healed. That should have taken days even with his healing.

Was that from the boy? Had he drawn on his life to heal himself somehow? Kit had killed before. You had to on the streets but it hadn't ever felt like that before. Smoke began to fill the corridor so Kit slammed the door shut.

Guilt washed over him. Killing someone standing in your way was one thing but to *use them* was another. Kit didn't know how to feel. The guard had just been a boy.

The sound of heavy boots clomped down the corridor. More guards coming to find out what the noise was. He had to move and find Bas and Wenson. He had to shake this from his mind. Distraction was death. Kit took off, running back the way he came.

How did anyone get around this palace? *All the corridors look the same,* Kit thought as he shot around a corner. There were two guards ahead so Kit slowed and put his head down. If one acted like they belonged, they could blend in anywhere. The guards passed without a word.

Kit made his way back to the intersection he was sure Bas and Wenson had turned off at. Bas had formulated a rough map of the palace for sneaking in. He said that despite the fact that the passages and hallways changed, the main rooms were always in the same place. So if one knew roughly where they wanted to go they could head in that direction and find it. Impractical, Kit thought but he could see the defence tactic in such a set up.

Making his way down the flight of stairs, he crept quietly and strained to listen for guards. Sconces marked the walls some lit and some unlit. The map Bas had sketched for them had the palace cells near this area. Kit was sure of it. If he kept wandering in this direction he should—

"Feed them? They killed that boy on the streets! They need a beating, not food," said a female voice.

"We follow the rules, Amme," a gruff guard responded.

Found them.

Kit peeked around the corner to see a female guard standing at the cell door while the older male guard was passing a tray of gruel through the opening. Kit shivered remembering eating that same gruel last time he was in the palace cells.

He needed a way to get past them. Could he lead them away with a distraction? It was unlikely. This wasn't like the stories when one could run up and tell them that there was a fire. These were palace guards. They would need to be lit on fire themselves before moving from their post. Kit glanced to his hand and remembered the feeling of that boy dying under his touch. There was a hunger in him now to feel that again. No. He only killed when he had to.

Kit cleared his throat and walked down the corridor. He didn't have many skills but talking enough nonsense to confuse someone into doing what he wanted was one of them. These weren't the same guards at the gate. So at least they wouldn't recognise him. Kit straightened his back and walked with an air of superiority. Amme, the female guard arched an eyebrow as he approached.

"I'm here to see the prisoners," Kit said.

Both guards stared at Kit, unsure what to make of him. "On who's orders?"

"My own."

"I don't know what you're playing at kid," the guard said.

"Sir," Kit corrected.

"Sirs don't wear half burnt clothes," Amme said.

Kit glanced down. He forgot about that. It was hard to pull off a regal look when your clothes were falling off of you.

"What I do in my spare time is not to be questioned by some palace guard," Kit snapped.

The guards looked at one another. They were sceptical, Kit knew, but no street kid would use a tone like that and mistaking a noble's son or someone of importance for a street kid would be detrimental to their career.

"Let me pass," Kit said.

The male guard stepped forward. "Unfortunately, we can't do that… sir. I didn't catch your name."

"I never proffered it. The fact you haven't recognised me is an insult unto itself," Kit said.

The guard rolled her eyes. They were getting annoyed now. This was going nowhere. New tact. "I'm the boy this man killed. Climbed out of the furnace to take some revenge, you see."

"That's ridiculous. That boy had no pulse."

Kit held out his hand and Amme looked over to the other guard who gave a curt nod. She held his wrist for a moment and then went white. "He's not got a pulse."

Both guards went to draw their swords and Kit lunged at Amme. She squealed as they fell to the floor. They tumbled but she pinned him down without much difficulty. Kit clasped her wrists trying to throw her off but he couldn't move her. The cold tip of a sword touched Kit's neck and he froze.

"I don't know what your game is, but you'll regret this," the guard said.

Anger and frustration flushed through Kit as a heat from deep inside. If only he wasn't so weak!

Amme's voice caught.

"Get him up," the older guard said. But Amme's face was contorted in pain. "What's wrong?" he asked.

Her skin started to go grey.

"What're you doing to her?" The guard brought the sword back to Kit's neck.

"I..." Kit noticed the greyness was coming from her wrists, spreading from under his hand. Her skin peeled and flaked like ash. The guard slashed down on Kit's hands. He screamed and pulled back, gashes bit deep into his wrists.

Amme collapsed. The guard dropped to her side and checked her pulse, keeping the sword pointed at Kit. The gnawing pain in his cut wrists was sharp and burning. He couldn't take his eyes off the puckered flesh. If the guard hadn't been terrified of Kit, he was sure he would have cleaved off Kit's hands.

Then the same rush as before came again.

Pleasure flooded Kit as a warm wave. He trembled and exhaled. Then the surge of energy travelled through his body and to his wrists. Kit watched as threads of tendons and flesh knit themselves together.

The other guard watched too. Kit waited for it to heal and then tested his hands by balling them into fists. They weren't even stiff. He stood and rolled his wrists. What kind of monster was he?

"What are you?" the guard's voice was quiet and small.

"I'm sorry." Kit picked up Amme's sword and rammed it into the man's chest. "I'm so sorry."

The guard didn't fight back. He choked as his lungs were pierced and blood trickled down the side of his mouth. Then he was dead. Kit reached out and felt the last of his life sap away and moments later, that same pleasure seeped through him. He hated how good it felt.

After it passed, Kit took a minute to come back to himself. He glanced down at the guards and felt sick.

Don't think. Don't think.

Kit pulled the key free from the man's belt and stepped up to the door. He fumbled the key. His breaths coming short and sharp. *Click.* Kit threw the door open to see Bas sitting in a meditative position against the far wall. Wenson sat on the bench his head in his hands.

They both glanced up.

"What's wrong?" Bas asked.

Kit swallowed. "I killed the guards." It was all he could manage.

Calmly, Bas stood and walked past Kit.

"You did what you had to," Bas said. "Someone might see them. Help me drag them into the cell."

Kit wanted to tell him. Warn him about his strange touch. The memory of the woman's skin decaying was too much. Kit balled his fists to stop them from shaking. Verses from the translated tome came back to him.

Bound to death, it stalks the deathless like a killer in wait. It will steal breath and life drinking it in, all the while growing stronger.

He thought it had referred to *his* breath and life being drunk. Not only did this curse steal life from Kit, he could now steal life from others too.

But those who have promise in their heart and minds are given the gift of the deathless.

What kind of gift was this?

35

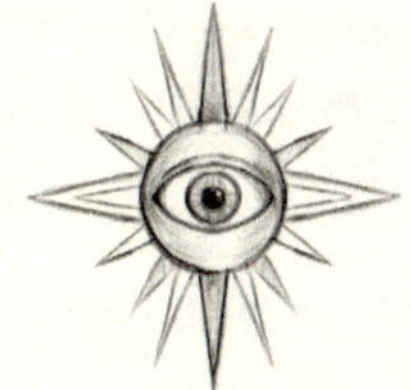

The Path of Blood

13 years ago.

The Moon Eye broke the horizon and lit the black sands in silver. Rai stood on the Verdin Temple plateau, the wind blowing through him as he teetered on the edge. The Deadlands Basin spread out before him. Once a terrorizing stretch of sand was now nothing more than his training grounds.

Rai breathed out and fell forward. He dropped headfirst down the side of the plateau. The rock wall was an incoherent blur of motion. As he came to the hard sand below, Rai shot a diera arrow. It hit the ground and Rai flicked his wrist. Refin blood ran up the arrow's length. Usually the blood was used to control and nudge the arrow but if Shesmu taught him anything it was that the blood arts had more than one application. The control seemed to be an almost magnetic pull and while training with Shesmu, Rai had learned that he could use the ground as leverage to move himself with that same energy. His fall slowed as he came closer to the arrow until it threw him forward. He flipped and landed on his feet, another arrow already nocked.

A pack of helix glanced up from feeding on a dead sand fox and hissed. He loosed the arrow and it tore through three of the beasts before losing momentum. The rest of the pack lunged at Rai. He drew his daggers. Swiping in a wide arc, flames burst from his daggers sending a plume through the helix. The force of the wave knocked them mid jump and they rolled about the ground alight and screaming. Rai trudged among them, slicing their necks. They may be vicious things but they deserved a clean death. He sent a prayer out to Ma-ilus, the deity of all wild creatures to care for them during their passing.

Rai whistled. The high searing note carried across the desert and, a moment later, a hyian tore from the hidden Verdin Guild stables built into the base of the plateau. It came to his side and dipped its head. Rai matched the gesture and leapt atop its back. Whipping the reins, they shot out into the black sand desert. Rai stayed low on the beast's back letting it stride across the dunes.

Small beasts chased them but a single arrow killed most of what could match their pace. Rai was hunting for something larger tonight, and he didn't have to travel far. Having spent most of the last couple years training out in the Deadlands Basin, Rai was growing familiar with its shape. A huge rock stuck out from the sand where it should not. Rai steered the hyian towards it.

Rai stood on the hyian's back and launched himself atop the rock. For a moment, the boulder remained still. Then it began shaking and rumbling beneath his feet. With a sudden jerk, the bouldon emerged from the black sand. The sand burst out like clumped rock as the bouldon woke. The hyian hissed and ran out of striking range.

The bouldon had a body of stone that the creature built around its wiry frame. Over time, it grew nerves and limbs into the rock until it could move like the stone was part of it.

Rai thrust his dagger into the stone as the bouldon tried to shake him off. Once that didn't work, the stone beast flopped forward hoping to crush Rai. Rai ran along the length of the bouldon's body as it fell. He unslung his bow and leapt. Midair Rai loosed the arrow that stuck between the joint of the body and arm. He hit the hard sand in a roll before pulling himself up and moving away from the bouldon.

BANG.

The explosion sent out a shockwave that knocked Rai from his feet. The bouldon, now free from its rocky exterior, screamed. It was an ear-piercing squeal. Rai covered his ears as he squinted in the dark. The bouldon's body was akin to a plant's roots. The main body was no larger than Rai's forearm with thin, fleshy tendrils reaching outward into the rock. Part of its body had been blown off and an iridescent liquid poured down the shattered rock.

Laying back, Rai pulled an arrow free and shot it right at the main body. With a hiss, the screaming stopped and the bouldon dropped to the black sand.

Rai stretched his aching limbs. *I need to get further before loosing those explosion arrows,* Rai thought, rolling his shoulder. At least another couple meters.

In the distance, another black sand creature howled. It had heard the commotion and was coming for Rai. He whistled and the hyian returned. Rai jumped onto its back and rode to meet the beast.

It was nearing dawn when Rai returned to the Verdin Temple. Dirt and blood stained his Verdin Guild jerkin. He nodded to Yor, the old man grunting and sending the platform lift firing upward. Yor wasn't a big talker.

The clatter of practice swords rung from the training grounds. Warriors trained at all hours in the Verdin Guild. Some sparred on the training grounds. Some entered the many halls to face challenges. And some, like Rai, travelled out into the Deadlands Basin to face down the monsters that roamed the night.

In the years since joining the Verdin Guild, Rai had spent every waking moment with Shesmu learning all he could about diera weapons and their practical applications. He trained with others too, of course. He had to keep his combat skills sharp. But he spent more time with Shesmu than anyone else at the temple.

Rai made his way to Shesmu's hall when Tys bumped into him from the shadows. "Another night on the sand?" he asked.

His jerkin was dusty, telling the tale of hours spent training in the sparring circles. Tys had chosen the path of fire and stone, the Verdani. It was no surprise to Rai as the man had always had a brutality to his fighting style. Quick, simple but strong movements that packed a punch.

"Yeah, I was testing the new bomb arrows," Rai said.

"Did you not see Quar out there?" Tys asked.

"Quar is back?"

Both Quar and Eril, the two warriors who saved them from the pack of helix on their trip across the Deadlands Basin, had been sent to Atef Palace. It wasn't uncommon for the emperor to ask for Verdin warriors for missions or for important guard duties.

"Came in just before you," Tys said.

"Where is he?"

Tys flicked his head towards the Verdin Temple. Despite his many years in the Verdin Guild, Rai had yet to step foot in the temple. It was reserved for those who were assigned to their path, and Rai was still an initiate with an unchosen path. He adapted his fighting style constantly to fit the diera weapon he used so he found it hard choosing one style over the other.

Tys had told him about the interior of the Verdin Temple and how it was similar to other temples but that didn't quell Rai's curiosity. It didn't help that they were only allowed to access the first floor, which raised the question of what was on the second and third floors of the temple?

"Did he say anything?" Rai asked.

"He said the emperor is getting more paranoid about assassins," Tys said. "Locked himself up in Atef Palace and refuses to leave."

Tys didn't have to explain the implications of the emperor locking himself away. This would be taken as a weakness from the other monarchs, making them more likely to move on the throne.

"Imayan?" Rai asked. Time and distance had slackened the bond between them but it never broke. Rai always asked how she was. They didn't write to one another but some of the other Verdin warriors told him she had asked about him too.

"She's doing well. Eril is still her personal guard," Tys said.

They were years off her ascension to empress of Tarris and Rai was set on returning before that happened.

Rai longed to wait for Quar outside the temple but Tys led him to the feast hall, lightening the conversation with talk of how his training was coming on. They ate and talked through the dark hour and the Sun Eye began its watch over the world. Genu and Ada joined them. Both were doing well in their respective training regimes and they both chose the Verdin path, the way of wind and water. Agile fluid movements focusing on technique and skill over brute strength.

Peering out of the open shutters to the feast hall, Rai spotted Quar marching back to his living quarters. Excusing himself, Rai stood and chased after him. The golden morning glow trailed long shadows across the plateau. The cool crisp of night already melting away in the Sun Eye's glare.

"Quar!" Rai shouted.

The man spun. He looked exhausted. Bags hung from his dark eyes. His frame seemed to droop like it had already fallen asleep.

"Rai," Quar said.

"How are you doing, brother?" Rai asked patting him on the back.

"Weary but well," he replied. "You?"

"Yes, yes, good," Rai said.

"You aren't here for pleasantries, Rai, so just ask." Quar sighed.

Rai cleared his throat. "How was Tansen?"

"Flourishing," Quar said in a mocking tone. It was rare for him to be sarcastic but it was a hard journey from the capital and he had been talking to Shesmu and Overseer Lieten for hours which was a drain unto itself.

Quar deflated. "Sorry, Rai. It's been a rough couple of weeks."

"What happened?" Rai asked. Quar was usually so positive. It was strange seeing him so defeated.

Quar glanced towards the Verdin Temple. His face was conflicted, flickering as if he were arguing with himself. Then he looked at Rai and nodded towards the gap between the buildings.

They stepped into shadow. The heat subsided, the breeze cut off and everything grew quieter. Quar continued to turn his head like he was expecting to be attacked.

"The emperor is getting more paranoid by the day," Quar said.

"Yeah we know. We were talking about it earlier today. He's been asking for more Verdin warriors to strengthen the palace guard."

Quar shook his head. "You don't know the half of it. He sees killers in every shadow. Old friends are tools for his enemies. After naming Imayan empress, the other monarchs have disrupted trade and troops in any way they can."

He fell silent as two warriors walked past the alleyway, waiting for them to vanish from sight before continuing. "He doesn't leave his quarters. He feeds part of his meals to his pet ferin to make sure it isn't poison."

If the emperor was this concerned with assassins, other matters would be falling to the wayside, which would allow the monarchs openings to wreak more havoc. It was a vicious cycle.

"What of Imayan?" Rai asked.

Quar strained his neck, stretching the muscle like he had to wring the words out of himself. "There was another attempt on her life."

Rai's heart dropped.

"Several, actually." Quar must have noticed a change in Rai as he lifted his hands and quickly added, "She's fine. I was on guard with her when the most recent attack happened. The damn assassin hit me from behind and knocked me out cold. Luckily, Imayan knew enough self-defence to fight back until nearby guards heard and rushed in."

Imayan hated combat training and avoided it, so to hear she had learnt enough to defend herself was reassuring.

"The emperor claimed I had *let* the assassin in and that I'm working for one of the other monarchs. Planned to execute me until another Verdin warrior helped sneak me out of Tansen and back here. Now the emperor is asking Overseer Lieten for my damn head and another warrior to replace me. He's lost it and even Lieten is worried about him. Lieten can't keep sending warriors at this rate or we'll have none left at the temple.

"Especially, if the emperor starts killing us off." He spat the last words.

Technically, the Verdin Temple was a separate entity from the Tarrisian monarchy. Since their founding, they made sure to remain free warriors and not to tie themselves to the throne. Too many tyrannical leaders had shown a need for them being separate. Overseer Lieten didn't have to do as the emperor asked but not doing so would further divide an already splintering country. There was no clear answer.

Rai turned and headed for the Verdin Temple.

"Rai!" Quar shouted after him.

Rai ignored him, continuing down the path. Blood red light painted the gaps between the shadows of the buildings. Jogging up the steps, Rai marched into the temple, unmanned by guards. Why guard a place no one would dare to enter?

Inside, there were two red pillars on either side of the chamber. A step led down onto a reed mat that covered the floor. A balustrade not unlike Shesmu's hall circled the centre of the room with an ornate boxy design. The conversation cut off the second Rai entered the temple but its faint echo lingered in the rafters above.

Overseer Lieten didn't look surprised when Rai walked out onto the reed mats. Shesmu didn't turn, however, he sighed and slumped forward when Rai approached.

Rai sat cross legged beside Shesmu, facing Overseer Lieten whose expressionless eyes locked onto Rai's. Overseer Lieten was an older woman, her hair greying at the sides. She wore it in a bun tied neatly atop her head. Wisdom shone as if through windows from her eyes. A glow only bestowed to those she saw worthy.

"Send me," Rai said, dipping his head in deference.

"And where might you be expecting us to send you, initiate Rai?" Lieten asked. A hint of humour lined her tone.

"The capital." Rai didn't want to reveal what Quar had told him but he would if he had to.

"Why would I send someone without a path to Tansen in such troubling times?"

"Because you know as well as I that I'm not set on either of the paths offered here," Rai said. One of the few rules of the Verdin Guild was not to question the overseer. It always felt contradictory to Rai. A guild with a focus on removing a hierarchy should take opinions from all.

"It has been an honour training among the Verdin Guild. I have learnt so much in my time here," Rai said. "But my path is not the way of the Verdani or the Verdin. It is not stone and fire or water and wind. It is a path of blood."

Overseer Lieten looked to Shesmu who nodded. "He has taken to the diera weapons quickly and together we've made breakthroughs that I wouldn't have come to without him." Shesmu glanced at Rai. "He has a hands-on and practical approach that age has made me wary of taking."

Rai nodded to Shesmu. They had grown close, despite his best efforts. This kept happening. Imayan and Tys. But he was glad to have befriended the old man who opened Rai's eyes to a new world. One tinted in red.

"This is all well," Overseer Lieten said. "But what makes you think we're sending anyone to Tansen?"

"Quar has returned and the emperor needs more warriors to protect himself and Imayan. Send me. I know Imayan and can protect her now," Rai said.

Overseer Lieten bit the inside of her lip, deep in thought. "You know of the manner in which Quar returned? The dangers of what you're asking for?"

Saying outright that the emperor ordered a Verdin warrior to be falsely executed was dancing on the line of treason. The carefully worded question told Rai all he needed to know. Lieten thought it was likely to happen again. Perhaps get worse. But that only strengthened Rai's resolve. He couldn't, in good conscience, put one of his Verdin brothers or sisters into the dark unknown where blades slipped and everyone wore a smiling mask. While there was more for him to learn here at the Verdin Guild, it wasn't meant for Rai. He spent longer with Shesmu than the warriors. Rai was here to gain the tools and abilities to protect those around him. Let them walk their paths and he would walk his.

Rai nodded. He would return to Tansen. And he was now strong enough to protect Imayan from any threat that may arise. His back straightened at the realisation, reinforced by a confidence earned through sweat and scars.

Overseer Lieten looked saddened by his decision. She bowed her head in acquiescence. "Very well. But know this Rai, the danger for you is higher than any other in our ranks. I would not have sent you had you not asked."

Rai screwed up his face. Why would it be more dangerous for him?

Before he could ask, Lieten stood. "Gather your things and I will meet you at the lift at the start of the Moon Eye's watch."

She bowed and stalked off to the staircase at the back of the chamber. Once she was out of sight, Shesmu spun.

"Did you blow a bomb arrow too close to your head!? To just march into the temple?" Shesmu shook his head in disbelief.

"Quar told me everything," Rai said. "I always planned to return eventually."

Shesmu blew out a breath. "I'm going to miss your bullheadedness, but it's going to be the death of you. You can't keep throwing yourself into the Deadlands Basin."

The saying made Rai smirk. "I can if I'm holding the right bow."

With a hard pat on the shoulder, Shesmu said, "Come. I have a parting gift."

36

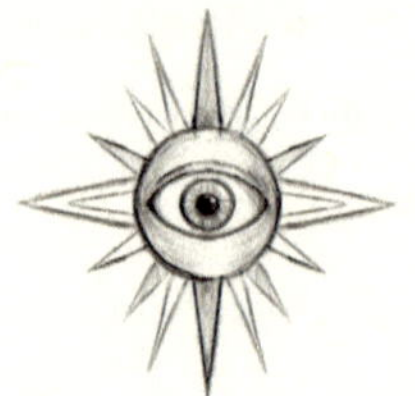

The Unforgotten Oath

13 years ago.

Shesmu led Rai back to the Blood Hall. They were deep into dark hour now and Shesmu spent some time lighting the lamps. Firelight flickered like stars among the eclectic mix of material laid sprawled atop the worktops and shelving surrounding the pit in the centre. Rai had spent years trawling through the oddities in this place and still didn't know what everything was.

"How were the arrows?" Shesmu asked.

"The shock-wave was a little larger than expected," Rai said. He had been testing a bunch of new iterations on the diera weapons during training the night before. One of them being a new bomb arrow mix. Rai remembered back to the chunks of rock from the bouldon blasting outward and the shock-wave that knocked Rai back in the heat of the explosion.

"Mmm. Perhaps stand further back next time?" Shesmu grinned.

"Yes, thanks for that." Rai picked through some of Shesmu's wares as he ruffled around his workbench. He picked up a discarded piece of diera shaved razor thin to a point. "What about the refin blood?"

Refin blood allowed one to nudge the diera weapon, usually fashioned into an arrow or throwing dagger. They had mainly been used as guided projectiles. Recently, however, they had been experimenting with how light the diera ore had to be to allow the user to lift the ore from the ground and have it move on its own. The battle capabilities of weapons that could move without one touching it was huge but they had yet to figure out a design that was light enough to move but strong enough to pierce skin.

"A botched attempt," Shesmu said waving off the discarded ore. "Come, come."

Rai wandered over to Shesmu who stood at his workbench. "Now as you know, diera is a very limited resource and I can't have you leaving with any of our weapons."

Rai froze. He hadn't thought of that. Shesmu allowed him to train with the array of diera weapons that they had at the Verdin Guild. But they only had a couple of each. He should have expected this.

Rai slid the bow from his back and placed it on the worktop. He unsheathed the daggers from his waist and laid the quiver filled with diera arrows beside the bow. Both the bow and arrows were made from diera ore. One could get similar effects with just one being made from diera, however, effects and some practices could be amplified with both being made from the ore. With the hiss of unsheathed metal, Rai brandished his diera sword. He always thought he could tell it was a diera blade by the resonance of pulling the blade free. It sang higher and longer than a normal sword.

Rai sighed and stepped back from the weapons.

"And Lintou's short sword I'm afraid," Shesmu said.

He had hoped since he had brought Lintou's blade that he could leave with it. With a pained expression, he placed the short sword that had saved his life three times already on the top.

"I'm sorry, Rai," Shesmu said. "I know what that short sword means to you."

"I understand. Short swords were never my preferred weapon anyway," Rai said. He rarely trained with the short sword but it had never strayed far from his side.

"Both Overseer Lieten and the emperor are extremely strict with the control of diera weapons. Few ever get to hold one and they would notice if you were to take one from our inventory. This doesn't mean I'd toss you out into the world undefended, however." Shesmu grinned. He bent down and pulled out a long case from beneath his workbench.

"Now, raw diera ore is harder to track. Some is made unusable by my experiments. Some is fashioned into materials that don't count as weapons. And, as you know, often there are shavings and extra pieces left over. If someone was to collect all these extra scraps, you could pull them together into, say, something like this." Shesmu unlatched the box and threw it open. Inside was a diera bow. No, not quite. It was Sen's bow but it had been shaved back and had diera casing along its length.

Rai's eyes stung, tears threatening. He hadn't seen this bow since the night he arrived at the temple. But the memories of Sen and the fight atop the basin's edge with the Dwellsand haunted his nightmares.

"An experiment. Can one use diera *plating* to enhance already formed weapons? Yes. Although to a lesser ability than a pure diera bow. It uses more blood and the abilities are slightly more subdued or sluggish depending on the blood but—"

"It's perfect," Rai said. He swallowed the well of confused emotions and wiped a tear from his eye. "I'm sorry. I thought I was stronger and past this by now."

Shesmu patted his shoulder with a warm smile. "Emotions do not make you weak, Rai. One cannot control a natural response. Strength is found in what emotions you act on and which you let wash over you."

Rai didn't trust himself to speak so instead, he hefted the bow, feeling its weight. The diera ore had been smoothed and carved to fit perfectly in his hand. But Shesmu had painted the curving wood of the bow a dark green, which blended well into the black diera plating along the centre of the bow. Even those who knew of diera weapons may not recognise this as one from looking at it.

"Blood will be harder to get out there than here," Shesmu said. "And you will have to do any distilling yourself. But you're part of the Verdin Guild and most cities will have guild representatives where you can top up with whatever blood they have stocked. If we stay in contact I can maybe have some delivered to you."

"You just want me to continue running practical experiments for you," Rai said and smiled at the man.

Shesmu chuckled.

He held out his hand and Rai took it. "I can't thank you enough for all that you've taught me. I will return when I can."

"Good. You're the only one crazy enough to take these half-baked ideas out into the basin," Shesmu said.

In the time Rai was with Shesmu, Overseer Lieten seemed to have summoned the entire Verdin Guild. A throng of over a hundred warriors crowded at the lift's entrance. A snaking gap was left for Rai to walk through to where Overseer Lieten waited. People reached out and clasped his shoulders and patted his back as he walked up to the overseer. They had done the same with Quar and Eril but they were Verdin warriors and had been at the temple for more than a decade, while Rai was just an initiate. Rai had been ready to disappear in the dark.

Reaching Overseer Lieten, Rai bowed, the overseer returning the gesture.

"Rai," Lieten shouted. "A quick exit to match your quick entrance." There were laughs from the crowd. Word of how they used a diera blade to ride across the black sand of the Deadlands Basin spread once Ada let it slip. They had been the fastest to make the trek from Tansen to the temple in the guilds history. Rai was still asked about it years later.

"But as soon as one has stepped foot into the Verdin Temple they are of the Verdin Guild. And once you are part of us you will always be part of us."

Overseer Lieten held out his palm. In it was a coin. It was gold with a band of verdant green around the edge and was inlaid with a symbol. It was a pointed temple with a huge eye behind it. Rai took the coin, inspecting it closer. The symbol was simple enough that only those who had seen the Verdin Temple would recognise it.

"This is a Verdin Guild coin. It will allow you certain connections. Just look for that symbol and know they are from the Verdin Guild and will help you in any way they can. And it is expected of you to do the same," Lieten said.

Rai dipped his head. "Thank you, Overseer."

"I wish you luck, Rai." Lieten held out her hand and Rai clasped it and she pulled in close. "The mind is more often one's downfall than the blade." Overseer Lieten whispered the words so only Rai could hear then released him.

Mulling over her words, Overseer Lieten stepped back and said, "May you be stone and fire, wind and water. And may your path lead you." The rest of the guild repeated the mantra and cheered.

Overseer Lieten stood back beside Shesmu, who grinned and nodded before letting the crowd flood in. Rai shook hands and received more pats on his back than he ever had before. It may have only been a handful of years he spent among the Verdin Guild but the kinship came from sweat and blood. He felt like he had a place here.

Tys, Genu, and Ada walked up as the rest started to disperse.

"I'm sorry that we can't come back with you," Genu said.

"That's okay. Your place is here," Rai said.

"Will you make it back without my sage advice?" Ada asked.

Rai smiled at the man. "I'll be fine."

"Good luck, Rai," Genu said. They bowed and stalked off towards the training grounds.

Tys approached last. He had been there from the start. Since his first day in Atef Palace. He was the closest Rai had come to a friend. One that had stayed long enough to be more than a passing spec in the desert's past.

"This isn't goodbye," Rai said, holding out his hand.

"Oh, I know it's not. You can't get rid of me that easily," Tys said. He shook his hand. "Tell Imayan I said hi."

Rai nodded while a voice in his head questioned what he was doing. Why would he leave the first place that felt like home? Why would he leave those who hadn't left him?

Rai stepped into the rickety lift and nodded to Yor, who flipped a lever, and with a sudden *chunk* the lift began to descend. Tys watched as he dipped out of sight and into the dark of the cavern below.

He left because he had made an oath. An oath that brought purpose when he had none. One that, despite the years and the distance, hadn't frayed.

Dark times were coming. And they were stronger together.

37

Cage of Shadow

Something or someone had to have trapped shades in this dark realm. But who? Why? What was this place? What were shades? It was simpler knowing less. Nya could pretend they were incomprehensible beings from another realm. But if they had originally come from Tarris. They were part of *her world*. Something tangible and real, unlike this place with its ever-storming sky. Did that mean the darkness in the black stone city had come from Tarris, too?

A growl perked Nya's ears.

She turned to see a small grey creature. It looked like a sand fox but it had longer ears that flopped to its chin rather than pointed upward. Its grey fur was matted and pressed against a scraggly body and its tail whipped back and forth kicking up rocks. The creature bared its teeth at Nya.

Nya took a step back. Behind her, she heard scratching. Another of the dark sand foxes burrowed out of the scree. Then the noise came again. Soon a whole pack of these creatures were digging their way out of the ground.

One of the sand foxes leapt at her.

Bom blasted a wave of shadow outward, upending the foxes and sending them hurtling through the air. At the same time, Nya turned and ran. More scraped at the rock as Nya threw herself over the uneven landscape. Further ahead, the rocks shifted as long claws sliced through the stone.

"They're everywhere!" Nya shouted.

Another launched itself at Nya and Bom slapped the beast away. The palace guards hadn't given Nya a weapon to defend herself with so she had to rely wholly on Bom. She pressed her back against a rock wall as an onslaught of the foxes approached. Bom appeared as a long black spike impaling some of the creatures but there were too many.

A fox made it past Bom and charged Nya. She raised her arms and screamed as fangs bit into her forearms. Nya flung the beast but its teeth were deep in her flesh. Bom fell back as a tendril of shadow and cut through its skull. The fox fell limp to the ground.

Too many, Bom thought as it battered several more foxes away.

"Just hold them off," Nya said.

Nya jumped and started climbing the rock wall. Her feet slipped and she slid down a couple of feet before digging her fingers into a crack in the stone and continuing upward. Bom fought off the foxes at the base of the wall as Nya crested the top.

"Bom! Come on!" Nya shouted before running along the plateau.

She felt the shade return a second later.

None made to climb up here, Bom said.

"Maybe they can't," Nya said. "If they're anything like Tarrisian sand foxes, they struggle with climbing steep surfaces."

The ground began to rumble. Nya's eyes went wide as an eruption of rock burst behind her and a fox clambered out. These foxes seemed to be able to burrow *through* the rock, so they had no need to climb. Nya sprinted across the plateau as Bom shot back to fight them off. Nya squealed as a fox dug its teeth into her ankle. She kicked wildly and flung it off the edge. Pain shot up her leg as she ran. Stumbling forward, Nya knew she couldn't outrun them.

Nya spun and faced the hoard. Bom moved as a blur of shadow, spiking out as a tendril and killing as many as it could. One burrowed out of the rock in front of Nya and leapt. Nya kicked out but the fox latched onto her calf and she screamed. Another barrelled into her chest and she fell back. Nya's vision went hazy. When it focused she saw a fox chewing on her leg while the other clambered to its feet. She writhed shaking the fox off by kicking it with her leg.

More were approaching.

The fox that had knocked her to the ground glanced at her bloody leg, painless in the buzz of the fight. Its eyes narrowed, coming to the realisation that she couldn't run. The creature made its way towards her.

She needed a weapon.

The dagger!

The fox lunged at Nya as she slid the black dagger from her waist band and slashed out. This might be it. She thought of home. Before her, the trail of the dagger sliced into the air and opened a rend. A black tear in the fabric of existence opened. That same warm darkness hung in the air where she had cut and the fox flew right through it.

Nya sat stunned. She had opened another tear. She glanced down at the dagger in her hand.

Bom sent a flurry of incoherent panic that stole Nya's attention. In the distance, the foxes were being killed, but not by Bom. Shadow spikes burst from the dark skewering multiple beasts at once. A feat that Bom couldn't manage.

If it wasn't her shade killing them then…

 "Troublesome one, aren't you," Adani said.

He emerged from a shadow to her right, stepping out of a shroud of darkness. His face was set and contemplative until he saw the tear and his expression twitched.

"Close it."

"What?" Nya croaked.

"Close that tear." Adani wouldn't take his eyes off it.

"How?"

Adani snatched the dagger and pulled it back over the rend following the arc Nya had made but in reverse. His eyes were closed as if in concentration and the tear stitched itself back together. Nya watched in wonder. Mirt was right. The blade could close the tear and shut off this world.

It was more than a hope now. They could do this.

Adani breathed out as the last of the tear disappeared. He faced Nya but didn't say a word. His eyes burned with a fury she hadn't seen from him before.

"Perhaps we were too lax with you," he said.

Terror flooded Nya's mind but it wasn't her own. It was Bom's. A tremor ran through her hand and her heart hammered in her chest. She would never get used to her body reacting to emotions she couldn't explain.

"What're you doing?" Nya asked.

"What I should have done from the start."

Adani's shade wrapped around Bom, constricting it in a cage of shadow. Bom thrashed in alarm.

"Stop, no please," Nya said. "Let it go."

Adani let out a breath. His shade was even more powerful here than when they fought in the palace. It had to be the darkness, Nya realised. Adani had left the connection to the voice open and it was lending his shade strength.

"You're a fool, Nya. Why can't you see the power to be gained? It's unlike anything you could imagine." Adani lifted his hand. Then he balled his fist and behind him hundreds of tendrils shot out of the ground and instantly killed the remaining pack of grey sand foxes. He looked down at Nya.

"That will slow us down."

For a moment, Nya didn't know what he was talking about. She followed his gaze to her injured ankle and burning pain flared.

Novi, the other scholar, looked at Nya's ankle. He cleaned and bandaged the wound claiming that she would be fine in a week or so. However it was painful to put her weight on that leg and with Bom being held captive, the shade couldn't assist with walking. So she leant on Blackcap as they continued further into the dark place and closer to, what Mirt had started calling, the Black City.

Adani's shade held Bom pinned down and dragged the shade along. Bom wasn't in pain and could talk with Nya but it couldn't move or return to her shadow. Adani had warned her that straying too far from her shade would bring unimaginable pain. So Nya stayed close, walking with the guard she had betrayed.

Mirt and Novi led the way with Adani close behind. The other guards fanned out around them watching the horizon. And Nya walked in the middle, strategically placed to make it harder for her to run. *Not that I'll be doing much running,* Nya thought as her ankle throbbed.

"You can't blame me," Nya said. Blackcap's muscled arm was under hers taking some of the weight off her foot. He stayed silent.

"You must know this isn't right. We don't know what this dark presence is," Nya whispered. "I think it's trapped here."

"Quiet," Blackcap said.

"I think it wants into Tarris. We can't let that thing through. You need to listen to me!"

The guard pulled her to a stop and Nya hissed as she went over her ankle. "Look. I don't understand any of this but I'm here to do a job. As are you. The scholars wouldn't be foolish enough to bring anything back to Tarris."

"What about the shades?" Nya raised an eyebrow and Blackcap turned away.

"The dagger. It can open tears like the one we came through," Nya said.

Surprise blossomed on the guard's face but he squashed the look quickly.

"You need to help me," Nya said holding his gaze.

"Keep up!" Adani called.

Blackcap cleared his throat and pulled Nya onward. Adani watched them a moment longer before continuing.

"How can I trust you? You just want to escape," Blackcap whispered.

"I want to close the tear," Nya said. "The dagger can close it and it'll end all of this. The husks entering the city, the—"

"Husks entered the city?" Blackcap asked.

"You didn't know?"

He shook his head.

"We stopped one the night of the Passing of the Nyfin," Nya said. "If one got through then so can others."

"You lie."

"Why would I lie?"

"To earn my trust and use my sense of justice to deceive me."

Nya looked up at Blackcap. Bags hung from his blackened eyes and his shoulders swayed. She thought of how Kyan used his sense of justice to use people. How he manipulated others into believing in him. She didn't want to be like that.

Nya sighed. "Believe me or not, I don't want to deceive you. I want to stop this and go home, but I can't do it alone. Not anymore."

It was Blackcap's turn to glance at her. Something shifted in his gaze.

"Do you really think it's trying to get to Tarris?"

Nya nodded. He blew out a breath and they marched on through the dark landscape.

The rocky formations started to disappear and the landscape became more open. It was still uneven and ridged making it difficult for Nya to traverse with her ankle but they did not slow. Provisions were handed out and eaten as they walked. Nya was sure they had walked for more than a day but the sky never dimmed and no creatures stirred. Mirt said the presence was keeping them safe and it was only because Nya had run that she was attacked by those strange sand foxes. This didn't seem to ease any of the guards' worry as they glanced around.

The party's energy started to wane. Nya was doing all she could to keep on her feet.

"We need to stop," one of the guards said.

"Not in the open," Adani replied. "You never rest in the open."

And so they walked on until they found some rock formations. Nya all but collapsed against the stone wall. Shooting pains ran up her leg and she grimaced. The guards dug out a crater for the fire as Blackcap dropped onto his haunches beside Nya. He looked over his shoulder at the others before turning back.

"These bandages need changed," he said. Without waiting for a response, he started peeling back the bloodied wraps.

"Even if I did help you, we wouldn't be able to get back with your ankle like this," Blackcap whispered. Nya tensed.

"Easy," he said. And Nya relaxed before the others noticed. "We would need a way to get back with the dagger. Incapacitate some of the others, perhaps."

"You want to help?" Nya asked.

He tightened the new bandage around her foot and Nya groaned. Blackcap ignored her question. "The other guards have to have the option to come with us. But when we get back, I can say Adani and Mirt were killed and that this place is dangerous. They will believe me. I'm well respected in the palace. If I freed your shade, could you stop Adani?"

Nya remembered how Adani killed all those foxes with one motion. She shook her head and the guard's expression went grim.

"He's too strong. The presence is making him stronger," Nya said. Blackcap watched Adani as he gazed out over the landscape. A smile curled the corner of his mouth as if he could see their destination already.

"He barely sleeps or rests. Sometimes he scouts the path ahead but never for long," Blackcap said. "Perhaps we can make him scout for longer. Give him something to look for."

The guard patted her leg and stood. "I'll bring you food. Don't walk on that leg."

Nya nodded as he left to help set up the fire. She reached out to Bom. The shade was getting more agitated the closer they got to the Black City.

I'll get us out of here, Nya thought to the shade. Bom didn't respond but she could feel its doubt.

Somehow.

A pot was placed over the fire and a broth was soon bubbling. The spiced scents of thyme soon permeated their makeshift camp. The guards warmed their feet by the flames while Nya sat back against a rock wall. Blackcap returned after a while and handed Nya a steaming bowl of stew and sat down beside her. She nodded gratefully. Nya hadn't realised how hungry she was until she started eating. It wasn't particularly flavourful but it warmed her and satiated the hunger.

"When will it get dark here?" Nya asked placing her bowl on the ground.

"Mirt said in a couple days, our time," the guard said.

"If we are to do anything, doing it under the cover of dark is our best hope."

"Won't he be stronger at night?" Blackcap asked.

Nya watched Adani eat. They couldn't fight him. They couldn't outrun them with her hurt ankle. But there was one thing they could do. "Yes, but we can't fight him anyway."

"So what're you thinking?"

"The dagger," Nya said. "When I used it to fight off those foxes it opened another tear."

Blackcap choked on his stew.

"Adani closed it again but I think I could open another one. I don't know where it'll take us, but if we can go through and close it then they won't be able to follow," Nya said.

"What if it doesn't take us back to the palace? What if it drops us somewhere even more dangerous?"

Nya shrugged. "I think it'll take us home. I have a theory. Don't you think this place is familiar in its shape? Almost like a reflection of Tarris."

"What?"

"Well when we came out the cave with the tear, we exited a huge rock formation that could easily have been the palace. And if you were watching the layout of rocks, they were almost grid-like. Like city streets."

The guard raised an eyebrow.

"And now we're out of the city limits this looks like the desert," Nya said.

"So what you think we'll appear in the desert?"

"Possibly."

They stared at one another for a moment. *"Possibly,"* Blackcap repeated.

"We'll have to open another tear to know for sure."

He rubbed his face. "Okay. I'll have Adani scout out when it gets dark in case there is something lurking but he'll have to take you with him since he has your shadow thing."

"Shade," Nya said.

"Right. Shade. I'll offer to come to watch you and then we can blindside him. We run back. Mirt is no fighter. Take the dagger, open a rift and offer safety to the other guards." Blackcap grimaced. "Well, possible safety."

"There's so much that can go wrong," Nya whispered.

Blackcap didn't reply.

Her mind ran through the possibilities. Adani killing Blackcap. The guards revolting and holding Blackcap and her prisoner. The tear taking them somewhere else.

Nya felt the draw of the Black City. It grew stronger each day.

This plan had to work.

38

War Camp

The war camp came into sight as a plume of dust and smoke on the horizon. Rai's shoulders eased at the sight of the war camp. Their rationed food had become scarce and the constant threat of unknown dangers left little time for sleep or rest. Rai had barely slept. After three days unconscious, he felt guilty spending any more time not watching for assassins. And even when he did, sleep was light and fractured. The slightest twinge of thought from Fax would be enough to startle him awake.

An envoy rode out to meet them. Soldiers clad in heavy jerkins and Yontar's crest emblazoned on their chest. Kleran shook hands and discussed numbers and their progress towards Asuriya as they made their way into the camp. Guards boxed them in a protective formation that they probably assumed would be comforting. But Rai felt caged.

In the dimming light, the soldiers set up tents in rows. Poles were buried deep in the sand before it hardened, supporting the thick canvas walls. Fire pits were dug out too before the black sand froze. The stink of many miles walked, a scent of sweat and dirt, permeated the camp as men and women carried supplies between aya and the tents. However, all bowed to their procession. The return of their monarch and the empress sent whispers through the crowd.

In the centre of the camp, one tent had already been erected. A massive dome-shaped structure. It was the same dark colour as the rest allowing it to blend in with the night sand. However, its segmented dome shape was distinguishable from the rest. Rai recognised it immediately.

A war council tent.

They hopped off their hyians which were led away by stable hands to be fed and watered. Imayani made sure that the servants knew they were to be treated with the upmost respect, as they had been pushed well past their limits and everyone in the company knew they would not have survived without them.

Imayani took her place at Kleran's side as they talked with the overseers while Tysar wandered off to talk with the captain of the guards. That left Mino, Yeru and Rai standing in wait. Rai was not in a position to join the conversation but watched with interest as Imayani, Kleran, and the overseers stood off to the side talking in hushed tones.

"You have a plan, right?" Mino whispered.

"A plan?" Rai gave her a questioning look.

Mino made sure Yeru was too busy with her pack to listen before continuing. "To stop Kleran if he tries to take the throne."

By marrying Imayani he already had the power of the throne, but power is addictive. Once one has a taste of it, they will crave more until they have gluttoned themselves.

"Imayani doesn't need me to have a plan. She's smart. She would only have agreed if it was the right thing for Tarris," Rai said.

"But what if she doesn't think her safety is the same thing?" Mino asked.

This made Rai pause. Before he could respond, they started to move inside the tent. Imayani beckoned them in.

Inside was an austere space. A table centred the room with a map of Tarris strewn across it. Not unlike the war room in Atef Palace, Rai thought. He had expected the monarch to be a man of luxuries but this tent told another story. Perhaps Tysar was right. Perhaps there was more of a soldier in the man than Rai had anticipated. After all, he had fought off the assassins and didn't cower to the black sand phantoms.

They spread out around the table as Kleran talked quietly with his overseer, who held a bundle of scrolls under his arm, containing assuredly numbers of soldiers within the camp.

The overseer was one of the tallest men Rai had ever seen. He had a narrow frame but his large hands and thumping footsteps would have made him a perfect soldier. And while the nashk he wore was banded in red and gold, it was clear by his thin build that the man was a warfare *adviser* and not someone who trained himself.

Some scouts haven't made it back, Fax said.

Rai perked up at Fax's return. He had gotten the shade to listen in to Kleran's conversation at the door. *They should have returned by now. The overseer said it isn't the first lot of scouts that they've sent towards*

Asuriya that have gone missing. They think Ossin spies took them out.

That's unlikely, Rai thought. They would have to have covered far too much ground. The strange mutated kiren came to mind. It wasn't surprising that the overseer hadn't thought of the strange wildlife around Asuriya. Most dismissed it as stories. Before venturing into the Bandor Mountains, even Rai had found the stories hard to believe.

When they had come across the blight-touched kiren they were still days of travel away from Asuriya. And the rumours spoke of the worst creatures being within the city's walls. Perhaps they needed a more scholarly approach to this. Rai glanced over to Yeru who was writing away in her notebook. She had gone quiet since the black sand phantom, spending all her time reading or taking notes. *Did something happen with Yeru in the three days I was knocked out?* Rai asked Fax.

Not that I saw.

He was going to have to speak with her later. She would know more about these blight creatures than him.

Kleran cleared his throat. "The army is making good time and are ahead of schedule," Kleran said. "This isn't a sprint but a marathon. We need to move quickly but not burn our soldiers or hyian out."

"What about the Ossin force?" Imayani asked. That familiar softness had hardened once more as she stepped back into her role as empress.

"Empress, if you will," the Overseer said. "I am Overseer Hemil. I've been tracking the Ossin force and I believe we should reach Asuriya before them."

"Believe?" Imayani asked. "I need assurances. I want to avoid combat if we can."

Overseer Hemil looked to Kleran. Imayani noticed his worried expression.

"What're you not telling me, Kleran?" Imayani asked.

The monarch forced a smile. "There is nothing to worry about. I've selected a smaller force to ensure we are faster and don't have to fight for the capital."

Imayani glared as only she could. It brought Rai some amusement to see Kleran start to sweat under her gaze.

"Kleran."

Kleran exhaled. "The Ossin force is larger than we anticipated."

"How large?" Imayani asked.

Kleran opened his mouth to speak when Overseer Hemil said, "Three times as large as ours."

Imayani scoffed as Kleran glared at his overseer. "I chose this size of force without consideration of theirs as it doesn't matter." He sat forward and clasped his hands. "Whichever force gets within the walls of Asuriya has won and a bigger army is more cumbersome and takes longer to move across the desert. Any larger and we wouldn't make it before them. This way we can retake the capital and fend them off at the walls."

It was a risk. The Ossin army had a head start but Kleran had sacrificed numbers for speed. He was right that whoever got to the ancient capital first would have the upper hand, being able to utilize the city's defences. But was it enough? Especially when Ossin's army was *three times* the size? Who was to say.

"Are we assured to reach Asuriya before them?" Imayani asked after a moment.

"We—" Overseer Hemil started.

"Yes," Kleran cut in.

Imayani raised an eyebrow.

Kleran sat forward. "It's close but I will ensure we get there first."

"How long?" Imayani asked.

"Two days and we should arrive at the city wall."

Imayani nodded and waved Mino to her side. "Very well. I want to survey the soldiers you brought."

"Surely you would like to rest for the night first. Have a hot meal and wash up. There is plenty time—" Overseer Hemil said.

Imayani tilted her head.

"I will escort her myself," Kleran said standing. "Show the others to their tents."

And with that, Kleran whisked Imayani out of the tent, Mino trailing behind.

There was a moment of silence before Yeru snapped her notebook closed and stalked towards the exit. Rai followed her out into the night air. Overseer Hemil called after them about showing them to their tents but neither looked back.

Dark hour settled upon Tarris and lanterns were alight around the camp. Still shadows pooled in the unwalked stretches between the tents. Fax watched Rai's back but since the black sand phantom, Rai couldn't help but feel on edge. Ahead, Yeru marched with purposeful steps towards the fire pits on the edge of the war camp where soldiers ate and talked.

"Yeru," Rai called as he caught up to her. "We need to talk."

She studied him. "Is that not what we're doing?"

Rai grabbed her arm and pulled her to a stop. He didn't want to talk about this at the fire pits. "Since the black sand phantom, you've done nothing but scribble in that notebook and avoid me."

She had the decency to look chagrined at that. Yeru started tapping her foot. "I don't like not knowing what's going on. I'm the scholar and Imayani, the empress herself, invited me on this"—she waved her hands around them—"and I have no idea what's going on."

Rai flicked his head towards a quieter part of the camp and they started walking between the tents.

"We're dealing with ancient lost libraries, other worlds, Asuriya and the wasting sickness that haunts the old capital. You can't be expected to understand what no one alive does," Rai said.

"Imayani asked for me because I've spent my life studying Asuriya and the cataclysm that took it. I *am* expected to understand or at least aid the empress in some way."

"You are."

Yeru bit her lip. Torchlight drew out the worried features on her face. "The worst part is that it's right in front of me. All of this is connected I'm sure. The black sand phantoms, shades, the old capital."

"What makes you say that?" Rai asked.

She stopped and glanced back to ensure they were alone before opening her notebook. "It's said that no one has seen a black sand phantom's true form and survived. They appear as fragmented memories to draw travellers off the path to be devoured. But we've seen one now. It's inky and smoky and not unlike your shade. Even the way it acted and moved was similar to Fax."

I recall fighting off that thing. Not being friendly with it, Fax noted.

416

"And you were able to fight it off. A feat that, if the histories are to believed, has never happened before. What if black sand phantoms are connected to shades or to the dark realm you described?"

"The tear is only five years old," Rai said. "I was sent to check it out not long after it opened."

"The tear is a door. One that can be opened and closed. I talked with the Yontar's scholars. They didn't open up straight away but over time I got some answers. They believe they can open and close the tear with a dagger."

"A dagger?" Rai froze. Nya had talked about a black dagger.

"The strangest part? They got the dagger from a treasure hunter who had raided *Asuriya* of all places," Yeru said. "What if this isn't the first time a tear has opened a rift between our world and this dark realm? It must have if they had a dagger in Asuriya that could do it."

Rai scratched his stubble. "Why would they want access to a dark world of horrors like that?"

"Your shade is powerful. It makes you a strong warrior. And we haven't explored enough of the dark realm to guess what they want from it. But when I asked the scholars working on expeditions into the pocket world they alluded to something powerful. When I prodded for information they shut up and I was told it was just theories but I think they've found something else."

The voice. The darkness that flooded through Fax in Ma-atan's temple.

"Nothing good, I'm sure," Rai whispered.

Yeru leant against a pole and faced Rai. "The most popular theory for the cataclysm is that our emperor fought off a God and that battle lead to the destruction of Asuriya and the creation of the blight. But what if the God wasn't killed? What if it was *locked away* in this dark realm?"

Bile rode up Rai's throat as he thought about the thrum of energy that came with the voice. Was that the voice of a God? Some ancient deity that they had woken like Ma-atan?

"We need to stop them from letting it through," Rai said.

"I voiced concerns with the scholars that taking the dagger into the pocket world could be dangerous and they agreed saying they didn't take it with them on expeditions."

"That's not enough!" Rai shouted. He felt a surge of fear. But it wasn't his. Yeru took a step back. "Sorry. I…" Rai raised a hand. "We need to close the rift."

"I agree," Yeru said. "I think they have left it open in hopes that it'll give them the upper hand for the throne. But Kleran is more focused on Asuriya and the marriage now. I think once we reclaim it, they'll be distracted and we can take control of the research and close it ourselves."

"When we take Asuriya, I can't leave Imayani."

"I know." She smiled then, and Rai hadn't realise how much he needed to see it. "I can close it. It's not dangerous as long as I don't enter the pocket world. If you keep them busy here, I can pose as a new scholar on the project and close it for good."

Rai nodded. It was a good idea. With their focus on Asuriya, it would be the perfect time to do it. "What about the shades and black sand phantoms?"

"I don't know. I think they are from the pocket world. Does Fax want to go back?"

Fax shot out of Rai's shadow in the shape of a crow and sat upon Rai's shoulder. *My home is here.*

It was the most serious Rai had ever heard the shade. He smiled.

"First, we need to retake the old capital," Rai said. "After that, we can worry about closing the tear."

One problem at a time.

39

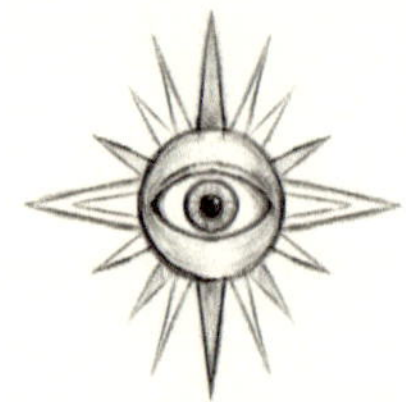

A Warm Welcome

13 years ago.

Rai rode through the outer markets of the Tarrisian capital. He was assaulted by the sights and smells. The barrage of life was overwhelming after the simplicity atop the Verdin Temple plateau. Sweet and herbal spices infused with the stink of the unwashed. The gurgle of pots clashed with the shouting of vendors and all was awash in colour.

Stalls were set up in lines corralling all those on their way to Tansen. Rai walked past a stand of bubbling pots. The sweet smell prickled the hair on the back of his neck and made his stomach growl. A man stood behind the stall occasionally stirring the food in the pots.

The outer markets worked as a buffer lessening the queues to the gates into Tansen. But Rai was later in the day than he had hoped to have arrived and the winding line led back into the stands.

Sliding off his hyian, Rai groaned. He stretched his weary muscles, waving away the plume of sand he kicked up. Rai joined the back of the line and watched the lively market. He was surprised at how much he had missed the city. If someone had asked him if he preferred the peace of the temple or the bustle of the city, he would have said the still of the temple. And yet, breathing in the city air, listening to the clamour of the crowds, Rai couldn't deny the charm and fullness of city life. He wondered if he would be welcomed with that same friendly familiarity.

Eventually, the city guards waved Rai in. Travellers were free to pass to and from the city. The checks were never to identify all that entered Tansen but to manage merchants and their trade.

Tansen sprawled out in front of Rai. A mass of towering buildings, tarp sheltered streets, and narrow alleyways. Atef Palace was deep within the city limits and protected by a palace wall. But Tansen was large enough that one couldn't see the palace upon entering the city.

Rai headed to the palace and brandished his letter from Overseer Lieten at the palace walls before being allowed past. Servants bustled around him in the late afternoon. Instinct led Rai to his old room that he grew up in with Tys. He didn't even know if it was still his. The door creaked as he pushed it open. The two beds were made, sheets tight around the frame. The hooks that Rai had attached to the wall for their weapons were empty save for a coating of dust. It hadn't changed a bit and looked to have been abandoned. Rai supposed it had been.

As he delved deeper into the palace, Rai passed through three different guard posts, the last of which wouldn't let him pass even with the letter from Overseer Lieten. However, after a quick trip to

Overseer Rikai, they let him through.

Rai's heart hammered in his chest as he approached Imayan's door. What if she didn't remember him? It was a ridiculous thought given how long they had spent together but Rai couldn't shake the feeling that he wasn't meant to be here. With an exhale, Rai rapped on the door.

A second later, Mino opened the door. Her eyes went wide with recognition. At least she hadn't forgot him.

"Hi, Mino," Rai said.

"You're back," Mino said.

"I'm afraid so," Rai said.

Mino ushered him into Imayan's chambers. Although perhaps *chambers* wasn't the correct term as she had an entire section of the palace to herself, with a bathhouse, kitchen, bedroom, and three sitting rooms. Why she needed three sitting rooms was unclear to Rai.

"She was so upset when she returned and you were gone," Mino said leading him into one of the sitting rooms.

Relief flooded Rai. So Imayan hadn't known he was getting sent to the Verdin Temple. So was Tys right? Had the emperor sent him away to get rid of him? How would he react now that Rai was back?

He has more important worries, Rai told himself.

"Sit," Mino said. "I'll go get her." She sped out of the room leaving Rai in silence.

The sitting room had a glass pane window letting in the sunlight. A bookshelf clung to the far wall and many chairs and tables lay sprawled throughout the chamber. Rai clutched the top of the plush fabric chair. It felt unbelievably soft after the meagre luxuries of the

Verdin Temple.

The room was not unlike Overseer Lintou's study. The similarities sent flashes of the last time Rai was in the man's study, when the assassin came for Imayan. Overseer Lintou's lifeless eyes begged Rai to save Imayan but in the end, she had saved him. In the tunnel with the duon, it was Imayan who held the beast off until the guards arrived.

But he was stronger now. He was a different man. And he wouldn't let anything like that would happen again.

"You!" Imayan stormed into the room.

She hadn't changed. Her slick black hair fell to her waist. One side was straighter than the other. Had she been in the middle of brushing it? That's when Rai noticed her fury. Her eyebrows only arched when she was furious.

She stalked up to him and slapped him across the face. Rai's head rung as he pulled back, his cheek stinging.

"You think you can saunter back here after years?" Imayan asked, hands on her hips. "You think you can just disappear and come back to a warm welcome?"

"I... I—" Rai couldn't say that her father had sent him away.

Imayan's front crumbled, tight expression releasing, and she swept into an embrace. Rai stood there, hands at his side, perplexed and trying to figure out what was going on. She had never hugged him before.

"I missed you," Imayan said.

Rai's muscles eased and he hugged her back.

Despite Mino's protests, they made their way to the rafters of the Iluian Blend coffeehouse like old times. Imayan explained that she wasn't allowed to leave her quarters without an onslaught of guards. Mino had convinced her to take Eril, who had become her personal guard, and was currently sitting with Jyun in the back of the coffeehouse.

Rai sipped his coffee. He closed his eyes savouring the taste and a snicker came from across the beam.

"What?" Rai asked opening his eyes.

"Have you not had coffee the whole time you were at the temple?"

"Yes but it was nothing like this," Rai said.

Imayan smiled and ran a finger around the rim of her mug. "What was it like being at the Verdin Temple?"

"It was hard." Rai thought back to the gruelling training sessions and brutal sparring. The Verdin Guild lived up to their name of harsh training, but it wasn't what he had expected. There weren't drills and exercises like with the palace guard, but seeing those around him pushing themselves to their limits was infectious.

"Did you like it there?"

Flashes of memory brought back the triumph of overcoming an opponent that had been beating him for months, and the elation of a breakthrough in the blood arts with Shesmu. He thought of the early mornings in the feast hall with Tys and the others. The camaraderie. Perhaps he had spent longer under stress and pain but he wouldn't have changed it for anything. And those memories would stay with him until the end of his days.

Rai smiled. "Yeah, I did."

"Then why did you come back?" Imayan asked.

The question came down upon him like a landslide. Rai swallowed and said, "Because I swore an oath in that infirmary to keep you safe, and I do not break my oaths."

Imayan stared at him. Her expression flitted back and forth between a creased worry and a bright joy as she mulled over his words. She sat back and sighed as if coming to a decision. "Well, I guess I can't deny a Verdin warrior to be my personal guard."

"What about Eril?" Rai asked.

"I can have two," Imayan said. "Father will probably be delighted to hear that I have double the protection." She spat the words. Talk of the emperor made Rai grimace.

"How have things been here?" he asked.

Imayan let out a shaky exhale. "It's been hard. With Lintou and you gone…"

"I'm sorry, Imayan. I didn't want to go."

"I understand. It was my father. He sent you away and made sure I was out of the city when it happened," Imayan said. Tys was right, then. It sounded ridiculous for the emperor to take notice of Rai and to coordinate something like that to get him to disappear.

"I confronted him and he told me as much. He thought we were getting too close and that assassins could exploit our friendship and use you to get to me." Imayan shuffled forward and lowered her voice despite the fact no one would be able to hear them. "He's getting worse, Rai. I don't recognise him anymore. We can't even have a meal together without him lashing out. He's had good men and woman killed claiming they were spies. And his duties as emperor have fallen to the wayside.

"Overseer Myain hasn't said anything about it but he's been

pushing me harder and fitting in extra training, both with weapons and my studies. I think he hopes I will take up the throne sooner if I'm ready faster. I don't feel ready, Rai. I still don't know if I want this."

She stared into her coffee.

"I heard about the assassination attempts," Rai said. "And how you defended yourself. Despite hating the combat training, you're stronger than you think."

"But is it enough?" It come out as a plea. She wanted to hear that everything would be fine. That she could do this. But he didn't know, and he wouldn't lie to her.

"I don't know," he said.

Imayan let out a quivering breath. She leant back against the roof beam. Fear bled from her face, leaving a resigned worry. He hadn't settled her mind but fear and stress kept one aware. Rai knew this better than most. And if they were going to survive this, they would need to be aware of the realities. Not muddled in half-truths to protect feelings.

They chatted for a while longer catching up on smaller things before they descended and returned to Imayan's quarters. Rai wished her a goodnight and left Eril to guard her, returning to his room. He was past exhausted as he dropped into his bed.

He was back.

He would do things right this time and keep Imayan safe. Rai looked over to his bow attached to a makeshift weapons rack. Even with only a diera-plated bow he was a lot stronger than when he had left. They drilled and sparred everyday atop the plateau at the temple. And Rai was ready to put those new skills to the test.

The room darkened as dark hour descended and Rai closed his eyes. He was ready to fall asleep when a hand covered his mouth. His eyes shot open to a room of shadowed figures. They pinned down his legs, others reaching for his arms.

Something hard cracked against his face and he drifted into the void.

40

Black Stone Arch

The sky roared and rolled in a grey sea of clouds, an ever-present reminder that Nya was far from home. Far from those she loved. She told Blackcap that they needed to make a move soon. He didn't understand, despite her best efforts to put into words the feeling of the encroaching darkness. It was always on the edge of her senses. Poking and prodding and waiting for an opening. And with each step further from the tear, further from home, it grew stronger.

However, it wasn't long until their plan was set in motion.

Time held little meaning in a place without night but eventually the sky started to dim. Nya looked to the clouds wondering if it was a trick of the light.

No. It is darkening. I can feel it, Bom said.

"Hey! The sky is getting darker!" One of the guards called.

"It is. It happens every seven days." Mirt gazed at the landscape like one might admire a painting. "This place truly is magnificent."

Why Mirt thought this dead landscape of scree and dark stone was magnificent was beyond Nya.

It was darkening quicker than in Tarris. Nya watched in awe as the world dimmed.

"What happens when it gets dark?" Blackcap asked from Nya's side. He continued to help her walk with her injured ankle.

The smile slid from Mirt's face. "The sky turns black and the clouds settle into a still sheet of grey. Then, the creatures come out."

"Best to hurry," Adani said.

They walked in uneasy silence after that. The rumble from the sky quietened as if in anticipation of the night and colour drained from the world. Nya felt Blackcap's arm tighten. The party slowed from a proud march to a skulk through a place they no longer felt welcome in.

And yet, with the coming dark, strength filled Nya's limbs. The pain in her ankle eased and she could put more weight on it. Her senses sharpened rather than dulled with the coming night.

Part of Nya knew she should be afraid. This vigour was coming from the Dark. She knew she should fear the hold it had on her. But instead, confidence and energy eased the tension from her shoulders and relaxed her mind. It was the voice. The presence in the Black City. Yet she couldn't muster up any concern for this newfound strength. It felt too pure. Too natural.

"Perhaps," Blackcap's voice was loud in the quiet, "Adani and I should scout ahead. If creatures come out from the dark, we will need somewhere to camp out and protect ourselves."

He squeezed Nya's arm. That was the sign. This was it. Their chance.

This was the perfect time with this newfound energy from the dark. However, that no doubt meant Adani felt the same surge in strength.

Mirt looked to Adani who chewed on his bottom lip. The palace guard glanced at his shade. It was a black blob on the ground beside him holding down Bom.

Adani liked being in the lead, scouting ahead, and making the decisions. Blackcap and Nya had discussed his regular scouting trips over the last leg of the journey, and if what Mirt said was true, they would need shelter for the coming dark and they had passed a rock formation recently. That meant they needed to make a decision: risk marching on in search of more cover or backtracking to the spot they had passed an hour ago.

Adani licked his lips. "Fine. Bring the girl."

Nya suppressed a smile.

The remaining guards set down their heavy packs and rolled their shoulders, delighting in the respite. Blackcap pulled Nya along as they trekked ahead of the others. Adani led the way.

"When I make my move, you pull back your shade and we run," Blackcap said. His face was tight.

"Loosen up a bit," Nya whispered back. "He'll notice."

With visible effort, Blackcap eased his face into a neutral expression.

As the light dwindled and sky settled, so too did the clamour of the clouds. Scree crunched underfoot as they made their way over the cresting black stone landscape.

"It's getting quieter," Adani said. He stood atop a rock peering into the distance. "It will make listening for creatures approaching easier but equally it will allow them to hear us."

Blackcap grunted.

Nya guessed that they walked for around half an hour when the rock formation appeared on the horizon and the others had slipped from sight. They had walked in relative silence listening for husks or other dark creatures.

Adani ran up a smaller rock and threw himself onto a higher ledge of a rocky arch. It was a bulbous rock and there were plenty of ways to clamber up. Which was good. Nya's ankle would struggle with incline. After a cursory glance, Adani waved them to join him.

"This is good," Adani said. "If we can get up there, we can hide amongst the rocks and get a good view of the path ahead." He pointed to the top of the arch.

"Should we climb up and see what the area around us looks like before we head back?" Blackcap asked.

"If you can bring Nya up. I don't want her left in case she runs off. It would be foolish with her shade captured but she is a foolish girl." He grinned at Nya who scowled back.

It was an easy climb with few sharp inclines but Blackcap supported Nya until they reached the top of the arch. Around them was open land that rose and fell like stone dunes made of scattered rocks. Nya stared in the direction they were walking. The Black City was too far to see but she knew it was there. She felt it calling to her even now.

Nya.

Nya shook her head and tried to force back the connection but it was getting harder and harder.

"You feel it, don't you?" Nya flinched at Adani's voice. "The call."

"I don't know what you're talking about," she said. Adani gave her a knowing smirk.

Nya wanted to wipe that smile off his face. Perhaps if she just opened herself up and took in some of the strength she could… No. If she did there would be no shutting it off. The surge of power and energy she had felt in Ma-atan's temple was intoxicating. If she hadn't fallen unconscious Nya wasn't sure she would have been able to sever the connection. And now that she was so close to the source, Nya knew there would be no turning back after opening her mind to the darkness.

"We should head back," Blackcap said.

Blackcap stood beside Adani on the edge of the arch. This was it. If he pushed him off, Adani would need to call his shade to catch himself and Bom would be free. Blackcap cleared his throat and stepped closer. He was sweating and not doing a good job of hiding his nervousness.

"Are you alright there, Werin?" Adani asked. He was looking at Blackcap an eyebrow arched.

The world froze.

Nya went cold.

Werin.

The name that had haunted her from birth.

The name that her mother revered and spat at the same time.

Bile rose up her throat as she spun to face the man who had left her mother. A wave of nausea sent Nya stumbling as she met his gaze.

How had she not seen it? She had never met the man but Nya always assumed she would *know* when she saw him. Her father. The man that kicked her mother out of the palace after she became pregnant with Nya. The man who left her mother to starve on the streets of Yontar. The man who stole mother's life from her.

"Nya?" Werin gave Nya a concerned look.

The sick feeling swelled into one of fury and without thought, Nya lunged.

She tackled Werin and they flew off the edge of the arch. Wind whistled as Nya punched him. He grunted, fear sharp in his eyes. She wanted to relish that fear but anger burned away all other thoughts and emotions.

Nya! Power surged through her like a warmth blooming from within. Bom was in her shadow once more. Nya commanded the shade to pierce the man's heart. Her stomach was in her throat as they fell and she could feel the shade's worry at the fact they were plummeting towards the stone but that didn't matter.

Before Bom could make a move, a blast of shadow separated Nya and Werin. It slowed their fall pulling them up just before they hit the ground.

Nya landed and her ankle collapsed beneath her. She ignored it. Nya hissed and sent Bom tearing across the space between her and Werin. He shouted and threw his arms up. Adani's shade threw up a wall of shadow and Bom crashed into it and the shade pinned Bom down. Bom thrashed feeding off Nya's anger but Adani's shade was too strong.

Adani appeared then, brows arched.

"What is going on?" he asked.

"Duat take you! Coward!" Nya shouted at Werin who looked equally perplexed. "You left her! You got her pregnant and threw her from the palace like a damn coward!"

Werin's face paled as recognition flickered across his face.

"Werin, what is she talking about?" Adani asked.

"You're Ven's daughter?"

Nya wanted to shout and curse at the man but hearing her mother's name sent a sob bubbling up instead.

Adani looked between them. "She's your daughter? And you're just telling us this now Werin?"

"I didn't know. I didn't know I even had a daughter," Werin said, standing.

"Liar!" Nya shouted.

He met her gaze then and creased his brow, his eyes soft with sympathy. She didn't want his sympathy.

"Nya, it's not what you think. Your mother is sick and—"

"Was."

Werin scrunched his brow.

"She *was* sick."

Realisation dawned and he turned away, taking a deep breath. "I'm so sorry."

"The dead have no need for apologies," Nya spat.

She had to free Bom.

The darkness. The connection. The voice. Nya opened her mind and let some of the dark in. It flowed through her like water through a shrivelled plant and her body pulsed with power. Adani must have felt it as he looked at her, eyes going wide.

"Now, Nya..." he started.

Darkness exploded outward in a wave of shadow. Adani's shade was thrown off and Bom weaved through the air as a dancing tendril aiming for Werin's heart.

"Enough!" Adani screamed.

The voice in her head laughed, a deep bellowing. It echoed in her mind and Nya felt Bom cower at its power.

Adani's shade wrapped around Bom and yanked it downward. The two shades pushed and pressed against one another vying for the upper hand. Nya felt Bom slipping as Adani's shade took control. She pulled more power from the dark and felt Bom bulk and regain hold of the other shade.

Okay. That is enough. Your quibbles bore me. You are my champions and I will not have you fight, the voice boomed in Nya's head.

Nya cried out as a sharp shooting pain ran through her mind. Suddenly, Bom and Adani's shade stilled, shadows frozen. Then they retreated into their hosts like scolded animals.

Adani was breathing hard but his shade recaptured Bom, pinning it down. The Dark didn't intervene.

"You will not hurt Werin. We are travelling across a dangerous landscape and we need all the men we have," Adani said.

Nya lay back on the ground. Exhaustion stole the fight from her limbs.

All the while, the sky continued to darken.

Adani watched over Nya as Werin returned to tell the others about the cover they had found. No one spoke. Eventually the others caught up and Nya was passed off to one of the guards. Without

Bom, she couldn't do anything but submit to their treatment. Nya refused to look in Werin's direction.

She couldn't fathom that the man who had left them, the man who had made her mother's life a living nightmare was *here*. Her mother spoke of Nya's father as a handsome guard with sharp features. Not this scruffy palace guard who couldn't even tuck all his hair under his cap.

He was the reason for mother's misery. Nya always wondered what her life would have been like if he hadn't thrown her out of the palace. They could have been happy.

And mother wouldn't be dead.

Nya vowed then that she would kill him. The first chance she got she wanted to watch the life drain from his eyes. For mother.

This new guard who supported Nya didn't speak as they made their way atop the arch. He was silent and Nya was thankful for it.

They all clambered onto the arch as the last of the light was sapped from the sky. It should have been like dark hour but there was a pale purple light seeping into the black from the further ahead. It was coming from the Black City, Nya knew.

Her newly opened connection to the darkness increased her senses and brought knowledge that she should not know. The others squinted and peered across the rocky landscape but Nya could see the horizon in detail, the stone ridges clear.

And if she listened, Nya could hear whispers on the wind, a warning to the husks and other creatures of the dark place. A threat to leave their company unharmed.

There was a name on the wind, too.

Kygian.

She shuddered and the shadows around her quivered. Even thinking its name affected the world around her.

Their fire flickered creating a flash of light in the dark. *That's all we are,* Nya thought. *A spec of light that will soon be extinguished.*

She wasn't sure how much of that was her thought or the Dark's.

Nya glanced up at Werin.

But he will be the first to go.

41

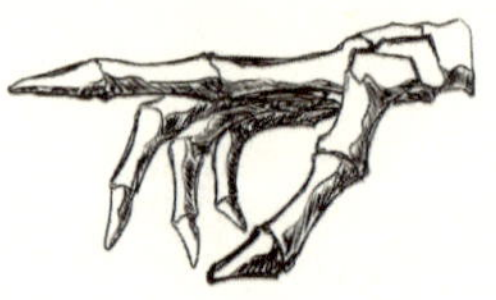

Dunes of Stone

B as led the way through the Thousand Floor Palace following, what he called, the essence. Kit still didn't quite understand how Bas could see this trail that was connected to the dark place but it hadn't steered them wrong yet.

His fists were clenched as they ran through the sandstone corridors. All it had taken was to touch the guard and her skin started to flake and turn ashen. Kit hadn't even meant it. He had to be careful.

"This way," Bas said turning up a flight of stairs.

Eventually they came to a familiar door. It was the same door the Doomed Others had passed through, into the room with the tear. Bas didn't slow. The guards looked up at the three of them. Before they could get a word out, Bas slid out his two spear hafts and leapt.

One guard went wide eyed and tripped back. The other, more

experienced guard by Kit's reckoning, reached for his weapon, but he was too slow for the Urdahl. The pointed end of Bas' broken staff stabbed straight through the man's neck. Blood spurted. Bas then flung the second half of his broken staff and it flew across the space and hit the other guard on the thigh. He squealed as he fell and a second later, Bas was on top of him gliding the same point over his neck while clasping the guard's mouth shut.

Kit watched, wide eyed. He knew Urdahl were meant to be incredible fighters but the level of ease and fluidity to Bas' movements was unlike anything he had seen before. Bas wiped his broken staff halves on the bodies and stood.

"They're in here," Bas said.

Wenson gawked. "How you do that?"

Bas scrunched his brow and Wenson gestured to the guards. "I will teach you but first," Bas pointed to the door.

"Do you think they went into the dark place?" Kit asked.

Bas nodded. "I only sense the essence here."

Pushing the door open, Bas quickly dispatched the handful of guards inside. The scholars scuttled away from the door that Wenson and Kit blocked. One scholar held her hands out in warning and pulled some of the others behind her.

"Hold the door," Kit said to Wenson and took a step forward. "You." He pointed to the woman. "When did they go through the tear?" The woman looked to Bas who was wiping the blood off his weapons. Her face twitched.

"Yesterday," she said.

"Was a girl with them?" Kit asked.

She nodded.

"And what did they go in for?" Kit asked.

One of the scholars stepped forward. His face was beetroot with rage. "Because that damn fool Mirt thinks—"

The leader scholar turned and slapped the man across the face and the man was stunned to silence.

"We don't know. Searching for something," the woman said.

Her eyes were stone. Kit knew that face. That level of solid resolve was rare and they wouldn't be getting anymore from her.

Kit scratched his chin. "We can make up on a day's travel. Come on, let's go." They strode towards the steps at the back of the room that led down to the tear. Bas and Wenson fell into stride as they made their way down the stairwell. A scholar sprinted out of the room, but it didn't matter. If they were going to the dark place again, more guards were the least of their worries.

"Wait!" the leading scholar called.

Kit turned.

"Don't bring anything back." There was a softness to her tone now.

"I'm just here for my friend," Kit said and her lips drew to a line.

"Then I'm sorry."

The scholar followed the rest out of the room. Her words sent a cold shiver through Kit. What else would they bring back?

It was exactly how Kit remembered it. The dark stone landscape reached for the crashing grey clouds above. The clamour of the sky a constant background noise. Blood drained from Wenson's face as he stared out at the dark place. Nya and Kit had explained to them what this place was like but nothing could prepare one for seeing it stretch out in front of them.

Without a word, Kit set off down the embankment. A day. Nya was a day ahead. They could make that up and catch them unaware, rescue Nya, return to the tear and close it.

It almost sounded easy.

That was never a good sign.

The dark place was a weight on those who walked there. It had an oppressive feeling as if you were being watched and it demanded quiet. Kit felt like an unwelcome intruder.

Bas carefully studied the landscape as they moved among the dark rock. Wenson, on the other hand, stuck close to Kit, eyes darting back and forth.

"What is this?" Wenson asked. His clipped Tarrisian was getting better.

"The dark place or 'pocket world'. I already told you this was where Nya, Bas, and I were thrown into. So keep an eye out for black dots in the sky or the sound of fabric being shaken hard. That's what the husks' wings sound like," Kit said.

"Can you see Nya as this essence?" Kit asked.

Bas kept watching the horizon as he spoke. "No. It's muddled here but it's stronger that way." He pointed north of their location.

"Do you think that's where they went?" Kit asked.

"The scholar said they were looking for something. I would bet that whatever it is, is what's causing the essence," Bas replied.

It was Wenson who spotted it first after a couple hours of walking. "There!" he called and ran ahead. Kit and Bas ran to catch up. As they approached, they saw Wenson bent down beside what was left of a fire pit.

"Ash cold," Wenson said showing the tip of his ashen finger.

"That means we're going in the right direction," Kit said. It wasn't that Kit didn't trust Bas's vision but having tangible evidence that they were on the right track eased some of his worry.

They continued on in the quiet of the dark place for an unknowable length of time. It was only when Wenson had stumbled for the fourth time that Kit called for a stop. They didn't light a fire. They weren't going to stop for long. Kit unslung his pack and handed out food. He placed it on the ground near Wenson and Bas, careful not to touch them. He was sure they wouldn't be harmed if he did touch them but he didn't want to risk it. Neither questioned the strange behaviour.

Wenson nodded and ate his meat strip as Bas reached out for his.

What kind of sorry company is this? Kit thought. *An Urdahl that barely speaks, a Nuian who doesn't know much Tarrisian and a dead man walk into another realm. It sounds like the start of a joke. And not a funny one.*

However, Kit was grateful Bas was here. His fighting prowess was the reason they had made it this far. Wenson, on the other hand… Kit had tried to explain the dangers of this journey but he was set on helping. Wenson wasn't a fighter and had no discernible skills that Kit had seen. They had grown close during their time at the Patched Cloak and Kit enjoyed spending time with him but this wasn't the time for friends. But no matter what Kit said, Wenson wouldn't take no for an answer.

A hand clutched his shoulder and Kit shook out of his daze to see Wenson smiling at him.

"We will find Nya," Wenson said in almost perfect Tarrisian. He stood and brushed off his hands on his tunic. "You show me now?" He waved his hands about in an imitation of Bas' fighting style.

"No. We need to get moving," Kit said pushing to his feet. They didn't have time for Wenson to train.

Wenson looked disappointed but he didn't argue and soon they were wandering the dark place once more.

Eventually the rocky landscape fell away to an undulating plain not unlike the desert dunes. This was further than they had trekked the first time they had come to the dark place. As they continued northward, they spotted remains of several other fire pits. And Bas confirmed the trail was pointing them towards the dark essence. A grey fox ran out in front of them before scuttling out of sight but other than that, they found no signs of life. And no husks.

They stopped for only short periods but it was wearing on them. They took turns napping each time they stopped but it was clear they couldn't keep this up for much longer.

Come on. They must be close.

Kit walked ahead watching for more burnt-out fire pits. Behind, he heard Wenson talking with Bas. He was asking questions about fighting forms and the best weapons to use in certain situations. Their voices grated on Kit. They should be keeping their strength up by staying silent. They weren't here to chat. They were here to save Nya and close the rift.

Just as Kit turned to say that he heard beating wings. The familiar *thwack*. Bas' eyes went wide. He heard it, too. Kit surveyed the landscape. Most of the area around them was flat but up ahead a rock formation rose into the sky.

"There!" Kit hissed pointing. "We need to take cover!"

They didn't question him and ran for the stone arch. Kit's head swivelled trying to glimpse the husks but he couldn't see anything and it was hard to find the source of the noise over the din of the storming sky.

Barrelling forward, they dove under the cover of rock as the sound of beating wings grew ever louder. They hid under a lip of rock just large enough to fit the three of them. Kit peeked out and in the distance he saw them. A black cloud breaking into many pieces.

"Back. Back," Kit said dragging the other two away from the edge.

Their breathing was hard from running. The husks were louder. They shrieked and howled. For a moment, Kit thought they had been spotted but the husks kept flying past, continuing their guttural screeching.

The husk's cries faded into the storming clamour of the clouds. The three of them glanced at one another until finally, Bas stuck his head out. He looked around before nodding.

Kit blew out a breath and pushed out from beneath the rock.

He took two steps, searching the sky for movement. Stabbing pain burst through his back as talons pierced flesh. Kit's breath caught and he was lifted into the air. A scream slipped from his lips and the husk matched his shriek as they rose. The blade-like claws tore through the flesh in his back sending a crackling burning rippling through him. His muscles ripped apart as his weight fought to drag him back to the ground.

The husk flew for a rock face. It was going to crush him against it. Terror kept the darkening corners of his vision at bay as Kit scrambled trying to free himself. He grabbed the husk's wing and yanked downward. They spiralled dropping away from the rock wall. Pain flooded Kit until his whole body was alight with it.

They crashed into the ground, bouncing across the scree. Sharp pains rang through Kit as he careened across the rocks. It was a welcome distraction from the pulsing throb of his back.

The world spun as Kit pushed up. The husk hurtled towards him. Kit threw up his arms as the husk sank its teeth into his wrist. He screamed. Its fangs dug deeper. Flashes of the guards decaying under his fingers came to his mind. With his free hand, Kit gripped the husk's head, its skin was leathery and cold. Kit focused.

Nothing happened.

The husk started kicking and clawing at Kit, its talons shredding his gut. The brutality was astonishing and sent Kit reeling, his mind an incoherent whirl. These were fatal wounds.

I might die, Kit thought.

The old texts Jirma and Kit had translated alluded to deathless not being immortal. He could die from wounds and they had no idea what that threshold was. If the husk tore through enough of him, Kit was sure he wouldn't be able to recover.

Kit let out a feral scream. He brought his attention away from the pain, trying to picture the skin of the husk flaking with decay. The darkness around his eyes crept over his vision. Everything was getting hazy. Kit stared at his hand on the husk's head willing it to work.

But there was nothing.

He didn't feel the spark of energy between his fingertips and he knew he was dead. Kit slumped forward, as relief bloomed. At least the agony would stop.

With a battle cry, Wenson tackled the husk. Kit's vision swam as he saw Bas fighting off another husk in the distance. He rolled over to watch Wenson hit the husk with a rock but the creature looked more annoyed than in pain.

It swiped its claw and left a bloody gash in Wenson's arm. Wenson fell back. He was no fighter and had no healing abilities like Kit.

A new kind of terror rose inside of Kit. Not the burning of pain and rage but the icy fear of losing his friend. He crawled over as the husk stepped towards Wenson. The husk was about to launch itself at him when Kit grabbed the beast's ankle. It looked down, startled.

It's now or never, Kit thought looking up at those burning eyes.

Nothing.

The husk brought its talon up to strike.

There was a tingle in Kit's fingertips and the husk froze. It looked down as its skin started to peel.

Wenson clobbered it with a boulder and the husk crumpled to the ground. Kit held its ankle as Wenson dropped on the husk and continued to smash husk's face in. The decay crept up its leg to its body. There it spread over to Wenson's calf. He screamed, looking down. Kit tried to let go but his body wouldn't let him. Not until he had drained more life to heal himself.

The blackened skin spread and started to peel. Wenson's eyes went wide. Kit shouted. He wanted Wenson to move, to get away, but his voice wouldn't work.

Bas reached out and yanked Wenson away while Kit siphoned

the last of the life from the husk. Energy ran through him as his wounds started to knit themselves back together.

Wenson grimaced but the decay had stopped spreading on his leg. There was a dark blotch of skin on his calf. Almost like he had gotten ash on his calf. Wenson held his hand out to get Bas to help him to his feet. Bas obliged and Kit was relieved to see that Wenson could still walk.

The pain faded to a dull ache and anger overcame Kit.

"What were you doing?" Kit snapped.

The others looked to him, brows furrowed.

"You can't fight. You can't heal. And you still threw yourself into the fight!" Kit said.

"I help," Wenson said.

This anger stemmed from fear. It would have been Kit's fault if he died. He couldn't blame Wenson for trying to help but the words tumbled from him anyway.

"Fool! How can you help? All you do is make it worse. I don't even understand why you are here. What good are you? You're just making it harder for us as we have to save you every time we get into any mess! You're nothing but a burden!"

With each sentence, Wenson's eyes grew wider. Once Kit was done, there was a moment's quiet.

"I go set up the fire," Wenson finally said and walked off.

Kit watched him go. Guilt washed over him drowning out the dulling agony of his wounds. He shouldn't have said that. Bas stared at Kit. His face was neutral but Kit knew he was scowling inside. The Urdahl left Kit lying there and went to assist in setting up the fire.

Kit lay on his back. The sky was a swirling storm of clashing clouds.

They set up camp and Kit passed out before the fire. He didn't know how long he had slept for but when he awoke, the majority of his wounds had healed. Kit inspected himself with astonishment. His back still ached and there were some minor cuts healing across his torso but the pain was minimal. This was the fastest and most drastic healing he had done so far and he was certain it came from draining the life from the husk. His wounds did heal with time but it seemed that if he killed someone with this new ability, he could restore himself faster.

Kit wasn't sure how to feel about that. He felt guilty about the guards back in the palace but this was a monster from another world. So it was okay then, right?

Bas was stoking the fire when Kit woke. Wenson was nowhere to be seen. A sudden flush of worry passed through him that Wenson might have left by himself, either further on or back to the tear. Both would be a death sentence by himself.

"He is atop the rock planning the journey ahead," Bas said. He must have seen the concern on Kit's face. The Urdahl was always good at reading others emotions.

Kit blew out a breath and moved closer to the fire. "How long have I been out?"

"A couple of hours, roughly."

Kit nodded and then drank from his waterskin. A couple of hours wasn't too much of a setback. They could make back the time. They had built a small fire under the rock they had used as cover from the husks. It kept them out of view from any others that might pass.

"We need to get moving," Kit said reaching for his pack.

"First, you must talk with Wenson."

Kit glanced at Bas. The bald man looked up from the fire, his gaze inscrutable.

"I know I was harsh. I just…"

I was scared. He didn't say it allowed. If one admitted to being afraid while living on the streets they died. Those same instincts clung to Kit and refused to be washed off with his new life.

"You were afraid Wenson would get hurt," Bas said.

Kit nodded.

"And in your fear, you lashed out and hurt him more than any husk could." Bas poked the fire. "I understand why you did it. But the threat of death can be a self-fulfilling prophecy."

There was a subtle tightness to Bas' face.

The fire crackled.

"Do you know why I am here?" Bas asked.

"To help save Nya and close the tear?"

"Partly." Bas hesitated before continuing. "We were raised not to talk with non-Urdahl people and I could be killed for mentioning this, however, my people and I do not always see eye to eye," Bas said. "Once we become of age we are shown visions."

Under different circumstances, Kit may have laughed at that. But he could see that there was no humour on Bas' face.

"I saw fragments of a future that did not bode well for my people or Tarris. I saw darkness flood Yontar and death came like a wave across the desert. Blood pooled and the Urdahl drowned in it."

A shiver crept up Kit's spine. Bas' voice was emotionless.

"I am here to save Nya, but I am also here to follow this darkness to the root. To close the rift to this dark place and put a stop to it."

"That's why I'm here too," Kit said. "The plan has always been to close the tear."

"But you're also here for Nya. We all have our reasons. Why do you think Wenson is here?" Bas asked.

Kit shifted uncomfortably. "For the same reasons as me."

"Wenson can't fight. He can't speak much Tarrisian. He's limited in how he can help with this. And still, he tries. He sees you and he sees Nya with her shade and he sees Illy running the inn. You asked him why he came? He came to prove that he can help. He came to prove that he is worthy of being part of this."

Kit stared at Bas. He hadn't considered any of that.

"He doesn't need to be worthy of being our friend," Kit said.

"Does he know that?"

The words hit Kit like a blow. How had he not seen it and Bas, who had only been at the inn for a month, did? Wenson had always been there in the background. He had helped gather supplies. He volunteered to infiltrate the palace and come to another realm. Now looking back, he could see why Wenson withdrew after Pio attacked the inn. He was annoyed that he couldn't help defend it.

And Kit had told him he was all but useless.

Kit stood and walked away from the fire. He made his way to the rocks and started climbing. It didn't take long to spot Wenson sitting at the edge of one of the plateaus looking at something in his lap. As Kit approached he realised that Wenson was mapping out the area ahead. There were many paths between the mountainous region ahead and despite Kit waving him off, Wenson was preparing and helping in any way he could. Kit dropped down beside him.

"These are good," Kit said.

Wenson made a noncommittal grunt. Kit looked at his hand. They used to be so close, but since Ma-atan's temple and becoming deathless, Kit hadn't spent much time with his friend. He had been too wrapped up in his own problems to see his friend's struggles.

"Wenson, I shouldn't have said those things," Kit said. "I was just… scared that you would get hurt saving me."

Wenson stopped his sketching.

"I didn't mean any of those things. I'm glad you're here. I wouldn't want anyone else with me delving into Duat," Kit said.

"I'm no help. You were right."

"No, I wasn't right. You saved my life back there, Wenson. If you hadn't attacked that husk, I'd be dead right now."

Wenson looked up.

"Like when Nya and you saved my life?"

Kit had forgotten about that. He and Nya had saved Wenson from some thugs out the back of the Patched Cloak before they travelled to Ma-atan's temple. Had Wenson felt like he had a debt to repay?

Tears threatened but Kit swallowed them back. "Even better. At least Nya and I were fighting off some thugs but you faced down a Duat-damned demon, Wenson."

He smiled at that.

"You're like a brother to me." Kit held out his hand and Wenson clasped it.

"Black sand fool," Wenson said as a smile touched his lips.

Kit grinned back.

42

The Greatest Lie

It was the day after she learned that Blackcap was her father when he approached her again. The urge to lash out tensed Nya's body. He held out a plate of dried meat and she snatched it from him.

They hadn't moved from the top of the arch. Nya was sure they had been there for more than a day but Mirt wanted to wait out the prolonged night here in the dark realm, claiming he was worried about someone misplacing their footing.

But Nya knew that wasn't true. She could feel it. Fear shrouded him and the others like an aura. An effect from opening up to the darkness.

Even now, as Werin stood there, she felt his apprehension and fear.

"Can we talk?" Werin asked.

Nya bit into the meat strip. He took that as an affirmative and sat just out of reach.

"Your mother and I…" He hesitated. "I don't know what she said but we weren't close."

Nya didn't look up from her food.

"She had a sickness of the mind. I didn't know or we wouldn't have…"

Nya's grip tightened on her plate. Werin was staring at his hands.

"Look, if I knew she was pregnant it would have been different. I would have helped care for you. I swear I didn't know."

Silence.

"I've seen him," Nya said.

"Him?"

"The Weigher of Souls. The Harbinger of Justice. Ma-atan. I watched as he tore the heart out of people I loved. How he held them up and inspected the hearts before popping them like ripe fruit. I'll be sad to miss the look on your face when he does the same to you," Nya said. Her voice was soft and emotionless.

Werin stared at her for a moment before getting up and returning to the fire. The other guards sat around it, laughing and playing cards. Only Adani and Nya refused to go near the warmth and the light. The dark was like a blanket, comforting and protective.

A voice in the back of her head said that this wasn't normal. That this was the darkness influencing her but she didn't care. Not anymore.

He's a liar, Nya thought. *Mother told me that they lived together in the palace. They were in love until she became pregnant with me.*

Bom grumbled in her mind.

What? Nya asked.

Lying makes humans spike in fear. He did not spike in fear when he spoke, Bom said.

No. He had to be lying. *He's not afraid because he knows I can't hurt him. For now*, Nya thought.

The night passed and light returned. At the break of that dawn they extinguished the fire and made their way down from the arch. By the time they were marching onward it was as bright as the day they had arrived.

The company fell back into a routine of walking until they could walk no more and then setting up a camp to eat and rest. This repeated over and over. The landscape barely changed and there was no conversation to be had with this new guard that helped Nya walk.

It was the third or fourth trek broken by naps and food that her foot healed. It healed faster than what should be possible and she knew it had to have come from the darkness that she had opened herself to. Still, Nya made a show of limping and getting the guard to help her. To be underestimated is to be given the upper hand, a lesson Nya learnt many times on the streets of Yontar.

With nothing to do but walk in silence, Nya was left with her thoughts. She had failed. Despair clung to her with that honest fact. There was no way for her to defeat Adani and close the tear. She would have to hope that Kit and the others found another way to close it from the Tarrisian side.

I'll likely never see them again.

The realisation came barbed and sharp. She didn't know what

awaited her in the Black City or what this Kygian wanted with her. But she was done with letting others choose her fate. Nya clenched her fist and felt the darkness thrum inside her.

She would use this strength until her last breath.

"I'll take her."

Nya glanced up to see Werin nod to the guard helping Nya. The guard screwed his face up. "Are you sure?"

Werin looked to Nya and then to the guard and nodded. With a sigh, the guard stepped back and let Werin take Nya's arm. She felt the heat of him under her arm. They walked for a while in silence.

"How did she die?" Werin asked.

The attic. Dark tendrils. Warm blood running down Nya's arm. Those empty eyes.

"Killed," Nya said.

Werin nodded as if he had expected as much. Living on the street was hard and few survived. What he didn't know was that she had killed mother. The scene still haunted her nightmares.

"She was a performer at a Night Theatre when I met her," Werin said.

Lies. She worked in the palace kitchens.

"I didn't usually go to the Night Theatres but my buddies and I made palace guard and we were celebrating." Werin stared out to the horizon. Lost in memory. "She danced on the stage for hours. The guy who owned the Night Theatre worked the dancers to the bone. Keeping them lucid with shock herb. You know what that is?"

Nya did but she didn't respond.

"Shock herb is its street name. I don't know what it's really called but a couple drops of that and you can be awake for days. Some watch guards take it. Anyway, I could tell your mother had been on it for too long. She stumbled and went over on her ankle but I caught her. The owner was shouting and screaming at her but I threatened to have him brought in and showed him my palace guard patch. He shut up at that. So I pulled her out of the Night Theatre and helped splint her leg. By the time I was finished she had passed out.

"I couldn't have left her there and I didn't want to take her back into the Night Theatre with that owner so I brought her to the palace and took her to the infirmary, where they nursed her back to health. I visited most days and stayed with her a couple of nights. She was friendly and grateful. We talked into the late hours most nights."

Then Werin's face darkened.

"One day after I got off duty I went to go see her and she was no longer there. I asked the doctors and they said she was fine so they set her free. I knew what this meant. She was a performer and the infirmary was for the palace guard so as soon as she could stand they threw her out onto the streets. I went out looking for her. It took me days to track her down. Eventually I found her stealing from a street vendor. I asked her to come back with me but she lashed out and screamed that I had abandoned her and that she wouldn't fall for my tricks again."

He fell silent for sometime. "I never saw her again."

Nya felt Bom's sense strain for a spike in fear that could indicate a lie. The shade felt nothing. Could it be true? Her mother had a sickness of the mind and often saw things Nya did not, but why would her mother lie to *her*? Could she have been lying to herself?

The greatest lies are those that one tells themselves.

Part of Nya believed him, but another part wanted to stay in the anger and the fury. It made more sense than this sadness and sense of loss for someone who was already gone.

"How can I trust you?" Nya asked.

Werin rolled up his sleeve to reveal a bracelet around his wrist. It was made of a coarse red fabric and weaved in tight knots in a style her mother loved.

"She told me she wanted to open an inn one day. An inn that sold travellers clothes, too. That way she could continue to sew and get to meet people." He looked at the bracelet fondly. "I'm not going to tell you that I loved her, Nya. I didn't know her for long enough. But I swear to you, I would not have left her if I knew she was with child."

Nya sagged into his grip. She didn't know if she could trust him but did it matter? He still left her. Mother still blamed Nya and now she was dead.

"I can't forgive you."

"That's okay."

They stumbled on in silence.

43

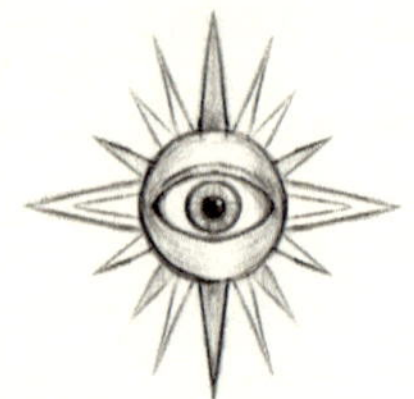

Atop the World

13 years ago.

Rai's head lolled as he searched through the bleary dark for clarity. The metallic tang of blood lingered on his tongue and he felt more dripping down his face. Pain surged as he became aware of it and Rai let out a groan.

"Shh now. Just a little further," someone said. The voice was almost a whisper, like a mother telling her child to go back to sleep.

A blur of burning firelight filled Rai's vision. It was so bright. He pressed his eyes closed against it. Sensations came to him in drips and drabs and Rai noticed that he was being dragged. Two palace guards in dark jerkins pulled him along by his arms. It was cool and Rai glanced to the night sky. The ethereal glow of the Moon Eye tinged the horizon but it was yet to surface. So it was still dark hour and he hadn't been knocked out long.

The guards tossed Rai to the ground. His head cracked against the stone spattering stars across his vision.

"You've done this to yourself, Rai," said a familiar voice.

Rai lifted his head. Everything was still a haze. The light of the city silhouetted the man who spoke. Realisation set in as Rai recognised the voice.

No.

Emperor Leondal turned to face him. Wreathed in firelight he rolled a dagger between his fingers. Suddenly, everything fell into place. He was on the Atef Palace roof. That's why he could see the city. The whistling wind masked the sounds of the city leaving them alone atop the world.

"If you just stayed at the Verdin Temple I would have let you live," Leondal said. "But to come back, and early? What monarch has you in their pocket, Rai?"

Rai coughed searching for his words. "None, sir. I came back to be of service."

The corners of Leondal's mouth lifted in a sinister half smile. "Of service? Would you give your blood for the throne?"

Rai nodded.

The Emperor took a deep breath staring at the dagger in his hand. "Hold him."

The guards swept in and propped Rai up on his knees. He didn't fight them. Leondal approached with the dagger.

"Wait!" Rai shouted pulling away from the blade. "It's true! I came back to guard Imayan. I protected her from the assassins before you sent me off, didn't I?"

The dagger stopped inches from his neck.

"Before I sent you off?"

Rai's heart dropped.

"Do you think I needed to *send you off?*" Leondal stood and laughed. "My advisors were right. People are thinking me weak. Let him go."

Rai flopped to the ground. He pushed up on shaking arms as Leondal turned back to the city.

"Beat him," Leondal said.

A foot slammed into Rai's side and he was sent careening across the rooftop. Rai gasped for air, clutching his chest.

"This is what the great Verdin Guild offers me? You cannot protect my daughter. You cannot even protect yourself."

Hands grabbed Rai by the scruff of his cloak and yanked him up as the other guard pummelled his torso. Spittle and blood sprayed from Rai's mouth. The guard let him go and he fell into an uppercut. Blinking, Rai was on his back again looking up at the night sky. His vision swam as the Emperor said something else lost to the ringing in his ears.

Rolling to his side, Rai curled up in a defensive position. The emperor truly had lost his mind. It wasn't that Rai didn't believe what he had heard but seeing it was different. A foot cracked across Rai's face. The sides of his vision darkened.

"I might have to rethink this deal with the Verdin Guild. Their warriors are not all they are told to be after all," Leondal said.

The Emperor grabbed a hunk of his hair and lifted. "You love her, don't you?" Leondal whispered.

The world seemed to slow. The pain subsiding as adrenaline flooded Rai's system.

"Yes, I can see it in your eyes," Leondal said. "I know you're not with another monarch. They wouldn't pick someone so weak. But Imayan deserves better than you."

The words stabbed like a knife. Of course she did. Rai knew that.

"She will be my family's legacy. I spent too long making safe choices to keep the peace. I would have been lost in the slew of past rulers. Just another pillar in the Hall of Strain? I don't think so. But the father of the first Empress of Tarris? The one who put her in power? Now that will etch my name into history books for all time.

"She will have to marry, of course. I've already selected several suitors that would strengthen the throne. And her Duat-damned personal guard isn't one." Emperor Leondal spat in Rai's face. The glob dripped down his cheek. Rai hadn't the energy to wipe it away. Leondal then smashed his face off the edge of the roof and let him crumple into a heap.

"She needs a man who is a born leader. One that will keep her right under a firm hand. Why can't the other monarchs see? Of course I wouldn't let her rule on her own. She would be guided! Black sand-footed fools."

Keep her right? Guided? The emperor had no plans to let Imayan rule. He wanted a figurehead. One that he could control. Despite all that Imayan was training for, despite all her effort and focus, she was going to be a puppet. She didn't even want the role and yet she put everything towards it. For her father. For Tarris. And this man didn't care. He didn't see her effort and that was worse.

Rage sharpened Rai's vision.

Emperor Leondal sighed. "Kill him."

Rai slipped his hand into his belt, masking the move with a roll. The guards had taken his weapons but left the small vial of blood.

After all, what could it do? Rai unstoppered the top and drained the contents. Curiosity curled the Emperor's face.

Blood had little to no effect on humans apart from a couple exceptions that Shesmu had discovered. Artengo blood could be boiled and inhaled for a euphoric effect. And that same blood could be ingested with diera ore shavings for a sudden kick of energy.

Heat burned through the pain and Rai's limbs thrummed with energy. It didn't heal him but it would mask the pain for a short time.

Emperor Leondal's mouth fell open as Rai leapt. He tackled into the Emperor, knocking him to the ground. The guards shouted and charged. Instinct took over and Rai tore the dagger from the Emperor's belt, plunging it into the man's chest. Leondal's eyes bulged as warm blood ran through Rai's fingers. Rai pressed the dagger deeper and watched the life drain from Leondal's eyes. He didn't scream. He didn't so much as shout out for help. It was too quick, the blade having pierced his heart. Shock flushed the Emperor's face the seconds before his death. The last thing he saw was Rai's grim face lit with the burning torches of the city he failed.

Panic swelled as Rai stepped off the Emperor and staggered backward. Realisation came like a punch to the face. His breath quickened.

He had just killed the Tarrisian Emperor. The ruler of the country. Imayan's father.

The rooftop was in silence. Rai glanced up to see the guards frozen staring at the body of their ruler. They shared a glance and burst into motion. One guard sprinted for the stairs back into the palace. Rai flung the dagger which caught the man in his calf. He collapsed grabbing his leg with a feral scream. The other guard barged into Rai knocking him from his feet. Agony flared before the blood took hold and suppressed the shooting pains.

The guard screamed holding his sword above his head, about to plunge it into Rai. He rolled at the last second, the blade clanging against the stone roof, then Rai kicked the guard's leg. He tripped, losing his balance.

Stumbling to his feet, Rai noticed the other guard had begun crawling towards the stairs, the dagger left discarded. Stalking over, Rai followed the trail of blood, snatching up the dagger. These were innocent men. Guards not unlike himself. But if one were left to speak of what happened, Rai would be the most wanted man in Tarris.

Rai stabbed the blade deep into the guard's back. He howled as Rai dragged the knife through his flesh. He felt it scrape bone as the guard flailed and screamed before finally falling still.

Slapping footsteps.

Rai spun just as the other guard swung his sword. Raising his arm, the blade sliced up his forearm and blood sprayed. But it stopped the sword from cleaving his head off. It was Rai's turn to scream now. It was a raw, feral sound that was more animal than man.

Fear flickered in the guard's eyes and he hesitated. That was all Rai needed. He tackled the man. The guard hit his head on the ground and his eyes unfocused. Rai punched his face and blood spurted. He hit again and again. There was no thought, just fury. Rai's face was drenched in blood; he felt it drip down like sweat on a hot day. He screamed as each impact cracked and collapsed the man's head. It wasn't until he was unrecognizable bloody pulp that Rai slumped and dropped to the ground beside the corpse.

He lay there breathing hard. The Moon Eye began its watch bringing a silver tinge to the bloodied rooftop. Rai could now make out more of the details of the roof and the gore that marred the ornate stone.

He felt sick.

Did he do this?

What had he done?

Facing away from the guard's body, Rai threw up. The stench of decay and voided bowels mixing with his dizzied mind left him nauseous. The strength from the blood started to ebb and the pain started to swell.

It was all too much. And then there was darkness.

44

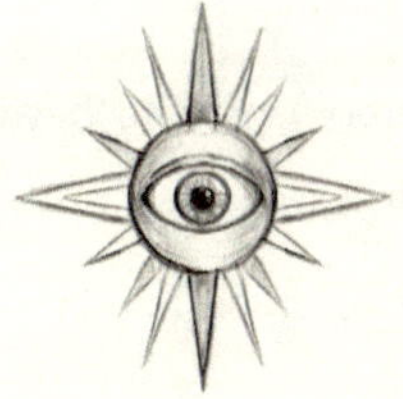

Mask of Lies

13 years ago.

Memory blended with reality as Rai woke where he had woken many times in days long past. The infirmary hadn't changed much in the years he had spent at the Verdin Temple. The same scent that Rai associated with places of healing wafted him to wakefulness. Throbbing pain echoed around his body making it hard to tell where it resonated from. Rai tried to speak, to call out but his throat was too dry. There was no water at his bedside. He glanced around the room. The other beds were empty. What had happened?

Hands in the night.

The city burning brightly.

Blood.

The crack of bone and spatter of blood under his fists.

He had killed the emperor.

Rai's heart rate spiked as the night came back in a flood. He killed the Duat-damned emperor. Lifting his arms, Rai note that he wasn't chained to the bed like he had expected to be. He was in no state to run. Even if he did, he would be the most wanted man in Tarris. He wouldn't make it far. His thoughts fell to the Verdin Guild. There was a divide within the capital but would they hide him? *No. I would put them all in danger*, Rai thought.

If they were found harbouring him, they would all be slaughtered, too. And while facing down the Verdin Temple was no mean feat, Rai didn't want more blood on his hands.

This is it then. The end.

He surprised himself surviving this long.

After some time, footsteps broke the silence. Rai braced himself as a doctor turned the corner. The woman hummed as she carefully placed down an array of bottles and cloths on the far table. Turning, she started.

"You're awake," she said.

"Water," Rai croaked.

She nodded bringing water to his lips and letting some trickle into his mouth. He was grateful beyond belief. He thought she might have denied him. The doctor turned to leave and Rai grunted. He didn't want her to go. While she was here he could pretend it was like years ago after a particularly brutal training session.

She tilted her head with a half-smile. "I'll be back. I was told to tell Imayan as soon as you woke." And with that she vanished around the corner.

Imayan.

Rai didn't want to face her. He didn't want to hear her berate him for killing her father. A scalpel lay across the other side of the room. Could he make it over and finish this now? Rai shifted his weight and his whole body screamed. No. He couldn't move.

Time dragged as he waited, straining his hearing for the patter of footsteps. They came as the clomp of heavy-duty boots. *Guards,* Rai thought.

Two palace guards crested the corner and fanned out across the room as Imayan and Mino stepped into the infirmary. Imayan's eyes were red from crying but none streaked her face now. She walked with Mino whose brow was creased with worry.

More palace guards followed, several hovering around the entrance to the infirmary. Imayan stalked up to his bed side. Now that she was closer, Rai noticed that her eyes were puffy and her hair was matted as if it hadn't been brushed.

"He's dead." Imayan swallowed.

Rai opened his mouth but what was he to say? Sorry? Sorry I killed your father and thrust you into a position you aren't ready for and don't want.

"He's dead, Rai," Imayan said, clutching his hand. It hurt but not as much as the look on her face did. "Did you see it happen? Did you get a look at those responsible? They're searching the palace but they haven't found anything."

Rai blinked. His addled brain was a whir as he tried to piece this all together. Did she think it was an assassin that got her father?

"I'm sorry. I know you're…" She waved at his battered and bloodied body. "How is he?" Imayan asked the doctor.

"He has fractures and broken bones. I can't see the extent of his injuries but he will live," the doctor said.

Guilt washed over Rai. He had to tell her. Tell her it was him who killed her father. Tell her she should send him for execution. That pain welled and bloomed threatening tears.

"Thank the Gods," Imayan said. She rubbed her face and took a deep breath before dropping down to his side. "I'm not sure what I'd do if I lost you, too."

Rai could see an inconsolable torment behind her brown eyes. She was putting up a front because so many were around her but he could see that she was a phrase away from collapsing and breaking down.

If he told her the truth, Rai would send her over the edge.

"They want me to take the throne," Imayan whispered. "They said Tarris is weak without a ruler and that it must happen this week."

Fear rang through her words.

"Rai, I need you by my side for what comes next. I need you to get better, and soon."

Her eyes pleaded with him. If he told her that he was the one that killed the emperor she would shatter. The monarchs would sweep in and a civil war would erupt all across Tarris. Imayan needed to be strong. She needed support from those around her. But could he live in a lie?

And so Rai never spoke the lie. His silence was his confession. It was his bloody truth.

It was the wordless lie that ate him up and left him a hollow husk.

As promised, Imayan became the first Tarrisian empress within the week. Rai stood by Mino as the crowds screamed. Imayan was draped in gold and black robes as she looked stoically over the throng from the pronouncement balcony. She wore no crown like leaders in other countries as a symbol to the other monarchs and the rest of Tarris that she was a conduit for them, the people.

From their vantage point, it seemed all of Tarris was here to show support for the empress. And yet as the advisers had warned her, there were some who pushed against her rule causing fights and riots. Imayan didn't seem to care. She had become despondent and distant in her mourning. They had talked little in the time between her father's death and her ascension to empress. This didn't bother Rai, though. Every time he looked at her, her father's shock-filled eyes stared back. Guilt sat like a weight in his gut.

As the doctor had said, his wounds were healing slowly. He had begun walking the day before and Imayan requested him to be at her side for this monumental day. A day Rai shouldn't have seen. A day that shouldn't have been. Not yet, anyway.

Mino told Rai of Imayan's breakdowns. An undirected anger at the world bubbled out of her when no one was around. She screamed and cried and swore at the World Turner. How could fate be so cruel? To take her father from her. To force her into a place of such importance when she wasn't ready. Mino hadn't left her side and was the only one she confided in. Rai could tell Mino was terrified for her mental state. She didn't know how to help. She didn't know if anything would.

She is hoping I know what to do, Rai realised once when Mino visited him. But of course, he didn't. He knew of the emptiness and knew it had no cure. There is nothing to cure. It is an absence of something.

Something that cannot be reclaimed. And as Rai had learned, the void can grow. It can take more of him, dragging him into a pit of pure darkness. A place where light and hope can't flourish because they do not exist in such places.

But there was none of that now. Imayan the first empress of Tarris, stood tall and regal. Her face trained to a relaxed pose of propriety. It was the same practiced expression she wore to the orphanage all those years ago. One that commanded attention and showed nothing but control. Back then Rai caught glimpses beneath it. But Imayan had mastered it now. A perfect mask of lies.

The Tarrisian people cheered. An era had ended. And a new one had just begun.

45

Sand and Steel

To Kleran's word, the army rode hard to the ancient capital. Two days passed in a blur of sand and steel. Cresting a sand dune, Rai caught the first glimpse of Asuriya. The ruins of the outer city were half-buried in sand. Derelict buildings had eroded to corpses of what they once were. Past that the walls of the city proper lined the horizon and the Bandor Mountains further still, reaching into the blue sky.

A scout reined in her hyian beside Rai. "Never thought I'd set eyes on the old capital."

Rai grunted surveying the desert. Fax saw it before Rai did. A plume of sand that could only be kicked up by a sizeable company of warriors. The Ossin army had yet to come into sight but the sand dunes obscured a lot in the desert and distances could be deceiving.

"Report back and tell them the Ossin army has been spotted,"

Rai said. He wasn't part of the Seventh Sceptre anymore, nor was he an overseer, but he couldn't help the commanding tone that leaked into his voice. The scout gave a curt nod and shot off back to their procession. He wasn't sure his part in all this. But he had made a promise all those years ago and he was going to keep it.

"What do you think, Fax?"

They'll reach Asuriya before dark hour, Fax said.

"It'll be close."

When is it ever not?

Rai whipped his reins and turned the hyian around riding back to their army. The procession pressed hard with news from the scout. Even before Rai fell into their ranks he saw the determination on the faces of the men and woman. He weaved through the fast front: a squad of soldiers on hyianback, their front line, meant to reach the walls first. Then he moved through the heavier, bulk of their force. Aya covered in thick leather jerkin armour surrounded by their own guard of hyian warriors and foot soldiers marched at their feet. Unlike those merchants used, these aya had thick tusks and were bred for battle.

Pushing through their forces, Rai pulled up beside Imayani and Kleran who rode near the centre of the army. Their honour guards circling them.

"They will reach Asuriya before nightfall," Rai said.

"Then we push faster," Kleran said nodding to his overseer, who left to pass on the orders.

"I will ride with the fast front and try to take the walls. This has become a sprint to the finish," Rai said.

"I'll come with you, like old times." Tysar rode up to Rai.

"Hold them off as long as you can," Kleran said.

Rai nodded and looked to Imayani. "Be careful," she said.

With that, Rai charged back to the front of the army, Tysar at his side. Like old times, Tysar had said. But there was no going back to those days.

Too much had changed.

Rai had gone to Imayani during one of their short rests where they set up camp. Few slept despite the breaks in the march but the respite was always well received. Imayani paced in her tent. Her tea left by Mino was laid out untouched and cold.

"Worry doesn't water growth," Rai said stepping into the tent. It was nicer than the soldier's tents with plush bedding and a rug. However, it was far from luxurious. "Isn't that what you used to tell me?"

Imayani glowered at him.

"I also told you not to enter without knocking," she said.

Rai moved to the table and started to brew a fresh pot of tea. Fax flew atop the table and imitated sniffing the different jars of herbs.

"I don't want tea," Imayani said.

"I do."

Imayani scowled "What do you want, Rai?"

Rai turned to face Imayani. She stood, arms crossed, one eyebrow raised. Once he wouldn't have needed a reason to spend time with her.

"Make me part of your honour guard," Rai said.

Imayani scoffed and waved him away.

"You know you can't trust Kleran. He is a monarch and he's been vying for the throne since your father was on it," Rai said.

"Rai, I sent you away. Do you think I'll just add you to my honour guard because you followed us?"

Rai set the water onto the small fire. "Do you think Kleran will be okay with sharing the power?"

"It doesn't matter. I secured his help to *keep* the throne. Without it, we wouldn't have an army close enough to Asuriya. If I didn't take his offer I would have already lost the throne!"

"Once, you didn't want it."

Imayani's shoulders fell and a tiredness drooped her features. "It doesn't matter what I want. There is no going back to those times. I swore myself to Tarris and I plan on keeping it in one piece. I can only do that while I'm in power."

"Did you not think about what Kleran wants? He could have taken his army to Asuriya without you and laid claim to the throne. Why then did he make this deal? To get you out of the way. With your marriage, he has the legal right to the throne and now if you were to fall in battle, it would all go to him."

"And you don't think I know this?" Imayani shouted. The pot hissed and boiled until Rai took it off the flames. Imayani looked around the tent noticing the thin fabric that contained their conversation. "You don't think I talked with my overseers about the different possibilities?" she said, quieter this time. "We have weighed the options and risks and this was the best one we could come up with given," Imayani gestured around her.

"Then let me protect you," Rai said. He reached towards her. "Like I vowed to do."

"That vow was broken before it was made." Imayani brushed him off. "You vowed to protect me when you had already caused the worst harm imaginable by killing my father.

"Sometimes I wonder what my life would look like if Lintou hadn't picked you at that orphanage. Would my father be alive? Would any of this have happened?" The last sentence came out quiet and small.

"I'm sorry, Imayani," Rai said. "When this is over I'll leave. For good."

A quiet held them apart as neither made eye contact.

"I'm not sure that's what I want now," Imayani said. "But I don't want you here, either."

What was he supposed to do with that?

"Seeing you brings back pain but it also reminds me of better times. You know, I hadn't talked about plants in years until you came back. And now," Imayani gestured to a piece of parchment on the far table. It had sketches of different plants. She sighed.

"You were right about charah flowers. Perhaps we are like them in some ways and opposite in others. While they fight in the sunlight and huddle in the dark, we do the opposite. We smile under the Sun Eye and share pleasantries. But it's in the dark, when we need each other most, that we turn on one another."

The Sun Eye beat down with a heavy heat as Rai pushed his hyian faster. There were only dark days now. What did that say for their people? This was a time when they should be pulling together to reclaim a past lost to the ages and here they were on a battlefield ready to kill one another over some title.

Rai and Tysar took position near the front of the charge. The commanding overseer nodded as they came up on her side. Her inky black hair peeked out of the cowl that covered most of her face. Fighting in the open desert kicked up a lot of sand so most soldiers covered their faces with cowls. Their jerkins were emblazoned with a downward facing sword, the sigil for Yontar's monarch, Kleran.

They rode hard, closing in on the outer city.

Fax, can you see their charge? Rai squinted at the plume of dust and sand that signalled the Ossin army.

Part of their army broke off for the last sprint but they aren't going as fast as they could, Fax said.

What do you mean?

Their fast front has slowed down on approach, Fax said.

"Overseer," Rai said. "Something is wrong."

The Ossin army were approaching from the west. A line of black on the horizon throwing up a cloud of sand like an oncoming storm. They should have reached the outer city at the same time but at their current pace Kleran and Imayani's force would be within the walls long before their fast front approached the outer city.

"What makes you say that?" the Overseer asked.

"They have slowed down," Tysar said. "They're planning something."

"It won't matter what they're planning once we have the capital." The Overseer flicked her reins and they sped up.

Buildings towered around them as they entered Asuriya.

Soldiers surveyed the lost capital's outer city with furtive glances. It was meant to be a city of the dead. Tarrisians spoke of the horrors of the calamity that stole them of their home. And yet, it was just a ruin. Eroded homes and collapsed walls. Rai knew treasure hunters often scavenged the outer city but he was surprised to see all that

through a scardrae. "Take my hyian."

Tysar gave him a questioning look but caught the reins that Rai threw to him. Rai then stood on his saddle and leapt into the fray. He landed in a roll and came quickly to his feet drawing his daggers at the same time. He sliced through a scardrae the moment it broke from the sand and then threw a dagger into another that launched itself at him. The nearby soldiers watched in awe.

"These aren't the nightmares you were promised as children!" Rai shouted. He spat out some of the beetles black blood. "These are scardrae that have been tainted with the blight! That is all."

Some of the strength returned to the soldier's eyes. All Tarrisians grew up seeing scardrae burrowing in the sand. Fear hides in the dark. A monsters mystique wrapped in the unknown. And Rai was shining a light upon it.

"The Ossin army released these to take us out! They are using your fears against you, but we will not fall!"

Rai darted forward and Fax flared outward skewering several scardrae with black tendrils. Retrieving his second dagger, Rai stomped on one burrowing out of the sand. Around him, soldiers stopped fleeing and took charge, fighting off the giant beetles. It only took a couple soldiers to face the scardrae for others to start following suit.

Good.

Fax stretched out in front of Rai painting the world black as Rai cut down scardrae left and right. Steel shone in the sunlight clattering against the beetle's hard carapace. Cries of pain clashed with screeching insects. It was chaos with the scardrae erupting from all around, breaking up their forces into the many streets of the derelict outer city.

Rai swung a dagger out wildly catching a scardrae mid-air. It screamed and hissed as it dropped to the ground. He spun to watch a soldier's head be torn clean off by the pincers of a scardrae. Behind him another was eating a corpse.

They're eating humans?

Rai watched in horror as the scardrae tore into the soldier's guts. It didn't make any sense. Why would a scardrae have a taste for *humans*? They lived out here where so few humans dared to go.

Unless the Ossins had been feeding them human to get a taste for it so they could use the creatures. The thought brought bile up the back of Rai's throat. Surely they wouldn't have. They wouldn't have gone that far.

But Rai knew they would. Anything for a leg up over the other monarchs.

Fury welled in Rai and he flicked his daggers towards the alley. Flames erupted from his diera daggers and billowed down the side street. He breathed in the shrieks from the scardrae as they burst into flame. He had to be careful using his diera blades in such close quarters and he hadn't brought much blood with him to top them up.

"Rai!"

Tysar reeled in his hyian at the end of the alley, pulling along Rai's steed. "The Ossins have reached the edges of the outer city. We need to get to the walls now!"

"They're trying to sneak past us while we're distracted," Rai said.

Rai leapt onto the back of his hyian and together they tore through the streets swiping at any scardrae they passed. He didn't like to leave the soldiers to face the scardrae alone but if the Ossins took the city walls, all was lost.

"They approached from the west, entering the outer city from the side to try and sneak past us," Tysar said. "The overseer led a small group to ride for the gates."

"How big was the force?"

Rai saw the strain on Tysar's face.

Larger than ours then, Rai thought.

46

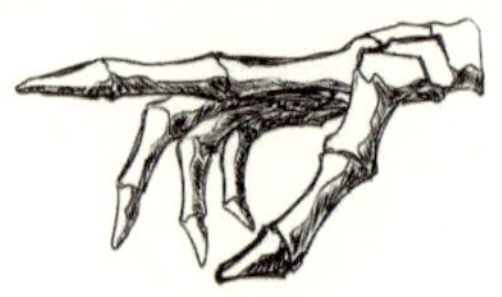

The Hand

"There." Bas pointed to a stream of smoke rising from behind a black stone plateau.

"Finally," Kit said.

It was hard to tell how long Kit, Bas, and Wenson had chased Nya across the dark plains. They had rested little and slept less. Only stopping when it was dark out. Bas had begun instructing Kit and Wenson on how the Urdahl fought. They went through sword forms and defensive positioning while they walked. Kit had asked about group formations and Bas gave him a confused look. The Urdahl fought as individual warriors. Bas spoke of Urdahl elders directing forces in large scale battles in ages past but they did not fight in groups like the street gangs Kit was used to. So Kit led Bas and Wenson through some basic street gang manoeuvres to see how they would fight as a group.

The energy had shifted from concern and trepidation to focus and preparation. Once they caught the first sight of Nya and her party, Kit felt like they were ready.

"He is the one with the shade," Bas said. He pointed to one of the men leading the party beside Mirt.

"Why Nya not fight?" Wenson asked. She plodded along beside one of the guards.

"She's favouring one of her legs. I think she might be hurt," Kit said. "We will need to wait until they set up camp."

They trailed behind the party of guards and Nya, wandering close to the towering rock walls around them for cover. After a couple of hours, their company slowed and nestled into an opening in the plateau. Soon after, a fire was lit.

"They do not hide from husks," Bas said.

"No, they're left exposed there. They must have a way to fend them off," Kit said.

"Or keep away." Wenson watched the sky.

Movement in their camp settled and Kit circled the enclosed space noting where they posted guards. They had enough guards to create a perimeter around their small area. However, Nya remained at the back of the space, away from the fire where the other resting guards talked quietly.

Kit picked out the leading guard. The one with the shade. Bas had talked about how he had disarmed both him, Nya, and her shade with ease. They were going to have to do this right. Kit crept back to where Bas and Wenson hid behind a rock.

"We need to wait for an opening. They aren't expecting us but we need to have an escape ready if this guard with the shade is as strong as you say, Bas," Kit said.

Bas nodded. "We won't be able to fight him."

They couldn't fight him but if Nya was injured they wouldn't be able to run, either. Kit could tell the others were having the same thought.

"We'll figure this out. For now, we follow them."

The procession of guards rested for a short time before they continued their trek northward. Kit's assessment had been right. Nya walked with a guard at her side to ensure she could keep pace despite her injury. It was no wonder why they left her without fear of her escaping whenever they stopped. She was barely able to walk herself.

They had been following Nya and the guards for a couple of hours when a thought occurred. Kit lay flat on a high ridge watching as Nya and company moved across an open stretch of black rock.

"Why isn't she using her shade to help her walk?" Kit asked more to himself than the others.

Behind, Wenson and Bas were going through some brawling drills. Bas swept in and grappled Wenson before throwing him to the ground. It wasn't a forceful attack but Bas didn't pull any of his attacks when training. Wenson puffed out, winded by the blow and Bas walked over and dropped to his haunches beside Kit.

"When he attacked us, his shade pinned down Nya's," Bas said.

Kit remembered him saying something about that at the time. "Pinning is one thing but does this mean he can capture her shade and hold it?"

Bas shrugged.

Ever since Nya had gotten the shade she had been the fighter in the group. Kit could fight street thugs but he didn't have a chance against a palace guard with a shade. Not even Bas could stand up to him.

Kit glanced down at his hand. If he could somehow summon that power again, perhaps he could kill this guard. Or at least distract him long enough for the others to sneak Nya out. It hadn't worked when he reached out to it during the fight with the husk. If it hadn't been for Wenson he'd be dead. And he wasn't going to get that second chance against a shade. *If only it was more reliable,* Kit thought.

Nya and her party were a spec on the horizon.

"Come on."

Over the following days they moved back into more rocky areas, where Kit, Bas and Wenson could follow closely among the pillars of black stone. They ran into no wildlife. Where before shadowed movement and burrowed scree shifted at the side of Kit's vision, now all lay still. Seeing creatures from this dark realm was unsettling but the eerie lack was even more so.

Wenson might have been right, Kit thought. Maybe they had found a way to repel the creatures of this place.

After some time, the sky began to darken again. The first time Kit and the others had hidden in a small cavern. Instinct overruled the necessity for speed. One did not travel the desert at night. Especially during the dark hours. That was when black sand phantoms and other creatures roamed Tarris. And they did not want to find out what horrors appeared in this dark realm at night.

The scholars must have had similar worries. Their party stopped at a small burrow. The guards went into the cavern first and once they appeared again, the others entered.

"They're setting up camp," Wenson said.

A guard unslung his pack and pulled out thick black fabric. The guards each took an end and stretched it over the cave entrance. The tarp was clearly made to resemble the black rock of the dark place. After it was set up, two guards appeared outside to stand watch. They made their way up the side of the rock to sit on a perch above their encampment.

"They're watching for husks," Bas said.

"What makes you say that?" Kit asked.

"If they were watching for people they would stand at the entrance. Not above it."

The pale light dimmed. The grey clouds turning black. Kit, Bas and Wenson hid behind a rock wall. They didn't dare light a fire this close. Not a word passed between them as they ate their meat strips and hard bread. Each of them watched their darkening surroundings. All Tarrisians had it burnt into their minds from childhood that when it got dark in the desert, you made for cover. So to so brazenly sit awaiting the dark to consume them set Kit's skin prickling.

"What is this place?" Wenson asked. His voice was quiet so as not to disturb the stillness.

"I have no idea," Kit said. "The last time we were here, it wasn't for as long and the sky didn't darken. How a place without Ova the World Turner can become light and dark, I don't know."

"Ova watches." Bas took a draught from his waterskin.

Kit and Wenson looked at each other before turning to Bas.

"Look," Bas said pointing into the distance. "It does not darken evenly. There is more light on the horizon just as it is when the Sun Eye dips in the sky. Ova watches over us from behind that cloud cover."

That should have been reassuring. A piece of home in this other world. But it only raised more questions.

"So then, this is still part of our world? How can Ova watch over us here and in Tarris and why do days last so long?" Kit asked. He didn't expect an answer from his friends as they all stared into the crashing clouds.

"Maybe Ova has given up on this place," Wenson said.

The dark came with an almost tangible thickness. A shroud that seemed to fill the air and smother the light. It was stifling. Each breath filling Kit's lungs. But it also brought opportunities.

Kit ducked behind a rock, Bas at his side. They watched the guards sitting atop their perch through a crack in the stone. A small lantern was placed between them. It was a spec of light in a sea of darkness.

Suddenly, there was a scraping of stone in the distance. The guards were too far for Kit to hear what they were saying but one was pointing to the source of the noise. After a bit of debate, one of the guards picked up the lantern and walked off in the direction they had been pointing.

"Damn," Kit said. "Only one fell for it."

Kit had hoped the guards wouldn't wander through the dark alone. The plan was to get in and out without anyone knowing. Wenson was to distract and draw the guards away without being seen. Kit felt bad sending him off by himself but after what Bas had said about him wanting to help and watching how hard Wenson had trained with Bas along the way, Kit needed to let him have the opportunity to help.

There was a shout and the remaining guard looked over his shoulder.

"Now," Kit said.

Kit and Bas ran on their haunches towards the cavern entrance. Bas grabbed Kit and pulled him against the rock and they fell still as the guard turned back. There was another cry and the guard cursed and stood. As soon as his back was to Kit and Bas they sprinted the last of the distance.

Hugging the stone wall, they caught their breaths. This was going to be the hard part. Kit pressed his ear against the tarp. He heard voices but they were muffled and far off. That was a good sign. Kit was sure it was a deep cavern before they blocked it off but if they had set up by the entrance they had no hope sneaking in.

Kit peeled back the edge of the tarp enough to peer inside. Firelight glinted off the black stone. At the far side of the cavern a small fire threw long shadows across the ground. Guards and scholars sat around it chatting in low voices. Mirt was waving his hands as he spoke. *The dagger will be with him,* Kit thought. Getting to Mirt's pack would be difficult but not impossible. It was thrown against the cave wall back from the fire. He traced the edges of the cave until he found her. Much like she had done the previous times they stopped, Nya was far from the flames, her head buried in her knees.

Kit let the tarp close. "Okay, they're far enough that we can sneak in," he whispered. "But once we're inside creeping to the back of the cave will be difficult."

Bas looked thoughtful scratching his chin. "What about the cave walls?"

"What about them?"

"Can we climb them? Back home we often climbed through the caves and tunnels beneath the sand. I escaped an irkan in the dark of a cave once," Bas said.

"An irkan?" Kit wanted to press for the story. He had been half convinced that the stone spiders were made up creatures used to keep travellers on well-walked paths. But they didn't have time for stories. Kit blew out a breath and stepped out of the way so that Bas could look inside. After a quick peek, he nodded.

"We can climb the walls."

"Lead the way then," Kit said.

Bas peered into the cave again. Kit started bouncing his leg as time ticked on. Finally, Bas motioned for him to follow and ducked into the cavern. They moved swiftly along the wall, among the stalagmites. Bas looked over his shoulder at the fire and then *leapt* at the wall. He clung to it and climbed higher into the darkened areas where the stalactites sheltered them from the fire's glow. Kit watched in awe. He hadn't considered that he might not be able to manage the same feats.

Kit reached up the wall, feeling for something to grab. *There.* He pulled himself up and dragged his body higher. Bas hung from the wall watching him intently. Once Kit had caught up, together they inched along the cave wall. It was difficult and Kit's arms ached with the strain but there were regular ledges he could rest his body weight on.

Bas stopped when they were in line with Nya. "I will go around and fetch the dagger. You get Nya and come back the way we came," Bas whispered. "The guards have been drinking. I can smell the odour of ale in the air and the scholars are too busy talking. The guard with the shade is sharpening his blade on the far side of the cave."

Kit nodded, not trusting himself to speak without a groan escaping his lips and Bas sped off into the dark. With a sigh, Kit made his way down the wall and behind a particularly large stalagmite.

"Nya," Kit called. Nya's head was still between her legs. An untouched plate of food lay beside her.

"Nya," Kit said a little louder. He looked around but no one glanced his way. He tried a third time and finally Nya stirred. She stared right at Kit. Her eyes went wide and he grinned. Kit gestured for her to come over but she shook her head. Nya flicked her hand as if to shoo him away. Is she worried they will be caught? Kit wondered.

Again, he pointed towards the cave entrance. She tapped the shadow at her feet and then pushed her fingertips down onto her palm. Her fingers were shaped like a cage.

Bom was captured, just as they thought.

It was the one part of the equation they hadn't figured out. Aside from attacking the too-powerful guard and no doubt dying in the process, they had no way to free Bom. But having Nya free was better than neither.

Kit glanced over to the fire where the guards continued to chatter. It was clear they had settled in for the long night to pass, so Kit crawled over to Nya. Her eyes went wide and she shooed him away again but Kit ignored her.

"What're you doing?" Nya whispered once he reached her.

"We're here to get you out and close the tear," Kit said.

"You fool! Adani's shade will see you," Nya said.

Kit ignored her. "Can you run?"

"Kit, they have Bom. I can't run."

"We can help," Kit said. "Remember, in Mirt's notes we saw some theories on the dagger being able to sever the connection with a shade?"

Nya shook her head. "That was just a theory he hadn't tested. And anyway, I can't leave Bom. Not here."

With a glance at the fire, Kit crept closer. "We can end this. Bas is getting the dagger."

"Bas is here?"

Kit nodded. "With it, we can close the tear. I know you've grown fond of Bom but this is the shade's home."

Her face darkened. "You don't know that."

Kit leant back. The darkness around her seemed to coalesce her skin.

"This is a prison, Kit. We need to bring Bom back."

Kit groaned. "Okay. We'll figure something out but you should come now. We'll come back for your shade."

"Go where?" a voice asked.

Kit spun and the guard with the shade, Adani as Nya called him, was just *there*.

Well his face was. It floated in darkness. Then suddenly he walked out of thin air and he stood behind Kit.

Kit grabbed Nya's wrist and made to run but before he could even stand a black tendril cracked him across the face. He scraped across the ground. Kit let out a groan as he righted himself. Darkness darted towards him like a snake. He kicked back from it but it was coming too fast. Just as it was about to wrap around his ankle, one of Bas' spear ends plunged right through it, dispersing the shadow.

Adani turned to look at Bas who clung high in the stalactites. A glint of the black dagger shone reflecting the flames of the fire pit. Kit grinned. Adani growled and a flood of darkness blasted at Bas, who dove from the cave ceiling.

While he was distracted, Kit yanked Nya up to her feet. "Wait!" she called but there was no time. They sprinted for the exit. Waves of shadow burst through the rock as Adani's shade chased Bas through the cavern. It sent up clouds of dust. Kit blinked against the dirt, unable to see.

"I can't go yet!" Nya said.

"We don't have a choice," Kit said. He felt in front of him until… *there*. The tarp. He pushed through and they were outside.

Kit stopped short.

Lightening flashed illuminating the sky. The clouds and darkness were taking shape in the distance as a huge hand. Long pointed fingers filled the sky only visible in the bursts of lightening. Nya stared too.

"It's Kygian," Nya said.

Kit wasn't sure what she meant but her tone held a strange weight. Whether from fear, awe, or acquiescence, Kit didn't know.

The tarp was brushed aside and Adani stepped out, his shade holding Bas aloft. The anger on his face dissolved when he saw the hand.

And then he started to laugh.

47

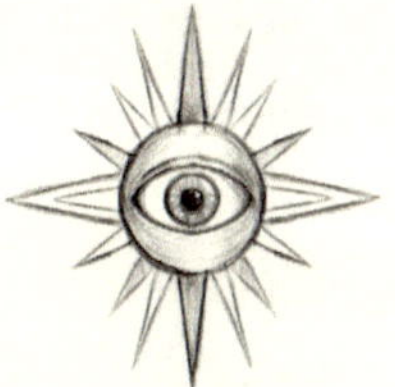

A Survivor

13 years ago.

Duty kept the darkness at bay. Imayan filled her days with the going on of the country and Rai remained a silent watcher. They spoke little and of little things. Imayan gave Rai more control of the palace guard. Being her personal guard allowed him certain privileges and power as well as the right to lengthen his name. However, there was no time for such semantics and Imayan bestowed him more than he deserved.

As expected, the other monarchs were testing their defences. They made things difficult and pushed to see where the throne was weak and how the new empress managed the fires that they set across Tarris, always making sure it couldn't be tracked back to them. Disruptions in trade routes, burnt farmland, noble families making alliances. They tried it all and Imayan was run ragged, finding her feet and battering off their veiled attacks.

All the while trying to hold together a crumbling empire.

"I don't think you understand," Jackl said. The rotund man ran one of the largest fighting pits in Rizu. His head seemed to want to blend into his body leaving him as more spherical than human shaped.

"Your father and I had a deal," he was saying.

"Yes, well, he is no longer here and you can't shirk your taxes any longer," Imayan said. She sat straight backed, the same stoic placidity plastered to her face that had remained fixed there since she had become empress.

They sat on a balcony looking over the palace gardens. Their table pressed against the ornate balustrade giving a fantastic view over flourishing greenery. But Imayan hadn't glanced once at the garden that had brought her so much joy in the past.

Jackl didn't hide his displeasure. A scowl creased his weathered face and he tapped on the table. Rai stood guard at the door into the palace, hand resting on the daggers at his waist.

"I am not *shirking* my taxes," Jackl said. "Your father and I had an agreement. He came to the pits free of charge whenever he wanted in exchange for *lowered* taxes."

The fighting pits were a distasteful business to Rai, having creatures and sometimes humans fight one another to the death for sport, but it was legal and profitable part of Tarrisian culture.

"And as he is no longer with us he will not be attending and therefore, the agreement is void," Imayan said. She was beginning to sound like Overseer Myain using terminology that Rai wasn't familiar with.

"This is when you need friends, Empress Imayan," Jackl said. "It is a mistake to push away those who support you."

"Is that a threat, Jackl?"

The man lifted his hands in mock surprise. "No, of course not. I'm simply pointing out a fact. Favours lead to favours."

Imayan was unperturbed. "If that is all."

Jackl cleared his throat and made his way to the door. He looked like he wanted to say more but bit his tongue.

"The missing payment will be sent this week," Imayan called after him.

He froze as he reached for the door and grumbled something under his breath before pushing it open and going inside.

The Sun Eye burned golden on the skyline. Imayan picked up her mug and sipped on her coffee looking thoughtfully over the garden. It was clear by her glassy gaze she was elsewhere and Rai let her have a moment of undisturbed thought before approaching.

"He may be right. You need these people at your back, not taking the side of the other monarchs," Rai said.

"You're taking his side?" Imayan's head snapped around to look at him.

Rai raised an eyebrow.

Imayan took a deep breath and deflated. "Perhaps you're right but I just hate the idea that people like him have these *special deals*. The more I learn of how my father ruled the more I question if I knew him at all."

Rai thought of Emperor Leondal's plan to use Imayan as a puppet on the throne. He was worse than she knew. "Ruling is a burden and sacrifices must be made." Rai regretted the words as soon as he said them. All Imayan knew was sacrifice. "I'm sorry. That's not…"

She waved it away. They had known each other long enough
now that Imayan understood his meaning.

"It doesn't matter. I don't need fools like him at my back when I
have you," Imayan said.

"Imayan… I'm not who you think I am." Rai resisted the urge
to air out his collar. Moments like this kept arising since Imayan's
ascendance to empress. A chance to tell her the truth. So far Rai had
found reasons to keep his silence but it was getting harder.

"I've known you since we were children," Imayan said. "I know
you better than you think. It was you who was with my father when
he died. You're a survivor, Rai."

Rai's heart sank. A survivor. That was true. And it haunted him
like a shadow.

"I haven't had a moment to truly thank you for being there with
him," Imayan said. "And for being there for me."

A wave of nausea swept up from Rai's gut.

"That was the last meeting for today?" Imayan asked.

Rai nodded fighting back the bile in his throat.

"Good. Come with me."

Imayan dismissed the other guards at the stairwell, claiming
she was turning in early for the night. They looked at one another
uneasily and then to Rai who gave them a confident nod. The guards
were placated that Imayan wasn't alone so bowed and wished her
a goodnight. In the back of Rai's mind, he thought about how this
looked. Imayan dismissing them and taking her personal guard to
her rooms alone but shook the thought away.

Once they were out of sight, Imayan turned off the path to her quarters and led Rai down a different corridor.

"Where are we going? You should keep the guards nearby if you're wandering the palace," Rai said.

Imayan rolled her eyes at him. It was a sign of the old Imayan and a warm surge came over Rai at the sight.

"You're sounding like my father," Imayan said. "They can't come. I'm taking you somewhere secret."

Imayan used to take Rai to secret spots. Often they were perches in the garden or nooks on the rooftops where they could sit in peace and talk. The idea of going to one of these spots and having a heart to heart was terrifying. He couldn't lie to her face. And the truth would destroy everything.

Rai followed Imayan like a man walking to the gallows. They walked down the quiet corridors that led deeper into the palace. He had never been down some of these corridors and he wasn't sure where they led to. The hour grew late and Rai expected to see more and more servants roam the palace but these hallways were quiet and they passed few others.

Imayan pushed open a door to a darkened corridor. She grabbed a torch and lit the closest brazier. It wasn't uncommon to find dark corridors this early, but Imayan knew where the spare torch was kept. She lit the braziers as they continued onward. The crackle of firelight and their echoing footsteps was all that could be heard. More passageways broke off and Imayan turned leading Rai through the maze of sandstone.

The brazier roared to life and Imayan pulled back her torch. The sudden spilling of light brought shape to something at the end of the corridor. Rai froze. The black shape didn't move but it was huge. He laid a hand on the pommel of his daggers. Imayan grinned at him and Rai relaxed. Setting the next wall sconce ablaze.

A glistening silver statue of a nightraven dominated the end of the passage. Its great wings outstretched in a fighting pose. It was common to find grand statues decorating the hallways of Atef Palace but this was a strange place to display such a beautiful piece. Imayan continued towards it and it was only when Rai followed that he realised the scale of the statue. The nightraven was almost twice as tall and about four times as wide as Rai.

"Wow," Rai said.

"Wait until you see inside," Imayan said.

"Inside?"

This was the end of the corridor and no doors or passages led any deeper. Imayan dropped to her haunches and stuck her hand behind the statue and with an audible click, the statue swung towards them. Rai took a step back so it wouldn't knock him over.

A path continued into darkness. Rai remembered Lintou's study and the hidden passage there but he didn't think there would be more secret passages. Now his mind whirled with the implications that there could be many of these pathways throughout the palace. If he was to protect Imayan, he would need to know of them.

Imayan walked in, her torch held aloft. The short corridor opened to a grand chamber. The aged musk hit Rai first. A smell of ages past. Pillars lined either side of them and a great skylight let in streaks of moonlight bright enough that Imayan didn't need her torch.

A sigil was engraved into the floor. It was a huge, swirling circle with tendrils of black smoke and seven swords surrounded the shape. At the far side of the chamber was a dais with a round stone table and behind it seven weapon mounts were attached to the wall. Engraved above the mounts was the phrase '*Bound by shadow, we are the dark.*'

Rai gawked. *What is this place?*

Imayan appeared at his side after hanging the torch in a holder by a reading corner where several shelves were packed with meaty tomes.

"This is one of the greatest secrets that the emperor holds," Imayan said. "The dark assassins of Tarris, the heroes thought of as legends."

"The Seventh Sceptre," Rai whispered. "They're real?"

Imayan nodded and pulled him towards a passage on their left. *How big is this place?* Rai wondered as they passed more openings before Imayan pulled him into another room.

This one was a training hall, not unlike those they had trained in with Overseer Rikai. A corner held a variety of weapons, some practice, some not.

"This is where I did some of my training," Imayan said. "The Seventh Sceptre isn't what most people think. It's a secret sect that takes care of the more sensitive missions. Missions that the emperor, or empress, doesn't want to be connected to or made public. The seven often hold roles as palace guards to hide their true identity."

Grabbing his hand, Imayan dragged him back out of the training hall.

"It is tradition for each new ruler to pick a new seven," Imayan was saying, but Rai couldn't focus. He glanced around a place that belonged in stories.

The Seventh Sceptre was *real*?

Rai peered into the rooms. They were all training rooms of different varieties much like the different halls at the Verdin Temple, but smaller. Coming back out into the main chamber, Imayan walked into the centre of the room arms outstretched.

"I can't believe this is real," Rai said.

She grinned at him.

"Well?" Imayan asked.

"Well, what?"

"Will you lead the Seventh Sceptre? It's not uncommon for the emperor's personal guard to be the one who leads the seven and," Imayan blew out a breath, "you're one of the few people I can trust."

Rai stared unable to formulate words. Imayan took his hand and led him over to the dais. "I have a couple of candidates already selected but you can pick out the other members of the seven." Imayan gestured to the weapon racks. The seven weapons were all different: sword, daggers, bow, axe, spear, glaive, and a war hammer. They were all the deep black of diera ore.

"Most of my picks are high-ranking guards. You will need a variety of people to accomplish the mix of missions. The old leader of the seven can help you pick the right people, too."

"Imayan I…" Rai trailed off. What could he say? He couldn't be her stone. She couldn't rely on him. He wasn't worthy of a place such as this.

I killed your father. The words danced on his tongue.

She stepped up to him and took his hands. "I know I said I wasn't sure if I wanted all this, but Rai, now that I'm here I think I can do some good for Tarris. I've seen how my father ruled and was bound to these deals. But I can start over. A fresh start for Tarris. Shift the focus from those like Jackl and onto those who truly deserve it.

"I need you at my side for this."

Spinning on her heels, Imayan pulled the daggers from the wall mount and brought them over to Rai, forcing them into his hands.

"The weapon of the empress," Imayan said.

Rai glanced down at the daggers. A weapon. He could be that. Rai rolled the familiar weapons in his hands. Diera ore. The power that he had sought handed to him.

The truth was a double-edged sword, one he could hold and save Imayan from the hurt. From the betrayal. Telling her the truth would bring nothing but pain and the downfall of Tarris. Rai could become the weapon Imayan needed. He could go back to the person he was in the Eye all those years ago. The one who could run until he collapsed. The one who would give everything. But this time he had purpose. He was the weapon.

"We will need to send a letter to the Verdin Guild. I know some warriors who would be perfect for the seven," Rai said.

48

Forgiveness

With every step closer to the Black City, Nya felt stronger. And it was amplified during the long nights of the dark place. With this newfound strength, part of Nya wanted to rip Bom free and escape with Kit and Bas but she knew that if she was feeling stronger, so was Adani.

After waiting out the night in the cave they continued their march to the Black City. Kit and Bas were prodded along separately, far behind Nya as to avoid any plotting. How they had managed to get this far into the dark place was a mystery. She thought herself too far gone for her old friends to reach her and yet they were always there. Nya was in another realm and still they found her. No matter how far she wandered, they were always able to reach her.

It should have been a comforting thought but all Nya could focus on was the danger that she had dragged them into once more.

Despite the added power fluttering in her stomach, the haze in her mind thickened. Every thought felt sluggish as if she were pulling them through thick sand. Seeing her friends should have brought elation, fear and joy. But she could only feel muted versions of these emotions, as if she were detached and looking at herself from above.

But maybe it was better this way.

Not to feel. Just be.

The voice that had been screaming that something was wrong was quietening, drowned out in the stillness of her mind.

The company made their way through a rocky passage. High walls of stone winding through mountainous formations. And before they passed out the other side, Nya knew they approached the Black City. She felt it, always like a cloud covering the Sun Eye. The closer they got, the colder and darker it felt.

They turned a corner, and it was there.

Even seeing the Black City in her vision was not enough to ready Nya for the real thing. The stone that crafted it was the same black rock that covered the dark place. A wall encircled the sprawling city of dark stone. It could have fitted Yontar within its walls several times over.

Bom pulsed in fear.

They had talked little. What was there to say when the shade was trapped?

At the back of the Black City, palace spires were carved into the mountainside. The front of the palace was cut into the stone like a door into the mountain itself. That was where *it* was. And that was where they were headed.

Audible gasps came from around their party. Mirt started to laugh.

"Look! It's as we thought. A structure clearly created as an imitation of Tarris," he said.

"That looks awfully like the illustrations of Asuriya, the old capital," the other scholar said.

"Why is that?" one of the guards asked.

"We believe whatever lives here is as fascinated by us as we are of it. It has moulded this as an interpretation of our world," Mirt said as they walked towards the city limits.

Nya knew that was wrong. She felt it through the connection to the presence. The dark here cared not for the Tarrisians, nor their culture.

The Black City has stood for hundreds of thousands of years, Bom said.

Then why does it look like a Tarrisian city? Nya asked.

How do you know that Tarrisian cities don't look like it? Bom replied.

They quested out over the last stretch of land and towards the Black City. The walls grew higher and the huge scale of the city became more apparent.

"Were they housing giants?" the guard helping Nya muttered.

A cracked maw broke the endless black stone where a gate might have stood. Beyond it, more rock formations led up the slope of the Black City to the secondary wall and the palace. Nya inhaled sharply. A shroud of inky smoke poured from the building as if it were on fire. But this was no fire. Her mind buzzed as she laid eyes upon the swirling shadow. Upon Kygian. The guard grumbled something and shoved her forward.

They passed between the crack in the wall. The landscape could have been mistaken as the base of a mountain with black rocks strewn atop the scree. But after what Mirt had said Nya saw the shape of it. The rough grid layout of the stone. It looked like a city turned to black stone and left to crumble through the ages. The company stalked through the Black City like unwanted guests. Silence lay like a mantle over them.

Nya searched for her friends. Kit walked with a guard, his eyes wide and darting around in disbelief. Even Bas' face held a tightness as he stared up the slope, to the Mad Palace.

That was what they called the palace in Asuriya and it was all Nya could think of as she gazed upon the pillars cut into the mountain. The endless, wispy dark leaking from the entryways and openings.

"In here," Mirt said. He gestured to a cave.

Adani shook himself and looked back at the scholar. He had been transfixed, like Nya. *No doubt he feels the same tug.*

"Why?" Adani asked.

"We can't just saunter up there," Mirt said. He glanced to the palace as he spoke as if afraid it was listening. "Let's rest here and decide how to proceed. I need to think about how we're going to introduce ourselves."

The interior of the cave resembled a home with many rooms and segments. Nya was thrown into one of the far rooms, a guard standing at the door to ensure she wouldn't run off. Not long after, Kit and Bas were dragged in and dropped by her side.

"You always keep such interesting company," Kit said, rubbing his back.

Nya glanced at the guard at the door who glowered back. She reached out to Bom who showed her the scholars and other guards in a similarly shaped room on the other side of the building. Through her shade, Nya could hear their conversation. Adani was pushing for them to leave immediately. Whereas Mirt clearly had more reservations. He was discussing with the other scholar on possible offerings. But Nya could feel his fear. It poured from him like smoke.

"What were you two thinking?" Nya said turning to Kit.

He shrugged, his eyes passing between her and the guard. "Oh you know, save a friend, fight the bad guys. Save Tarris. Standard stuff."

The guard at the opening leant against the wall, his face a mask of frustration. He was clearly annoyed being left on guard duty while the others planned their next move. He tilted his head towards where Mirt and Adani argued. More interested in the murmurs from the other room than the prisoners chattering. Nya inched closer to Kit.

"You need to escape now," Nya said. "Once they reach the palace, there won't be any turning back. Go now while the guards are distracted."

"Come with us," Kit said. There was pleading in his voice.

"I can't. I can't leave Bom and…" Nya hesitated. "I need to see this darkness."

The guard at the door grunted, fell against the wall, and then slid to the floor. Nya, Kit and Bas spun to see Wenson creep in. He was grinning.

"Side of head to knock out," Wenson said.

"Just like that," Bas said and smiled back. It looked forced as if he were testing an unfamiliar expression but there was no doubting that Bas was smiling. Nya had never seen the Urdahl smile.

"Wenson," Nya said. She stared at the knocked-out guard, mouth agape as Wenson ran over and started undoing their bindings. "You were here too?"

"Did you think that we wouldn't have a back-up plan for the back-up plan?" Kit said. He rubbed his wrists, marked by the coarse fabric. He then looked up at Wenson. "You saved us again."

Wenson grinned.

"Don't let it go to your head." Kit stood. "Let's get out of here before they come back. The faster we get back to the tear, the faster we can close it."

"You still plan on closing the tear?" Nya asked.

Bas slid the black dagger from his boot and spun it around his fingers.

"Mirt's dagger," Nya whispered. She waited for a surge of joy. Her friends came for her. They were able to escape. They could close the tear and stop all this. It was what they had been planning from the start. But Nya felt nothing.

The call of the dark beckoned her.

Bom knew what was happening. It could see through Nya as she could see through it. Fear emanated from the shade. It didn't want to be left.

"Come. Two guards are walking around," Wenson said peering around the corner. Kit and Bas moved towards him.

"I can't leave yet," Nya said.

The three of them turned.

"Nya—"

"There is something I need to do first."

Kit walked over to her and laid a hand on her shoulder. "We

need to stop this. This is about more than us."

"One of the guards is my father." The words were flat. Kit's eyes widened. "I can't leave without seeing him first."

Nya saw his face harden. Kit knew about her past. About how Werin had left Mother and her.

"Okay." Kit looked to Wenson and Bas. "You two get beyond the walls. I'll go with Nya to see her father. Once they've spoken, we'll catch up."

Wenson screwed his face up and opened his mouth like he was about to object when Bas nodded.

"But don't wait for us. Go back to the tear and close it," Kit said.

"Wait—" Wenson started but Kit nodded to Bas who shoved him forward and they were gone.

"Are you sure about this?" Kit asked.

Nya nodded. She couldn't leave without facing Werin and this would be her only chance. "I think he's watching the cave from outside."

"Let's go then."

Nya skulked through the empty cave, past the unconscious guard and to the entrance, Kit at her back. As they passed through the chamber, they heard Mirt and Adani's raised voices. Tuning into Bom, the words sharpened to an argument. It sounded like the guards were siding with Mirt to rest for a while before making their way up to the palace. They were afraid, too.

"We don't know what we will be facing!" one of the guards said.

Nya shook her head. Her connection to the shade had grown stronger as they approached the Black City. Now that they were within its walls, she could split her attention to see what the shade saw and heard at the same time as keeping to her own senses. But it was disorienting and Kit had to steady her before they continued.

Kit peered around and then gestured to Nya that there were no guards and together they stepped out under the pale storming sky. They crept along the wall, moving slowly and watching for guards. Of the four, one was knocked out, another was in the chamber with the scholars and Adani. That left two out here on patrol.

They didn't have to travel far to see Werin. He stood by himself overlooking the city. He was deep in thought, mind elsewhere, as he stared at the palace that leaked black smoke.

Kit faced Nya with a questioning look, no doubt wondering if that was her father. Nya pushed past him. A rock went skittering at her feet and Werin spun, hand on the hilt of his sword. Shock flashed across his face as he met Nya's gaze and then looked over her shoulder at Kit. They were prisoners and they had escaped.

"Father," Nya said stopping a couple steps away. Werin looked like he had been struck by the word. Wary eyes ran over Nya. He didn't remove his hand from his sword.

"We're going to leave and close the tear," she said.

"Nya!" Kit said but she ignored him.

"Why are you telling me this?" Werin asked.

Nya took a step closer. "I couldn't leave and lock you in here. Even after everything you are my… father."

Some of the tension fled Werin then. His hand fell from his sword.

"And I have to tell you what really happened to Mother," Nya said.

"Nya, we don't have time for this," Kit said.

Nya shot him a glare and he silenced. "It was me. I killed her."

Werin's eyes widened. His fingers twitched towards his sword again.

"Not on purpose," Nya said. Tears streamed down her face as she spoke. "I... It was the shade. She hit me. She always hit me and the shade tried to defend me and I didn't mean to and..."

Werin swept in and hugged Nya. It stole the breath from her lungs. "I'm so sorry, Nya. I wish I had been there for you. If I knew she had you I swear I would have been there. I would have done what I could to look after you both."

Nya closed her eyes and laid her head on his shoulder as hot tears stained his shirt. "I still see her in my dreams. She speaks to me. She tells me that it was my fault and she's right."

"You can't blame yourself."

"I can. Shades feed off emotion. Rai taught me that. It did nothing that I wouldn't have done. And when she was dead," Nya's breath caught and she had to steady her breathing. "I was happy. I was glad I did it. She loved me in her own way but she was angry. So very angry. At the world. At me. At you."

Werin stiffened in their embrace.

"Yes, she beat me and berated me. But she kept me fed and clothed and I loved her for it. She was just the way the world made her to be. Abandoned. Unloved. Alone. She had to fend for herself and her child all by herself. How could I blame her for the way she was? I grew up in the same world. I understand." Nya's words were hardening and her grip around Werin tightened. She hadn't ever spoken so openly to anyone about this. But he had to know the truth.

"And I'm what the world made me into."

Nya slipped Werin's sword from his belt. He realised too late as the blade plunged into his gut. Tears streaked down Nya's red, sweaty face as she pushed the sword in further. Werin gargled and blood spilled form his lips.

She leant in close to his ear and whispered, "Tell Mother, I'm sorry and that I hope she likes her gift."

Kit yanked Nya back and her father toppled to the ground, blood pooling at their feet. Werin stared at Nya like she was a husk about to tear his throat out. Terror tightened his face and permeated from him like a cloud.

All fear death when it comes knocking. Nya breathed it in and it tasted like the fresh scent of cooking from the morning markets. She smiled then. The tears cooling on her skin.

"Nya," Kit whispered.

It was only then that she realised that Bom was with her. Her shadow pulsed around her and strength surged through her. It broke free the moment she killed Werin, her emotion too strong to remain caged.

"Don't," Adani said.

Nya glanced up to see Adani standing with three guards, swords held to Wenson and Bas' throats. Bruising and cuts covered their faces. They must have put up a fight.

Nya's fists tightened. Her shade was tense. Ready to lash out and kill the rest of them. But she knew Adani wasn't bluffing. He would murder her friends without blinking.

Nya breathed out and fell to her knees splashing some of her father's blood, as exhaustion took hold. Adani's shade pinned Bom down once more and the guards approached her and Kit.

It was over.

49

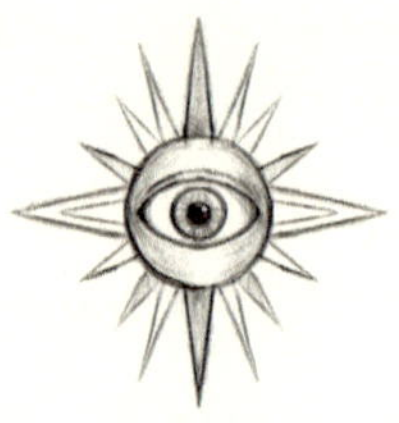

A Note

6 years ago.

Akarai perched high within the rocky mountains watching the valley below. A company of merchants were nestled against the side of the cliff. There must have been over a hundred in their party. Merchant carts pulled by hyian and aya lined either side of the fire pits as dusk settled.

A crackle of rock. Akarai spun to face Tysar who bowed and dropped to his haunches beside Akarai.

"A hundred and twelve," Tysar said. "We can't get a look at what's in their carts as their aya are skittish. But they're heavily armoured for merchants."

"We need to be sure," Akarai said.

"Shall we send the boy?" Tysar asked.

"And Neyla."

Tysar shifted uncomfortably. The motion was subtle but Akarai could tell his attraction to Neyla was affecting his judgment.

"You promised you're relationship with her wouldn't affect any missions," Akarai said.

"Of course," Tysar said but he wouldn't meet Akarai's eyes.

"Send them in before it gets any darker. They will be suspicious of two travellers who are out during dark hour," Akarai said.

Tysar nodded and disappeared down the other side of the rocky ridge.

Their spies said that Kleran, the Yontar monarch, had been sending soldiers disguised as merchants to Tansen in preparation for an attack on the capital. It was unlikely the attack was planned anytime soon, if it was planned at all. It had been over a hundred years since a monarch made a move so bold. Imayani and the overseers discussed that it was more likely to be used as leverage for better trade deals or to put favourable legislations in place with the threat of their position.

Smoke billowed from the merchant's fires. Laughs of revelry echoed up to Akarai.

These men and woman will never make it to the capital.

Akarai went to join the others.

The desert darkened as Neyla and Kyan rode towards the merchants on a single hyian. While this valley was a little off the beaten path, two travellers getting lost at this late hour wasn't unrealistic. Neyla's slick black hair bounced as the hyian trod up to the company. Heads spun and several of the merchants' hands fell to weapons hanging from their waist with a swiftness that spoke of experience.

Many of them looked to one of the merchants who was deep in

the company near the centre. He flicked his head and two woman and a man went to meet Neyla and Kyan. *Their leader*, Akarai thought studying these 'merchants.'

The three talked with Neyla and Kyan who didn't hop off their hyian but gestured wildly. On the mountainous ridge the merchants were nestled against, Ada jumped from ledge to ledge. He was right above them, too close to be seen, and dressed in a tan cloak like the rest of the seven, blending into the rock.

The closest blade cuts first. It was an old adage with many different interpretations.

Ada leapt atop one of the merchant's carts and dropped to his stomach. Akarai watched for any indication that he had been spotted but none glanced his way.

Thank the Gods he checked the carts, Akarai thought. While Ada was undoubtedly a skilled assassin and perfect for these missions, he unsettled Akarai and animals also seemed to have an aversion to him. He was sure to have alerted the merchants by setting off one of their aya if he had targeted the crates on their platform. There was a flash of his cloak and Ada disappeared inside the cart.

The merchants around the fire were growing bored of Neyla and Kyan now that they knew they were no risk.

A glint of light caught Akarai's eye. *The signal.* Although Akarai couldn't see him, that light meant Sebhan was in position on the plateau near the end of the valley. The hulking man was one of Imayani's picks for the seven. He was the brute force for the Seventh Sceptre and swung his war hammer like it was a toy.

Another glint of light came from the opposite side of the valley. Tysar was in position now, too.

The merchants were trapped.

The final flash of light came from above the merchant's campsite, where Genu had set up on the rock face.

The Sun Eye leaked bloody crimson into the sky.

Its watch was almost complete.

The shouting started when some of the merchants noticed one of their carts was on fire. Flames crept up the side and consumed the cart in a brilliant red glow. Suddenly, all the carts were engulfed. The aya squealed and tromped about, their reins cut free from where they had been tied up. The merchants ran about in the ensuing chaos attempting to put out the flames and calm their aya. The three merchants spun to face their camp and Neyla whipped her spearhead around decapitating all three in one swish. Their heads hit the sand as the Sun Eye dipped from sight and the dark descended upon the desert.

Bound by shadow, we are the dark.

Akarai nocked an arrow and aimed it at one of the fire pits. The one right in front of the leader. The arrowhead crackled with energy and Akarai loosed. The diera arrow flew across the space and hit the middle of their campfire. At the same time, Genu loosed her arrow and it embedded in another fire. The fake merchants glanced at them, dumbfounded. Then the arrows exploded in a shower of embers. A plume of flames expanded from the fires and screams turned to howls.

Crack!

A piece of the mountain broke off and a huge boulder crashed into the passageway blocking the way forward. With another ear shattering boom, the other end of the valley fractured and blocked the way back.

Panic flared as the soldiers scrambled for their weapons. More than half had already died. Neyla and Kyan charged, engaging the soldiers before they could grab their weapons.

Akarai smiled and threw himself from his perch.

Catapulting towards the camp, he let loose an arrow and using the refin blood he pushed on it, slowing his fall and flipped into a forward roll. As he rose, he unsheathed his daggers and swiped at the closest soldier. The soldier grabbed his chest as blood bubbled and ran down his torso.

An impact shook the black sand and a fissure opened up running through the middle of the camp. Several called out as they fell into the crack. Akarai looked up at Sebhan who heaved his diera war hammer from the cracked black sand.

Wind whipped and threw soldiers against the stone as Tysar stepped in spinning his sword. An arrow wound through camp cutting through soldiers as Genu controlled it from above. Ada laughed as he sent out waves of flames burning soldiers alive.

Neyla spun her spear a crackling energy zapping anyone it got near. And Kyan followed similar motions with his glaive that had the same buzzing energy as Neyla's spear.

The soldiers were all dead within minutes. Hard chunks of black sand and bodies littered the ground as the stench of decay permeated the camp. No matter how many Akarai killed he never got used to that smell.

Akarai stood at the epicentre of the slaughter and whispered a prayer for those killed. They were just soldiers, after all, doing what they were commanded to do and Akarai held no malice towards them. They were weapons, like him. Following orders. Tysar stalked up through the devastation as the rest looted what they could carry.

"They had enough weapons to arm more than triple the amount of soldiers here. And they have enough provisions to last this lot several months," Tysar said. "I think Overseer Myain was right. It looks like they were planning a siege."

Akarai finished his prayer and opened his eyes. "We will double the scouts around Tansen and send more to these less wandered paths."

Tysar nodded and followed Akarai as he stepped over the corpses. Akarai dropped to his haunches and prodded some of the bodies. The bomb arrows caused quite the explosion. A little larger than Akarai had expected but that was probably from the extra fuel from the fires. He found the body of the presumed leader. He was nondescript. Average height and build. And probably short brown hair. It was hard to tell with the ash and blood.

Akarai patted the man down and checked his pockets. He carried nothing save for a rolled-up piece of parchment. It was burnt around the edges. Akarai unrolled it and blew off the ash.

O,

We continue our studies but are in need of more soldiers. The research is more dangerous than we thought. However, this may be a good thing. The weapon applications could be grander than we had hoped. I understand your need for soldiers but if you have any you could spare, please send them to where the dark is drawn.

M.

"It's not coded like most correspondence," Akarai said, passing Tysar the note.

"A scholar, perhaps?" Tysar asked.

"It's possible given the subject of the letter," Akarai said.

"But why would a researcher need soldiers for a study?"

Akarai scratched his chin where stubble had started to grow. He had been so busy recently that he hadn't had time to shave.

"I don't know but if it has weapon applications, we need to get this to Imayani," Akarai said.

The cool morning breeze blew in from the balcony and into the war room of Atef Palace. Upon returning to the capital, Akarai and Tysar sent word to the empress and waited in the war room. Akarai tapped his finger on the stone table etched with a map of Tarris. Small, coloured pieces showed the placement of soldiers across the country. They were already spread thin and now that they needed to increase their scouts to watch for parties of soldiers it would be even worse.

The stone doors swung open and Overseer Myain and Empress Imayani strode into the room. She wore a long white dress trimmed in gold. A pure gold nashk hung around her neck. It was tradition for the emperor to wear a gold nashk for official meetings but Imayani had taken to wearing it every day. She said it was to ensure she was ready for any important duties, should they arise. However, Akarai thought she wore it to look the part of a ruler. Despite years of rule, there were still sceptics and those who believed a woman shouldn't rule Tarris. And while Imayani brushed it off, Akarai knew it bothered her.

Overseer Myain placed his hands atop the war room table. He wore a simple navy robe and an overseer's nashk. It was gold and turquoise. The same that Overseer Lintou had. The gold indicated the highest position an overseer could ascend to and the turquoise placed him as an adviser.

"What news?" Imayani asked leaning against the table.

"The spy was correct. There was a party of soldiers moving through the mountain passes. We took care of them but they had enough weapons to arm three hundred," Akarai said.

Imayani blew out a breath. Overseer Myain barely reacted as if he expected as such.

"If I may, Empress," Tysar said. "They also had enough supplies to last them months. Now, if that was just for the company of a hundred or part of a bigger movement of supplies to feed a larger force, there is no way of knowing. But it does all lean into the idea of an attempted siege of the capital as we predicted."

It was early morning and the sky was bloody pink but already Imayani looked exhausted. Sweat beaded her brow and Akarai wondered if she had slept last night.

"I suggest we send out more patrols on the less frequented passes. We need to know if more parties are smuggling soldiers or supplies to the outer villages," Akarai said.

Myain nodded. "I will let Overseer Dalana know. Anything else?"

Akarai and Tysar met eyes and Akarai pulled out the half-burnt note. "We found this on the leader of the company."

Imayani took the note and Overseer Myain stepped to her side to read it over her shoulder.

"What does this mean?" Imayani asked.

"We don't know," Tysar said.

"A research project with battle applications? I will send out word and see what our spies can learn," Overseer Myain said.

"It could be something to aid their siege," Tysar said.

Overseer Myain's normally neutral face was scrunched in concern. He didn't like not knowing things. Even Imayani, who had been trained to hide her emotions, slumped against the war room table. There was too much they didn't know.

Imayani took a deep breath. "Send word out among our spy networks. I want to know if there is a secret research project going on. We will reconvene once we have more information. We can't do anything until we know more." Imayani tossed the note onto the table then glanced up to Akarai and Tysar. "You must be tired from your mission. Go, bathe, eat, rest."

Akarai and Tysar bowed and walked out of the war room. Just before the stone doors closed, the faint whispers of Overseer Myain's voice reverberated through the gap.

Akarai loosed the arrow and it tore through the air hitting the target in the centre. Now that he led the Seventh Sceptre he could have asked for a pure diera bow to be made for him, but Akarai preferred Sen's, even if it was less potent than a true diera bow. Each time he held it, the bow reminded him of those who had died because he wasn't strong enough.

Drawing another arrow, Akarai let out a slow breath. He closed his eyes and cleared his mind. Training was one of the few times that he could silence his thoughts. He loosened his grip and the twang of the bow sent a ripple of energy through his body. The arrow pierced the centre of the target.

"You know, enemies won't be standing still when you're firing arrows at them," Imayani said.

Akarai started.

"I also expected the leader of the Seventh Sceptre to be more aware of his surroundings," Imayani said. She stood in the door frame to the training room having changed into loose fitting trousers and a simple tunic. It was of the highest quality and considered ornate to most with the edges stitched with red and black but in comparison to her normal attire, this was simple. Clothes she only wore to train in.

"We all need a place to retreat to where we don't have to look over our shoulders," Akarai said, nocking the next arrow.

Imayani stepped up to his side. He could hear her breath whistling. He loosed the arrow and it hit the rim of the target. Dropping the bow, Akarai sighed.

"The Iluian Blend used to be that place," Imayani said. It had been years since they sat high up in the rafters above the coffeehouse. There was no longer any need to, now that Imayani was empress and could demand a room cleared with the click of her fingers.

"I thought you had a meeting with the Nuian official tonight," Akarai said. He walked over to the weapons table and laid down his bow.

"I pushed it to tomorrow. Their party arrived later than expected and I thought it best to let them rest."

Akarai nodded. Imayani stared at him a question in those brown eyes.

"What happened?" Imayani asked.

"What do you mean?"

"With us. We used to be so relaxed around one another and now it feels so forced and formal." Imayani ran her hand over the daggers lying discarded on the table. "Is it because I'm empress now? Is it because I send you off on missions?"

A knot formed in Akarai's gut. "Nothing has changed. We just aren't children anymore. We have duties."

Imayani crept closer. Each step she took was like watching an approaching sandstorm.

"Then why aren't you at my side for these meetings?" Imayani asked. "You've been drawing away from me. I thought it might be because of the new responsibilities and things would go back to how they were after we adapted. But they haven't."

"You dismissed me," Akarai said. "You have a company of guards at your back. You don't need me to be there all the time anymore. I'm better here." He raised a hand gesturing to the Nightraven training hall. "Preparing for the next mission."

She stopped moving towards him and some of that building pressure eased. Imayani bit her lip. She searching his eyes, scouring for the truth.

"Is this what you want?" Imayani asked. Echoes of a question asked a long time ago. There was a weight to it. The weight of a phrase that carried more than the sum of the individual words. Is this what he wanted? No. But he had no choice. To let things go back to how they had been before the Verdin Guild would be living a lie.

Akarai glanced away.

"Yes."

Imayani's face stiffened. She nodded before turning and leaving the Nightraven.

50

The Battle for Asuriya

Rai and Tysar rushed out of the tightly packed streets of the outer city. Ahead, the great gates of Asuriya stood open. Its walls wrapped around the inner city connecting with the Bandor Mountains behind it. In front of the gate, their overseer and a small company fought back the Ossins. Most were on hyianback and the forces clashed in a spray of blood and dust.

They're outnumbered, Fax said. The shade was right. With most of their soldiers trapped in the outer city fighting off the blight-touched scardrae, only a few had found their way to the inner city.

"We need to go to the gates!" Tysar said.

"We can't leave them to die," Rai said.

"If we join that fight, we will die with them and lose the city."

Rai grimaced. Tysar was right. Even if he could fend the Ossin force off for a time and save some of their soldiers, there were too many Ossins and they would overwhelm Kleran's force eventually unless they secured the gates.

"Go to the gate. I'll fight," Rai said.

Tysar shook his head. "Don't be a fool, Rai. We don't have the seven at our back this time."

"We cannot hope to hold the inner city ourselves," Rai said. "Be ready at the gates and I'll get us the soldiers we need!"

Rai flicked his hyian's rein towards the fight. Tysar cursed before setting off for the gates.

Rai crashed into the fight, his hyian ramming into an Ossin soldier and sending them toppling off their steed. Fax flew through the enemy force as a shadowy bird slicing through sword arms and necks. Sickly spurting noises broke through the din of steel on steel and blood spattered the soldiers. Rai dodged a spear grabbing its shaft and pulling the young soldier from his hyian. The soldier hit the sand, his own hyian trampling over him and he fell still. It had been a rookie mistake but now that the soldier's helmet had come off, Rai could see that he was just a boy. A boy dragged into a civil war he didn't understand.

Behind, the gates groaned as they started to close. *Tysar is lowering the gate,* Fax said.

"Good," Rai said. "Now we just have to get some soldiers behind it."

Rai searched the fighting for the overseer. He had to tell her to pull back to the inner city. Eventually, Rai spotted her corpse being dragged by her startled hyian at the side of the battlefield. With the overseer dead, their force was breaking formation and being picked off one by one by the Ossin army.

Damn it, Rai thought.

"To the gates!" Rai called. If he could retreat and rally the soldiers some may yet survive. Years of commanding the Seventh Sceptre leant a power and sense of authority to his voice that the men and woman reacted to. Some soldiers turned to ride for the gates but the Ossins were relentless and harried at their backs cutting down the fleeing soldiers.

Thud.

An arrow embedded itself in the woman in front of Rai. Her body went slack and she toppled from her hyian.

"Archers!" someone shouted.

Enemy archers appeared on nearby rooftops and arrows began to rain down upon the retreating company. Now that their soldiers were breaking off from the battle, it was easier for the Ossin archers to avoid hitting their own troops.

Arrows hit some of their hyian sending the beasts crashing into one another and throwing soldiers from their saddles.

Rai unslung his bow as he skirted up the outside the surviving soldiers. He nocked an arrow and loosed. The diera arrow hissed through the air catching one of the archers in the chest. Another archer loosed an arrow in response but Fax shot over to deflect it before it hit Rai.

They were almost at the gate.

Just a little further, Rai thought.

Another arrow whistled past Rai to catch the hyian at his side. The beast shrieked and bucked and the soldier held on for dear life. When another arrow hit the hyian's leg, the creature crashed into the sand. Rai pulled hard on his reins and circled back, holding out a hand to the fallen rider. Her eyes were frenzied and alert beneath her helmet.

The gate continued to lower.

"Come on!" Rai shouted.

The soldier shook her head coming back to herself and grabbed Rai's hand. He pulled her up onto his hyian and they rode for the inner city. Ahead, the last of their remaining company burst through the gate.

"Close it!" Rai shouted loosing arrows at the oncoming Ossin force. He flew through the gap under the gate entering the inner city of Asuriya.

A handful of the closest Ossins burst into the courtyard and crashed into their force. The gate clattered to the ground severing two Ossin riders and their hyian in half. The fighting continued within the walls as men and woman fought in the open courtyard. The soldier hopped off Rai's hyian to join the battle. They were evenly numbered now but if that gate were to open they would be overrun with Ossins. Bodies fell from the wall above as Tysar fought off soldiers attempting to reopen the gates.

Low on arrows, Rai leant down and grabbed a fallen soldier's spear. He hefted it feeling its weight before plunging it into a charging Ossin soldier. Breathing hard, Rai surveyed the courtyard. Tysar was fending off three soldiers on the steps up to the contraption that opened the gate. But he was becoming overwhelmed as the Ossins focused their efforts on getting the gate open to let in the rest of their army. Rai twirled his spear around to clatter it against an approaching soldier's head.

A behemoth of a man charged at Tysar. He clipped Tysar's side with the sharp of his blade and cracked him across the face with the pommel of his sword. Tysar's eyes rolled back into his head and he dropped off the wall, landing atop a pile of corpses.

"Tysar!" Rai stood on his saddle and threw his spear. It shot through the air and caught the man in the chest. He stumbled back into his fellow soldiers sending four of them tumbling down the steps.

As Rai approached the wall, he leapt from his hyian's back and onto the staircase. Above, six soldiers were on the wall and two were working the mechanism to bring the gate back up.

The metal started to groan.

Fax flew up to meet them. A wall of shadowy tendrils that cut through the first three soldiers with ease. A man stared, wide-eyed and shouted for those opening the gate to hurry. Rai launched himself through the black shroud that Fax left in its wake, daggers flashing in the dying light of day. Fax acted as cover and surprise flashed across the face of the closest man as Rai buried his daggers deep in his gut.

He slid them out, rewarded with a gush of blood that slicked his hands as he threw up his daggers to catch an oncoming sword. Rai gritted his teeth as he pushed back, overpowering the man and then swiping his daggers across his face. The man screamed clutching at his head as he fell back and off the wall. An arrow grazed Rai's shoulder. Rai hissed and took a few steps back. He looked up to see the last soldier standing with a bow.

The man nocked the next arrow.

Rai didn't have time to cover the distance between them and this next arrow would find its mark. Just then, a black spike tore through the soldier's skull and his face softened as death took him.

Rai blew out a breath and ran up the last of the steps to the mechanism. The two soldiers had managed to draw the gate up a little letting some of the Ossin force crawl beneath it. Rai loosed the latch and let the gate snap shut once more. Cries of pain came from the gate as those halfway under were pinned beneath it, bleeding out onto the sand.

Fax landed atop the wall as a crow.

Are you not going to say thank you? Fax asked. *That second arrow was sure to hit you.* The shade hesitated. *Although it might have helped your looks. Battle scarred and interesting.*

Rai ignored the shade and stumbled to the edge of the wall. The courtyard below was a battlefield. But not enough of the Ossins made it through the gate and Rai could tell the remaining Yontar force would come out on top. He made his way back down the steps to Tysar who was sat against the bottom step.

"Not dead then," Rai said.

"Not yet." Tysar looked up and grinned. A bruise already blooming on the side of his head.

Rai glanced around the courtyard as the last of the Ossins fell. It was a huge space with a second smaller wall and open gate leading into the inner city. Through it, Asuriya spread out before them. It looked much like other Tarrisian cities with buildings of varying heights stacked together with winding streets between them. At the far side of the city, the Mad Palace was cut into the Bandor Mountains.

"We need to secure the walls for Kleran and Imayani." Tysar groaned as he stood, swaying on his feet. "Where is the overseer?"

"Dead."

Tysar closed his eyes.

"That puts you in command," Rai said. His old friend looked to him. Rai could tell that Tysar had expected him to try and take control but he had no position in the army. Not anymore.

Tysar nodded. He took a couple deep breaths, straightened, and steeled his expression. "Secure the walls! Bring all the wounded to the far side of the courtyard and those fit enough, take to the walls! This isn't over yet."

They watched from atop the walls of Asuriya's inner city as the two armies clashed. Kleran's army made it to the city first taking the advantageous positioning among the buildings but that also meant they had to face the scardrae. From the wall, Rai could see the beetles scuttling through the streets and thinning their forces. But the army was huge. As soon as the aya tromped into the streets there was little the scardrae could do and slowly they were cut down.

The remnants of the Ossin fast front retreated back to their main army, aware that if they stayed at the gate they would be trapped between the army and the wall. That allowed a procession with Imayani and Kleran to reach Asuriya's inner city without falling under attack.

The gates were opened and hyian and aya stormed into the courtyard, now cleared of corpses. Archers were positioned along the wall.

Kleran, Imayani, Yeru, and the honour guard handed off their hyian to the stablehands as Tysar and Rai approached.

"The walls are secured but we have had heavy casualties. This reinforcement is welcomed," Tysar said.

Kleran glanced around noting the soldiers positioning and nodding appreciatively.

"You've done well," Imayani said. Blood speckled her face and clothes.

"We haven't delved deeper into the city yet but we set up two patrols so that we aren't ambushed from within the walls," Tysar said.

Kleran snorted. "The Ossins won't get behind the walls now."

"It's not them we are worried about," Rai said. The monarch raised an eyebrow.

"Mutated wildlife," Yeru said. Despite this being a battlefield, she wore her usual light travel gear, a notebook tucked under one arm.

Rai nodded. "I think the Ossins are releasing some captured blight-touched creatures in a hope that they will thin out our army."

It was Yeru's turn to look surprised.

"We saw the scardrae in the outer city," Imayani said. Was that where the blood had come from?

"They appeared just as we did," Tysar said. "And Asuriya's inner city might hold more surprises."

Imayani looked thoughtful. "We need to focus our army on defending the walls but we can spare some soldiers to scout ahead. I want to take the palace before dark hour."

"I'll see it done. We can leave in an hour or so." Tysar bowed and stalked off to pass on the commands.

An overseer waved to Kleran catching his attention and Yeru walked off surveying the courtyard. That left Imayani and Rai. She sniffed.

"I want to see the battle," she said and headed for the walls.

Imayani marched up the steps, her honour guard and Rai in tow. At the top, a soldier hesitated before saying, "They are drawing closer, Empress. It may be best to stay behind the walls in case there are archers."

Imayani shot him a deadpan look. "And how would I both see the battlefield and oversee my army?"

It was unusual for an empress or emperor to be on the front lines. That was normally an overseer's job. However, no soldier would question their empress so he stepped aside.

Archers lined the walls loosing arrows onto the enemy army. Imayani pushed through the crowd, Rai at her side. The outer city was a blood bath. Kleran's soldiers were being slaughtered. With more than two thirds of Kleran's army now within the walls of Asuriya, the Ossins had the greater numbers. The remaining Yontar troops were falling like flies.

Imayani's face tightened as she came to the same conclusion.

"They knew their fate when they stayed to fight," Rai said. "It's the duty of a soldier." The words came out monotone but he couldn't hide the bitterness from his face.

They stood in silence, watching men and woman die. Aya charged through streets crushing soldiers to death. A woman jumped off of a rooftop and onto the aya killing its rider, just to turn the beast around and crush more soldiers. They all wore similar jerkins making it hard to distinguish between the Yontar and Ossin armies. In the end, they were all Tarrisian and they shouldn't have been fighting. Blood stained the sand and the smell of decay rose from the dead city.

What's that? Fax asked.

The shade sat atop the battlements as an inky black crow. Shadow broke off Fax like smoke. Soldiers did a double take before backing up and giving them some space. No doubt stories of shadow magic had made its way through the ranks by now.

Rai turned to see what the shade had spotted. He squinted against the red light of the low Sun Eye. It was a korhin. The huge shiny blue creature sauntered through the streets.

"A korhin?" Rai said.

"Where?" Imayani asked.

Rai pointed the beast out. The pot-bellied creatures were usually used in palace dungeons as guards as they filled corridors and their huge fists could fight back any intruders.

Realisation dawned.

"It's headed for the gate."

Imayani's eyes went wide. "Reinforce the gate! They're going to try to bring it down!"

"One korhin won't be able to bring down these gates," a battle-scarred overseer said patting the battlements. A gold and red nashk hung from his neck revealing his experience and high position as a combat and warfare overseer.

Rai, that looks different than the korhin we fought, Fax said.

"Fax is right. That's no ordinary korhin."

As it drew closer, the scale of the beast became clearer. And it was huge. Normally korhins were three times a grown man, but this korhin was *three stories* tall. A third arm stuck out of the right side of its lower belly.

"A blight-touched korhin," someone whispered.

The overseer did all he could to hide the shock on his face. "Reinforce the gate! I want men and woman stacked behind it! We cannot let that gate fall!"

Soldiers rushed past Rai and Imayani as they pushed back down the stairs to the gate. Spears and shields blocked behind the gate and soldiers stabbed through the grate at any who got too close.

The enemy soldiers pushed through the remaining company standing guard outside the gate and parted letting the massive korhin through. It did not run. The beast walked like it had all the time in the world. That permanent curling of a korhin's red lips making it look like the monster was smiling at them as it approached.

The korhin threw its weight against the gate and the Ossins cheered. Tremors ran through the wall and Imayani grabbed the battlement to steady herself. It bashed into the gate again sending another jitter through the stone.

Fear washed over the troops like a wave every time the korhin hit the gate. The creak of metal bending and snap of mechanisms breaking sounded loud over the quiet of the soldiers. They stabbed through at the korhin, spears impaling the beast and yet it didn't seem to notice. With each crash, the Ossin army cheered louder. A war cry filling any void of silence.

Kleran appeared from the steps and grabbed Imayani. Tysar, and the monarch's honour guard stood at his back. "We need to go farther into Asuriya!"

The *thwack* of bowstrings made Kleran hard to hear. "Come, Empress Imayani. We have to retreat into the city!"

"We can't keep running, Kleran."

"It's a tactical placement. That gate is going to fall." As if to prove his point another shudder shook the wall. "And we have more space to fend them off in the inner city if we place our soldiers right. That korhin will just run us through in this tightly packed courtyard."

The monarch was right. Once the gate was open that blight korhin would bulldoze through their lined-up soldiers. Imayani turned to her overseer who nodded.

"Okay. Let's go."

With both Imayani's and Kleran's honour guards, they had a battalion of soldiers surrounding them as they moved into Asuriya. Both Yeru and Mino clung to the Empress as she marched confidently into the city. Rai and Tysar walked a couple paces in front of the empress and monarch watching the city streets. More soldiers filtered out into the alleyways and took positions atop buildings, preparing for their last stand against the Ossins.

The derelict inner city was much like the outer. The desert had reclaimed much of it. Sand filled the streets and buried the doors into homes. They passed a temple entrance. The design work scrawled into the walls was faded and barely legible after ages of erosion. Mutated sand foxes ran off as they passed but nothing attacked them. Shadows stretched long. It would be dark hour soon. Rai hoped they would be in the palace by then.

Crash.

They all spun back towards the wall where a new wave of noise erupted.

"The gate has fallen," Tysar whispered.

"We must hurry!" Kleran said.

With renewed vigour they made their way up the incline of the city and towards the Mad Palace. The palace protruded from the mountainside and was cut deep into the Bandor Mountains. Some said it was built using the bones of a God and continued to grow within the mountain even to this day.

Grand ornate pillars towered above them with a great staircase leading into a gaping black maw. Several stories up a balcony stuck out. The throne room, Rai remembered. He had read it in a book once that the throne room had a balcony that overlooked the city.

A crater was cut into the bottom of the stairs. Part of the pillars and balcony had been shattered in what must have been a huge explosion. But it was the pieces of rubble hanging suspended in the air, as if frozen in time, that caught the attention of the company. They passed underneath a massive chunk of stone that hovered in the air, unmoving. No one knew what had happened and how pieces of stone seemed to be frozen mid explosion. Few believed the stories but there was no doubting it now that it was before them.

One of the soldiers reached out towards the floating debris.

"Don't!" Tysar said and the soldier withdrew their hand.

They walked in a silent reverence, afraid that speaking might upset this ancient place. All that could be heard was the furious scratching of Yeru writing in her notepad.

A surge of noise came from the lower city as the Ossin army advanced into the inner city. However, no one sped up or urged the company on as they ascended the stairs. There was a wariness among the soldiers about entering the Mad Palace. Rai stared at a chunk of rock that had once been part of the balcony's balustrade floating above him. He couldn't fault their caution.

The honour guard entered first fanning out through the entry chamber. It was dark but soon they had torches burning as they delved deeper into the Mad Palace.

"There's no sconces," Yeru said, breaking the quiet. Rai gave her a questioning look and she gestured to the walls. "No skylight, no sconces. How did they see in here?"

"Maybe they carried torches," Tysar said.

"Every time someone entered the palace? That seems impractical."

The entry chamber was not unlike the Hall of Strain in Tansen. Pillars filled the room, carvings of ancient events etched into them that Rai couldn't decipher. At the far side of the chamber a staircase led up to blinding white light.

"The throne room must be up there," one of the honour guard said.

"So close to the entrance," Kleran mused. "Not the most strategic placement for a throne room."

The honour guard kept their hands on their weapons as they started up the stairs. After they confirmed it was clear, the rest of the company followed. There was an eerie quiet with only their footsteps ringing around them. Yeru muttered under her breath as her fingers trailed over the stone. It was dark but Rai could just make out the beautiful mural that covered the walls.

"What is it?" Rai asked.

"The War of the Seven Armies," Yeru said. "We have references to it but there's some debate on if it truly happened."

Everyone was quiet listening to the scholar. "There was said to be a war between seven armies that covered the world. Most scholars brush it off as myth. A war that great would have serious effects on everything. And why would seven different armies all want to fight one another? Wars usually start over a bid for land or resources. But seven factions fighting across the world? It doesn't make sense. What would an army here in Tarris fight the frozen Trosan Empire for, for example."

"Power. Dominance." Imayani whispered. It was what her father used to say. The greatest weakness of men is the power they hold and the power they do not. They continued in silence until they reached the top of the stairs.

The throne room was a massive hall; one side open to the air with a balcony sticking out overlooking Asuriya. The other faded into darkness as it stretched deep into the Bandor Mountains. Murals covered the walls here too. A swirling pattern with people bowing and making offerings in between the swirls.

"Fascinating." Yeru ran over and started drawing in her notebook.

"Yeru! Be careful," Imayani said.

The honour guard spread out to inspect the throne room as Kleran and Imayani walked to the edge of the balcony. They gazed down at Asuriya, the lost capital now a battlefield. The Ossin force hadn't made it far into the city. The korhin had fallen and now its corpse blocked the main thoroughfare limiting how many soldiers the Ossins could bring into the city. This allowed the Yontar forces to hold them at bay while picking off those who made it around the korhin.

"We did it," Kleran said. "We reclaimed the ancient capital and the throne!" His voice reverberated through the hall.

"We haven't won the battle yet," Imayani said.

"All in good time. But for now, I have to take my place as

emperor," Kleran said.

The shine of sunlight on metal caught Rai's attention as a blade was levelled to his back. He noticed too late that each of Imayani's honour guard had one of Kleran's guards standing right behind them, swords drawn.

The Empress faced Kleran wide eyed.

"I'll keep you alive, Imayani. Killing you would only cause uproar," Kleran said.

The dull rasp of blades sliding from scabbards echoed around the throne room. Some of Imayani's honour guard managed to pull out their blades but they were too slow. Kleran's honour guard was perfectly positioned behind each of Imayani's guards. Before Rai could take in the scene, Imayani's honour guard cried out as blades plunged into their backs.

Fax deflected the sword at Rai's back and skewered the guard as Rai turned to Kleran. *Traitor*. He lunged, Fax darting ahead as a spike of darkness.

A shadow battered into Fax, dispersing the dark tendril.

Another shade?

Rai followed the trail of black smoke to Tysar. His old friend met his gaze.

Tysar had a shade.

A wave of naseau hit Rai's stomach. The shock on Imayani's face told Rai that she hadn't known either.

"You," Rai said.

"There's more going on than you know, Rai," Tysar said. "But you'll see soon enough."

An explosion of darkness catapulted Tysar into Rai. He was

too shocked to react as Tysar tackled into him and together they launched off of the balcony and into the city below.

51

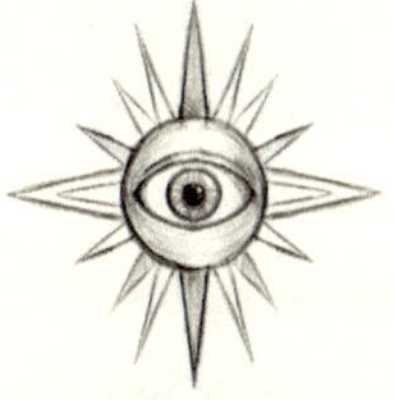

A Ghost

5 years ago.

The errand boy barged into the coffeehouse, toppling over a table. It clattered to the ground along with several chairs. The patrons gasped as onlookers swept in to help the young boy. He bounced to his feet seemingly unaffected by his dramatic fall. His body jittered as he surveyed the room, landing on Akarai. Of course the message was for him.

The boy scuttled over.

"Akarai sir, this is for you," the boy said, handing over a sealed roll of parchment. Others around the coffeehouse stared. He broke the seal and read the note. It was encrypted. A simple code for short messages that they could decode in their head.

Important news, Akarai read. *Meet in war room.*

Standing, Akarai cleared his throat and gave the boy a coin. "Maybe watch for the table next time."

"Yes, sir. Thank you, sir," the boy said, bowing as he ran off.

Those in the coffeehouse had returned to their seats but watched Akarai from the corner of their eye. Ignoring their questioning gazes, Akarai strode out of the coffeehouse and deeper into the palace.

Two guards stood at the great stone door into the war room. They saluted and pushed on the doors. Groaning under the weight, the doors finally creaked open and Akarai passed inside. Imayani was on the far side of the war room table, her brow furrowed as she studied the parchment laid out before her.

"And you're sure this is accurate?" Overseer Myain asked a scruffy looking servant. His hair was ruffled with a spattering of flour marring his grey clothing. A kitchen servant, then.

"Yes, yes, I swear it!" the boy responded.

Also around the table were two other overseers. Overseer Rikai nodded to Akarai as he entered. He looked more interested than worried as he scratched his chin, which was a good sign. And Overseer Dalana. She wore a battle-ready heavy brown jerkin and a sword at her waist. Her long blonde hair was tied up in an intricate bun. Her nashk was gold and red indicating her as an overseer of combat and of the highest ranking. Overseer Rikai also had red on his nashk, but he was only a silver ranking. Whereas Overseer Dalana was in charge of all of the soldiers in the capital.

Overseer Myain ground his teeth. "Very well. You can go."

The boy bowed and sped out the room.

"Do we have any idea what it is?" Imayani asked.

"What *what* is?" Akarai asked.

Imayani snapped her head up and looked at him like she had just realised that he was here.

"The weapon, Akarai," Overseer Myain said. "One of my spies in the Thousand Floor Palace has been delivering food to a heavily guarded room of researchers."

"Do you know what the weapon is?" Akarai asked.

Overseer Myain blew out an exasperated breath. "That's what we are here to figure out."

Running her hand over the parchment, Imayani bit the inside of her lip. "Do we know if it's dangerous?"

"Other than the note that the seven retrieved, we have no information about what they might be studying," Overseer Myain said.

"Can I see this note?" Overseer Dalana asked.

Myain slipped his hand into his pocket and pulled out the note, handing it to Dalana. She studied it for a moment, Rikai reading over her shoulder.

"Training a beast, perhaps?" Rikai offered.

"I can't think of any creature that we have yet to try and domesticate or use in a battle scenario," Dalana said. "Although from the note, it sounds like soldiers are dying from this study."

The others grumbled their agreement.

"Or a vaporous poison," Akarai said. "We have read about such things in ancient scripts. Perhaps they have learned of how to create one."

Dalana screwed her face up. She hated employing any weapon that wasn't made of steel. Even diera ore was a contentious topic with the woman. Dalana explained that raw strength and strategy was the honourable way to win a fight.

"We need to find out, and soon," Imayani said. "You retrieved the note months ago but who knows how long they had been studying this before then."

"I can send in some assassins," Dalana said.

"No, we'll go," Akarai said. All eyes fell on him. "This is the Yontar monarch. If we assault the Thousand Floor Palace to learn this is nothing more than a simple weapons test that they will claim to have forgotten to inform you about, then we will light the fuse for civil war.

"Send the seven," Akarai said.

"That makes the most sense," Myain said. "This requires a subtle touch."

Imayani mulled over her options. "Okay. We'll send the Seventh Sceptre. But I want this to be silent. Minimal killings, so rein Ada in." Ada did have a tendency to kill anyone he could get his hands on. "Sneak into the palace, find out what they're researching and get back out again."

Akarai nodded. "We'll go tonight."

Those around the table nodded.

"May this just be a weapons test," Rikai said under his breath. "Otherwise, it may set off a civil war anyway."

Akarai summoned the seven to the Nightraven. They sat around the stone table not an hour after the meeting in the war room. The piece of parchment Imayani had been studying was a map of the Thousand Floor Palace, crudely drawn by the cook servant but it gave them the general vicinity of where this research project was taking place.

"Shall we take the same path as the cook?" Genu asked. "We

could break in and disguise ourselves as servants."

Akarai took the parchment and ran his finger over the path the cook had drawn out. "This may not be an option anymore."

"What do you mean?" Neyla asked, sitting forward.

Sometimes Akarai forgot the others weren't in the private meetings with the empress where he learned many of the secrets of Tarris.

"People believe that the Thousand Floor Palace got its name because it has a thousand floors. Others say this is just a guess as no one would count the number of floors but the truth is more complicated. The palace doesn't have normal floors despite what it looks like from the outside. The rooms are built at different heights within the stone, some only a couple meters of a difference. Between them are a multitude of corridors and staircases connecting rooms at random and many of them are blocked off by walls." He pointed to a dead end on the drawing.

"A lot of the time there are more passages behind the stone. And there are builders that pull down and erect these walls at regular intervals. So what was once a stairwell could now be a dead end. It's why so many say it is disorienting to wander and why some rooms you will find yourself going up a flight of stairs only to come down another flight not long after," Akarai said.

Sebhan rubbed his temples groaning as he tried to keep up.

"But why?" Genu asked.

"To stop people like us from breaking in," Kyan said.

Akarai nodded. "Before the cataclysm, Yontar was the centre for managing Tarrisian soldiers as they had the biggest barracks. It was built as a last line of defence should Tarris ever be invaded."

"So how are we going to find this room?" Neyla asked.

"We split up," Akarai said. "Move in from different directions. Sebhan can go with Kyan. Tysar with Neyla. And Genu, Ada and I." Akarai made sure to group himself with Ada to keep an eye on the man who didn't always do well with the stealth missions. "Do we agree?"

The others nodded.

"Gather supplies. We leave tonight."

The empress sent word for Akarai to meet her on the rooftop before they departed. The same rooftop where the emperor was murdered. Imayani had taken to going up there to think as that was where she felt closest to her father. Akarai, on the other hand, hadn't returned there since the night he killed the emperor.

He nodded to the two guards and pushed open the door. Stepping out onto the roof, he felt no breeze. The night was still and silent.

The Moon Eye peaked over the horizon. Silver light tinged the edges of Imayani's silhouette as she stood overlooking the city. She wore a long red dress that contrasted the dusk.

Akarai came to her side gazing over the city alight with torchlight.

"The others are ready," Akarai said after a moment.

Imayani didn't reply.

"We will find out what they're hiding," he said.

They watched the city come to life as the Moon Eye lit the streets. Merchants flooded the squares, men, woman, and children laughed as they walked to their local coffeehouses or Night Theatres. The coming of night breathed new life into Tarris. Where other cultures feared the dark, Tarris celebrated it. The burning days left the people revelling in the cool nights.

Bound by shadow, we are the dark.

Akarai assumed this was a reference to the seven being the blade in the dark but now he wondered if it had another meaning. One that all Tarrisians could relate too.

"What happened that night?" Imayani asked.

Akarai was pulled back to the moment. "What night?"

"The night my father died. I read your account in the scrolls but I've never heard it from you. When it happened… it was just too raw and soon that I didn't want to know. But I think I'm ready now."

Akarai swallowed. "I don't remember much. It was a long time ago."

She turned to him, an unreadable expression on her face. "Try."

He cleared his throat and looked over the city. "The emperor asked to speak with me and we came up here when two figures appeared from nowhere. It gets fuzzy then but they attacked and I woke up in the infirmary."

"We never found any trace of the assassins," Imayani said.

What was this? Why was she bringing this up now, after all this time?

"What did he want to speak to you about?" Imayani asked.

"I don't know. We never got past pleasantries," Akarai said. Flashes of the emperor spitting in his face and of him kicking Akarai bloody. "What is this Imayani?"

She looked surprised at his tonal shift and took a step back. "That's when we changed. I've been thinking about it and I think that was the point we started to drift apart. I wanted to know why.

What happened that night? What did my father say?"

"Nothing, Imayani. I just told you." Akarai rubbed his face. He was too tired for this.

"Then why did everything change?"

"Nothing has changed!" Akarai shouted the words and the two guards came pushing through from inside. Imayani forced a smile to reassure them that everything was okay and waved them away.

"I'm sorry. I'm just thinking about the mission," Akarai said. How could he let himself lash out like that?

"You're not telling me something. You've been keeping it from me," Imayani said. She stepped closer to him. "I can see it eating you up inside. Why won't you let people in? Whenever something happens you withdraw. It happened in the orphanage with Kon too."

The name stabbed into Akarai. He hadn't thought about the boy in years.

"You did the same in the Eye. You haven't mentioned Sen. I had to hear from Tysar that he had died. Despite that, you've spent every moment since training in archery with *his bow* and declining a more powerful diera bow. I can see the hurt no matter how well you mask it. And after that night with my father you completely stepped back from the world. You stepped back from me. And I don't know why. I don't know how to help if you don't let me in."

Akarai felt cold. He thought something would surge up within him. That he would feel something from her words. But there was nothing. He had spent his life silencing the pain until it had become part of him. He thought keeping this to himself was saving those around him but he could see the hurt and concern on Imayani's face.

He hated that. He hated himself for causing that.

"I don't deserve that pity," Akarai said.

"I'm not pitying you, Akarai. I'm your friend. I want to help."

There. The curling guilt in his gut.

He couldn't keep living like this. The truth had been simmering in him for years.

"You can't help me," Akarai said.

"I can try. Please Akarai. I need to know."

Like the bile coming up his throat, words clawed their way up from the dark recesses deep within himself.

And then the truth bubbled out.

"I killed your father."

Imayani froze.

"He brought me to this rooftop to kill me. He thought I was getting too close to you. That was why he sent me to the Verdin Guild and he wasn't happy that I returned." The words flooded out of him in an uncontrollable torrent. He couldn't stop now, not even if he wanted to. "So the guards dragged me from my bed and beat me bloody. He was going to kill me and I… I don't know. I just broke. I didn't mean to kill him but before I knew it my dagger was buried in his chest. The guards made to run and I panicked. Then they were dead, too."

Fear crawled onto Imayani's face. A tremble shook her hand.

"The guards head was caved in," she said.

"I know how it looks but—" Akarai stepped towards her and Imayani scuttled back from him, opening a chasm between them. She drifted away like a ship on an ocean, covering distance that he could never close.

He knew then that they would never be able to return to how they had been. No lie or truth could rewrite the past. A part of Akarai felt relief. He knew he was a monster and didn't deserve her. And yet another part of him whispered that she might have understood, that they might have been able to go back to the way things were. That voice died in the rift she tore open between them.

"Imayani you need to understand—"

"Guards!" Imayani shouted. The two guards burst through the door and rushed at them. They grabbed Akarai and kicked the back of his legs so that he dropped to his knees. He didn't fight them.

"He tried to kill me, Imayani," Akarai said. She was petrified. Eyes wide and condemning. "He killed other innocent people. You know this. He was paranoid and saw everyone as an enemy."

The fear didn't shift from her expression but a recognition flickered in her eyes. The guards shifted uncomfortably. They didn't know whether Akarai was a threat or a friend. All went still as Imayani measured him. Tears brimmed in her eyes.

After a long pause, Imayani spoke. "Escort Akarai to the stables."

The guards dragged him towards the door. Akarai strained his neck to look back as Imayani clasped her mouth and tears streaked down her cheeks.

He glanced away.

This day was always going to come. Akarai couldn't shake the look of horror on her face. He dipped his head in shame.

The guards did as they were asked, leading Akarai to the stables. They let him stand and walk with them as to not attract attention within the palace. Holding the door open, they waited until he was several steps into the stables before slamming it shut behind him.

Akarai's leg grew weak and he collapsed against the stone wall breathing hard. *Come on, get a hold of yourself,* he thought. The others would arrive within the hour and they were to start their journey to Yontar. But would there be a place for him when he returned? Or was this Imayani's way of saying don't come back? *Did he want to come back?*

The bond that had stretched and survived years of strife had snapped. It had grown more and taut over the years with the lie straining it but the silence had kept it from breaking completely. The truth was out now and it had shattered under the weight.

The door to the stables swung open and Tysar and Neyla walked in, laughing. Akarai struggled to compose himself and forced himself to his feet. They went quiet upon seeing him. The light of the corridor painted him in a strip of firelight surrounded by the dark stables.

"I'll go pack my hyian," Neyla said and bowed to Akarai as she passed.

Tysar approached with a look of concern. "Akarai are you okay? You're so pale."

He let out a shaky breath. "Fine."

Tysar didn't look convinced but nodded. Akarai pushed off the wall and trudged into one of the hyian's pens. He took a deep breath and grabbed the saddle from the wall attaching it to the beast.

You're a survivor. The seven need you. Focus. He screamed the words in his head fighting to keep down the swell of unfettered panic that threatened to overwhelm him.

52

The Black City

The Mad Palace, or the dark realm's version of it, was cut into the base of a mountain of black stone. In Tarris, this would be the edges of the Bandor Mountains, Nya thought, imagining a map. But the mountain was not made of the warm tan stone of Tarris but the black rock of the dark place. Pillars rose at either side of a grand staircase leading up to the gaping maw of an opening. Spiralled towers and ridges crawled up the side of the black mountain to a ledge high above. Darkness gathered there in a thick smog. And while it did not stir, Nya was sure it was watching.

She stood at the base of the stairs staring upward. The guard at Nya's back shoved her and they started to ascend.

Nya felt numb. After killing her father there was no rush of justice. No sense of rightness. But neither was there guilt. She just felt tired. Nya saw how Kit looked at her. But she couldn't find the energy to care.

"You feel it, don't you?" Adani waved her guard off and took position at her side.

Nya did feel the pulling sensation. She wanted to go to the darkness. Nya wondered if the reason she had failed to escape was because at her heart she didn't want to. Was it the Dark that kept her here? Was it the Dark that made her kill her father?

No, Nya thought. *He got what he deserved.*

"It's like the draw of a warm hearth during the cold desert nights," Adani said. "And the power. You must have felt the strength that the dark has given you. Imagine what it'll be able to bestow once we reach its heart."

Adani was grinning. Nya turned away.

"Nya, Nya, Nya," Adani said. He lowered his voice so only Nya could hear him. "We will be Gods among men. Can't you see it? Can't you *feel* it? You and me. We will hold power beyond imagination."

"Why would it give us power?" Nya said.

"Because it told me so. It must be speaking to you too."

Nya stayed silent. There had been a presence pressing on her mind. It didn't speak words to her but fed her impressions and knowledge. The closer they got to the Black City the harder it was to tell it apart from her own mind and now that she was within the city limits, there was no telling what came from the Dark and what was her.

They passed beneath the arch and into the Mad Palace. The entrance was a crude opening that resembled an eroded cave mouth. Inside was a thick darkness. It reminded Nya of the cloud that surrounded the Ahmune that roamed the lost library of Nenelan.

A shadow that was more than a lack of light. It had an essence, a thickness like smoke.

A quiet reverence held the company as they peered inward. Their echoing footsteps told of a large chamber but they could make out little by the light coming from the entrance.

"Light the torches," Mirt said.

Firelight led the way between the stalactites. As they wandered through the cave-like chamber, Nya's sight improved and the dark lessened allowing her to see their surroundings better. The others still squinted relying on the torches. All apart from Adani, who had a confidence that spoke of someone who could see more than the others also.

Welcome, champion.

Nya spun looking back and forth. The voice sounded like it had whispered into her ear. It was deep and gravelly. The guard at her back gave her a confused look.

That word again, *champion*. It was what the Ahmune called her in the library too. She reached out to Bom but the shade had no answer.

On the far wall a staircase led upward. *Towards the throne room,* Nya thought. She didn't want to think about how she knew that.

The walls of the stairwell depicted ancient murals faded by the ages. Nya had no doubt that if she didn't have this connection that she wouldn't have been able to make out the dulled shapes on the walls.

It was a war. Seven armies clashing together. It held a level of detail Nya had never seen before. If she stepped towards it, Nya could make out individual soldiers fighting. Sword and spears pressed against one another. At the front of each of the sections were seven armoured figures for each of the seven armies. Each clad in the colour of their army.

Nya searched her mind for a war of seven armies but couldn't recall any. *If only Rai was here,* she thought. He would have known.

They came to the top of the stairs and wind blew in from the open far wall. It was brighter here with a balcony letting in the light from the clouded sky.

However, on the opposite side of the chamber was a wipsing shadow that sat like a creature at the back of the throne room.

At the edges of the darkness, shadow broke off like black smoke. There, Nya could see the through the dark to the murals depicting people worshipping on the walls. But as Nya brought her eyes closer to the centre of the mass it became a void of pure black, reminding Nya of the tear. A level of darkness that seemed to be nothingness itself.

The company gasped and several of the guards fell backwards at the sight. Even Mirt, who had been rambling with excitement the whole way here, had trepidation marring his features.

Welcome.

The voice boomed around the high-ceilinged chamber. Shock flashed across everyone's faces. *They heard it this time,* Nya thought.

It took Mirt a moment to compose himself before stepping forward towards the darkness. He cleared his throat.

"I've come to your call, mighty Aspect," Mirt said. His voice cracked.

You did well bringing my champions to me.

Two specs of purple flared to life in the shadow and then a torrent of black smoke darted out towards them. It circled around the party. The two purple eyes forever fixed on them.

The shadow laughed as it trailed smoky black clouds around them. The company pulled in closer. No one spoke.

Why, they are even better than I had hoped, Kygian said. The throne room was smothered in an oppressive darkness. It surrounded them in a shroud of pure black and the party all pulled together in the centre, eyes darting back and forth. Nya sucked in air finding it hard to breath.

First, we have Adani. Born with darkness in his heart, it's all you have ever known. Is it not?

Adani didn't shy back from the dark. He dropped to one knee and dipped his head. "Yes, dark one."

And you, Nya.

The hairs on the back of Nya's neck prickled at hearing the voice say her name.

The dark is always strongest around that which is light.

She felt it press against her mind. Nya couldn't hold it back. Not here where it was so strong. But before it broke through the Dark Aspect withdrew.

Do you submit to me, Child of Darkness? You can only join willingly. I cannot force you to become my champion.

"Nya," Kit said. He was at her back. A reassuring hand clasped hers.

Mmm. You tried finding peace with them, did you not? You thought returning to the Patched Cloak with your new friends would settle the unease. You thought that it was as easy as wishing the dark away and distracting yourself.

But you were wrong, weren't you?

556

Kygian's words grated against Nya, though she felt the truth in them.

Darkness does not dissipate. It is always there, under everything. For the second the light turns away, it returns.

You are a part of it now.

Did you not have a chance to run back with your friends? Did you not use that chance to instead kill your own father?

Warm blood pouring through her fingers. Pooling at her feet.

"Don't listen to it," Kit whispered. His voice was softer than the Dark's. Nya didn't know who to listen to. She didn't know how to respond to either of them. She was so tired. Tired of trying to say the right things. Tired of trying to *be* the right thing.

The Dark let out a breathy sigh.

Let me show you.

Darkness flooded Nya. The black filled her mouth, ears, covered her vision until she swam in shadow. Nya couldn't breathe.

Then she was in the Patched Cloak. The doors and windows barred. Illy was pressed against the door and it rattled against something pushing on it from outside. Screams came from the street.

Nya stepped forward.

Lem lay behind the bar. His stomach was ripped open, guts pulled out and eyes glassy. Dust stood at his side, her fur matted in his blood. The sand fox looked up and Nya saw pieces of Lem hanging her mouth. Then Dust went back to eating.

Nya felt nothing at the sight as she kept walking through the inn.

Wenson was sprawled out in a booth. Blood vapor filled the air around him as he laid back in a daze.

Nya continued through the inn.

The door burst open and a husk charged into the Patched Cloak. It swiped, clawing through Illy's throat. Blood spurted over Nya's face as Illy's eyes bulged before she dropped to the floor.

Nya passed out into the street.

The city was overrun with husks. The sky was a black swirling storm. People ran through the streets to be cut down by the flying monsters. No one helped one another. They ran for their lives uncaring to those around them. A mother abandoned her child darting down a side street as her son was tackled by a husk and eaten alive.

Tears fell down Nya's face and yet she felt nothing. Still, she walked on.

You see it now, don't you? You may think the husks are the monsters but they are just like those you're trying to protect.

You fight.

You kill.

You do not care for whose blood is spilled if your own still flows.

Nya turned down a main thoroughfare. Around her was chaos. Screaming. Dying. Palace guards shoved through the people uncaring to their plights.

I feel your pain. I know you blame yourself. You think your mother was pushed to madness by your birth.

But you are wrong.

Walking past a side street, Nya glanced down to see her mother. She was younger. Youth glinting in her eyes. She held a dagger in shaking hands as a man lay at her feet.

You think you are the one hurting those around you.

But you are wrong.

Nya stumbled onward. She didn't want to see anymore. She didn't want to hear anymore.

"Stop!" Nya shouted. She covered her ears but it did nothing to block out the voice in her mind, so she ran through the streets until she found a quiet backstreet that she dove into and curled up into a ball.

A gargling cough brought Nya's head up. Ahead, Yontar burned and outlined in that fiery light was Kit. Nya dragged herself to her feet and ran towards him.

"Kit! We need to get away from here!" Nya grabbed his shoulder and pulled him back. He was laughing.

Nya squinted against the light in the street. Bodies lay strewn across the thoroughfare. They hadn't been ravaged like those that fell to the husks. These bodies were ashen, decaying, faces of torment frozen at the precipice of death.

She turned to Kit. He clutched his hand.

"Did you do this?" Nya asked.

Kit laughed louder now. Almost hysterical.

He reached out towards her and Nya drew upon Bom. It returned to her and threw up a wall of shadow, pushing everything and everyone away. She just wanted to be alone. A dark shroud leaked off of her filling the streets until it covered all of Yontar.

Then, she was back in the throne room, surrounded by the company that brought her here.

Do you see? Everyone has darkness, Nya. They cannot help you.

There is no escaping one's shadow.

Nya dropped to one knee and bowed her head.

Then the dark took her.

53

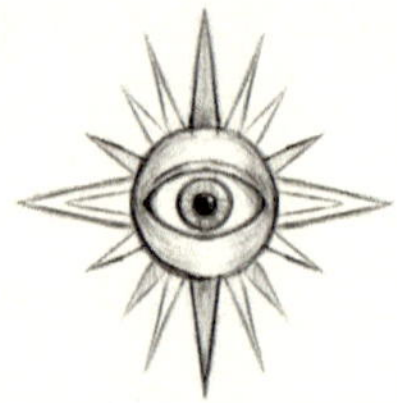

The Research Project

5 years ago.

Raucous laughter rose above the buzz of the city night life. The scent of coffee blended with the herbal smoke of furthing leaf pipes that poured from the shuttered windows of the coffeehouses. Akarai sat with Genu and Ada at a table outside the Curled Steam; a coffeehouse on a street corner near the palace walls. Above was the Strip, a band of shops placed along the top of the wall encircling the Thousand Floor Palace.

Sipping his coffee, Akarai cleared his mind and took in the city of Yontar. The Moon Eye's watch had just begun but already people filled the streets. Ada and Genu flicked a small rock back and forth across the table. Genu cheered as it hit Ada's mug of coffee.

Akarai downed the last of his coffee and stood.

"Let's go."

Patrols around the palace walls passed regularly, making it

impossible to climb during the short time between guards passing. At least, by normal means. Turning into a quiet alley, the three waited until a patrolling set of guards passed. The second the two guards stepped around the corner and Akarai ran at the wall. He loosed an arrow that had a specially designed grappling hook tip. The arrow flew upward, attached to a piece of rope and caught on the lip of the wall. Akarai tugged the rope to ensure it stayed in place before pulling himself up.

They only had minutes before the next patrol appeared. Not long enough to climb the entire wall by hand. After clambering up a good bit of the way, Akarai unsheathed a diera short sword and twirled it. A gust of wind blasted from the end of the blade launching Akarai up the side of the wall. Guiding himself with the rope, the torrent lifted Akarai all the way to the top of the wall where he grabbed onto the edge and pulled the rope up just as the next patrol appeared.

Genu and Ada repeated the process between patrols until they all clambered onto the Strip. It was quieter up here with only a few shops and cafes still open. Using the window ledges, they climbed onto a closed fruit merchant shop and from there they gazed upon the Thousand Floor Palace. The menacing monolithic building was lit up in firelight from within. The first several floors didn't have balconies but after that they circled the entire palace all the way up. Below a busy courtyard was bustling with guards and nobles coming to and from the palace.

Akarai launched an arrow across to one of the lower balconies. They were several stories up now, and with the Moon Eye still low in the sky the darkness hid them. Tying the other end of the rope to the rooftop, Genu pulled the curved metal bars from her pack and handed one to Ada and then one to Akarai.

Akarai nodded and pointed to Ada, who grinned. He leapt from the rooftop, the metal bar catching on the rope as he dropped. The rope went taut and he shot across the courtyard towards the palace. Genu went next zipping down to where Ada had signalled was clear.

After Genu sent the okay, Akarai slipped from the rooftop. The bar hissed as he flew down towards the balcony. The speed made his eyes water. Glancing down, Akarai noted that he wouldn't survive a fall from this height. His hands tightened on the bar. He crashed into the balcony beside the other two and he was sent tumbling across the ground.

"We really need to find a way to slow these things down," Genu said rubbing her shoulder. Akarai pushed to his feet and peered over the edge. No one in the courtyard seemed to have seen them. He tossed the bar to Genu, who put it back in her pack.

The balcony was a wide walkway that curved around the building and out of sight. Further to their right was an opening that led deeper into the palace. Akarai pulled out the map from his belt pocket and unfurled it.

"I think we need to get higher and further right," Akarai said. He turned and the other two had already changed into their servant outfits. Ada handed Akarai his and he quickly changed.

"Follow me and don't kill anyone unless I say to," Akarai said and stalked towards the opening.

Equidistant braziers lit the sandstone corridors. They took corners at random and had to double back more than once to find a through path. At each corner they left a mark cut into the stone to make sure they weren't walking around in circles, and to allow the others to follow their path should their party be the ones to find the scholars first.

All the corridors looked the same further adding to the disorientation. It was all by design of course. Most of the servants and guards they passed had tight expressions as if they were concentrating on a difficult problem. *No doubt remembering the route they've been told to walk,* Akarai thought.

As Akarai had hoped, the other servants didn't give them a second glance. With a palace of this size, there was no way they could all know one another.

They wandered for what seemed like hours. No one stopped to question the three of them as they strode with purpose. They climbed several flights of stairs and Akarai was convinced they had to be close to the research room and yet they didn't come across any guards. In fact, they could walk down some stretches of corridor and not hear or see a soul for the best part of an hour.

It was eerie. Like being alone in a stone maze. Irrational thoughts started to bubble up in the isolation. Could they find their way back out? What if they got lost wandering the corridors of the Thousand Floor Palace forever?

They were walking down one of these long, empty stretches when Akarai felt a pull at his belt. Glancing down, he saw that one of the pieces of diera ore shook. The small ore spheres were infused with refin blood. The same blood that could be used to control the flight of arrows. Akarai had suggested that they could also be used as short-range communication devices. By having one party keep a drop of the same refin's blood that infused the sphere they could use it to move a shard of the same ore in close range. Each party had two spheres for each of the two companies and whoever located the research room first could use the blood to shake the other ore and indicate they had found the target. They weren't sure how far the bloods range could reach but it looked like they were close.

Akarai pointed to it and Ada clapped. "About time!"

"That's Sehban and Kyan's ore right?" Genu asked. Akarai nodded checking the markings on the black sphere.

"They entered from the far side. So the room must be accessible from that direction. We'll head straight through and try to pick up their trail," Akarai said.

Breaking into a jog, they pushed through the palace to reach the other side. Before they reached it, Genu spotted the first mark. Akarai felt the two indentations on the corner. Two swipes chipped into a sandstone corner at ankle level.

They followed the marks. Much like they had done, Sehban and Kyan had meandered through the corridors, up flights of stairs just to come back down after a corridor or two. Several times Akarai followed the marks to dead ends just to learn they had doubled back and they had to retrace their steps to find where Sehban and Kyan redirected. Eventually, other servants and guards started populating the passageways again.

Passing around a corner, Akarai spotted Kyan arguing with two guards at a doorway. Sehban met his gaze but was smart enough to keep his face neutral.

"I don't know what to tell you," Kyan was saying, "We were told to clear empty dishes."

"And as I've told you, they have yet to have their meals so there won't be any empty dishes," one of the guards said.

"What about snacks? Coffee mugs?" Kyan asked.

Akarai, Genu, and Ada walked past the confrontation without so much as a glance. Then, once they were out of sight, they waited around the corner.

"What now?" Genu asked.

"Wait for Kyan," Akarai said pressed against the wall, ears perked. The arguing continued for several more moments before the guard gave up and threw the doors open.

"You have thirty seconds," the guard said. "And don't bother the scholars."

Akarai smiled.

A minute later Sehban and Kyan came around the corner. Kyan was holding a single coffee mug.

"Two guards at the door, four inside. There must have been six scholars rushing about. I couldn't see anything resembling a weapon but there was a staircase at the far side of the room that led down and two guards were blocking the way," Kyan said.

"They must have a separate room for the weapon," Akarai said.

"But how do we get in?" Genu asked. "They won't fall for the servant clearing dishes again."

"Killing time?" Ada started bouncing.

Akarai sighed. He had hoped it wouldn't come to this but it had taken too long to locate the room. They didn't have enough time to figure out another way in. He nodded.

"Yes!" Ada shouted.

"Not the scholars," Akarai said. "Just the guards. Quick and quiet."

The others nodded. Tysar and Neyla hadn't caught up yet but

they wouldn't be far behind. The company turned the corner and stalked back towards the guards.

"Now, I told you once," one of the guards started. Ada thrust his sword into the man's chest as Sehban swung his war hammer shattering the other guard's skull with a sickening crack.

Standing in front of the door, Akarai counted to three before kicking it open. The others swept into the room weapons raised. Genu loosed an arrow and it tore through the jugular of one guard then arced around and embedded itself in another's gut.

Ada howled with laughter as he launched himself onto the closest guard, two short swords spinning in his grip. The final guard screamed as Sehban's war hammer ripped through his shoulder and collapsed the man's torso.

"If you're quiet, we won't hurt you," Akarai said to the scholars. They whimpered and cowered by their desks but nodded acquiescence. The chamber was as Kyan had described; a small room with desks against the walls on either side and a huge staircase leading downward straight ahead of the entrance.

Kyan raked through their notes as Akarai approached the scholar who was shaking the least and dropped to his haunches beside the woman. "What's down there?"

She wore a simple grey tunic and trousers. Her long black hair was streaked with grey. "The... the tear."

"Tear?"

She nodded.

"What's that?" Akarai asked.

"A doorway," Kyan said holding aloft some notes. Akarai inspected them. It described a dark landscape with strange creatures they had named husks hidden behind a portal to another realm. It was ridiculous.

"Wrangle them up," Akarai said. "I want to see this tear."

The scholars claimed there were no guards down the stairs. To be safe, they sent the scholars down first. A draft carried up the staircase, howling. The seven clasped their weapons moving silently downward. Despite claiming that it was safe, the scholars moved with furtive steps, nervously glancing at one another.

"What do you think?" Akarai asked Kyan. His eyes had glazed over as they often did when he was deep in thought. He came to, focusing on Akarai.

"I don't know." He clutched the notes but he hadn't looked at them again. "They call it a doorway to a cave and this strange black landscape. But that's impossible. We're in the middle of the palace. It doesn't make sense."

"No, it doesn't."

Reaching the bottom of the staircase, Akarai raised his daggers as the scholars stepped into the room. They all stopped short gawking at what they found, their weapons falling to their sides.

The chamber was empty aside from a black tear. It was like someone tore into the air as if it was made of fabric. The black rend pulled in the nearby light, darkening the entire far side of the chamber. The flames in the braziers leaned towards it like they were being drawn into that black rip in existence itself.

"What is *that*?" Kyan asked.

"We don't know," one of the scholars said. "We've been studying it."

"Is it safe?" Genu didn't move any closer towards it.

"Yes, we've had people go through it and they appear in another place," one scholar said. "You should go in and see."

"The dark place is dangerous," another scholar said.

"Rikt!" the other scholar snapped.

"What? I don't want to be responsible for more death," Rikt said. "I didn't sign up for this."

"What's inside?" Akarai asked.

"Bat-like creatures. Other things too. Things we've never seen before," Rikt said. "They keep killing the parties we send in. Few have made it back."

That's why they were asking for soldiers in the note, Akarai realised. *They have been sending them inside.* But what was it? How could they use it as a weapon? Were they training these husks? They had to enter and see.

"Let's move," Akarai said.

"What?!" Genu asked. The others looked equally concerned.

"We can't return until we know if it's a threat," Akarai said. "Scholars in first."

"No! We'll be slaughtered!" one of the scholars screamed. With a hiss of movement, Ada held his short sword to the man's neck. He went quiet then.

There was no way to tell if the tear could be opened and closed, and while the scholars claimed they couldn't be locked inside, Akarai wasn't going to trust their word. So he asked Genu to stay watch in the chamber. She would also update Tysar and Neyla when they caught up.

Akarai, Sehban, Ada, and Kyan walked in a line, corralling

the scholars towards the rend. As they moved closer Akarai felt heat emitting from the black tear. It was like a black Sun Eye. The darkness seemed to swirl but it had to be an illusion because it was too dark to hold shape. And yet it was transfixing as they moved ever closer. The scholars glanced to one another, no doubt contemplating their chances of facing them or these *husks*. Ada prodded one of the scholars with his sword and they cringed as they stepped into the tear.

Akarai watched with fascination as they stretched like they were being sucked into the tear until the scholar had completely vanished. He had never seen anything like it.

One by one, the scholars disappeared and next it was Akarai's turn. Wandering up to the rend the heat was becoming unbearable. It burned more and more with each step until he worried that it would burn his skin off before he even reached it. He let out a slow exhale and plunged into the black.

For a moment, everything was dark. But then reality faded into view. The scholars were nothing more than shadowy shapes but he recognised the six of them. And it was now cool. Almost cold. A whistling wind bustled through them.

"Where are we?" Akarai asked.

"It's a cave," a scholar said. "The exit is that way." Akarai could just make out the scholar pointing onward.

The others passed through and they pushed on through the cave. Blinding light indicated an opening and they crept out wary of their surroundings. Outside was not Tarris. It was a landscape of black rock and grey scree. The sky was a tempest of swirling clouds. It was rare to get any clouds over Tarris but here there was no sky, just a roiling cover of dark clouds.

"What is this place?" Sebhan asked.

"The pocket world," a scholar whispered. "We had a camp set among those rock formations but the researchers pulled back after an attack. I think it's near a nest."

Akarai surveyed the horizon for movement but he didn't see any sign of life. It was like the dead black sands of night but during the day. *If you can call this day*, Akarai thought looking at the ever-storming sky.

"Keep your eyes open for movement," Akarai said.

"We aren't leaving the cave!" the scholar said. "They'll come!"

"I want to see this nest," Akarai said. Sebhan, Ada, and even Kyan—who was fascinated by study of this kind—shifted uncomfortably. They thought they'd seen enough too, Akarai realised. They could take back what they knew to Imayani. Why risk going deeper into this unknown land?

Akarai thought of returning to Tansen. Of what might be waiting for him. Banishment? Death? What if she pretended like nothing happened? Somehow that was worse. He couldn't live like that. No, he wasn't ready to return yet.

"We go on."

The scree was sent skittering down the bank from the cave entrance as they crept downward and the sky rumbled.

"What have you been studying?" Akarai asked coming to the side of one of the scholars. She looked nervously about, unsure if she should be talking to him.

"Uh. Everything, really. The rocks. Any creatures we find. We've explored pretty far."

"How long has this been here?" Akarai asked.

"The research project started a couple months ago and this hadn't been here long before that. But I don't know how it appeared. Only the head scholars know," she said.

"Are any of the scholars here head scholars?"

She shook her head.

That would have been too easy, Akarai thought.

They arrived at what was left of their encampment. Remnants of black tents lay strewn against a plateau of rock. There were no bodies or research equipment but there had clearly been an attack. Akarai lifted the torn fabric. Gashes had been ripped through the sturdy material. He thought back to his classes under Overseer Rikai of the many creatures that could have caused this. But there was too little information. He looked toward the horizon line.

"Where do you think this nest is?" Akarai asked.

"Do you have a death wish? Look at what's left of the camp! They even ate the bodies!" one of the scholars shouted. Another forced their eyes closed as tears streamed down his face.

Kyan stepped up to Akarai and leant in. "I think they're right. This isn't worth the risk. We aren't going to figure this out ourselves. We need to return to Tansen and let Imayani know of what we've found."

Akarai sighed and looked around the others. "Ada, hold the scholar." Ada glanced up and grinned. Bounding into action, Ada grabbed one of the scholars by the hair and pressed a throwing knife to their throat.

"No! Please!" another scholar ran for the man that Ada held but Sebhan blocked the scholar's path.

Wandering up slowly, Akarai let the scholar sweat a little. "What battle applications have you been using this place for?"

The scholar's eyes went wide.

"Ada," Akarai said and Ada added some pressure to the blade, drawing blood.

"The creatures! The husks! Some of the overseers think they can be trained," the scholar cried out. She collapsed to her knees. "Please. We are just researchers and they don't tell us everything. We've been told to study the flora and fauna for battle applications."

It was as Akarai suspected. He looked to Kyan who glanced away. The boy was still young. He would need to learn that results often came from questionable means.

"Ada, release the scholar. We need to find this nest."

They marched further south. The ground became more uneven and huge black rock formations towered around them. The sky growled making it difficult to listen out for movement.

The scholars claimed the nest was likely around these tall stone pillar-like formations. Then, they heard a rustle of movement. Akarai lifted his finger to his lips silencing the others. They looked around uneasily. Kyan pointed upward. Glancing up, Akarai noticed movement atop one of the black rock towers.

The party rushed up to the rock pressing against it.

"They must have a nest atop these plateaus," Kyan whispered.

The scholars looked petrified, eyes round and mouths agape. The rustling stopped and everything went quiet. They waited a moment longer before Akarai turned to the group.

"Kyan, Ada, stay here with the scholars. Sebhan and I will climb up to get a look."

54

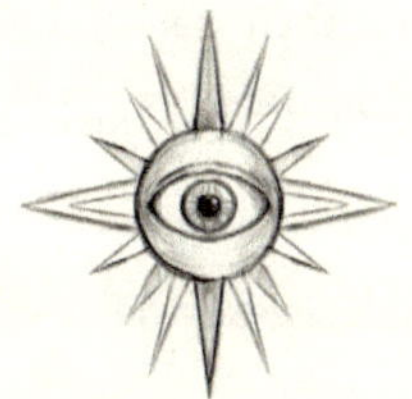

Backs Against the Wall

5 years ago.

Akarai pulled himself onto a ridge with Sebhan close behind. They were halfway up the plateau of black rock. It was unlike anything Akarai had ever seen. The dark stone had a purple tinge to it and it was smooth and almost glass-like to touch. From their perch, Akarai got a better look at the landscape around them. The rock formations looked to be natural and random from ground level but from up here he could see what looked to be remnants of structures. A lot had eroded but the way it was all laid out spoke of a design and not naturally occurring shapes. In the distance, everything was darkening on the horizon. All light seemed to be pulling into a single point.

"What is it?" Sebhan asked.

Shaking off the thought, Akarai turned back to the tower they were climbing. "Nothing." They clambered the top of the plateau and hung by their fingertips, listening. Above everything was quiet. Akarai signalled for Sebhan to stay put and then lifted himself up.

He froze at the sight before him.

The plateau's top was shaped like a crater and spaced out around the bowl was more than thirty bat-like creatures. The husks. They lay unmoving their eyes closed. Their bodies were black as night, ragged wings hung from their backs, and they had razor sharp talons curled up beneath them. The husks face was almost human-like but their nose and mouth stuck out in a short snout.

Sebhan came to his side, eyes wide.

"What are they?" he asked.

"*Shh*, they're sleeping," Akarai said.

He was about to gesture for Sebhan to climb back down when something stirred. Akarai spun toward the movement but it hadn't been one of the husks. In the centre of the crater was a pool of inky blackness. He hadn't realised it before because it blended into the rock. It shifted like water. Ripples of pure black. *What is that?* Akarai wondered.

He had to know what it was.

Akarai sidestepped towards the centre of the nest. Sebhan hissed his name but Akarai waved him away as he crept among the sleeping husks. They let out quiet growls in their sleep. His heart hammered in his chest. What was he *doing*?

He came to the epicentre of the crater and ducked. The black was even more mesmerising up close. It wasn't the same as the black of the tear. The tear was a void into eternity but this puddle of darkness was… comforting. Before he knew what he was doing, Akarai reached out and touched the shadow. It shot up his arm and

Akarai stumbled backwards suppressing a shout.

Then the darkness vanished.

He glanced over his shoulder trying to see if it clung to his back. It wasn't there but he felt it. It was on him like an icy hand on his neck. Akarai flailed in an attempt to shake it off. Something caught his foot and he was sent tumbling. Akarai tripped over one of the creatures and the husk squealed. He glanced up to a confused creature opening beady red eyes.

"Akarai," Sebhan said.

The husk howled and others stirred.

"Run." Akarai pushed back towards the edge as the husks came to their senses and stretched their wings. "Run!"

In a rush of motion, Sebhan dropped out of sight, Akarai kicked backward and clambered to his feet. The husks screamed. One shot towards him in a black blur. Akarai whipped out his daggers catching the creature's talons more by instinct than thought. He shoved hard and the beast was pushed back.

Akarai sheathed his daggers and leapt from the plateau.

Husks took to the air in a flurry of black and red. Falling backwards, Akarai unslung his bow and loosed an arrow at the husk who dove after him. It tore through the creature's wing and it squealed crashing into the stone. Turning, he loosed a diera arrow that displaced some of the momentum letting Akarai land unharmed.

The others were running back towards the cave mouth when the husks descended. Akarai ran towards them loosing arrows at any husk that got close. One dove at the group but Sebhan swung his war hammer battering the creature away. The sky was filled with the beasts. Their wings flapping and claws gleaming in the pale light of the storming sky.

The husks rushed at their group and circled the party. Akarai could only watch as he ran towards them, feral screams sounding from within their cloud of black wings.

He barreled into the swirling husks. Inside was a cacophony of high-pitched squeals. Kyan spun his spear around as it pulsed with energy. Akarai tried to push to Kyan's side but Sebhan's scream stole his attention. He spun to the behemoth of a man protecting one of the scholars. The husks glided past leaving gashes along the man's arm. They were wearing him down as he moved back and forth trying to keep the husks away from the innocent scholar. Akarai charged towards him flicking his diera blades in a wide arc. Flames plumed outward and the husks howled breaking their formation.

"Run!" Akarai shouted at the scholar. Her frenzied eyes met his and she sprinted for the cave mouth. In the distance, Ada was with the remaining scholar. Four of the six were already dead.

Sebhan nodded his thanks and they fell in back-to-back. Akarai was about to shout to Kyan but he was *gone*. His spear lay discarded on the stone and he was nowhere to be seen. Akarai's breath caught at the sight.

They even ate the bodies!

The scholar's words came crashing down. A pit opened in Akarai's gut but he steeled himself. He couldn't breakdown now or they would all die. Grief clawed its way up the back of his throat.

Focus! Akarai screamed in his mind. He had to focus on the task at hand.

"Sebhan," Akarai said and gestured to their feet. The big guy grinned in understanding. He lifted his hammer above his head and cracked it down on the ground. Fissures opened along the stone and a puff of dust billowed into the air blinding the beasts. Then Akarai twirled his daggers. He didn't have time to swap out to the blood in his diera weapons but he could make this work. Spinning his dagger, a swirling vortex of fire sucked in the dirt and dust and drew the husks in. Their screams rang in Akarai's mind. Then the vortex blasted outward in an explosion of dead husks and embers.

Husks flew at his back but Sebhan swept in with his war hammer and smashed them into pieces. Together they sliced flesh and shattered bone but the husks kept coming. It was endless. Akarai twisted his blades but no flames erupted from the end of them. His blood had run out.

In the distance, Akarai saw more black dots appear against the grey skies. They were going to die here. The realisation came with a sense of calm. Akarai began to slow, his muscles aching. Behind him, Sebhan grunted as he fought on. Guilt flared in Akarai's mind. Sebhan was another he couldn't save. Akarai would die failing another of his friends.

A talon ripped through Akarai's shoulder. He screamed spinning with the force of the blow and toppling over. Another husk swooped in.

The flash of silvered talons. Akarai closed his eyes.

A feral scream. A moment passed.

Opening his eyes, Akarai saw Tysar standing before him swishing his blade back and forth against the darkness.

You aren't dead yet, a voice whispered. Akarai turned assuming it had been Sebhan but he was crying out as he killed husk after husk. His imagination perhaps.

Neyla laid a hand on his shoulder. "Are you hurt?" she asked.

"No."

Dragging himself to his feet, Imayani's words rang in his mind. *What else is there?* What else was there but to get up? Was he going to lie here and let his friends die? Was he going to betray the years of training, his life's mission?

Moments of weakness are inevitable. It isn't that strong people don't have moments where they question everything. It isn't that they don't slip up. What makes them strong is taking the hit and getting back up.

The four of them stood back-to-back. Akarai glanced at Sebhan, Tysar and Neyla. He felt like he should say something. Bolster them. But when he met their eyes Akarai saw that it wasn't necessary. They were resigned to fight to the death. As was he.

The husks barrelled towards them.

Weapons lashed out in a seamless flow battering away the creatures. The torrent of husks around them squealed and howled in frustration as one by one they fell from the sky. Neyla used her diera spear which was charged up with energy. The power shocked the husks then arced and zapped those around it too. The ground shook with Sebhan's war hammer. And gusts of wind, sent out by Tysar, threw the husks off course.

But they kept coming.

"We need to inform Imayani!" Tysar called over the screams.

He was right. If the Yontar monarch learned a way to train these things, they could attack the capital. Akarai's mind whirled. They weren't all going to make it.

"Sebhan, throw up a dust cloud and Neyla zap them with your

spear! I'll hold them off as you all run for the cave!" Akarai shouted.

"We can't leave you!" Neyla said.

"Imayani must know. Just cover me and I'll catch up," Akarai said.

Tysar looked conflicted. He knew that Akarai had no intention of catching up but he also knew this was the only way any of them were getting out alive. Akarai gave him a reassuring nod and Tysar steeled himself. Then Akarai pulled back a latch on the bottom of his diera daggers and poured the contents of a vial inside. This blood wasn't meant for daggers and he wasn't sure of what the effect would be like but it was all he had left.

"Sebhan, now!"

The war hammer cracked the ground sending out a fissure and plume of dust clouds. Neyla stabbed into the mass of husks her diera spear sending arcs of energy jumping between the beasts. The husks shrieked. Some backed off and others were caught in the dust cloud whipping back and forth uncontrollably.

"Run!" Akarai shouted.

Tysar nodded and grabbed Neyla. Together they sprinted for the cave. "Sebhan, you too," Akarai said.

"No," he replied. "I stay with you."

Akarai was about to argue but thought better of it. Sebhan's expression told him that he had made his decision and there was no changing it. The big guy heaved his war hammer and Akarai readied himself.

"What's the plan?" Sebhan asked.

"We burn them to the ground."

"Good plan."

"Put this in your war hammer." Akarai tossed him his last vial of blood.

Tysar and Neyla had made it a good distance towards the cave.

"Ready?" Akarai asked.

Sebhan closed up the end of his war hammer and threw away the empty vial. The dust cleared and the husks regrouped. Some squawked as they noticed Tysar and Neyla had escaped. Just before they shot off after them, Akarai shouted, "Now!"

He thrust his daggers into the nearest husk and Sebhan slammed his hammer into the ground.

Everything went white in the explosion.

He had used the bomb arrow blood but they had never tested it on weapons like this as it was too dangerous.

Akarai was weightless as the blow sent him flying through the air. The explosion blew out his ears and there was silence. He felt something crack as he hit a rock. His ears rang as the world came back into view. Some of the husks were far enough back that they avoided the blast and were darting towards Tysar and Neyla. They had their backs turned. Akarai tried to call out. No sound came.

A husk ripped into Neyla, cleaving her head from her body.

The ringing masked Tysar's scream but Akarai saw the pain on his face. Bulging veins pulsed on his face and neck. He attacked the husk stabbing it over and over again as it fed on Neyla. The husk writhed and then fell, unmoving. Tysar breathed hard, eyes wide and unseeing.

Akarai managed a rasped shout. His friend looked up. Something registered in his dead gaze and he stumbled into the cave. Good.

At least Imayani would learn the truth.

The horror of what had happened numbed the pain. Akarai understood that he was in shock but couldn't find a way to shake it.

A hand yanked Akarai upward. Sebhan appeared in front of him. He shook Akarai and screamed something. Before Akarai knew what was going on they were hurtling towards the cave with the tear, husks hounding at their back. The scree spat out behind them as they ran. The looming presence of the husks above them was worse than the pain of their claws shredding into their backs.

Approaching the cave's mouth, Sebhan shoved Akarai inside and turned to the husks, blocking the entrance. Akarai watched as his friend was ripped apart in front of him. He died in an instant and they set on devouring him.

Splashes of blood and gore sloshed as it hit the stone. Akarai kicked away from the cave entrance scrambling into the dark. He groaned coming to his feet and pushing through the black.

The sound of crunching bones silenced. Akarai sped up. The warmth of the tear told him he was getting close. A too close howl from the husks told him they were in the cave. Akarai screamed as a talon pierced his arm and he tripped into the rend.

Then the palace chamber came into view.

The warm torchlight was a familiar comfort compared to the pale light of the pocket world. Akarai stumbled away from the tear not taking his eyes from it. But after a few moments, it was clear that the husks hadn't—or couldn't—follow him through the tear. Akarai didn't know how long he lay there as his mind caught up to him.

So many dead. Sebhan. Neyla. Kyan.

He didn't know if Ada had survived. Tysar and Genu were the only two he was sure had made it out alive. And the rest had died because of him. He had forced them into the rend. He had forced them onward when they made it clear they didn't think it was the right choice. Akarai had always listened to them before. Why hadn't he this time? What was wrong with him?

You need to move. Guards will arrive soon, a voice said.

Akarai spun, eyes searching for the source of the voice. He looked back to the tear.

Nope. I'm in your head.

The black blur.

"What are you?" Akarai asked.

We don't have time. Quickly, before the guards come.

Part of Akarai told him to stay. To let the guards take him in or kill him.

I can hear your thoughts, Akarai.

Another part of Akarai ached to move. To escape. Imayani had been right about one thing when she asked him to join the seven.

He was a survivor.

Pushing to his feet, the pain flooded in. Akarai reached for his belt. He took out a vial of blood and downed the draught. It would quieten the pain for now.

Akarai skulked through the Thousand Floor Palace. He dipped into the shadowed corners as guards passed. None ran towards the tear. They didn't seem to be aware of the seven yet. That would change very soon.

He found the closest open balcony and stepped out into the cool night. The Moon Eye stared at him accusingly. He should have died. It should have been any of the others that escaped and yet it was him. Again. Why did he keep surviving? Why did everyone around him always end up dead?

Akarai clasped the railing with both hands and dipped his head.

"I can't."

You can't what? the voice asked.

"Go back. Nothing waits for me there." Tysar would inform Imayani of the tear and the dangers it held. He wasn't wanted there any longer.

And yet…

The seven had been tasked to learn more about this weapon. And Akarai now had something from it in his head. He could study it. Learn all there was about the black blur and the dark place behind the rend in existence.

He was running from everything and everyone. It was cowardly and he didn't care. This is what he needed to do. If he learnt anything useful he would return to Tansen. He was still protecting Tarris. Protecting Imayani. And this way he wasn't a danger to them.

He could cut all ties to his past. Over the years, bonds formed no matter what Akarai had done to avoid them. Connections. Friendships. Love. And one by one, they snapped and stole parts of him. He had nothing left to give. No, he wouldn't go back. He couldn't go back.

Akarai dies tonight, he thought.

Rai fired a grappling hook arrow into the stone above and leapt over the edge.

55

Smoke and Shades

Rai crashed into the crater. The air was knocked from his lungs even with Fax softening the blow. Tysar floated down after him. His shade lowering him slowly to the ground.

"You might have been stronger than me back in the day," Tysar said. "But you've spent five years wandering around Tarris. I spent that time training."

Fax burst into shadowy tendrils but Tysar's shade cut each down in turn. Rai pushed to his feet and slid out his daggers. Now was as good a time as any to use his diera blades. He flicked the daggers sending a wave of flames at Tysar. Then he charged.

Rai dove through the fire as it hit Tysar. Tysar's sword sent a gust of wind deflecting the worst of the fire away from him. But he didn't expect Rai to barrel into him. Tysar stumbled, battering back Rai's daggers.

"You side with Kleran? After all that Imayani has done for us?" Rai roared. He hadn't realised the anger that his friend's betrayal brought out in him until he heard the rage in his voice.

"This isn't about Imayani or Kleran," Tysar said.

"Why, then?"

"You can't tell me you don't feel it." The two circled one another. The cracked crater of Asuriya their arena. "Your shade knows. It can feel the presence in the pocket world."

"What has that got to do with abandoning your empress?"

Their shades threw out cracking lashes at one another, testing their guards. "They're just people, Rai. Have you ignored the voice calling to you? Imayani is a good woman and leader. While Kleran is a power-hungry fool. But the Dark is returning. It is our true emperor."

Rai shook his head. He couldn't believe what he was hearing. "You're letting it infect your mind, Tysar."

"We will see."

Tysar shot at Rai with unnatural speed using his shade to thrust him forward. Rai threw up a wall of shadow knocking them out of the air. As Fax intercepted Tysar's shade, Rai lunged whipping his daggers around in an ancient complex form, but Tysar had known him for most of his life and knew all his tricks.

They were locked in combat, only scoring light slashes on one another. But with each back and forth Rai was losing ground and being nicked more than inflicting any damage.

They're strong! Fax said and Rai tuned in to feel it struggling against Tysar's shade as much as he was against the man.

We need to draw them into the city, Rai thought. With the chaos of battle they could even the odds.

Fax slid under the cracks in the crater. Tysar's eyebrows raised as his shade must have told him about Fax's retreat. A second later, the ground beneath him erupted in a shower of stone. Rai dove back letting a cloud of dust plume before turning and running into Asuriya's inner city.

Buildings were alight and bodies lay strewn through the streets. Rai coughed, waving away the smoke that left little to see by. He narrowly avoided a stray arrow that came from the haze. Rai leapt over a body and ducked into an alleyway.

Slow footsteps echoed from behind.

"Don't be a coward, Rai," Tysar said.

"A coward is one turning on all they love for a promise of strength," Rai said. Fax sent the vibrations of his voice through the shadows around the street dispersing it and making it impossible for Tysar to locate the source. It was a simpler version of what Kyan had done at the inn all those months ago where his shade created a projection of himself. Rai hadn't managed to master that trick but Fax *could* send his voice ricocheting through the darkness.

The ring of steel and howls of war surrounded them. Two men burst out of the smoke, swords clashing against one another. Black spikes struck them from the shadows and both fell to the ground dead. One must have been Kleran's soldiers and yet Tysar killed them both anyway.

Rai crept around the building, doubling back.

"Don't pretend you care about the throne. You love Imayani, that's all," Tysar said. "I was there, remember? You said yourself that she didn't want to become empress."

"And yet she took up the mantle anyway."

A black whip lashed out snapping at the corner Rai had been standing at moments before.

"You've seen it!" Frustration was leaking into Tysar's words now. "The other world. You've felt the power of the dark there. You can't still think men are meant to rule when such power exists."

"What did it promise you, Tysar?" Rai cut down another alley and peeked around the corner.

"Peace," Tysar said.

Rai hesitated.

"Aren't you sick of this war? Even in times of peace those leading are at each other's throats. They drag orphans from the orphanages and train them up to become soldiers. Then they throw them into bloody battles over titles and money that they will never see. Why should we care who sits upon the throne? We could have had a peaceful life. We should have a peaceful life. Instead we've become weapons for those who ensure us they are our betters."

He was right. Flashes of the brutal training they had gone through growing up flitted through Rai's mind.

He frowned. This felt familiar. And yet… something about this situation was wrong.

"The histories say we've had hundreds of years of peace in Tarris but we both know that is a lie. The ruling powers squabble like children hiding it from the people," Tysar said.

"You know Imayani is fighting to stop that."

Tysar laughed. "For now. They're just people, Rai. You know as well as I that it won't last."

Suddenly Rai realized why this felt so familiar.

"You sound just like Kyan," Rai said. It was more to himself than to Tysar but Fax sent the words skittering through the shadows anyway.

"The boy was always smart," Tysar replied.

"No, you don't understand. I agree with you in many ways. Tarris deserves better. But we're being manipulated. This darkness infects our thoughts and preys on our weaknesses. You've had your shade long enough to know that it feeds on emotion, flaring when you're upset or angry. They're in our heads, Tysar. This *darkness* from the other world is in our heads. It's trying to divide us. Influence us into following its will.

"It did the same with Kyan. The boy was always fixated on the injustices of the world but Kyan would never have endangered others without outside influence! That was the Dark, Tysar. And it's doing the same to us!"

His friend went quiet.

"Perhaps you're right. Perhaps it is strengthening certain thoughts. But just like with shades, they cannot put ideas into our heads, only enhance them. Which means they can still be right," Tysar said. "We have to end it, Rai. This war in the shadows will be the end of Tarris unless we stop it."

Rai peered back around the corner and Tysar was right there, facing him. Rai jerked back as a swish of shadow whisked past his face. Then Tysar pushed around the corner. Steel clashed against steel and shadow against shadow as the two friends traded blows. They moved out into the main thoroughfare.

Tysar's sword slipped beneath Rai's guard and tore across his side. It was only a graze but a blinding pain shot through him. Rai knocked the sword away and attempted to get a hit on Tysar as he relished his blow. Tysar had always been one to celebrate too early. But his cross guard whipped around and deflected Rai's daggers.

"Old tricks won't work anymore," Tysar said, grinning.

Rai growled and lunged. Every attack was parried. Every guard broken. Rai hated to admit it but he was no match for his old friend. They both drove forward, blades grating against one another as they drew closer.

"You've gotten slow in your old age." Tysar was inches from Rai.

Tromping footsteps were followed by an aya charging out of the smoke and down the thoroughfare. Its platform was alight in flame and there was no rider upon its back. Rai shoved Tysar and leapt backward as the aya stormed past them. The second it passed he darted at Tysar in a wave of shadow.

They tore down the street, their shades keeping their forward motion. Blades clattered to the ground in the close quarters and they resolved to a fist fight.

"Can't you see that this isn't us!" Rai shouted.

They barrelled down a thoroughfare riding a torrent of shadow, battering against fighting soldiers and hyian.

"You're stubborn, Rai. I won't ask you to join me because I know you won't. However, I am sorry it had to end this way."

Their shadowy tendril burst through a wall. Stone erupted in all directions as they crashed out the other side. The damage was enough to destroy the foundations and send the top two floors of the building crashing to the ground. Dust mixed with smoke and shadow.

They bounced against buildings, spinning around so the other would take the brunt of the collisions. Tysar forced Rai down. He pressed Rai into the ground as they skidded through the sand-strewn streets. He screamed. Fax slid under Rai's back to minimise the damage but rocks, bodies and whatever else lay on the ground scraped against Rai as they flew down the thoroughfare. Agony burned through his back and sent his mind reeling. Tysar gritted his teeth as he held Rai down and the world blinked in and out of focus.

Eventually they slid to a stop, their shades dispersing and returning to their shadows. Rai dragged in breaths and his body trembled and throbbed.

Tysar stood over him. He knew Rai was spent.

Rai lay there waiting for Tysar to try and convert him. To ask Rai to join him. To try and convince him that this was the only way. Instead, he spat a glob of blood off to the side and said, "You don't know what it's like to live in your shadow."

Tysar's shoulders slumped.

"You don't understand what it's like to never be good enough. I trained so hard." His voice was hoarse. "I out competed everyone. Everyone but you. You're so damn stubborn. You never gave up no matter how hard I pressed. You couldn't fall behind me once!"

Rai's mind was reeling with the pain and confusion of Tysar's words. "I—"

"Don't say a word. I don't want to hear it. You pushed yourself because that was all you had. Is that what you are going to say? None of us had anything! And none of us could gain anything because you were always on top. Selected by the emperor's daughter right from the start." Tysar was breathing harder than he had been as they fought.

"The emperor asked me to kill you." Tysar's voice was quiet.

The crackle of flames and cries of battle still rung around the city. But they all fell away as Rai forced his eyes to focus on Tysar. He couldn't believe what he was hearing. Why wouldn't Tysar have told him? The betrayal stung more than any wound.

"He asked me to kill you during training. Before we left for the Verdin Guild. Make it look like an accident, he said." Tysar glanced down. "I told him I couldn't kill a brother. I begged him to just send us away. I said I'd make sure you never came back.

"We never earned our place at the Verdin Guild, Rai. I think he expected us to die on the way. But you got us there. Despite everything, it was you who made sure we survived. And I hated you for it. And loved you like a brother for it. I knew then I could never be as good as you.

"Why couldn't you have just stayed dead?"

Those words stung like no lashing ever could.

"Go back to wherever you've been the last five years, Rai. Please. I don't want to have to put you down properly this time."

Then he turned and stumbled into the smoke of the city.

Rai lay there dazed. The broken buildings spinning around him.

Both Tysar and Imayani had sent him away. They expected him to run off. To return to where he had been the last five years. But he hadn't been anywhere. He hadn't been anyone.

Why couldn't you have just stayed dead?

He could leave. Rai could get up and walk away. He had the chance many times now. But that was not who he was.

Rai groaned as he sat up.

They were wrong about one thing. He did not flee all those years ago. He continued his mission of learning about the tear and shades. He was a soldier. A weapon. And he did not leave his post.

Everything throbbed. Blood ran down his back as Rai pushed to his feet.

Once Rai had thought that the bonds he made could be broken. Snapped by circumstance. Severed by death. But this wasn't true. The only bonds that truly fail are those that one lets break.

And Rai would not allow his ties to those he loved to snap.

He reached into his belt and pulled out a vial. Unstoppering it, he threw back the contents. The blood of the artengo burned as it made its way down his throat. It was the only blood that affected humans that they knew of. Energy flooded through Rai and the pain subsided, dulling to an ache.

His old master, Shesmu at the Verdin Temple, warned him of the dangers of artengo blood. It did not heal, only suppressed pain. This made it easy for one to overextend themselves and as the effects of the blood faded, the pain came back tenfold.

Are you ready? Rai asked Fax.

No, but when did that ever stop us? Fax replied.

He was no longer welcome as Akarai. But he had always preferred the name Rai anyway.

Mimicking Tysar's move, Fax exploded under Rai's feet sending him flying through the smoke in a swirl of black and grey.

A stumbling silhouette appeared among the fog of the burning city.

Rai tackled Tysar. They bounced off the ground sending dirt billowing around them. Rolling to a stop, Rai pressed Tysar into the ground. His friend looked at him as if he were a black sand phantom.

Eyes wide, mouth half agape.

"Why do you keep getting up?" Tysar whispered.

"Because my brother needs me."

Rai could see it now. The Dark preyed on one's emotions. It pressed at Tysar's insecurity of always being second best and promised him something more. The Dark promised an end to the fighting. It pained Rai to see that he had caused this.

"But he's a fool," Rai said. "He thinks his worth is tied to meaningless metrics like training and influence but he doesn't see that without him, there would have been no strength in the seven. There would have been no Akarai.

"I'm sorry I didn't see how you felt. To me, you were the person holding everything together and I thought you knew that. I only pushed myself at training *because* you were by my side. Why would I stop when my brother tried so hard?

"I made sure we got to the Verdin Temple because it was your dream.

"And I wanted you at my side in the seven because you saw things in people that I did not," Rai said.

Tysar searched his face as tears rolled down his cheeks.

"You ask why I keep getting up? Because I gather strength from those at my side and they are some of the strongest people I know. They are the only reason I *can* get up."

The words poured out of him. Thoughts he hadn't even known were true until they were voiced. Rai stood on shaky legs.

"My strength comes from the rest of the seven. It comes from Yeru. It comes from Mino. It comes from Imayani. It comes from you. Once I was terrified that friendship and that connection could be severed. I tried to stay a step back from you all to avoid the pain of bonds broken. But I see now that I was just blocking the strength and life that those same bonds could breathe into me. Without you all, I'm a husk of who I could be. I was lost all these years. I can see that now that I'm back. And I'm not going anywhere.

"If you truly desire it, strike me down. I won't stop you. Return to the Mad Palace, free this shadow God and claim the power. I already lost one brother to this darkness. I can't lose another," Rai's voice broke on the last sentence. Memories of Kyan and the realisation of his mistake as Ma-atan killed those Kyan had brought there. The guilt that had weighed Rai down that he hadn't been there for Kyan. It wouldn't take Tysar, too. "But you'll have to kill me first."

Tysar stared at him, unmoving.

Rai waited for him to speak. Fax watched his shadow for a sudden attack. But nothing came.

Eventually, Rai held out his hand. Tysar reached out and clasped it and Rai helped pull him to his feet. For the first time since he had returned to Tansen, Rai saw his old friend. Like a fog had lifted, he recognised the glint in Tysar's eye.

They were soldiers, guards, weapons, brothers. They hadn't ever spoken about their feelings like this before and yet Rai felt their connection strengthen because of it. He felt tensions ease from merely words spoken. And he saw the same in Tysar. There was a mutual understanding and neither needed to say anything else. Tysar dragged Rai into an embrace.

Their silence faded as the sounds of the dying echoed around them.

What now? Fax asked perched as a crow on Rai's shoulder.

"Back to the Mad Palace so we can stop this," Rai said.

A grave look came over Tysar's face. "We can't."

"Why not?"

"It's too late."

"Tysar, tell me everything."

56

Coming Home

Kit watched as black veins crept over the whites of Nya's eyes until they were completely black. Her body convulsed as shadowy tendrils picked her up off the ground. Kit called out. He leapt to grab her but the darkness slapped him back. Then her head dropped forward, body going limp.

She hung suspended in the air surrounded by a shroud of shadow.

"Nya?" Kit stepped towards her.

Nya's head shot up. "Yes?" Her voice was raspy and soft.

It was then that Kit knew that this wasn't Nya. She was grinning. Not the joyful smile of his friend but a crooked, warped attempt.

Kit didn't know what to say as she floated back down to the ground. He glanced at Bas and Wenson and noticed that Adani had gone through the same transformation. Their eyes were voids of pure black and their shades seemed to pulse around them.

Ah, it feels good to have champions again, the voice said.

The Dark flew around them. Its purple eyes fixed on Nya and Adani. That thing had gotten into Nya's head. He had to get it out. Kit stepped up and grabbed Nya's arm pulling her to face him.

"Nya, you have to fight it," Kit said.

"Get off me." Nya shook her arm free.

"It's in your head. Fight it, Nya!"

"Fight what?" Nya squinted her black eyes at him like she didn't understand. "The shape of your face." She reached out and touched his cheek. "It's familiar."

Kit stared at her. Did she not recognise him?

Then her face tightened as if in pain. "No, no. That life only brought pain. I know no humans. Not anymore."

"Nya, it's Kit," he said.

Recognition flashed through her eyes, like lightning. She looked like she might say something but then it was squashed and instead Nya snarled at him.

"I know no humans!"

A wave of shadow blasted outward throwing Kit and the others back. Kit skittered across the stone scraping the skin up his forearm. Hands pulled him up and Bas and Wenson were at his side. Kit made to walk back over to Nya but Bas held him back.

"Not now," Bas said.

"That thing has done something to her!" Kit fought against his grip.

"And you cannot force it out with words," Bas whispered the words as if afraid that he would be heard. Kit saw the sense in what the Urdahl was saying but he couldn't leave Nya to that thing.

"One can only cast the darkness out of themselves," Bas said.

"We need to do *something*," Kit said. He glanced at the dark shroud. It filled the end of the throne room roiling and shifting like a smoky shadow. How could they face that?

Frustration boiled up inside of Kit as he watched Nya stand with Adani beneath the swirling darkness. It was talking to Mirt, who was now cowering away from the… what had Mirt called it? The Aspect.

Did you bring the dagger? the Aspect asked.

Mirt looked taken aback. "Dagger?"

Don't act coy. The black blade that opened the rift.

"Why, yes, of course." Mirt fumbled through his pack and pulled out the black dagger.

The Dark Aspect laughed and it echoed through the chamber.

Ahh, this is a good day.

Nya took the blade from Mirt without a word. It pained Kit to see his friend being used like a puppet. She then returned and handed it to the Aspect. Shadowy claws formed and gripped around the hilt.

How I want to cast this damn thing away, it said. *But that would not do, now would it?*

Mirt cleared his throat and stepped up to the Dark Aspect, mustering the last of his courage. His hand was shaking but then he balled it tight.

"We have come to you oh great one for guidance and answers, as you promised," Mirt's voice faltered on the last few words.

The Dark Aspect laughed.

It is guidance that you wish for? Yes, I think that is right. Your people have been free for far too long. It's time you're reminded of your God.

The darkness convulsed and expanded. The shadowy claw lifted the dagger high into the air and then it was thrust through the very fabric of reality itself. The blade tore downward and a new rift was ripped into the world.

And all they could do was watch.

Yeru's heart thundered as she ran her finger over the walls of the Mad Palace. She tried to silence Imayani arguing with Kleran. He had betrayed them as Yeru had guessed he would. She had warned Imayani about the risk. But at the time they had little choice.

Yeru was no fighter or diplomat so she did the one thing she could do. Search for the truth. She scoured the walls as this might be her only chance to piece together the secrets of Asuriya and the cataclysm that destroyed it. However, as she made notes on what the illustrations depicted, Yeru only grew more confused.

She held her torch aloft. Firelight danced across the stone. The carvings were intricate. Swirling lines filled the space around the main illustrated panels.

But the carvings didn't make *any sense.*

Yeru had expected to find depictions of the emperor's celebrated deeds. Much like temples dedicated to deities had illustrations of their remarkable events, the Mad Palace was said to contain artwork of what past emperors had done for Tarris. Instead, Yeru found images of men and woman bowing down to some sort of God. It closer resembled a deity's temple mural than one from a throne room. To begin with Yeru thought they might have been metaphorical until she found panels of this God doing extraordinary things that no man would ever be able to do, like slaughtering entire armies with the wave of a hand.

"More metaphors and exaggerations?" Yeru mused as she tapped on the carving.

"What's that?" the guard at her back asked.

"Nothing," she replied.

But then why did it not depict the man? Surely they would want to highlight the emperor who did such great things. But instead of showing the many emperors who had ruled Tarris before the cataclysm, these carvings all had the same likeness making it impossible to tell what emperor did what great deed.

It didn't make sense.

Yeru wandered deeper into the throne room, torch held high.

She would find the truth.

Rai and Tysar tore through Asuriya. Around them soldiers clashed. Thick smoke added to the chaos with stray blades and arrows appearing in the blink of an eye. The sickly stench of death covered the musk of the ancient city and fresh blood spattered and pooled, a place untouched for thousands of years. This had to have been the largest battle in Tarrisian history.

Aya and hyian shrieked and charged down the streets ploughing through soldiers on both sides.

Using their shades they launched themselves over the crater and into the Mad Palace. They sprinted up the stairs and barreled out into the throne room. Imayani's honour guard hadn't been moved, their dead bodies littering the floor. Kleran's, however, had fanned out. There were a couple beside Imayani and Kleran and another by

Yeru who was inspecting the murals hiding in the shadows of the far corner of the throne room. And a handful of other armour-clad guards stood around the chamber.

Shock registered on Kleran's face when he saw Rai and Tysar entering side by side. Two of his men marched forward, sword tips levelled.

"Stand down before I kill them all," Rai said. Fax flared out to emphasize his words.

Kleran quickly wiped the worry from his face with practiced ease and smiled. He knew he couldn't hold Rai back. Not without Tysar.

"Tysar, back so soon?" Kleran asked.

"I do not kill brothers," Tysar said.

Kleran nodded to his guards and they dropped their swords. "Pity."

"You need to stop your scholar from opening the rift and freeing the darkness from the other world," Rai said. They didn't have time for preamble. Tysar had already told him of Kleran's plan to use the power of the deity in the pocket world to control Tarris. Kleran wanted more soldiers with shades. An army of shadow soldiers ready to take on any threat. But he didn't understand. Both Rai and Tysar *felt* the darkness. They knew that it didn't care about the whims of humans. It just wanted to be free.

"Free it? My, my, my, what has Tysar been telling you?" Kleran said. "I have no plans to free the Dark Aspect. I merely want to… converse with it."

"What do you think it'll want in return?" Rai asked.

"You." Kleran said. "It wanted me to bring it those who already had a shade." He shrugged. "It called you its children. I said I would.

Two of you are probably already with it."

Nya.

Fear surged inside of Rai. He should never have left her. Not when she had a shade like him. Who was the other? Rai walked closer to Kleran and the guards tensed.

"You don't feel it like we do," Rai said. He kept his voice low and threatening. "It wants free, Kleran. It doesn't care about you or your soldiers."

Kleran snorted. "Why would it come here? *How* would it come here? We aren't stupid enough to let that thing into Yontar. My scholars are under strict instructions not to draw it towards the rift."

"You think you can outsmart a deity?" Rai asked.

Imayani had been watching the confrontation. She cleared her throat. "Deity? I don't understand."

Kleran blew out a breath. He opened his mouth to speak when Yeru yelped. Everyone spun towards her.

"We were wrong," Yeru said.

Red firelight flickered in the depths of the throne room. A burning silhouette of the scholar was all that could be seen.

"Yeru are you okay?" Imayani asked.

"We had it all wrong."

Imayani pushed past the honour guard and ran towards her. The guard was about to grab her when Kleran signalled to let her go. Rai and Tysar made their way to the darkened back of the chamber too. Even in the warm firelight, Yeru's face was pale as she held up a torch illuminating the wall.

The etchings showed people praying and worshiping. A swirling pattern filled the gaps between the different panels. Another sketch had what looked to be a sacrificial ritual with a human bleeding out into a bowl.

"What is all this?" Imayani asked.

Yeru blinked in surprise as she often did when those around her couldn't follow her thoughts. "Follow me." She led them further through the dark, to the back wall where they passed more murals of worship and sacrifice.

"Tarrisians created the monarchs and emperor to fill the role of the fallen emperor who sacrificed himself by defending us against an evil God. Because of that, our emperor or empress, wears no crown to show they are secondary to the true bloodline."

"I don't understand why this has anything to do—" Kleran started.

"The old emperors were said to fill their throne rooms with their great deeds just like with deities in their temples," Yeru cut in. "And what do you see here?"

Yeru raised the torch, lighting the back wall of the throne room. The swirling pattern that had been between the illustrations all accumulated and led back to this far wall. It was a vortex of dark lines and in the centre were two purple gems.

Rai's stomach dropped.

"I don't understand," Imayani said.

"Our ancient emperor didn't *fight off* a dark God. Our emperor was the God," Yeru said.

They stared at the mural on the wall and those two purple markings in a sea of black lines. They didn't need Yeru to make the connection between this defeated God emperor and the Dark Aspect that acted as a puppet master from the other realm.

"It's been manipulating us from the beginning," Rai said. Fax had receded deep into his mind, much like it had in Ma-atan's temple. "It leant into our insecurities to use us. Kyan was set on freeing Ma-atan which would have wreaked havoc across Tarris. It tried to turn Tysar against me. It promised Kleran shade soldiers and the throne."

"What about you?" Imayani whispered.

"It drew me back here. Back to a past I wanted to leave behind." Rai could see those words stung Imayani but it was the truth.

"But then what does it want?" Kleran asked.

"To be free," Tysar said.

"We can't free it," Kleran snapped. "I sent my scholar into the dark world to *communicate* with it. If all of this is true how does it plan on coming to Tarris?"

Of course, Rai thought. "The dagger. What did you do with the dagger?" Rai marched over to Kleran and grabbed him by his collar. His guards stepped in but Fax shot out and cracked them in the face.

Kleran stuttered, eyes bulging. "I don't know! They might have taken it with them." Rai tightened his grip. "Really, I don't know! There's no way to communicate with them once they're on the other side!"

"Then we're doomed," Yeru said. "It has moved us like pieces on a board."

There was a moment of silence as they took this in.

Rai threw Kleran aside. Defeat leaked into the party and shoulders slumped and faces dropped. There was nothing they could do. The threat was an entire realm away. And Nya was there facing it alone. How could he be so foolish?

Kleran rubbed at his neck. "If this thing is as smart as you're making it out to be. Why did it bring us here?"

It was Yeru who answered.

"It's coming home."

Just then the air began to tremble.

57

Child of Darkness

They turned to see a blade slice through the air and trail its way downward, opening a huge black void. The black blade hissed and sizzled as it opened the rift before disappearing again. Warmth permeated from the tear. It was just like the rend in the Thousand Floor Palace in Yontar but three times the size.

Silence. Everyone stared at the rift.

Then shadow flooded into the throne room.

It flowed through the tear like water, pooling and filling the chamber. There were shrieks as everyone moved away from the oncoming darkness.

"Everyone, get to the balcony!" Rai shouted.

Rai felt something tug on his mind. On Fax. They ran through the throne room, leaping over wherever the darkness touched.

One of the honour guard's feet touched the edge of the shadow and it leaked over his foot like an ooze. He shouted for help but no one slowed for him. The black essence ran up his leg and covered him until he was a flailing shadow. Then the darkness squeezed and the man *popped*. Blood and guts rained down around where he had stood moments before. This elicited more screams as the last of the party ran to the balcony's edge.

Rai glanced down. They were several stories up. It would take time for his shade to lift them down one by one. Too long even with Tysar.

The shadow continued to reach for them as a wave of darkness. Everyone cowered against the lip of the balcony. It was crumbling away and one more step would send them falling to their deaths. Then the shadow stopped. Inches from them, the dark essence froze and began to recede.

It was toying with them. The thought came from Fax.

Can you fight it? Rai asked the shade.

Defend maybe, Fax replied. *Fight? No.*

The shadows swirled into a clump and two purple eyes opened. This had been their emperor? This dark God had been the ruler of all of Tarris before the cataclysm? That couldn't be true.

It feels good to be back. Its voice reverberated around the chamber. It was low and harsh. The purple eyes bobbed among the darkness and Rai noted that a clump of thick shadow always remained around them. A body, perhaps?

Yes, it has a body, Fax said. *It shrouds itself in shadow to protect it.*

If it has a body, it can be killed, Rai thought.

They tried once before and couldn't kill it, Fax said.

How do you know? Rai asked.

I... I don't know.

Others started to come through the rift. A man in palace guard uniform, his eyes black as the tear itself. He came through upon a wave of shadow and Fax confirmed that he had a shade. There was something familiar about him.

"Ada?" Rai asked.

Ada glanced up and grinned at Rai. Rai turned to Tysar but he wouldn't meet his gaze.

Ada had been a member of the Seventh Sceptre. Highly trained, unpredictable and unstable even before the darkness took him. Rai thought he had died. He was going to call out to Ada and try to reason with him when the tear rippled and another passed through.

Nya appeared.

Rai's stomach dropped when he saw that she had black eyes too. They both landed in front of the swirling shadows as others piled through. There were guards, scholars, as well as Kit, Wenson, and an Urdahl. They looked around in awe at the throne room. Kit's eyes went wide when he saw Rai.

"Rai! That thing has Nya!" he shouted.

A dark tendril shot out and smacked the boy across the room and he crashed into the stone wall. The Urdahl and Wenson ran to the boy's side.

The black shroud moved around the chamber. Everyone watched it in silence.

I can taste your terror, but you have nothing to fear. I'm back now.

In the distance, the sounds of the battle raged on. The armies fought on oblivious to that which happened in the Mad Palace.

You humans can't care for yourselves and you've been alone for far too long. The Dark almost sounded regretful. *Fear not, I've returned to take back Tarris. I'll stop the fighting.*

I'll bring peace back to my empire, the Dark said.

Rai ran through his options. He had to stop this. He had to kill this dark God before it reclaimed Tarris. But… wasn't there some truth to its words? Tarris had been fighting a war in the shadows *since the cataclysm.* Since this dark God was locked away in that Duat-forsaken realm. Tarrisians always believed that one day the true bloodline would take up the crown once more. Perhaps—

Rai shook his head. "Get out of my head!"

The dark God laughed. *Oh, you will make a fine champion, Rai.*

He couldn't trust his own thoughts. They were tinged in darkness through his connection with his shade.

Don't you want an end to this pain and suffering? the voice asked. The party looked around at one another.

Can't you hear their cries?

Below, Asuriya roared in battle as thousands fought and screamed and died.

Don't you want me to stop the fighting?

I can do just that. I'll show you.

There was a pause and then a low rumble. It was coming from the tear.

Hundreds of husks burst through the tear in a sheet of black wings, red eyes and gleaming slivered claws. People screamed and ducked as the husks shrieked and flew overhead heading for the city below.

They arrived in seconds and Rai watched as a husk dove for a soldier lifting him high in the air. It ripped the man apart. Pieces of him fell back into the city and other men and woman looked up, terror written on their faces.

"They're going to kill them all," a guard said.

Rai glanced around, wild eyed. There had to be something they could do to help them. A hand slipped into his. He glanced around to see Imayani at his side. She was smiling as tears streaked through the thick layer of dust on her cheeks. She winced as a surge of cries came from Asuriya.

Then she faced him and said, "I forgive you. I want you to know that."

The world was spinning out of control but everything seemed to fall away at her words. Rai stared at her.

"I need you to know that I understand, before we die. I'm sorry it took me so long," she said. Her hand was warm in his. "And I'm sorry that I ruined everything. I should never have sent you away and now I've destroyed all of Tarris, too."

"Don't say that. It's not over yet," Rai said.

She smiled then. It was a sad smile like the ones she gave him when he said it would get better and she knew that it wouldn't. That terrified him more than any dark God.

Kit was coming to on the far side of the throne room, staring up at the flood of husks pouring out into the city. The Urdahl and Wenson were at his side watching with defeat in their eyes. Yeru was staring at the shadow God, mouth agape in disbelief. Even Kleran stood speechless listening to thousands of Tarrisians dying in the city below. Innocent men and woman just doing as they were commanded were being slaughtered by beasts from another realm.

I have missed that sound, the Dark said with a satisfied sigh.

Rai saw acceptance in the eyes of those in the throne room. Postures slumped as they huddled close together. They had given up. This was the end and they accepted their fate.

He looked to Imayani again. She turned away from Asuriya, eyes pressed shut as the tears continued to fall.

It was then that Rai realised that he had been wrong all these years. He thought of himself as a weapon, but weapons had to be wielded by others. And while the others laid down their swords, Rai wasn't going to lay down and die.

Perhaps once he had been a weapon. But now he was more.

"Tysar, take Ada and hold him back for as long as you can," Rai said.

His friend didn't question the order. He didn't ask what the plan was. Tysar nodded and readied himself.

"We'll go back to the garden once this is all done," Rai said to Imayani. Her eyes widened and he squeezed her hand before letting go.

Then Fax threw Rai towards the black dagger.

Other than the thicker patch of darkness around the eyes, Rai had spotted another blotch that moved within the shadows and he had been tracking it. It had to be the black blade. If he could force this deity back through to the other realm, he could use the blade and close the rift ending this before Tarris fell.

I hope you're right about this, Fax said.

I have to be, Rai thought.

Rai shot through the air over the shadow pooling on the ground. But as he drew near, Nya barrelled into him and together they crashed into the wall of the throne room. The air puffed out of Rai's lungs as he tumbled to a stop. He sucked in a breath. Glancing up, Nya was walking towards him. Shadows poured from her. More than a single shade should have been able to conjure.

"Nya, you need to fight it," he said.

"Join us, Rai. Let the darkness in. It smothers the pain and the weakness and leaves only strength." Her voice had a strange duality to it, like a deeper version was mimicking her words as she spoke.

The dark God was too deep in her mind. Rai just had to hope that closing the tear would free her from its grasp.

Fax shot out as a tendril and whipped Nya sending her flying back into shadow. Rai pulled himself up and started running. If it was using Nya to protect that patch, he had to be right. It had to be the black dagger.

Incoming, Fax warned.

Spikes of darkness burst from the shadows around Rai. He ducked and threw himself out of the way of another and Fax battered back a third that would have split him in half.

Nya erupted from the swirling dark snarling and charged at him. An explosion of darkness launched Nya at him and Rai threw up a protective wall of shadow.

Fax and Bom clashed. The dark energy crackled and sputtered against each other. Nya stood in the centre of her shadow bubble baring her teeth. Rai lent Fax his strength and he began to see Nya's shade give a little. But then a surge of energy rushed into Nya. She threw her head up and went stiff as more darkness burst from her shadow. The Dark was using her.

They weren't going to be able to win this. Rai glanced to his side. The darker patch was right there. As Fax fended off Bom, Rai reached out towards what he hoped was the dagger.

I can't hold them back! Fax said.

Just a little longer. Rai plunged his hand into the shadow.

The patch of darkness was so close.

Rai reached out.

Almost.

A curling of shadow ran up his outstretched arm.

Give in, Rai.

Rai groaned as he pushed closer.

Why fight this? I can give you what you want. A silence to the pain. A country of peace. Why won't you…

LET.

ME.

IN?

Each word felt like a punch to the face as the God seeped further into his mind. He felt it in his thoughts.

Oh.

For her? It laughed. *I'll tell you what, join me and I'll let her live.*

Rai hesitated.

That's right.

If he could get away with Imayani they could regroup and come back better prepared to face this evil. This could be their only chance to escape… *No,* he thought. *Get out of my head!*

Why do you keep fighting? The darkness sounded confused now.

Rai stretched out further. His fingers touched the edge of the black blade.

"What else is there?" he said.

What else is there? The Dark said in a mocking tone.

Rai wrapped his fingers around the hilt.

Oh, Rai. My poor, Rai. There is peace from all that haunts you, the Dark said.

A shock ran through Rai followed by flashes of Kon in the orphanage. Sen at the Deadlands Basin. Kyan at Ma-atan's temple. Then images of Tysar lying dead at Ada's feet. Rai screamed and let go of the blade. He gripped his head as shooting pains rang through his mind with each memory. The emperor a bloody pulp beneath him as Tansen burned.

What else is there? The Dark repeated.

There is the power to never lose anyone you love again. Isn't that what you've been searching for? Its voice lulled Rai to open up. It was mesmerising.

STOP! Rai shouted. He wasn't sure if he said the word out loud or not.

Rai pressed against the voice but he could feel it slipping through. There was no way he could keep holding it back. He needed Fax back. It couldn't hold Nya back itself anyway.

Recalling the shade, Rai thought towards it, *Fax, it's getting in. We need to find a way to break whatever hold it has on you.* They had known from the start that the connection to this dark God was through their shades. They needed to find a way to block it.

The shade was silent for a moment.

I'm sorry, Rai, Fax said. *I can't break a connection with myself.*

Rai faltered and more of the dark God slipped into his mind.

That's right, Rai, Fax's voice mixed with that of the dark God's. *What did you think shades are? They're a part of me. My essence come to life.*

Numbness bled through Rai. An uncaring wave that washed away worry and fear and left nothing behind. He knew it was the Dark, but he could not muster the interest to care. All the turmoil and agony of his past was being erased before his very eyes and it left a serenity that Rai had never felt before.

You no longer have to worry, it whispered.

You no longer have to feel pain.

You no longer have to put that pressure upon yourself.

You are a Child of Darkness, and these human concerns are nothing to you.

Why was he still fighting? All it did was cause pain. Rai let go and everything eased. A knot in his shoulder relaxed and his mind went blank.

Imayani ran to Rai and grabbed his hands. She mumbled things and cried out.

Pathetic human sounds.

Then he felt it. He felt the power of the Dark Aspect through his too-dark shadow. It was an ocean of power that he could tap into. Rai would never be too weak again. His shade's abilities had been a mere fraction of what he could pull on now. And through the connection he saw what the Dark Aspect saw. The husks tore through Asuriya and killed without mercy. They were purging the city of pain. Why had he been against this?

Rai felt his brothers; Tysar and Ada, and his sister, Nya nearby.

Now, kill the guards, the Dark Aspect commanded.

Shadowy tendrils broke from the pooling black and cut the armoured guards in half. The humans screamed and grouped together. All apart from this empress who clung to him. Rai brushed her off but she came back pleading.

"Rai! You need to fight it. Please!" she said.

Champions, the Dark Aspect said. *Go down into the city and tell the remaining humans to either bow before their God or perish.*

Nya, Ada, and Tysar shot out over the balcony and into Asuriya. Rai made to join them but the empress would not let go of his hand. The other humans were calling her over.

A broken one, Rai thought turning to her.

Rai plunged a shadowy blade into her gut. More cries from the humans.

The human didn't cry out or fight back. She fell against him breathing hard as her blood stained his clothing.

"I guess you were right about us being like charah flowers," she panted. "Maybe we are born to kill one another. Always striving more."

A flicker of… something in Rai's mind. Was something wrong? He had the feeling that he had done something wrong.

"Charah flower," Rai repeated. The sound was familiar.

Her grip was weakening on his arm as she bled out. "But there is no sunlight anymore. And charah flowers pull together in the dark," her words came out as little more than a whisper. "Don't let Tarris fall."

Then she dropped to the ground. Rai stared at her corpse feeling wrong. This wasn't right. He should be doing something.

The thought was stamped out before Rai could think more on it.

Rai, go to the city. Tell the people their God has returned.

That's what it was. That's what he was to do.

A burst of dark energy threw Rai over the balcony and into the capital of Tarris. A voice was screaming in his mind. But it grew quieter and quieter until silence took it.

Epilogue

The screams coming from Asuriya grew louder after Rai reached the city. Kit peered over the balcony and watched as shadows filled the street and husks tore people apart. The Dark Aspect's '*champions*' ravaged the remaining forces on both sides of the conflict. It was like a scene from a nightmare.

Tarrisians had been told Asuriya was a place of monsters and now those stories had proven true. Horrors stalked the streets. They set upon unsuspecting soldiers and blood stained the sand of this once ancient place. Kit spotted Nya as she cut a man in half. He turned away feeling sick.

Bas tugged on his arm. "Come."

Mirt and Kleran were trying to reason with the Dark Aspect, asking the God to be lenient to those who freed it. The scholars ran for the staircase leading out of the throne room and Bas gestured to follow.

Sudden anger overtook Kit. Why should they run? This was humanity's last stand. He looked to his hands and thought about his death touch.

It was time to see if this truly was a gift or a curse.

Kit brushed Bas off and started walking towards the Dark Aspect. Bas called out after him but he ignored the Urdahl. If this truly was the end, then he would die fighting. He was done running.

Wenson stepped in front of him.

"No."

Something about the steel in Wenson's eyes made Kit hesitate. "We fight another day," he said.

Kit looked over to the Dark Aspect as it sliced through Kleran's neck. His decapitated body toppled over to lie beside the empress. Rai had done that. Kit couldn't wrap his head around anything that had happened. Nya and Rai had turned to the darkness. Now they were out there killing those they set out to protect.

Wenson laid a hand on Kit's shoulder. "We will get them back."

He was right. Attacking now would mean death. And he couldn't save his friends if he was dead.

Kit deflated and nodded. Together Kit, Wenson, and Bas crept across the throne room and down into the Mad Palace. As soon as they were out of sight they broke into a run. Their thundering footsteps rung throughout the entry chamber. And then they were out.

They darted between buildings. Dark hour had descended upon Asuriya. The flames of the burning city painted Asuriya in a harsh red. Darkness coalesced with the smoke making everything a haze of indistinct shadow. The stink of decay made Kit's eyes water as they sprinted through the streets like they were being chased. A glance over his shoulder showed no pursuit, but they did not slow.

Around them, the howls of pain were lessening. "Do you think some are escaping?" Kit asked running alongside Bas.

He returned a grim look. No. They are all dead. Kit could tell by the look on Bas' face that that's what the Urdahl was thinking. He was probably right.

Wenson screamed as a husk shot out of nowhere and pinned him against a building. Coughing on the smoke of the fires, Kit threw his weight against the husk but all he did was bounce off the beast. Blood poured from where the husk's talons pierced Wenson. His face was going pale.

A broken staff end stabbed into the husk's back and it shrieked, letting go of Wenson. Bas dragged the staff end through the leathery skin of the beast. It turned on him fangs bared but Bas buried his second staff half into the husk's mouth and the beast went limp.

Kit came to Wenson's side and pressed on his wound. Blood leaked through his fingers as his friend sat there dazed. Nearby there was a feral scream and then a sickly splatter.

"We need to move," Bas said. He was watching the street. More husks could be upon them at any moment and with the thick smoke from the fires, they wouldn't know until it was too late.

And there were the champions roaming the city. Kit tried not to think about that.

"Can you walk?" Kit asked Wenson. He nodded and together with Bas they pulled him to his feet. He swayed but didn't fall. Wenson's eyes focused and went wide looking at the sky. Kit followed his gaze.

A wispy shadow poured out of the Mad Palace. It bloomed outward filling the sky like an oncoming storm, stretching over Asuriya and then beyond. The light of the fires seemed to darken as it passed above throwing them into a deeper darkness.

"My vision." Bas' face was grave. "I've failed."

Illy sat atop the Patched Cloak. She gazed out over the city towards the Thousand Floor Palace. She had spent most of her breaks up here staring at the monolithic building, trying to will her brother and the others to return. It had been weeks since they had entered the palace.

"I hope they're okay," Illy whispered.

Dust stirred in her lap and nuzzled against her. Somehow the sand fox knew when she was upset and followed her up to the rooftop to sit in her lap. Illy smiled.

"You must be worried, too. I'm sure they're fine. They'll come back soon and I'll make some stew and close the inn for a night. How does that sound?"

The words were as much for herself as they were for Dust. Below, Illy heard Lem serving some of the guests. There was a clatter. They had two guests staying at the Patched Cloak inn and she should be down helping Lem. Something smashed.

With a sigh, Illy stood. Dust hopped off her lap and shook out her fur as Illy made her way back to the steps. Just as she was about to descend, the sand fox hissed.

Illy frowned and turned to see Dust standing at the far edge of the rooftop looking northward.

"What is it, Dust?" She rarely ever hissed. Illy squinted against the dark but she couldn't see anything amiss. She waited a moment and then she saw it.

It looked like clouds in the dark but it moved as one covering the sky. There were no breaks in its perfect black shroud. It reached out like fingers quicker than any cloud cover Illy had ever seen. In moments, it was overheard and threw Yontar into a thicker darkness. Illy ducked as if this wave would reach down and grab her. Instead it passed overhead stretching out in all directions.

Dust growled.

The strange darkness continued to cover Tarris like a black mantle.

ACKNOWLEDGEMENTS

Writing a sequel can be daunting. With expectations from the first book, there's a lot more to consider. Luckily, I had a team of people that helped bring this story to life.

Firstly, I want to thank my beta reader team; Katrina, Ben, Tim and Ross, for digging through the rough sand and helping me bring this story to the surface. And my ARC reader team who helped get the word out about the book.

My patrons who help fund these books. Including high tier patrons; Brett, Karl, Scott, Shannon, Sophia and Don.

My cover artist, Felix Ortiz, who continues to knock these covers out of the park. I don't think I've ever sent as many '*no notes*' messages to draft covers before.

My editor, Sarah Chorn, who is one of the most supportive people out there. I've learnt so much from her.

My family for their continued support. From being my first readers to just wanting the pretty covers, I couldn't do it without you all.

And lastly, the readers. Without readers, stories are nothing but mad ramblings. It's the reader who imagines the world and characters, and makes them real.

So thank you for making my story real.

ABOUT THE AUTHOR

Andrew Watson lives on the outskirts of Edinburgh where he rambles about made up people and places. He has a first class degree in Digital Media from Edinburgh Napier University and currently works as a freelance video editor and author. Andrew can also be found on YouTube and Instagram where he jumps around excitedly shouting about books.

Follow Andrew at:
andrew-watson.co.uk
@the_fools_tale